DEAD TO RIGHTS

Longarm called out, "Freeze, Mister Baker. I got the drop on you at can't-miss range and you are purely under arrest, if you know what's good for you!"

The swarthy owlhoot rider froze still as a wooden Indian, but kept his hands down. As Longarm caught the drift of that gun hand he said in a calmer tone, "Don't try it. Just unbuckle that gunbelt and let it fall as it may."

Brazos Roy quietly replied, "All right. My mamma never raised a total fool and I know your rep, Longarm."

Longarm continued to cover the professional gunslick as the gunbelt fell around his ankles, open, and Brazos Roy took one step away as if to clear his feet.

Then the fat lady came out in the yard to call out, "What's going on Roy? Why are you standing there so strange?"

The gunslick must have thought Longarm's attention would be drawn away from him for at least a split second. Brazos Roy whirled like a ballerina, raising the derringer in his right hand . . .

TABOR EVANS

AND THE
HANGMAN'S DAUGHTER

JOVE BOOKS, NEW YORK

LONGARM AND THE HANGMAN'S DAUGHTER

A Jove Book / published by arrangement with
the author

PRINTING HISTORY
Jove edition / January 2001

The Penguin Putnam Inc. World Wide Web site address is
http://www.penguinputnam.com

ISBN: 0-515-12999-2

A JOVE BOOK®
Jove Books are published by The Berkley Publishing Group,
a division of Penguin Putnam Inc.,
375 Hudson Street, New York, New York 10014.
JOVE and the "J" design
are trademarks belonging to Penguin Putnam Inc.

PRINTED IN THE UNITED STATES OF AMERICA

10 9 8 7 6 5 4 3 2 1

Chapter 1

It's hard to sleep late in a strange bed when they're building a gallows near your open hotel window. So Deputy U.S. Marshal Custis Long of the Denver District Court swung his long legs off his hired bed and rose to a considerable height to pad barefoot across the braided rag rug to shut the damned window.

But as he stood there with the morning breeze off the western slope goosebumping his bare hide, he didn't feel sleepy of a sudden, staring out across the Courthouse Square of Ambush, Colorado. For, come Monday morning, the county aimed to hang four bad boys in a row and, whilst they likely had it coming, those four steel hooks in the overhead beam of fresh-milled pine reminded a man how long everybody was fixing to sleep before that great getting-up morning the sky pilots kept trying to sell.

So Longarm, as he was better known to friend and foe alike, left the window be, rinsed himself wider awake at the corner washstand and got dressed to go on down and see how they made chili con carne in such a remote corner of the Centennial State.

Mexicans and Texicans had a contest along the border to see who could swallow the most peppersome chili con carne without crying. As one ordered it north or south of the border it got peppered less and less until by, say Monterrey in Old Mexico or Denver in the U.S. of A., they made it just the way Longarm liked it. North or south of

1

temperate zone it tended to taste too bland. So as he strode out onto the streets of Ambush to find out, he was hoping he wouldn't be served the glorified pork and beans they called chili con carne north of Cheyenne.

The mushroom town of Ambush still smelled of raw lumber and fresh paint. It had sprouted from what had been camus meadows of the White River Utes until said Utes had made the awful mistake of rising under Colorow and Nicagat.

The mistake had been more in the methods than the motives. Many a white who agreed the hitherto friendly Utes were being pushed around by the B.I.A. and foolishly arrogant Indian Agent Nathan Meeker, had been outraged when the Utes had not been content to murder Meeker, but then go on to massacre perhaps a dozen other B.I.A. men, ambush an army column and, above all, rape three white women in the process.

So all but a handful of Southern Utes who'd helped Kit Carson fight the Navaho that time had been removed to Utah Territory for the Mormons to worry about and that had likely been just as well, for placer gold had been struck in the nearby Ambush Creek the bitty mountain town was named for. The squaw serving behind the stand-up counter of a beanery down the slope was likely Arapaho. The Arapaho hadn't riz in recent memory and the ones who hadn't been removed east to the Indian Territory had learned to get along tolerably with decent white riders. Riders who weren't decent didn't get along with anybody and that was how come they were erecting that gallows platform up the way.

As a federal officer, Longarm hadn't come to Ambush about the young killers they aimed to hang on local charges. The mushrooming seat of a remote and newly incorporated county in Western Colorado was served by a stage line down to the railhead in Durango and its coaches had been packing U.S. mail when they were robbed eight times in going on nine weeks. Dirty as hell.

Instead of stopping the coaches at gunpoint, some sneaks

2

had set off charges upslope of the mountain route south and poked through the wreckage for fun and profit as the dust from their landslides and any moans from their victims drifted off on the thin mountain air.

They'd sent Longarm in as a lawman who knew the West Slope after a postal inspector called MacPhillips had wired he might be on to something, just before he was dry gulched out in the hills by a person or persons unknown.

Longarm had refused the offer of a posse to back his play. He liked to work alone because it was tough enough to watch your back when you knew nobody on your side was in back of you. After that, as Longarm had pointed out, it hardly seemed likely he'd be up against any wolf pack of stand-up gunfighters. Men who lay in wait in the pre-dawn dark to landslide an early morning coach, eight times, were more likely to pussy-foot around you in tricky light at uncertain hours.

His Arapaho waitress slid his order across the zinc countertop to him as she asked him to repeat what he'd just muttered.

Longarm smiled sheepishly and confessed, "I was talking to my fool self, Ma'am. A man can get to talking to his fool self, spending too much time with nobody prettier to talk to."

She sighed and allowed she'd just spent a lonesome night, her ownself, and added, "I get off at sundown and my name's Jenny Crowfeather. What was that you just said about wanting to know for certain who stepped on a twig behind you?"

Longarm busted some oyster crackers over his steaming bowl of chili con carne as he explained, "I ride for the law. Sometimes I ride in uncertain surroundings. When you know you're riding alone and you hear somebody pussy-footing after you in the dark, you know whose side he'd be on and what you'd want to *do* about it, see?"

Jenny Crowfeather nodded soberly and said, "In our shining times it was said a young man stealing ponies was safer alone in the dark. You sound like a young man I used

3

to know. He went under on the Washita, where your blue sleeves shot the ponies, too."

Longarm joshed, "You're making that up, no offense. You can't be old enough to recall young men who fought the Seventh Cav on the Washita back in eighteen sixty-eight, Miss Jenny."

So she flustered and told him he was the big fibber, which was true enough, but it didn't hurt to make a no-longer-young lady with a weight problem feel good and sundown was too far off for him to have to worry about her taking him up on her smoke signals.

When she let him be with his chili con carne he found they'd made it about right and the coffee was even better. So he left the beanery feeling bright-eyed and bushy-tailed enough to pay the courtesy call on the local law that went with toting a federal badge.

The modest settlement of Ambush wasn't laid out four-square like Dodge or Tombstone. It couldn't be, because of the lay of the land. The mostly east-west main street and the contour-line cross streets branching sort of north and south perforce snaked about as straight as they could and that wasn't too straight. As Longarm forged back up Main Street past his two-story frame hotel by the stage depot to the lower western side of Courthouse Square he spied some other assimilated Indians watching the county carpenters preparing for the festivities come Monday, as if they were enjoying the notion of four white boys hanging. Longarm repressed a grimace of distaste as he passed them and forged on toward the shadows of the gallows. Had it been up to him the mass execution would have taken place that evening, seeing the gallows were just about finished, or the morning to come, seeing that would be a Saturday with plenty of folk off the surrounding range in town to watch. But the powers that were in those parts had decreed the four doomed youths would have to sweat out the whole weekend in the small stone county jail because some kin of a murdered madam couldn't get up from the railroad

4

stop at Durango any sooner than Saturday night and it wasn't right to hang men on the Sabbath.

Longarm circled the freshly whitewashed courthouse on the far side to make for the attached office of the county sheriff's department across a narrow lane from the hewn granite jailhouse. He didn't know why. The recently elected sheriff and his own deputies hadn't offered an educated guess as to who might be stopping the U.S. mail in so nasty a way. And Longarm wasn't the only lawman who'd ever heard how that sheriff in Montana had masterminded the monotonous robberies betwixt Bannock and Virginia City. They'd strung Sheriff Henry Plummer up back in '64 but that wasn't saying history couldn't repeat itself, and there just weren't that many strangers passing through the remote new settlement of Ambush and the modest belt of truck farms and stock spreads around such a dinky market.

The last Longarm had heard, they'd failed to find the mother lode such color as they'd produced from the sands and gravel of Ambush Creek might have washed out of, way the hell up any of a dozen smaller mountain streams. So the economy of Ambush was more like one of the larger California gold camps of the '50s, such as Angels Camp, Poker Flat or Placerville. At a higher and drier elevation, Ambush, Colorado, likely looked more like folk back East *pictured* the gold camps of the '49ers. The ridges all around rose rockier, and both the trees and the grass grew taller and greener than one really saw in the browner and softer hills of the California Mother-lode country. All the more serious trees within an easy haul of Ambush had been cut and hauled by now, of course. Ambush Creek wound down through what had been marshy open camus flats in Indian times. The onionlike camus plants the Utes had valued so highly were long gone, replaced by the town and such garden plots and grazing as one saw to either side of the now mighty muddy creek dammed every few dozen yards to run through yet another gold sluice. Longarm knew from experience as well as his last few hours in a Concord coach

5

the evening before that more impressive homesteads or cattle spreads lay in the folds of the "parks" or mountain glens in all directions. Colorado folk called grassy glens in the Rockies "parks" as they called any stream too small to call a river a "creek." Longarm had no idea why folk back in West-By-God-Virginia had called the same sort of mountain features "hollers" and "runs." He figured folk who lived in a country were entitled to name their surroundings to suit themselves.

He knew that less than half a day's ride in any direction the small hill farms and even rougher cattle range would give way to plain old west-slope wilderness, with lush grass and sedge where the park bottoms flooded most, alder hells and aspen groves where tree roots could stay stuck in the ground during high water, and mostly evergreens everywhere else. The way of the winds with the rain clouds from the west had a heap of say whether a particular slope was covered with pine, fir or spruce. Longarm was more worried about the *folk* they were growing in these parts, these days. Until they got down to serious mining, there'd be little more than a few hundred placer miners and their dependents, with just the few merchants, whores and gamblers it took to staff a small but free-spending town and the handful of less fortunate country folk who rode in with food and fodder, some to spend their own pocket-jingle in turn. Longarm knew that unless they hit serious paydirt in the near future, Ambush figured to be yet another mountain ghost town by the time any roofs needed repairing.

A tall but not bad-looking gal of around twenty in a tan whipcord riding outfit and matching hair was fussing with someone in the jailhouse doorway across the street as Longarm opened the sheriff's door and strode on in. He found a young squirt sitting at ease behind the desk out front, with his booted feet up on the desk and the boots genuine Justins with fancy-stitched uppers of green Morocco leather.

6

The kid deputy said the sheriff wouldn't be in until later and suggested Longam come back around ten if it was important.

Longarm replied as casually, "It ain't important and having made my *pro forma* I won't be back unless I can come up with a better reason. I'd be Deputy Marshal Custis Long, riding for the justice department and to tell the truth I doubt you boys can tell me anything we don't already know about those stage robberies up this way."

The county lawman swung his high heels to the floor to sit up more businesslike as he replied, "I'm sure Sheriff Peabody will want to jaw with you about them fiends, Deputy Long. Ain't you that Deputy Long they call Longarm and send all over creation on the tougher cases?"

Longarm modestly replied, "I've talked to Reporter Crawford of the *Denver Post* about the silly tales they print about me. I'm checked in at the hotel next to the stage depot if Sheriff Peabody really has anything to say to this child. From here I'll be headed for the barber shop, the municipal livery, hardware outlets and such. I investigate one unknown gang of road agents much the same as any other until I cut some sign worth following. Unless you local lawmen have been holding out on us, all we have to go on, so far, is that they've been begging, buying or borrowing dynamite, or even more black powder, to landslide coaches, passengers, crews and teams to Kingdom Come."

The sheriff's deputy pointed out, "So far they've yet to stop a coach that wasn't carrying gold dust from the creek out back in its strong box."

Longarm nodded soberly and said, "That, too. Albeit they haven't neglected the gold watches and even the gold teeth of more then one of their victims. Road agents almost always case a stagecoach before they rob it. You get just as much time at hard, or in this case as high a hanging, for stopping one stage or the other."

Noting the chagrined expression on the younger lawman's face, he gently added, "You're on the right track.

But it's devilish hard to cull a finger man from the whole bushel of onlookers seeing a stage worth stopping out of the depot. Tell the sheriff I'll try the Maryland rye and free lunch in that Bighorn Saloon across from my hotel. My own boss, Marshal Billy Vail, don't approve of us drinking on duty earlier than high noon."

He stepped back out in the morning sunlight to head for the barber shop as he'd said. That tall gal in the riding habit loped across the lane on foot to grab hold of him like a soldier home from the wars as she sobbed, "Mister Longarm, you have to help us. My Rick is innocent, innocent I tell you!"

To which Longarm could only reply as he hugged her back, "I've no doubt of your sincerety Ma'am. But I don't have the least notion of what we're talking about!"

Then that jailhouse turnkey from across the way came to Longarm's rescue, hauling the hystericated shemale off him as he told her in a gruffly gentle way, "This gent can't do nothing for your Rick, Miss Joy. Ain't nobody can do nothing for your Rick, now, and you know your daddy don't want you hanging about down this way."

She was blubbering while protesting as he half led and half carried her around the courthouse corner, warning her she was only making it tougher on all concerned. The young squirt from inside had come to the sheriff's door to see what all the noise was about. So Longarm asked him about the young woman.

The kid in the green-topped Justins and Navy Colt conversions shrugged and said, "Oh, that was Joy Norwich, the hangman's daughter. She's tetched in the head. She keeps saying Rick Robles, one of them killers we'll be hanging come Monday morn, is innocent. Ain't that a bitch?"

Longarm whistled softly and asked, "When did the young lady take such a shine to the condemned man, before or after he wound up on her daddy's shit list?"

The local lawman shrugged and said, "Before, I reckon.

Miss Joy says he was in bed with her the night of the killings. But would you let a Mexican off on the word of a bewildered maid, if the maid was your own white daughter?"

Chapter 2

Longarm didn't need a haircut and knew how to shave himself as well as most grown men. But next to a beauty shop there was nothing like a barbershop for small town gossip, and Longarm would have felt silly going to a beauty shop.

He seemed to attract much curiosity as he loomed in the barbershop door, dressed in the tobacco tweed suit and vest they'd made him wear on duty since President Rutherford B. Hayes and Miss Lemonade Lucy, the tea-total first lady, had moved into the White House back East with their reforming ways. Plenty of town businessmen in the high country wore three piece suits, a lot of the same wore low-heeled riding boots and coffee brown Stetson's telescoped in a Colorado rider's crush. But not as many packed a double-action Colt .44-40 crossdraw under the tails of their coats. Longarm loomed more sun-tanned and trail-hardened than your average windmill salesman as well. So a certain silence fell over the small crowd in the barbershop until Longarm had a seat, picked up a recent copy of the *Police Gazette* and casually declared he was a federal rider, come to see about those stagecoach robberies and in need of a hot towel shave because his jowels were commencing to itch from soft soap, hard water and a dull razor he'd just thrown away.

The barber said he'd shave him and sell him a new kit when they were done if he'd like to take his turn. So Longarm settled back, secretly pleased there were three gents ahead of him. But after they'd all agreed it smelled like thunder and lightning before sundown the conversation got around to blood and slaughter. Longarm couldn't keep them on those smashed and looted coaches he'd been sent to study on. Everyone agreed a stagecoach and its softer-living components looked like a stomped-flat beetle-bug after someone rolled tons of rock and gravel down a mountain over it. But after that nobody had any notion who might have been doing such dastardly deeds, while they were all agaggle about the mass hanging they were fixing to enjoy, come Monday morn. So Longarm held his peace and let them ramble on, hoping to at least get the political lay of the land in those parts. He'd found there was often an undercurrent of local rivalry, with witnesses coming forward or holding back in accordance with which local newspaper they favored.

Down Tombstone way you could almost tell whether a man buttered his bread from mining and small-business, or beef, by whether he read the *Tombstone Epitaph* or *Tombstone Nugget* with his breakfast. Meanwhile, over Denver way, readers of the *Denver Post* or *Rocky Mountain News* were less likely to be set in their ways and surly to strangers than readers of the *Denver Tribune*. He wasn't at all surprised to hear the locals in the barbershop, as well as the barber, felt it was a crying shame about that greaser and the hangman's daughter.

Pretending to be more interested in the pink pages of his magazine but asking occasional leading questions, Longarm soon had the reasons for the coming rope dance sorted straighter in his own head.

Longarm had rode herd for more than one outfit between coming west after the war and signing on with the Justice Department eight or ten years back. So he could picture the sordid saga of four young bucks in a cut-rate cathouse on another Saturday night, likkered up and showing off for one another with their kid peckers and, when that wouldn't work, their harder sixguns until, all of a sudden and unplanned by any of 'em, the madam, the professor, and one of the working gals lay dead under a haze of gunsmoke as others crowded in, drunk or sober, to disarm the three blind-drunk and scared-shitless cowboys still on the premises.

Everyone agree one of the wildmen had lit out right after he'd shot Madame Frenchy, if not everyone else. A score of late-night celibrants had heard the sound of galloping hooves, headed hell-for-leather back for the Triple 8 they'd rid in from earlier.

Some black coffee and a little pistol whipping had established the quartet had consisted of Hank Brewer, Will Pulver, Buck Wylie and a drifting *vaquero* called Ricardo or Rick Robles, the one who'd gotten away. When the posse got out to the Triple 8 they found the lying son of Mexico in the bunkhouse, insisting he'd been there all night. But other riders had allowed he'd just rid in an hour before the posse showed up and so there the four of 'em were, fixing to hang together as they'd rid together, after a short trial with all but Robles pleading guilty but getting no breaks from a world-weary circuit judge.

Longarm allowed he was confused about their hangman and his daughter. The barber, snipping away at the gray head of an older client paused to explain, "Limey Norwich ain't a full-time hangman by trade. The county only hires him at piecework rates when they need someone hung because he used to work for a full-time scientific hangman over in London Town."

Another waiting customer offered, "We call him Limey because he hails from London Town. Came out Colorado way during the gold rush of the sixties. Wound up selling mining supplies and hanging folk for a living. Old Limey Norwich has never had a lick of luck at spotting color. Some say he don't see too good."

Another younger man in the shop snorted dirty and simpered, "That's for damned sure! Old Limey ain't never noticed his daughter, Miss Joy, screwing half the riders west of the Great Divide, the way I hear tell."

The barber shot him a severe look and asked, "Are you

saying for a fact you've screwed the hangman's daughter, Johnny?"

The dirty-mouthed rider looked down at the floor to sheepishly confess he wasn't speaking from personal experience.

The barber said, "There you go. What a man hears told and what he knows for a fact ain't always the same and you don't want Limey Norwich hearing you've been mean-mouthing his only child, Johnny. Limey may need specs and he may talk funny, but he has a temper and he's killed more than one man the hard way, without his rope."

There was an uneasy murmur of agreement. Longarm waited, saw nobody was fixing to answer his next question, and asked the room in general, "How did that story about Robles and this hangman's daughter get started?"

The barber shrugged and said, "Oh, Miss Joy came forward at the trial to witness for the greaser. She said the reason he'd fibbed about being out to the Triple Eight all evening was that he'd been with her, in bed, at the hotel. Lord only knows why she told such a whopper, but she did, owning up to rutting with a Mex just to save his greasy hide. Ain't that a bitch?"

Everyone but Longarm chuckled. Longarm quietly asked, "How come you all thought it was a lie? Wouldn't such an admission constitute a solid alibi unless it could be proven a lie?"

Another customer said, "It would have. I was on the jury. Trouble with Miss Joy's exercise in self-abasement was that it never happened. The three repentant young squirts who'd been with him at the whorehouse, shooting whores, all swore he'd been there with *them*. And then the night clerk at the hotel said he'd never hired a room, that night or any other, to any damn Mex or an unwed maid he knew on sight as the daughter of a man with a temper and a rep to back the same."

The barber said, "There you have it. The poor young gal has some sort of romantic vapor about Rick Robles. He's a handsome devil in that greasy way some of 'em have.

13

Folk around town recall him sparking her at the Greenup Dance the month before last. But that's all there is to it. A romantical maid with no swain of her own trying to save the neck of a murderous Mex at considerable cost to her own reputation."

"What might her daddy, your local hangman, have to say about all of this romantic bullshit?" Longarm calmly asked.

The barber sounded calm as he replied, "Old Limey don't beat Miss Joy, herself. But he's been known to horsewhup whistling cowboys and she once beat the shit out of two other gals who mocked her."

Longarm whistled softly and muttered, "Remind me never to fool with your hangman or his daughter! Where do you reckon those other rascals have been getting the dynamite or blasting powder to landslide those coaches out along the post road?"

The rider who'd heard tell about the morals of the hangman's only daughter sounded just as certain when he volunteered, "Dynamite. Takes pounds of blasting powder to move as much rock as ounces of dynamite."

An older man waiting objected thoughtfully, "I've lifted many a stump out of a field with the black powder you could carry in a beer schooner. Outlaw could pack eight or ten pounds of black powder in his saddle roll and nobody would be the wiser unless they lit a cigar too close to his ass."

The others argued both sides until Longarm was sore at himself for ever raising the question. There were advantages and disadvantages to either method and Longarm didn't join the jeering laughter when the old man in the chair suggested they might be doing it Apache style. Just getting behind a really big boulder and *shoving*.

You'd have to start much farther upslope to get a good landslide the most primitive way. After that, the crew of the intended target would have way more time to see all that rock and dusty scree coming down at them. But how much time were they talking about and what was a driver to do about such a nightmare situation in such time as he

14

had to work with? Longarm couldn't honestly say, himself, whether he'd brake or try to outrun an avalanche, even half-expecting one on a trail where they'd hit before.

He hadn't learned a useful thing by the time it got to be his turn and he got his first hot-toweled lazy shave for weeks. But when it was done Longarm respectfully declined the barber's offer to show him their line of razors and shaving soaps. The shaving kit he had saddled-bagged over the foot of his bedstead at the hotel would have done him fine if he hadn't needed an excuse to gossip in a local barbershop.

Clean shaven, save for his heroic mustache, smelling of more bay rum than he usually used, Longarm put on the federal badge he normally kept pinned in his wallet to save tedious identifications and introductions as he indulged in more gossip up and down the winding main street of Ambush. There were usually half a dozen hardware, feed and general stores selling dynamite or black powder in a mining camp. Shops in mining camps by definition sold things needed around mining camps and that old timer had been right about the need to blow tree stumps as well in fresh-settled country. But after that, try as he might, Longarm couldn't find anyone who recalled a customer asking for explosives with a view to stopping an Ambush to Durango coach.

He picked up a tad more gossip about the handsome Rick Robles and Mexicans in general around Ambush as he jawed with merchants and their customers. Robles was said to be one of those American citizen Mexicans created by the Treaty of Guadalupe Hidalgo, ending the Mexican War in Uncle Sam's considerable favor.

In exchange for most everything west of El Paso, Washington had said the residents of former Mexican territories who'd suddenly found themselves north of the new border could be U.S. citizens if they wanted to and most had wanted to because, for all his faults, Tio Sam, as they called him, wasn't any meaner to them than your average Mexican government and, when you got a government as mean as the current one run by *el presidente* Porfirio Diaz, other Mexicans snuck across the border to be American citizens as well.

As was always the case where one tried to mix oil and water, folk of one ancestry or another got along or didn't get along, as things worked out. Folk with Mex surnames were treated tolerable out on the West Coast, *bragged* about their ancestry in New Mexico and tended to be treated with ill-concealed contempt in Texas. So the way Colorado folk felt about Mexicans depended some on where they'd come from in the first place. Most seemed willing to tolerate Mexicans in modest numbers as long as they behaved themselves. Shooting up whorehouses was condemned by one and all, while Longarm got the impression some locals might have wanted Rick Robles strung up just for sparking a gal with tan hair, hazel eyes and an English surname.

Longarm ate a stand-up noon dinner of steak and home fries, served by the same plump Jenny Crowfeather at that same beanery, sent a progress report to his home office from the nearby Western Union, and headed back to his hotel to dig spare smokes from his saddlebag and have another sit-down read of those reports on the grim coach crushings.

When he got to the hotel the room clerk said, "One of the federal witnesses you've rounded up is waiting up in your room, Deputy Long. She said you'd said she was to wait in your room, discreet, so I sent her on up with an extra key."

Longarm gravely nodded as if he knew what the jasper was talking about and headed up the stairs as he reached for his own key. Like most experienced travelers, Longarm pocketed a hotel key and hung on to it rather than fume and fuss at the desk every time he went in or out. Most hotel clerks approved. Whether it was official hotel policy or not, it saved them a heap of work and he'd seldom had anyone give him a hard time about it.

He never stayed a second night where they gave him a hard time about anything. He paid what they asked, didn't

16

burn holes in the mattress and felt no call to take shit off anybody.

As he approached the door of his hired room with the key in his left hand he naturally drew his .44-40 with his right. He favored the Colt double action Army '78, chambered for the same .44-40 rounds as his Winchester '73, because it could self-cock so quietly in dark woods or a deserted hallway.

He silently slipped the key in the lock to discover the latch was open. So he flung the door open and followed the muzzle of his .44-40 in, fast, crabbing to one side and ready for most anything.

He hadn't expected to see a long-limbed naked lady reclining across his bed covers with a pillow propping her shapely rump higher to offer him a mighty interesting view of the gaping pink slit between her widespread thighs as she suggested he shut the hall door.

He did. He certainly didn't want any of the hired help to see his uninvited guest in that position.

When he politely asked if she was sure she had the right room the hangman's daughter calmly replied, "I hope I have. They tell me you like the ladies, and vice versa, Mister Longarm. So why don't we get that part out of the way so we can talk about my true love?"

Longarm had to laugh. Then he had to ask, "Do you usually commence a conversation about your true love by spreading your crotch open to another man entire, Miss Joy?"

To which Joy Norwich calmly replied, "If I have to, to save his life. My Rick is innocent. Those other riders accused him to protect a real pal by pinning the blame on an outsider they never really liked. So why don't you take off your clothes, throw the blocks to me, and let's see how we can get my poor innocent lamb out of that awful fix he's in. They say you're the best lawman in the West and I like to think I'm the best lay West of the divide. So why don't we put our bodies and brains together and get my poor lover-lamb out of that awful fix my daddy's preparing?"

Chapter 3

Once he'd gotten to gazing in other directions Longarm had noticed she'd draped her tan whipcord riding habit over the McClellan saddle he'd laid over the foot of the brass bedstead. As he drifted that way, holstering his six gun, he noticed she'd smoothed the whipcoard neatly, as if she'd been taking her own calm time. As he drifted, she put her thighs together and sat up, which only helped some because her bare breasts were bodacious in the afternoon sunlight bouncing off the windowsill to light 'em from below. She stared up with the puzzled eyes of a housecat regarding a stranger as Longarm picked up her duds and tossed them to her, saying, "I'd be obliged if you'd make yourself more decent, Ma'am."

She demanded, "What's the matter, don't you like girls?"

Longarm smiled ruefully and replied, "More than my boss approves, as a matter of fact, and later tonight I'll doubtless be playing my own banjo and cussing myself for a sissy. But I'd rather act the sissy than the fool, Miss Joy. So, like I said, I wish you'd get dressed, now."

She leaned back on her elbows to spread her thighs again and buck and grind her tempting pelvis as she purred, "Come on, you know you want some of this, Handsome!"

Longarm stood with the brass rails of the bedstead between her offer and the bulge in his pants as he truthfully replied, "I want *all* of it. I'm a natural man and you're a handsome woman. But the thing that makes a natural man a man instead of a hound dog or a kid shooting up a whore-house is the common sense it takes to see we can't always have what we want when we want it, Miss Joy. By this time half the town of Ambush knows you've come to pay this call on me and I'd sure feel the fool if your daddy was to bust in right now, even with me on my feet and dressed total. So do you aim to put your damned duds on or do I have to leave you up here acting silly all by your ownself?"

As he half turned toward the unlocked door Joy Norwich sat up to grope for her riding habit, pleading, "Hear me out! You have to help me save my true love and I was only trying to make friends the best way I know how, Mister Longarm."

As he saw she was hauling the folds of whipcord over her tan hair, he relented enough to say, "My friends call me Custis and, no offense, you weren't out to make friends. You were out to wrap this child around your little finger and does your true love, Ricardo Robles, know how sassy you've been acting on his behalf?"

Smoothing the riding skirts down over her bare legs Joy bent forward to gather her boots and calf-length socks from the braided rug as she confided, "I'd gang-fuck the posse that brought Rick in and take on the judge and jury if I thought it would get him off. Fucking one man is a lot like fucking any other. But I really *love* my dusky latin lover!"

Longarm didn't ask if the Mex et pussy. He figured it had to be something like that, or better. Seeing she was hauling on her boots like a proper witness calling on a lawman, Longarm fished out a three-for-a-nickel cheroot and thumbnailed a matchhead aflame for himself. No gent raised under the social rules of Queen Victoria ever offered a lady he'd never screwed a smoke.

As he stood there, lighting up, the gal seated on his bed-stead tried to sell him the same tale she'd told at the trial of her true love, with little more luck.

He gently but firmly pointed out, "You say you and this notorious Mexican flash shacked up here at this hotel, on a payday night with a whole lot of drinking and hell-raising going on? No offense, Miss Joy, but you'll have to do better than that. I know you weren't over to the barbershop with me earlier, but both you and young Robles have folk gossiping about you as much or more than you might deserve. Had Rick Robles been here in the center of town with you instead of over in that house of ill repute in less well-lit parts of Ambush, you'd have had more luck selling your story at his trial."

She sobbed, "All right, I wasn't with him here that night. I wasn't with him anywhere. But I know he wasn't with Will, Buck and Hank at that cathouse. Rick didn't need to pay for pussy, mine or any of the other girls he had in these parts, the adorable scamp."

"Where do you reckon he was, then?" Longarm asked, pressing on to suggest, "With some other gal who didn't admire him enough to testify to her shame at his trial?"

Joy looked away and said, "He was riding with other pals. I wasn't supposed to tell anyone. He said he'd come to me after midnight, once they'd finished some chore they had in mind."

Longarm blew a thoughtful smoke ring. Joy stared up through it at him. "You have to believe me, Custis! This time I'm telling the simple truth. Rick didn't ride to town with the other hands off the Triple Eight. That might have been why the three who got in trouble that night in town set out to frame him. Rick was more grown-up than your average young cowboy. He rode with other like-minded men on what he said was more serious business."

Longarm started to ask what serious business, serious *honest* business a top hand off a cattle spread and some like-minded pals might have on a payday Saturday night if it wasn't in town or on their own range. But Joy Norwich had just said she wouldn't tell him, assuming she knew. So Longarm blew smoke out both notrils like a bull making up its mind to charge and declared, "I want you to go on about your own beeswax, where the town gossips can see I ain't groping at you, Miss Joy. In the meanwhile I'll be headed up to the county jail for a talk with your true love about his true whereabouts on the night in question."

Joy Norwich clapped her hands, leaped to her feet to circle the foot of the bedstead and, being such a tall gal, only had to stand on her toes a tad to haul the cheroot from his mouth and plant a big, wet smack under his mustache.

Longarm kissed back. Most men would have. When they came up for air she thrust her pubic bone forward against his fly to growl, "Now aren't you sorry you passed on my earlier offer?"

He was, but he laughed and led her out into the hall so's he could lock up. He didn't perform his usual trick with a match stem wedged in a door hinge. Secret tricks weren't secret when you performed them in front of folk.

Longarm got Joy downstairs and out the front entrance, where he performed a polite public parting on the plank walk so's any old biddy hens watching would have to report they'd gone their seperate ways, no matter what they'd been jawing about.

Longarm legged it back up to the small but thick-walled county jail as, sure enough, the clouds sweeping upslope from the west commenced to darken and clear their throats from time to time.

At the jail house Longarm flashed his wallet warrant as well as the badge he'd pinned to his lapel, earlier, and said he had to speak to Ricardo Robles in private.

The county turnkeys obliged with no argument. Longarm soon found himself alone in a dinky interrogation cell across a deal table from the condemned Ricardo Robles, a good-looking young gent in his early twenties, with more Spanish than Indian blood, but still more Mex than Don Quixote in those book illustrations. His jailors had stripped Robles down to his bare feet, bell-bottom pants and undershirt, as if they feared he might hang himself in his cell with his boots. Lots of Anglo riders liked those fancy Mex boots.

When Longarm introduced himself and held a hand across the table Robles shook, polite enough, but said, "I don't see why the U.S. government would want to talk to me about that dumb whorehouse shooting I took no part in, Deputy Long."

Longarm nodded gravely and replied, "Your true love, Miss Joy, told me you weren't there that night, Rick. She told me where you were that night and who you were really riding with. I know you told her not to tell anybody and she didn't want to tell me until I pointed out it was your only hope."

It didn't work. Rick Robles cocked an amused eyebrow at Longarm to reply, "Nice try. Joy couldn't have told you toad squat because I never told her toad squat. I learned long ago that the three most rapid forms of communication are telegraph, telephone and tell a woman. I'm sticking to my story that I was out at the Triple Eight, night riding some new bobwire fencing, whilst Buck, Will and Hank were raising hell at Madame Frenchy's. I can't tell you why. I've never been there. I am not inclined to frequent such places."

Longarm said, "I believe you. Miss Joy's a handsome woman and she says you have others willing to dance the fandango with you. But let's try her another way, Robles. Had you been with Joy Norwich or any of your other gals in town you'd have been seen, and noted. You're one of the only Mex riders in these parts and you likely know you ain't too popular with some of the local riders."

Robles shrugged and replied, "I spit in their mother's milk. None of them have *los huevos* for to tell me how they feel about me to my face!"

Longarm smiled thinly and said, "*Sin duda, pues* I put it to you that you weren't in town, you weren't out at the Triple Eight, so you were night riding with a person or person's unknown on the Saturday before last."

"Meaning what?" The Mex accused of shooting up a whorehouse shrugged.

So there it lay like a gob of spit on the unpainted pine between them and the only way Longarm could put it was, "Meaning the very last stagecoach smashed flat whilst packing the U.S. mail was hit by night riders that same payday night. They doubtless hit it with payday in mind. I understand there was paper money as well as specie and gold dust in the strong box that was never recovered, Robles. Would you care to tell me where you boys left it after you dug it out of all that mountainside you swept it downslope with?"

The condemned man looked incredulous and replied, "You're as *loco en la cabeza* as Joy Norwich! Are you accusing me and my true friends of robbing those coaches?"

Longarm nodded soberly and said, "Yep. But I'll allow I can't prove it. So I was wondering if you might care to confess."

Rick Robles laughed dryly and asked, "Would you care to take a flying fuck at a rolling wagon wheel or, better yet, *tu madre*?"

Longarm stood up and replied, "Suit yourself and let's leave our mothers out of this. I don't mean to say that twice. Seeing you seem bound and determined to enjoy the rope dance with those others, come Monday morn, I'll be on my way and we'll say no more about it."

But as he turned to leave Robles said, "*Un momento, por favor.* Are you saying I won't have to die if I confess to killing and robbing all those others out along the post road?"

Longarm shrugged and said, "We all have to die, sooner or later. If you stick to your guns you'll get to die next Monday. If I ask them for you on a federal warrant the county prosecutor will likely make a fuss and Lord only knows how long it will be before we can even get started for the federal court in Denver."

"What happens after you get me to Denver?" asked Robles, cautiously.

Longarm truthfully but not unkindly replied, "Oh, they'll hang you high for interfering with the U.S. mails so mean."

"You sure don't offer a man much, Tio Sam."

Longarm shrugged and said, "Things are tough all over.

What were you *expecting* anyone to give you for premeditated murder by landslide, a fucking *medal*? You're going to hang here, sooner, or yonder, later. The boys who stood trial with you for a local killing will be dead and buried by the time my outfit can even set a date for your trial over on the far side of the divide."

Robles thought and then demanded, "What if I should be found innocent of robbing those coaches?"

Longarm said, "You won't. I ain't about to charge you with a federal crime until such time as I can present some evidence in the form of a signed confession with some exclusionary details."

When Robles asked what he was talking about, Longarm explained, "We get heaps of *pendejos* ready, willing and anxious to confess in general. They say that after Lincoln was shot and the identity of his killer was known, men lined up to confess they'd done the dirty deed at Ford's Theatre. So we like to have admissions to guilty knowlege, or things only the guilty could know, before we arraign anybody on a confession alone. You're going to have to convince me you're sincere about those smashed up and looted coaches along the post road. The names of your accomplices would make a fair start."

"*Veta pa'l carajo*, do you take me for a *paloma de la banqueta* who would sell his friends to save himself?"

Longarm said, "It happens. The lawmen out front know where to find me should you decide to come clean with us. If you don't, I'll likely see you Monday morning as they lead the four of you up those thirteen steps."

He moved to the oak door barred on the outside and kicked it some to attract the turnkey as Robles insisted, "You have to make me a better offer than you have, so far, Deputy Long. Wouldn't it count in my favor if I gave you the whole gang and named the leader?"

Longarm repressed a grimace of distaste as he soberly replied, "I ain't the judge you'd be appearing before in the Denver District Court. He might let you off with Life at Hard in exchange for such testimony. He might not. Speaking from experience, once you turn your leader in he's likely going to accuse you of being the leader. Everybody thought Cole Younger led the James-Younger gang until Cole and his brothers got captured back in Minnesota and old Cole explained he'd only been taking orders from Frank and Jesse. Frank is the oldest, with the most wartime experience, but whether he or his kid brother, Jesse, are leading the gang right now will likely depend on what any living survivors say. I can only promise to deliver you alive in Denver long after your pals are dead and gone."

The turnkeys came to let Longarm out and frog-march Robles back to his death cell. As they did so the doomed *vaquero* called after Longarm, "Get me some more time! I need more time to think your grim offer through!"

Longarm half turned to call back, "They're giving you plenty of time. They ain't fixing to hang you until Monday morn. But get word to me by tomorrow afternoon. I don't see how I could wrangle you a stay of execution on a sabbath, with all the judges and Governor Pitkin Lord knows where."

Then he turned to leave before Robles could argue further. Longarm had done his best and figured the odds were two to one in his favor that the kid would crack Sunday night, with the fancy last meal most of them ordered untouched and turning cold, as the sands of time ran down his spine.

Longarm had sat many a death watch and eaten his share of apple pie a la mode forced upon him by a condemned man who'd suddenly lost his appetite and wanted to be friends with everybody in sight.

Of course, as he'd just warned Rick Robles, the wee small hours of a sabbath night would be way too late to wire Denver. So Longarm headed for the Western Union near the stage depot to wire that Friday afternoon, while he still had plenty of time and Rick Robles had no way of knowing.

Chapter 4

Standing at the Western Union counter with a stub pencil, Longarm worded his wire to the home office with care. That song about the old boy out in the jailyard, down on his knees, asking the warden to pardon him, please, only went to show how little most lawbreakers knew about the way the law really worked. A stay of execution was tougher than that to wrangle, once invites to the hanging had gone out.

Longarm didn't have enough, yet, to pester Judge Dickerson in the federal court down the hall from the marshal's office. But Longarm's boss, Marshal Billy Vail, had enough pull with the local machine to ask for a stay from Governor Pitkin, based on likely new evidence. Hardly anybody on the side of the law approved of those bloody stagecoach robberies and so, as disappointed at the local crowds might be, Colorado ought to be willing to hold one of the four condemned men in reserve, for now.

Longarm sent his wire direct at a nickel a word, having meant what he'd said to Robles about the hours bankers and politicians kept.

Leaving the telegraph office, Longarm headed next for the combined livery service and corral up the way from his hotel to strike another bird with the same mosey.

The Associated Hostlers of Ambush Inc. appeared to be managed by a tall, rangy tomboy a tad too calloused and tan for a gal and a mite too pretty for a boy. She shook like a boy who'd pitched some hay growing up and said he could call her Meg Connors. After that she was sun-bleach blond with eyes of cornflower blue that matched her mannish shirt. Her split riding skirts were a duller shade of blue denim. She wore her hair parted and braided Arapaho style with no hat. Her feet were encased in low-heeled army boots as stern as Longarm's, with a lot more dust and horse shit rubbed in. The rest of her smelled of castile soap and lavender toilet water, with just a hint of honest recent sweat. He liked her even before she smiled and said, "Proud to meet you and what can we do for you, Deputy Long?"

He said, "My friends call me Custis. I'm trying to cut the trail of those road agents and might you keep tight enough records to be worth my poring over 'em, Miss Meg?"

She asked what kind of records they were jawing about and when he told her she shook her blond head ruefully and explained, "It saves a heap of bookkeeping when you just tally up daily profits against a week's expenses. We hardly ever buy straw and fodder by the wagonfull as often as once a week. I'll show you how we tally charges if you'd want to come inside with me."

He was starting to want to come inside most anybody after not having come at all since leaving Denver a few nights back. But he kept his thoughts and his hands to himself as he followed, admiring a very shapely rump filling blue denim nicely under the concho belt the gal had cinched around her trim waist.

Meg Connors led him inside the cluttered office off the tack room it shared in a wing of the rambling one-story stable complex of sun-silvered pine. Atop a rolltop desk stood two paper spikes, impaling two stacks of paper slips. Meg explained that when a customer came to stable or hire a horse she wrote down the terms of the deal as the customer and Associated Hostlers of Ambush Inc. understood them.

Meg said, "We don't require a deposit from repeat riders

27

we know well enough to trust. On the other hand you've heard the poem about Little Dapple Gray?"

Longarm nodded and soberly recited,

"I had a little pony, his name was Dapple Gray.
I lent him to a lady, to ride upon one day.
She whipped him and she lashed him,
She rode him through the mire,
I will not lend my pony, now, for anybody's hirel"

Meg nodded grimly and said, "You can't always tell, just looking, who's likely to be hard on horseflesh and who ain't. So we ask two bits a day with a ten-dollar deposit from strangers. If they bring the critter back in good repair we just charge them the two-bits a day. As I see your problem, you're asking about mysterious strangers hiring mounts on mayhaps the day before one of those stage coach robberies. Sheriff Peabody has already asked. I had to tell him the same as I'm telling you; I ain't sure for certain it's really going to storm before sundown, but I'm a fair hand at guessing. So I guess I'd recall if anyone made a habit of hiring livery mounts at the time of yet another robbery and at no times between. We keep a note of the customer's name, the pony's name, and the times off and away on this left-hand spike. When they bring the mount back we make a note of that time and put the slip on this other spike, along with a note as to any monies paid or owed. At the end of the week all the profits are lumped as a single figure against consolidated costs in our business ledger. Sheriff Peabody, the old fuss, said it was a primitive way to keep books but, as I asked him to no avail, what law says we have to keep any books at all? Can you name anyone, public or private, who'd have any right to poke through the private records of an honest business?"

Longarm shook his head and said, "I ain't here accusing you and yours of anything, Miss Meg. You'd have recalled when the sheriff asked if you'd held back any records of unpaid claims against more likely suspects. But could we try her another way?"

When the whipcord firm but not bad-looking tomboy nodded Longarm said, "Assuming Sheriff Peabody and me are following the same process of eliminating, we've both suspected the crooks we're after may be two-faces holed up right in town, pretending to be something other than road agents or even full-time riders. Riders working regular for a cattle outfit might have more trouble accounting for where they've been with a particular pony, see?"

She nodded brightly and said, "Of course, it's up to the wrangler in charge of each spread's remuda who rides where aboard what. Sheriff Peabody already explained how the rascals could be hiring ponies for some night riding but, as I told him, not from us, unless I'm missing something."

Longarm thought before he decided, "There's more than one way to skin a cat or change from shank's mare to saddle on short notice, Miss Meg. Don't many a merchant or mining man board a now-and-again mount for riding now and again?"

She nodded and said, "Many of the poor brutes suffer sore from the lack of exercise. I have some boys who run 'em around the paddock out back from time to time and some few townsmen are smart enouth to let us hire their mounts out for livery riding, with us deleting our fees from their own. But we'd have noticed if anybody made a practice of taking their ponies out for night riding on all the nights you and the sheriff seem so interested in."

Longarm asked if Rick Robles or any of his friends made a pracitce of coralling their ponies there, when in town. Meg shook her head and said, "Not hardly. Dollar-a-day cowhands tend to leave their ponies tethered in front of the card house or wherever whilst in town, hard as it may be on horseflesh. We do board the big thoroughbred of that lady both of you seem so interested in, however."

Longarm blinked and asked if she'd back up and drive that past him some more. When she said she was talking about the handsome gelding of Joy Norwich, the hangman's daughter, Longarm protested, "Hold on, Miss Meg. Miss Joy may be *his* gal. Whatever in blue blazes might have given you the notion *I* was interested in her?"

The tall, tanned tomboy grinned like a mean little kid and demanded, "Wan't she alone with you in your room at the hotel, and has Miss Joy Norwich in living memory been alone with a man she didn't like, a lot?"

Longarm laughed incredulously and protested, "My only interest in Joy Norwich is as a suspect in . . ." then he caught himself, remembered that as far as anyone but the road agents knew, Rick Robles was only slated to hang for a whorehouse killing. He lamely finished, "She did come to me at yonder hotel to ask my help in getting her true love off. I told her the federal government had no juristiction in local hangings and I'd be obliged if you'd spread the word that a two-faced room clerk has a vivid imagination about government witnesses!"

Meg Connors dimpled up at him to reply, "I'll tell them, but those few who believe me will say you passed on a sure thing."

As they went back outside she confided, "I'm glad for you both. My opinion of you just went up a notch and poor Joy could surely use the rest."

He smiled uncertainly and asked, "Speaking as a woman, would you say it was usual for a lady as indiscriminate with her favors as they say she is to be so desperate to save one lover at some cost to her own reputation, time and trouble?"

Meg Conners shrugged and said, "Speaking for myself, I'd never go for a womanizing dollar-a-day cowboy to begin with. I can't say why she carried on like that in court for Rick Robles. The day I stand up for a man who was cheating on me in a house of ill repute will be the day the people from the funny farm come to carry me away!"

Before Longarm could answer there came a distant roll of thunder from somewhere off to the west. So Longarm allowed he had to get it on down the road and they parted friendly, albeit not as friendly as a man who hadn't been getting any lately might have chosen. It sure beat all how a pretty gal kept getting prettier as a man went on jawing with her.

It was getting late and the sky was darkening more by the minute. So Longarm headed for his nearby hotel, knowing the day was about shot and his slicker was lashed to his saddle at the foot of his bed if he thought of anywhere he just had to go in a mountain thunderstorm.

But he was stopped on the walk by a skinny little gent in an undertaker's outfit who said he was Matt Greene, running the north end of that victimized stage line.

Longarm held out a hand, said he was glad to know Greene and allowed he'd been planning to drop in on them.

Greene shook without enthusiasm and said, "We've been expecting you, a heap. How come you got off our coach last night and went direct to the hotel without even sticking your nose in our depot office along your merry way?"

Longarm said, "I was tired. It was late. It's been my experience that after six or so in the evening the bigger frogs in the puddle have gone home and the little frogs can only chirp without telling a lawman a whole lot. So instead of chirping with little froggies I had my mighty late supper and went to bed early. I got up early and I've been talking to all sorts of folk and you were just about next on my list."

Greene growled, "In that case let's belly up to the bar in that Bighorn Saloon across the way. I was commencing to suspect you might suspect me and mine of something."

"The thought never crossed my mind," lied Longarm as they strode across a clearing street as the winds picked up. Some cowponies out front of their destination were fighting their tethers and trying to bust loose from the hitching rail, as anybody but their likely drunken riders inside could see there was going to come a gullywasher.

Longarm's opinion of Matt Greene went up as he followed the little cuss through the swinging doors to hear him yell, "Seth Warren and Jack Fennel, get away from that bar and get your ponies under cover before that storm breaks outside. Ain't neither one of you got ears?"

As the sheepish hands ducked out into the gathering storm Longarm followed Greene into the spaces they'd left at the crowded bar. Seeing only two of the crowd had tethered mounts out front, it was safe to assume most of the regulars at that hour worked in town or over in the placers along Ambush Creek.

Longarm could have told the stage-line manager about that other boss down in the Four Corners masterminding stagecoach robberies. Greene doubtless knew how Sheriff Henry Plummer's confederates, working for that Montana line, had chalk-marked those coaches worth stopping by gang member out along the trail. He felt no call to bring either up.

He let the wiry little fuss drone on about their own more recent robberies as he absently studied the sun-bleached skull of the bighorn mountain sheep mounted over the back bar's grimey mirror, idly wondering what it was doing there but not really caring. Until recently they'd had a *human* skull over the back bar of the Cosmopolitan Saloon over in Bodie, California. The grim display was the skull of the prospector who'd made the town of Bodie mushroom on the east slope of the Sierra Nevada. His name had been Waterman Body, not Bodie, but he'd pronounced it Bodie and so, after he'd been dead a spell and they'd named the place Bodie they dug up Bill Body's bones and mounted his skull over the back bar in the biggest saloon in town. Longarm had never gotten a very clear answer as to why they'd done that, either.

Matt Greene was going on and on about the sort of yellow-bellied rascals who'd aim a landslide instead of a gun at a Concord they were out to stop.

When Longarm suggested dead men told no tales on two-faces known to coach passengers and crew, Greene moaned, "Jesus H. Christ! Are you saying the killers could be anyone from the boys spitting and whittlng on the depot steps to one of the regulars in this saloon, right now?"

Longarm shrugged and replied, "If I knew who they might be I might up and arrest 'em, Matt. My job would be easier if crooks were not by definition so damned crooked. Crooked and sneaky mean the same thing."

They made short enough work of the round Greene bought and then the round Longarm had to buy in return. Longarm spoke little and let the worried stage line man do most of the talking, despite the fact that Greene didn't have a thing to say that Longarm didn't already know.

When Greene proposed a third round Longarm stopped him by saying, "No offense, but I got to get back to the hotel. I cast some bread on the water earlier, and I'm hoping to hear from somebody by bedtime."

Green allowed he had to get on home to bed with his own little woman. Longarm didn't ask if Greene had heard some gossip about himself and what seemed to be the town punchboard. As the two of them got back outside it was dusk and some rain had commenced to fall. Then a bolt of lightning rent the dark sullen sky above and in the gloom to follow Longarm decided aloud he could make it almost directly across from his hotel for one wet dash by working his way along store-front awnings on their side of the now muddy main street.

Before the wiry little Matt Greene could answer a much bigger man with an Able Lincoln beard, only straw-colored, upped to Longarm to declare, "My name is Cedric Norwich and I am looking for a man they call Longarm."

The even taller deputy so addressed noticed Norwich had pronounced his name like "porridge," the way folk did in Limey Land. So he knew he he was talking to Limey Norwich, the county hangman, and replied, "I'd be the man you're after, friend. What would you want with me?"

To which Norwish coldly replied, spreading his boot heels and opening his frock coat to expose ivory gun-grips, "What would *you* want with the man who's been black-mailing your daughter, an invitation to dance? You'd better step to one side, Matt Greene. I've nothing against you, but a father has to do what a father has to do at times like these!"

Chapter 5

Matt Greene had vanished into the wind, rain and gathering dusk by the time Longarm could say, "Hold on, Mister Norwich. Before one or more of us dies dumb as hell, you have my word as an enlisted man and gentleman that I have never made a play for your daughter!"

To which the hangman replied with a weary sigh, "Good Lord, I'd have been hung on my own gallows, long ago, if I started shooting the men who've only *tried* to diddle my daughter. Her poor mother and I tried to raise her properly. But I fear Joy would flirt with anything in pants and lead the poor bugger on, the naughty child. But I say, we know that you know and all that rot. So fill your fist, as you bloody Yanks put it!"

Longarm protested, "One of us is *loco en la cabeza* as Miss Joy's better friends might put it, no offense! Before you kill me would you please explain what you're so sore about if you don't gun men just for chasing after a known flirt, as you fucking Limies put it?"

Norwich was getting tougher to see in the dank darkness along the awning-protected walk as rain ran betwixt them and the street in solid silvery sheets. But Longarm could see enough to know it was time to soothe the savage beast or go for his own gun any time now, as the outraged Englishman demanded, "Are you going to say you didn't tell my daughter you could arrest her on a federal charge unless she came to your hotel room, tonight, ready to service you

34

in perverse fashion down her throat and up her bum?"

Longarm laughed incredulously and said, "I sure am! What sort of a federal case could this child build against a gal who admires Mexican cooking and likes to tell fibs?"

Longarm sensed he'd struck a nerve when the outraged father sort of flinched and asked, "Are you implying my Joy would say you'd demanded perverse sexual favors in your sordid quarters if you hadn't done so?"

Longarm replied without mercy, "Ain't implying. Saying. If Joy told you I made any sort of play for her I can see why a jury of her peers paid no attention when she said Rick Robles was with her on the night of that stagecoach robbery!"

Norwish sounded surer as he growled, "That bloody cowboy is ancient history. I've been soaking stout Kentucky hemp for the four of them and whether or not my Joy ever sullied herself with that Mexican is a moot point. We were talking about you and your own vile intentions for a girl who may be wild but has never been *queer*, God damn your eyes!"

Before Longarm could come up with a reply for the bodacious charge he felt a soft arm slip into the crook of his left elbow from behind as a soft shemale voice purred, "Sorry to keep you waiting out here, lover. But I told you how my boss feels about my sparking with custom, and I still need the job."

It was Jenny Crowfeather, the pleasingly fat Arapaho waitress from that nearby beanery. She'd changed to a sort of Navaho blouse with gathered skirts. Longarm was as surprised as Limey Norwich, but he tried not to let it show as he grinned down at her like a shit-eating dog and said, "It's about time you showed up. This older gent thinks I was here to meet another gal entire, honey."

The Arapaho gal sounded pure Quill Indian as she wailed, "Who is she? I'll snatch her bald-headed! I'll shove a broom up her ass and make her sweep the streets clean out of town! You told me *I* was the gal you meant to spend the whole weekend with, lover man!"

Longarm patted her wrist with his gun hand as he smiled sheepishly at Limey Norwich to confess, "I was trying to keep the two of us our own little secret. As one man to another, could you sort of forget this whole awkward situation?"

Norwich naturally knew the waitress at the beanery near the stage depot. He still sounded confused as he asked nobody in particular, "Am I to understand the two of you had been planning on your own hotel tryst this evening?"

Jenny replied, "I don't know what a tryst is, but we're going over to my place, now. I ain't the sort of gal who goes up to a hotel room with a man after dark!"

Then she nudged Longarm to add, "Let's go, lover man. I got cold cuts and a warm nature waiting on us just across the creek."

So Longarm let her lead him away, with the spot between his shoulder blades itching like hell as Limey Norwich moaned aloud, "By God's little whiskers, this time you've gone to far, Joy, megirl!"

As they drew out of earshot Longarm murmured, "I'm much obliged and that was mighty rapid thinking, Miss Jenny! How come you thought so rapid back there, though?"

She answered simply, "I was on my way home. I heard you talking. I stood in a doorway and listened until I understood what you were talking about. I thought maybe Limey Norwich wouldn't think you were out to meet his daughter at your hotel if you were coming home with me. I hope I didn't make you feel foolish back there, Deputy Long."

Longarm gripped her arm tighter with his elbow as he assured her, "If you didn't just save my life you sure saved me an even sillier conversation with the county coroner and my friends call me Custis, Miss Jenny. How could your fast-thinking have made me look foolish, just now?"

She sighed and said, "I have a mirror on my cabin door. I hate what I see in it. But I have to make sure my hair don't need more brushing and my duds are hanging on me

36

right as I go out the door in the cold gray light of dawn. When we get to the end of the awnings you can run for your hotel and I'll run from my place in the same dark. Nobody will know you were only desperate to avoid a fight when you allowed you had something going with a fat squaw."

Longarm knew "Squaw" wasn't considered as insulting to Algonquinoid Arapaho as it was to Ute or NaDéné speakers. But from the way she said the word he knew she meant it as all too many white men did. He told her, "There's no reason to low-rate yourself just for being an Indian, Miss Jenny. You had no more to say about being what you are than I had to say about being what I am and I got plenty of Indian pals. Some of 'em Arapaho. There's a Denver bakery run by an Arapaho family living like you, off the Great White Father's grub line."

"How many of them are old, fat and ugly?" She sighed, as they neared the end of the plank walk to hear Ambush Creek growling in the dark ahead of them.

Longarm soothed, "You can't be more than thirty. I'll allow you could afford to lose a few pounds. But you know you ain't ugly, on the outside or inside. What you just done for a stranger in need was downright beautiful, ma'am!"

They reached the end of the walk and the last of the overhead pine planking. She turned to face him in the dim light. He could barely see her face but he could hear the tears in her voice when she told him, "I'll always remember you saying that, Custis. It was sweet of you to try and I can make it the rest of the way from here, now."

He held on to her bare arm as he insisted, "I have to see you all the way home. I wasn't brung up to let a lady who'd just saved me from a gunfight ford a torrent alone in the dark."

So she allowed it was his funeral if they both got drowned and for a time it looked as if they might. The usually ankle-deep current that the petering-out cinder path forded north of town was now closer to crotch deep and they were talking about a tall man's crotch as Longarm had to literally haul Jenny most of the way, once she was in as deep as her waist with her pudgy legs swept from under her by the foaming rainwater. But they wound up laughing as Longarm half dragged her out on the far side and as they stood there laughing in the rain-swept darkness it somehow seemed only natural to kiss, and then kiss wilder. But as she felt his free hand cupping a melon breast through her sopping wet cotton blouse Jenny husked, "Not here. In my cabin, where nobody can see. Not even us!"

By then it was so dark, all over, that she needed lightning every few paces to lead Longarm along a twisty path through some granite outcrops to her modest but clean-smelling and neatly kept cabin of shingled frame construction. A man who hadn't been getting any tended to grope a friendly gal some as they staggered through a thunderstorm. So he had Jenny hot as himself under her soaking-wet duds and cool clean hide. He struck a match and got to see what things looked like in her two-room cabin for as long as it took her to blow it out and plead, "Don't light my lamp. Take me right to bed and shove a log in my poor cold stove!"

So he did. They undressed along the way and Jenny said she'd hang their duds to dry later. So Longarm only hung his gunbelt over a bedpost and then they were at it hot and heavy, or clammy and heavy, at least, as he mounted her in the dark to discover he needed no pillow under her ass, thanks to her ample rump, and no lubricant to get it in, despite her tightness, thanks to the good wetting both their crotches had endured, fording Ambush Creek.

Her amazingly childlike hairless love-slit might have worried him more if he hadn't known how many Indian gals plucked their already sparser pubic hairs, and if she hadn't moved that tight little twat in such a womansome way. She threw her plump thighs to the four winds outside and hugged him tight with her palms flat on his buttocks as she babbled sweet but incomprehensible Indian love words, her moist lips pressed to his own while they went deliciously mad for a spell.

Then they'd somehow wound up on the floor with Longarm flat on his back so's Jenny in all her considerable naked glory could slide her tight, wet twat up and down his raging erection as she squatted on her bare heels and hefty haunches, Horse Indian Style. Longarm had suspected she'd come to womanhood in a tipi if she still felt wistful about a Quill Arapaho who'd gone under in the Washita Fight.

White folk who hadn't thought things through were inclined to fault Mister Lo, the Poor Indian, for reversing some of the notions Queen Victoria had about the way a gent was supposed to treat a lady. An Indian walking ahead of his heavily laden squaw, packing no more than his weapon, wasn't out to do her dirt. He led the way so he'd be the one to meet the rattlesnake or worse on the trail ahead. So he wanted to be able to move up, down or sideways with his light weaponry when, not if, he had to. The gal trudging after him with all their stuff wasn't supposed to worry about getting killed along the way if her man was worth trudging after.

As for the notorious Indian custom of "making" the woman get on top, it was usually the Indian gal's own notion because it was a lot easier on her tailbone than taking it on the bottom, with seldom more than a few layers of hide or blanket between one's ass and sod set in solid soil. It seemed safe to assume that having learned to tickle her fancy in a tipi, Jenny just naturally liked it better on top. He had no complaints because his own tailbone was safer with his legs together betwixt Jenny's bare ankles and, even if it hadn't been, she sure moved nice atop a man, with her elbows to either side of his head while her tawny melon-sized breasts smoothed the halves of his mustache with their steady bobbings.

Later, back up in her bed to share a cheroot, Longarm knew she'd been harking back to her tribal days when she suddenly blurted, "You won't tell anybody where I work about this, will you, Custis?"

Longarm dryly replied, "You've ruined my morning

plans. I was set on breezing in to declare I could go for some ham and eggs after coming in their waitress seven times."

She laughed, uncertainly, and said, "I'm serious. Nobody in town must know and I only counted three times, you big silly."

He laughed more sincerely and snuggled her closer as he gallantly assured her, "Me too, so far, but the night is young and I ain't the one you have to worry about if you'd prefer me as a secret lover. I can only speak for myself. What about old Norwich back in town?"

Jenny shrugged, massively, and demurely explained, "Limey Norwich isn't about to spread it all over town that his harlot of a daughter lied to him again! We both heard him say Joy told him you were out to blackmail a screwing out of her. What's he supposed to do, now, tell all his friends he was about to draw on you for trying to screw his daughter when all the time you'd made plans to screw an Indian squaw?"

Longarm removed the cheroot from between his teeth and kissed Jenny friendly before he said, "Don't low-rate yourself like a sob sister writing for the papers back East. Squaw ain't a bad word where you come from or where I'm coming from and your quick thinking surely saved me and that hangman a whole lot of trouble. I'm surely sorry it only hit you later that you were laying your own rep on the line for me, Miss Jenny."

She shrugged some more and replied in a small bitter voice, "I'd do it again, now that I know what a natural man I may have saved from a shooting, and I know how much respect any woman of my kind can hope to get from . . . Oh, have it your way, *most* of your kind. I just don't want any of *my* kind to know about this. Some say bad things about me because I serve *food* to you *waya-bishki-wah* for *wampum*!"

Longarm took a drag on the cheroot and offered her a puff as he mused aloud, "I've seen more than one assimilate up this way, now that all you Wild Indians have been

40

cleared off this slope. How many of 'em might be 'Rapaho, Ute or Mex? It's tough to tell when a dusky cuss in Anglo riding duds is staring at you sort of sullen."

Jenny exhaled and declared, "*We* can tell. Don't ask me how unless you'd care to explain how your kind can tell your Englishmen and your Irishmen apart."

He said, "Sometimes we can't. I'm only asking for a rough guess."

She decided, "About half the folk around here who look Mex are really Mex, drifting north out of New Mexico Territory with Spanish livestock. Most of the others would be Arapaho. Some of our warriors and their dependents came over the divide with your blue sleeves, as scouts, while you were putting down the Ute and Shoshoni more recently."

She sighed and bitterly added, "They sneer at me for serving your kind food while they help the pony shooters fight the Ute who once helped Kit Carson fight the Navaho!"

Longarm took a thoughtful drag and said, "The ancient Romans said Divide and Conquer worked most every time. But you can't cheat honest men and there's two sides to every story, no offense. So before we get into why the cavalry never shot the ponies of the Pawnee or evicted anyone from the Taos pueblo, let's stick to how many Mex or assimilates a certain suspect of the Mex persuasion might have been riding with if the Anglo boys he works with out to the Triple Eight can't cut the mustard with him."

She repeated her guess there were few if any Ute, with the other nonAnglo riders about evenly divided betwixt Mex and 'Rapaho as he snuffed out their smoke and forked a leg between her soft ample thighs. She laughed and demanded, "What are you doing with your palm on my pussy? I thought you wanted to question me about federal crimes!"

He kissed her as he got a better grip on her off-side tit. Then he pointed out, "I *am* questioning you and what I'm doing to you would be a federal offense if we were on a reservation and you were on the BIA rolls as a ward of the government."

She spread her thighs to coyly croon, "I knew there was a lot to be said for living off the Great White Father's stingy blanket!" Then they hissed in mingled pleasure as something gave and he suddenly slid into her tight, hairless slit to enjoy those old familiar yet always sweet surprises of the first few strokes. As he ground it around, deep in her moist depths, Longarm mused aloud, "I might narrow things down a heap if I start with the local Ute riders. In their shining times the Ute were notorious for rolling rocks down mountainsides at folk they were sore at and Lord knows that nation has a lot to be sore about in recent memory."

Jenny gasped, "Don't tease. Move it in and out of me faster and don't worry what breed of Mex or Indian rider might hate your kind the most. They all hate as hard and, speaking of hard, could I get on top some more?"

He growled, "Later. I'm fixing to come again and, like I said, the night is young."

She sighed and replied, "Not as young as you might think. The rain is blowing over and if I don't get you out of here well this side of cockscrow we may both learn more about moody redskins than either of us ever wanted to know!"

Chapter 6

The dark hotel lobby was deserted as Longarm sloshed through it in his sopping wet tweeds and squishing boots. He was glad he'd held on to his room key and that once he got upstairs he found the match stem he'd lodged in the bottom door hinge still in place.

He ducked inside, lit the coal oil lamp on the bed table and hung his wet duds up to dry. He knew wool dried fast in the high, thin air of the West Slope when it wasn't raining. If it stayed wet outside he could use the excuse to change into clean, dry denims from his saddle bags and to hell with the present dress regulations out of Washington.

In the meanwhile some clock outside had just struck four and for some reason he felt a mite tuckered from his visit across that creek. So he whipped the flannel top sheet and quilted comforter down to hit the sack bare-ass and wake up six hours later with the weather outside bright and sunny while he pondered a morning erection and a growling gut.

Nobody but a total pessimist jerked off in the morning before he'd learned who he might be having lunch with. So he ignored his wayward organ grinder as he washed up, shaved himself and hauled on a mostly dry outfit with fresh socks inside his only clammy leather boots. His hatband felt refreshingly cool after the hat had spent the morning on a bedpost with his barely damp gunbelt and holster. He checked his Colt .44-40 for signs of rust, of course, but found none, thanks to the mix of whale oil and dubbing he wiped his weaponry down with now and again.

As he passed through the lobby a tad after ten in the morning the beefy bewhiskered jasper behind the desk called him over. Longarm was trying to come up with a sensible excuse for sleeping so late when the hotel clerk said, "You just got a second love letter from the county jail. Couldn't help noticing the handwriting on both envelopes seems the same."

Longarm smiled thinly and explained, "I was hoping I might get some messages from the jail. Can't say I was expecing love letters, though."

The crusty hotel clerk chuckled and replied, "Same turnkey brought 'em both past that gallows up the slope and according to him that Mex they're going to hang, come Monday, seems mighty hot for your attention, Deputy Long. I just now told them I thought you'd gone out. I thought you had, seeing you seemed to have turned in alone, up yonder."

Longarm took both envelopes with a muttered remark about the preacher man's wife leaving early. As he tore them open and scanned both terse but not at all similar messages, he added with a confidential wink, "It's best to take your time answering messages from the county jail. They get more urgent as time goes by."

The hotel clerk nodded soberly and replied, "Turnkey said something about the greaser pacing his cell all night after sending you that first envelope around midnight. Night man left it in your box when he failed to rouse you at such an ungodly hour. You reckon that Mex was afraid you weren't fixing to answer the first one at all?"

Longarm nodded tersely and confided, "I'm glad I never did. This last note sets fewer conditions. I'm off for some late breakfast, now, should anyone else come calling."

"Ain't you going to answer that latest letter from that doomed Mex?" asked the older man.

Longarm shook his head and said, "He ain't doomed total until they had him up them thirteen steps and I mean

44

to have a good breakfast whilst he's deciding on what he'd like for his last meal."

He strode out into the bright sunlight, swinging the other way as he hit the plank walk. For whether Jenny had meant what she'd said about them acting natural at her beanery or not, he felt more like eating than play-acting and by later that afternoon he'd have a better notion on just how discreet his 'Rapaho pal would really be. Longarm had been shocked and chagrined at a tender age back in West-By-God-Virginia to discover gals bragged just as bad as boys about getting laid. So he meant to play his cards close to his vest until he found out whether his walk in the rain the night before was a secret or general knowledge in Ambush.

As he strode up the walk, staring straight ahead, he was reminded once more of that old Irish jig that went:

"As I go walking down the street.
The people from their doorsteps blather,
There goes that Protestant son of a bitch,
The one who shagged the Rileys' daughter!"

But nobody gave him the fish eye or grinned like a shit-eating dog by the time Longarm made it to the Associated Hostlers of Ambush Inc.

He spied the lean but far from boyish Meg Connors out in her dusty corral, fighting a sunfishing paint at the far end of her throw rope. The blond tomboy had her low heels planted well and she shifted her balance graceful but the cantankerous paint was a tad too much horse for even a strong gal's body weight. So Longarm vaulted the rails in his clean but faded denim jeans and jacket to remark, "I got a few pounds on you, no offense, and I could use the practice."

Meg Connors let him have her end of the disputed rope. She was no fool. As Longarm surprised the living shit out of the sunfishing paint with a sudden savage jerk she laughed and said, "I was wondering why you'd changed to work duds, Custis. I can start you at a dollar a day 'til we see whether that's beginner's luck or not."

Longarm laughed and played the mean bronc closer, as if reeling in a leaping trout. When he had it close enough for it to decide on some new devilry Longarm kept it from rearing to box with him by jerking it off balance toward them and whipping it across the eyes with the gathered loops of the now much shorter rope they were still arguing about. The big paint was no fool, either. As some long-ago horse on the steppes of Eurasia had decided long before written history could record the exact details, this one decided that when you couldn't lick the little two-legged bastards, you might as well join 'em.

As Longarm patted the paint's sweaty neck and Meg fed it a dried apple she said, "You're pretty good with ponies, too. How tough was Joy Norwich to handle, last night, in that thunderstorm?"

Longarm handed her the rope as he soberly assured her, "Tolerable, once I had a Spanish bit in her mouth and raked her good with my spurs. I would tell you the man who's been spreading such toad squat about me and Miss Joy is a flat-out fibber. But I am so looking forward to my telling him in person. I don't reckon you'd care to tell me who I might be after, Miss Meg?"

She turned to lead the now-calm paint toward the stable as she told him, "Don't go off half-cocked. Nobody out and out accused you directly. Some deputies were clearing the streets last night as that thunder and lighting commenced with Limey Norwich on the prod for yet another man who'd trifled with his damned daughter. Knowing you were new in town I simply assumed you were more likely to get in that sort of trouble than anyone else I could think of. Who was Joy with last night if she wasn't with you?"

Longarm snorted, "How in blue blazes am I supposed to know? You and your county hangman have my word she wasn't with me!"

He was braced for Meg to ask who he might have been with, in that case. But to Longarm's relief she mused,

"Hmm, her latin lover, Rick Robles, has an alibi as well. An alibi for last night, I mean. Nobody believes Rick was with Joy Norwich instead of those Triple Eight riders when they shot up that house of ill repute."

That reminded Longarm. He said, "I might drift over for a word with Robles, once I have some breakfast. Might there be another place to eat, up the way a ways?"

Meg said, "No. But I don't blame you for avoiding the beanery down the other way. Let me stable this brute and I'll rustle you up some ham and eggs. It's the least I can offer a man who just saved me or this paint a busted neck. He knows the vet's coming this afternoon. Lord only knows how a horse could fathom what the vet plans to do to him. But sometimes I suspect they read minds."

Longarm didn't ask what the vet was planning to do to the spunky stallion. He sort of hoped he was wrong. The poor brutes had to be cut down to geldings if anyone expected to ride them safely in bunches but Longarm enjoyed his own virility too much to begrudge it to a fool sparrow bird. They said most of the bees in a hive were born sexless to just fly around from flower to flower. It was small wonder bees were such mean little stinger-bugs. What better chore could a worker bee come up with than to just sting some happier critter and die?

A stable hand met them near the doorway to help them get the wall-eyed dancing paint secured in a stall with blinders on. Then Meg led Longarm across her main paddock through a whole remuda of calmer horseflesh and sat him down in her kitchen whilst she put the coffee on to perk and rustled up a handsome meal of Canadian bacon and scrambled eggs for the two of them.

As she did so, Longarm brought her up to date on his increasingly urgent messages from Rick Robles, over to the county jail.

Meg said her mamma had told her to always keep boys guessing just a tad and added, "That poor *vaquero* must be getting frantic by this time. He must know that even if he agrees to turn state's evidence nobody who can grant a stay of execution may be available on the sabbath."

Longarm dug into the grub she'd placed before him. He didn't know her well enough to say he'd already asked for a stay from the state governor. Her cooking was fine and she smelled swell in spite of the horse shit ground into her boots. But when he wanted Rick Robles to know he might not hang on Monday morning after all he'd tell the son of a bitch himself, not another soul in a small town looking forward to a rope dance.

Since both of them were country bred, they polished off their grub and washed it down with her Arbuckle brand coffee before he told her how much he admired her ways with a kitchen range and added, "I might be able to throw some government livery trade your way if things pan out over to the county jail, Miss Meg. How much would it cost Uncle Sam to hire say two ponies, a pack saddle and a hackamore with trail line by the day? I already have my own McClellan and bridle over to the hotel."

Without hesitation Meg replied, "Let's say a dollar a day and not itemize. Do you really think Rick Robles is likely to give you any of his *compadres* to save his own neck?"

Longarm shrugged and replied, "Stranger things have happened. If I have to go out after anyone he gives me, I'd as soon travel sitting down."

She asked how far he figured he'd be riding.

He said, "If I knew that I wouldn't be waiting on that fool Mex to tell me, Ma'am. He might not tell me anything. I still ought to have some riding stock lined up, no matter how things pan out at the county jail. They wouldn't let me bring a pony half-fare from Denver and who told you I'd been trying to cut a federal deal with that Mex and that Mex alone?"

That didn't catch her off-balance. Without batting an eye she told him, "Most everyone in town knows Rick Robles has been trying to reach you since late last night. Anyone can see the law *has* the two riders convicted along with him for those killings here in town. What other sort of deal would a federal lawman want to make with an already con-

48

victed killer? You're trying to get him to confess to those stagecoach robberies, aren't you?"

Longarm smiled sheepishly and conceded, "Only if he done it. Just confessing to some other crime don't cut the mustard when you've got one foot on the gallows steps. As everyone in town seems to know, I told Robles he'll have to convince me he knows toad squat about those other killings before I'll lift a finger to stop old Limey Norwich in the cold gray dawn of Monday."

He leaned back from her kitchen table to ask in a desperately easy tone, "How is the sporting crowd here in Ambush betting on my chances with that murderous Mex, Miss Meg?"

"They don't think he'll talk. He wasn't behind the door when the brains were passed out. Rick's smart, for a furriner. So he has to know he'd only be gaining a few more sunny mornings by betraying his pals and going to his grave as a yellow dog. He has to hang, sooner or later, no matter who he owns up to killing, right?"

Longarm said that was about the size of it and offered to help her with the dishes. When she said she had hired help that washed and wiped better than she did, he allowed he'd talk to her later about the hire of that riding stock. They went back outside and parted friendly. She didn't ask where he was headed next. So he never had to lie.

He headed down toward the Western Union to see whether Billy Vail had wrangled that stay out of Governor Pitkin. Longarm wanted to know exactly where he stood before he mosied over to the county jail and the longer he took, the less likely Robles was to horse around.

The sun stood high and dry in contrast to the day before. Longarm was glad he'd had an excuse to change into a thinner denim jacket as he felt the noonday warmth on his shoulders. The Western Union wasn't far, but the other side of the north-south main street was still way shadier. So he cut across the now-dry dusty gravel as he considered what Meg Conners had just told him about a whole town betting whether or not Robles would talk.

What she'd said about the *vaquero's* grim choices were backed up by the simple fact that Robles *would* be branded a yellow dog by everyone for miles around. So a heap hinged on how much Robles cared about the opinion of the other local riders. On the one hand he might feel proud of being a top hand. On the other he might feel he'd always be an outsider to the mostly Anglo top hands of the Western Slope. As he reached the far side Longarm fished out a fresh smoke, muttering to himself, "Shit! Even if he gives you some names you won't know for a fact whether he's telling you true or stalling for time!"

He stopped and ducked into the windless shelter of a sunken store entrance to light his cheroot as a buzzing .52 caliber bullet thunked into the pine siding where he'd been heading, followed by the dulcet roar of a buffalo rifle.

Longarm crashed into the boot shop beyond the sunken door, door and all. As he rose from the shattered glass and splintered wood, .44-40 in hand, he yelled, "Stay back! I'm the law! I'll tell you when it's safe to stick your heads out!"

Someone in the gloom behind him was stammering stupid questions as he peered out into the noonday dazzle to make out a thinning cloud of gunsmoke drifting above a rooftop across the street.

Despite Longarm's orders, a store clerk joined him in the doorway with a drawn Navy Conversion .36 to breathlessly demand, "Are they after us or after you, Deputy Long?"

To which Longarm could only reply, "If you know who I am you know the answer to that fool question, Pilgrim. But looking on the bright side, they just answered a question that's been vexing the shit out of *me*!"

Chapter 7

Gunplay in even a small town tended to draw a considerable crowd. Longarm didn't care at first. He was back out
on the walk, telling the boot shop owner how to bill the
justice department for his dive through their door when the
tawny-haired Joy Norwich suddenly sprang out of the gathering crowd to plaster herself against the front of him and
sob, "You have to believe Rick's alibi, this time! I just
came from visiting him in durance vile and there is no way
he could have been shooting at you from inside the county
jail!"

Longarm found it awkward to disengage from the hangman's daughter with his six gun in one hand as he protested, "Unhand me, Madam. You never heard me accuse
a man in jail of sniping at me from that roof across the
way!"

But she chortled, "Can't you see who it must have
been?"

To which he could only reply, "Not hardly, Miss Joy.
The coward fired a single shot and ran. Are you saying you
know who it was?"

She ground her pelvis against his blue denim jeans,
oblivious to the sniggers from the crowd around them as
she told him, "It must have been the one who shot and ran
that other time, six weeks ago at Madame Frenchy's. Buck,
Hank and Will said it was Rick who rode in with them that

night. I told them and told them it couldn't have been Rick but nobody listened!"

Still clinging to Longarm like a limpet, the hangman's daughter turned to the crowd to jeer, "Laugh if you like, you provincial hay seeds! Then tell me why anyone but the real killer, still at large, would want to kill the only lawman who's been listening to me about another Triple Eight rider being the one who got away that night?"

Longarm could tell from scattered murmurs in the crowd that she'd posed a good question to more than one of them. This hardly seemed a time to bring up other possible motives.

A shorter lawman with a beer belly, a low-slung Schofield .45 and a gilt star pinned to his white shirtfront elbowed through the crowd to join Longarm and the hangman's daughter in the doorway as he said, "I'd be Lem Peabody. They told me you was in town. Who did you just shoot it out with?"

Longarm holstered his six gun to shove Joy Norwich away with both hands as he wearily replied, "Nobody, Sheriff Peabody. As you can see by the shattered glass all around, I ducked considerable when somebody pegged a buffalo round my way from the roof of that notions shop across the way."

The older lawman nodded soberly and said, "We'd best go yonder and question the ladies in the shop below, then. Let go of Deputy Long, Miss Joy. I heard about his winning ways with you sweet young things, too. But this is neither the infernal time nor place and I've warned you more than once you're fixing to get your dear old daddy shot or hung by carrying on so bold!"

She stepped further back from Longarm but followed the two of them as they crossed the street together. There was nothing Lem Peabody could do about it. Everyone else seemed to want to tag along and it was an election year.

The two old dears who worked in the notions shop were dithering in their own doorway about hearing a horrendous roar above them and being terrified by male boot heels running across their very roof.

After that they had no notion which way he'd went or what he'd looked like. But they sure sold some ribbon-bows and yard goods by the the time half the town had crowded in and out of their shop to ask the same questions.

The disgusted Sheriff Peabody led Longarm to the only place in town they could talk alone—his office behind the courthouse. More than one slack-jawed cowhand or poker-faced Indian seemed to be staring in at them through the front windows as they talked, but the grimey glass kept the conversation more private as Sheriff Peabody found a bottle of rye filed under R and poured them heroically stiff drinks in hotel tumblers.

They clinked and took seats on opposite sides of the booking desk as the older lawman said, "I heard what Joy Norwich said as she was trying to screw you with your fly buttoned. Would you want to gun a federal lawman if you were guilty of doodly-shit and they were fixing to hang another man in your place and forget the whole deal?"

Longarm sipped his rye. It was real rye and any man who could take Tex-Mex chili con carne without bawling could inhale his whisky neat without making faces. He said, "This is good stuff, Sheriff. Would a man prone to shoot up whorehouses for no sensible reason be expected to reason like a chess master about any lawman sniffing around Ambush about anything?"

Peabody said, "Nobody's shot at me and my own deputies, recent, and Joy Norwich has been pestering us longer than yourself about an unknown killer those three doomed Triple Eight riders might be covering up for."

He sipped his own drink, grimaced, and added, "I thought you were over on this side of the divide about them stagecoach robberies in the first place."

Longarm said, "The robberies and the murder of Postal Inspector Mac Phillips. It was one of your deputies who found Phillips dead on the trail about a week ago, right?"

Peabody shook his gray head and replied, "Wrong. It was

53

a homestead family hauling butter and eggs into town who came upon that rider for the post office a mile or so this side of the site of that last landslide robbery. They left him lay and I sent some boys out to fetch him in aboard a buckboard after they'd reported the crime to us. He'd been shot in the back with a .52 caliber buffalo round. Bled to death, internal, as he lay there knocked out from the hydrostatic shock. Never knew he was dying as he lay there dying."

Longarm said, "I read your coroner's report. Whatever happend to the pony Phillips would have been riding?"

Peabody looked surprised, smiled sheepishly, and allowed he'd just never thought of that, adding, "He should have begged, borrowed or hired a trail mount once he got up here from Durango, right?"

Then Peabody brightened and said, "Anybody who'd hired him a mount should have reported one missing when he never brought it back, right?"

Longarm nodded, sipped more rye, and replied, "They should have. But I've been over your officious county reports and we both know nobody ever asked you to find any missing riding stock. Horseflesh has a way of finding its way home for supper. That works better for me than the killer making off with some innocent third party's property and none of us ever hearing about it."

Peabody whistled thoughtfully and agreed, "Works for me, too! What sort of riding stock are we talking about, Uncle Sam?"

Longarm sighed and said, "I don't have the least notion. I wasn't out this way when Postal Inspector Phillips left town to search for sign along the Ambush-Durango Trail. He might have brought his own saddle, the way I've done. He may have hired a saddle here in Ambush along with one or more ponies. I don't know what he was expecting to find out in the hills, riding what, for how long. I don't know whether he cut sign or not. Somebody must have suspected he had, or might, when they laid him low with possibly that same rifle somebody just aimed at me. I sure hope you ain't fixing to ask what sign poor Phillips might have cut seven or eight days ago, before at least one serious rain storm."

Peabody smiled thinly and said, "Three. We've had three hard rains in these parts since Phillips was brung in dead as a turd in the milk bucket. The trail had been under more rain and repairs than that by the time the postmaster general sent Phillips out our way to scout it. We'd already scouted it our ownselves, no offense, and I'll be damned if I can think of any sign we could have missed that a stranger to this slope would ever notice!"

Longarm saw he'd put away enough of the rye to avoid insulting his host. So he set the tumbler on the desk and reached for two cheroots as he said, "Sometimes gents looking at familiar surroundings overlook details that eyes gazing in wonder might not. A lady stage magician I met a spell back told me stage magicians hate to perform in front of children or idiots because a heap of their magic depends on grownups looking at what seems natural to them as you point a magic wand at it. It's the bitty kid or village idiot in the audience who's most likely to spot your assistant doing something sneaky, away from the spot light, as their minds and eyes wander, see?"

Peabody grimaced and grudgingly allowed, "All right. Let's say your village idiot from the U.S. mails was letting his eyes wander where at least one outlaw didn't want them to wander. Have you asked Meg Connors or any of the smaller livery owners whether Mac Phillips ever hired say a horse and saddle from them?"

Longarm shook his head and said, "We've agreed any honest owner of any stock Phillips had lost out along the trail should have come forward, whether they recovered their stock or not. I did question Meg Connors about less mysterious livery services and she sure makes swell coffee and grub. What else can you tell me about her, Sheriff?"

Peabody looked confused and asked, "What would you expect me to tell you about anybody I barely know in a spanking new gold camp? I understand Meg Connors is a widow woman who drove her remuda of riding stock over the divide about the time they'd finished the first card house. Don't ask me how she got to be a widow woman. But I did hear tell she and her man ran a livery down Trinidad way until he up and died on her a spell back. Are you suggesting Miss Meg hired Phillips some riding stock before somebody else dry gulched him down the line?"

Longarm made a wry face and replied, "If she did she was in on it with the dry gulcher. That's how come I ain't asked her or anyone else in town. Like I said, there's no argument against any honest owner volunteering such information to the law. Meg Connors didn't strike me as too stupid to notice if she'd hired trail stock to a murdered man everyone in these parts would have heard about."

Peabody looked relieved and said, "Meg Connors keeps books casual as hell and I've told her so. But she ain't stupid and neither she nor her stable hands would have held out on me unless they were guilty as all get out. So which do you want it to be?"

Longarm thought back to those scrambled eggs as he sincerely told the older lawman, "It would hurt like sin to find out I'd been sold a jug of snake oil by such a handsome woman. But it happens. If you ever met Miss Belle Siddons of Denver, Deadwood and other parts you'd take her for a high-fashioned lady of quality. But during the war she was about the best spy the Confederacy had and, more recent, she's been running houses of ill repute all over the West. So before I judge a book by its cover I like to browse around inside it, some."

Sheriff Peabody grinned like a dirty schoolboy as he told Longarm, "You wouldn't be the first gent in these parts who wanted to look inside Meg Connors's covers. They say Rory Logan off the Triple Eight wasted enough on flowers, books and candy for her to buy two squaws. But she seems content with her ponies and her memories of Trinidad. Some widow women are like that."

Longarm said, "I've noticed. You say yet another rider off the Triple Eight has been courting Miss Meg?"

Peabody belted back the last of his second drink before he shook his gray head and said, "No, I never. Rory Logan don't *ride* for the Triple Eight. He *runs* it for yet another widow woman down in Durango. He's the resident ramrod of the spread, quartered in the big house and riding by his ownself when he rides into town at all."

Longarm asked, "Is it safe to say this foreman who cottons to blond widow women in denim can be eliminated as a tight pal of either Robles or those other three cowhands who claim he was with 'em at the Madame Frenchy's shootout?"

Peabody muttered something about Rory Logan being too old by half for such randy riding with his underlings. Then he didn't say anything at all for an awkward spell. Hundred-proof whisky could hit you that way after you'd thought you'd stopped drinking it in time.

Longarm said some polite words to make sure he was alone in there. Then he rose to ease over to the windows for a look-see.

He saw the crowd outside had evaporated. Trying to lip-read through grimey glass when the more interesting stranger in town has his back to the windows didn't sound too interesting to Longarm, either.

As he stepped out into the sunshine the only one left seemed to be the village idiot, judging by the way he was staring at Longarm like a goldfish regarding a housecat. Longarm nodded as he passed the pasty-faced and pudgy youth in bib overalls and a derby hat. The bewildered looking cuss managed a howdy in an odd accent Longarm had heard before, if only he'd been able to place it.

The West had been full of furriners from the beginning, from the Sons of Han who'd come from Far Cathay to labor in the gold fields and along the railroads of a booming new land to English-speaking gents such as Limey Norwich and the Thompson brothers.

As he legged it back down the slope across the courthouse square Longarm kept a wary eye on the rooftops all around while he felt glad about not having to fib to his elders. Fellow lawmen tended to resent it when outsiders from another juristiction held out on them. A heap of other locals were fixing to resent it when they found out he meant to cheat them of a rope dance for the least popular of the quartet doomed to dangle on Monday morn. But Longarm was used to doing what had to be done and just taking his cussing like a man. So he was more worried about the wobble in his legs as he made it down to the main street and almost staggered when he changed directions. Hundred-proof took its own sweet time grabbing hold, or letting go.

But by the time he made it to the Western Union, Longarm had his legs behaving tolerable and his tongue only felt a little numb as he soberly asked the telegraph clerk if Billy Vail had wired back to him from Denver, yet.

Billy Vail had. After that it was all headed for hell in a hack. Vail's wire said both the governor and Judge Dickerson down the hall had left town for the weekend early. That was the trouble with having those new mountain resorts so temptingly close to the state capital as high summer was coming on.

Vail had added,

I AM SORRY AS DELETED BY WESTERN UNION STOP BUT DONT DO ANYTHING ILLEGAL TO SAVE THE DELETED BY WESTERN UNION STOP I MEAN THAT STOP MARSHAL WILLIAM VAIL OF DENVER DISTRICT COURT AND DONT YOU FORGET THAT EXCLAMATION POINT

As Longarm was reading it over a second time the clerk behind the telegraph counter asked in a distant voice if he was coming down with some ague. The clerk added, "You look like you were just punched in the stomach Deputy Long."

To which Longarm could only reply, "Now that you mention it, I'd say it feels more like a kick in the balls."

Chapter 8

Few if any government offices stayed open past noon on Saturday and most of the big shots in charge left earlier. But Longarm had the home address of one of the best lawyers and great lays working the state and federal courts back in Denver.

Of course, Portia Parkhurst, Attorney at Law, had told Longarm never to darken her door again. But a long shot seemed better than no chance at all. So Longarm spent more than a day's pay composing a wired appeal to a good lawyer's sense of simple justice.

At a nickel a word he never tried to explain those other ladies she'd likely heard about. He simply told her about the fix he was in and what needed to be done before they strung Rick Robles up, come Monday morn. He didn't tell old Portia how she was supposed to get Robles a stay of execution. He knew she knew more than him about the law and he didn't want to consider how such a flat-chested but trim-hipped brunette won so many cases on appeal, personal appeal, back in the judge's chambers. She'd told him those stories about her weren't true. Just like he'd told her he and that widow woman up on Capitol Hill were just friends.

Paying up from his own pocket, Longarm asked the Western Union man behind the counter to get the long wire off as soon as possible and stepped back outside into the sundazzle as a thunderous rumble rolled across the clear cobalt sky from the south.

It sure as shooting didn't *look* like more rain, but his duds from the day before were barely dry and it wouldn't kill a man to tote a light slicker around 'til the thunder bird made up it's mind. So Longarm ambled back to his nearby hotel to unlash the same from his saddle. As he passed through the lobby the room clerk called him over to say they were going to have to ask him to move out of that room he'd hired from them.

Longarm shook his head and firmly but not unkindly replied, "I ain't done with that room and there's nothing wrong with it. So I fail to see why I'd want to move out of it just yet."

The older and more anxious sounding clerk explained, "It ain't what you want or what I want, old son. We just got word that the duchess of Durango and her anchorage are coming to town this afternoon and she always takes over the whole top floor for her anchorage, see?"

Longarm said, "Not hardly. But I suspect the word you had in mind would be *entourage*, not anchorage. After that you'd better tell me a mite more about this one-woman wonder with the power to evict paid-up customers from hotel rooms."

The clerk morosely explained, "Her full name would be Widow Slade. Sharon Rose Slade née La Verne. Her late husband was a money-lending man. Miss Sharon Rose has continued the family business with awesome skill and that's how come they call her the duchess of Durango. She owns a considerable part of Durango and at least half of Ambush, including this hotel, even as we speak. So about that room . . ."

"I reckon I'll just hang on to it, for now." Longarm cut in, adding, "You can tell the duchess I'll let you know when I am ready to vacate the premises. Until such time as I'm ready to leave the statute laws covering public accomodations in the state of Colorado say no paid-up guest can be

60

evicted without just cause and you can tell your duchess a lawman told you that."

The clerk sighed and said, "I'll tell her. But she ain't likely to like it and some of the riders who tag along in her anchorage can play rough with gents their boss lady don't like."

Longarm snorted incredulously and replied, "I'm going up to fetch a slicker. Don't go shoving a French key in my lock whilst I'm out if you don't want that fucking door kicked in after I wreck this fucking lobby, speaking of playing rough!"

He went on up for his yellow slicker and Winchester '73. When he got back to the lobby nobody seemed to be behind the desk anymore. So he grumped outside for another thoughtful stare at the roof tops all around, considering where he wanted to head with more serious hardware.

Until his sometimes pal Portia wired back that she was willing to entertain his request, Longarm couldn't in good conscience offer Rick Robles any promises. Meanwhile it was likely to be a while before he heard one way or the other from old Portia. He'd jawed with everyone else in town he could think of, and so mayhaps a ride out to the spread those doomed riders had ridden for was in order.

He started to go back inside to fetch his own saddle, but decided it would be as handy to hire a stock saddle with a livery pony off Meg Connors. So he ambled on up to the Associated Hostlers of Ambush to see how the denim-clad blonde might feel about fixing him up.

Meg Connors met him in the doorway of her livery with her blue eyes ablaze and her face white with cold rage as she spat, "How *dare* you stand there, smiling like a shit-eating dog, after low-rating me and Rory Logan to the sheriff behind our backs!"

Longarm blinked and honestly replied, "I never and the one who told you different is a cotton picking liar, Miss Meg! So who might this unfortunate individual be?"

She demanded, "Do you deny you and Sheriff Peabody

were talking about me and Rory, or that Sheriff Peabody said Rory had been courting me?"

Longarm thought back before he told her, "Sheriff Peabody made some mention of you being an honest and upright widow woman who didn't seem interested in anybody courting her. I never said toad squat about a lady I respect or a gent I've yet to meet, Miss Meg. But speaking of widow women, what can you tell me about this here Widow Slade who's got so many local folk afraid of her and her own gentlemen callers?"

Meg Connors snapped, "You know very well Rory ramrods the Triple Eight for the duchess of Durango and don't try to change the subject. I was talking about you and Sheriff Peabody talking about me. Deaf Dave has never lied to any of us yet and he was right there when . . ."

"Hold on!" Longarm cut in, adding. "Might this Deaf Dave you got the story from be sort of slow-witted as well as lip-reading-deaf? Might he favor bib overalls and a derby hat whilst he's at it?"

When she nodded, mutely simmering, Longarm laughed and told her, "Your lip-reading gossip was only reading half the conversation and guessing dirty about the rest. My back was to the window. Deaf Dave put his own words in my mouth and he sure seems to have an imagination. Neither me nor Sheriff Peabody said anything about you or Rory Logan we'd be ashamed to say to your faces."

The tomboyish young widow demanded, "Where did either of you get the right to discuss my love life, or the lack of one, at all?"

Longarm's soothing smile faded as he shrugged and said, "Have it your own way, then. I asked your local law to tell me everything he knew about a logical local suspect. You do hire riding stock and the road agents who've been stopping them stages have to be hiring or boarding riding stock somewheres close."

She gasped, "That's not fair! This isn't the only livery here in Ambush and even if it was, who's to say those road agents can't be holed up out on the range or working off some farm or cattle spread?"

Longarm soberly replied, "Nobody, for certain. After that, Sheriff Peabody and others have searched high and low for hideouts in the hills all around. Outlaws working as honest farmers or cowhands betwixt jobs would have to account for themselves and any riding stock when they lit out to stop another stage."

She didn't sound as sore at him as she asked, "Couldn't the leader of such a gang *be* the owner or manager of some neighboring spread?"

Longarm nodded and replied, "Yep. Anybody with a heap of horseflesh on hand to be dealt out at short notice makes as handy a suspect. So, like I was telling Sheriff Peabody, earlier, I'm in the market for as much local gossip as he might have to offer on anyone in these parts who owns more than one horse. Your Deaf Dave forgot to tell you the sheriff said you were honest and upright and true. I never asked him about the foreman of the Triple Eight courting you. But I'm glad the two of you don't seem all that thick."

"Good grief!" She gasped, "Are you saying poor Rory Logan is on your list of suspects, too?"

Longarm cheerfully replied, "Well, sure he is. Four of his riders are over in the county jail, even as we speak. For reasons I ain't saying, I've reason to suspect at least one of them knows more about those stagecoach stoppings than he's letting on. Their foreman might or might not have known they were riding in to visit Madame Frenchy on company stock. He'd know for certain if anyone riding for the Triple Eight went in for night riding on certain nights in question."

Meg pointed out, "At least one robbery took place after sunrise."

Longarm nodded soberly and said, "I read the reports. That makes my point even better. I don't see how any outlaw pretending to be a cowhand could get time off to stop a stage without asking the permit of his ramrod, do you?"

She shook her blond head but insisted, "That's not possible. Rory can make a pest of himself around a girl but he's a harmless loon, not a two-faced killer!"

Longarm had long since decided life was too short to waste much of it arguing with women. So he never told her a two-face by definition was a villain acting innocent. He just told her he'd come there in the first place with the hire of a horse and saddle as his intent.

She softened some and said, "I was wondering what that Winchester were for. We're in business to hire horseflesh. So I reckon we can fix you up with such stock as you might need. What sort of riding did you have in mind?"

Longarm said, "A Tennessee walker would be nice. But I ain't seen one in your remuda. So I'll settle for a steady trotter with an easy-going disposition. I ain't out to rope no strays nor jump no fences. I only need to cover some ground and get back by supper time."

She stepped out into the sunlight and led the way round to a corral gate as she said, "I've a big privately owned gelding who could use the exercise. I suppose I'd be wasting my time if I asked just where the two of you meant to spend the afternoon?"

Longarm soberly replied, "You sure would, no offense. I don't like to lie to pretty ladies. So ask me no such questions and I'll tell you no such lies."

She warned, "Watch that pretty ladies bullshit. Sheriff Peabody told you true when he told you I wasn't in the market for sweet talk from any man."

Longarm opened the gate for them as he quietly observed that Sheriff Peabody had mentioned her man dying down Trinidad way. He added he'd heard some widow women took considerable time to get over the shock.

Meg Connors sounded more whupped than shocked as she quietly told him, "I wouldn't say it came as a shock. They told my Steve he had a cancer eating at his guts nearly a year before he went down fighting it, wasted away to skin and bones and begging me to forgive him for the smell as the blood and crud oozed out of his poor brave flesh!"

Longarm resisted the impulse to reply he knew what such a sick room smelled like toward the end. He'd only had to visit a couple of pals dying slow and dirty. He could only imagine what it had been like for their closer kith and kin.

Meg pointed at a chestnut gelding standing sixteen hands as she told Longarm, "Yonder's Comanchero. The druggist who owns him dosen't get to ride him often enough, and Steve was not the first I'd loved and lost. My first husband was a drunk. Need I say more?"

As she took a coiled throw-rope from a nail driven into a corral post Longarm softly replied, "When you say a married man is a drunk and his woman ain't married to him no more you've told the whole sad tale."

She shook out a loop as she grimly replied, "I don't know just what happened to the poor sick puppy, once I'd left him back East to sleep it off. My point is that having lost one love to booze and the other through no fault of his own, or mine, I don't think I'll ever be ready to start over again with anybody."

She threw underhanded and gracefully caught Comanchero on her first try. As she gently but firmly reeled the big gelding in she went on in a conversational tone, "I doubt I'd be tempted if a fairy tale prince on a white stallion rode in to declare his undying love with an offer to carry me off to his castle in the clouds and make me his princess forever after."

She patted the muzzle of the easy-going Comanchero and suggested they head over to the tack room as she calmly but bitterly explained, "You see, I know now that none of those girls in those fairy tales lived happily ever after with their fairy tale princes. I know now that all too soon they wound up old and sick and one or the other was left all alone, if they were lucky. More than one Cinderella must have wound up married to a prince who beat her, betrayed her with other fairy tale maidens, or just got fat and sloppy and forgot to change his underwear. Nobody ever got to live happily forever and ever."

Longarm had no answer for her morose observations. So

he helped as she saddled and bridled Comanchero for him. The roping saddle she'd chosen for the comfort of man and beast had no gun scabbard. He lashed the slicker across the skirts to ride with the gun in his lap with a round in the chamber in any case. So he and the Winchester mounted up before Longarm smiled down at her to remark, "I'll try not to marry up with any of the ladies I pass on the trail this afternoon. Remind me to tell you about my reasons for riding alone, some day when you really need to feel gloomy. But, no offense, I got to get it on down the road."

So she opened the corral gate for him and he neck-reined Comanchero out on the sun-baked main street, with a trot out to the Triple Eight in mind. But a hell of a commotion seemed to be taking place down the other way. So Longarm swung his hired mount's head that way and stood tall in the stirrups for a look-see.

What he saw was a dusty Concord coach braking to a stop in front of the stage terminal behind its team of six mighty lathered mules as others, mounted or afoot, gathered around the jehu and shotgun messenger standing in the boot, like a pair of preachers calling two congregations to account for their sins at once.

Longarm settled back in the saddle with the Winchester across his thighs as he heeled the gelding toward the confusion at an easy walk.

As he did so some other gents were helping a considerable helping of shemale curves in a tan travel duster and big picture hat out of the dusty coach. She had the hat tied on with a mile or so of dusty silk scarf that might have started the day white. So Longarm had a time making out her hair color or features as they led her up the plank stairs and inside for whatever, bitching like a mermaid who'd been taught to cuss by a whaling crew.

As he and Comanchero drifted into the crowd Longarm asked a rider who'd been there longer what was up. The other rider, who looked to be part Indian or Mex but talked American, said, "Those road agents hit again this afternoon! Came within a whisker of killing the one and only duchess of Durango! The jehu was just explaining how he spied a whole slope landsliding their way and drove on at full speed down a providential slope! Says more than one good-sized rock hit them along the way. Him and the shotgun messenger can't seem to agree whether some of the bigger rocks rolled under them or sailed over them as they drove for their lives."

Longarm decided to split the difference as he spotted more than one big scuff mark in the maroon and yellow paintwork of the Concord stagecoach. Then a local lawman Longarm recognized as one of Sheriff Peabody's senior deputies came out of the terminal to announce they were forming a posse comitatus to ride back to the scene of the crime and see if they could cut some damned sign for a change.

When somebody asked where the sheriff was his deputy allowed the sheriff was feeling poorly and meant to command the manhunt from his office desk.

Longarm turned to the rider he'd been jawing with to declare, "I reckon I'll tag along. How about you, pard?"

The dusky but otherwise American-acting rider shook his head and replied, "I got other fish to fry and they ain't going to cut no sign. They never do. Those road agents know what they're doing."

Longarm replied with a sardonic glance at the battered but still intact rolling stock, "They say the longest route march starts with a single step and the downfall of many a slicker starts with a single mistake. So can you tell me how any road agent who knew what he was doing could have planned the way things turned out, this time?"

Chapter 9

Traveling light on a big horse, Longarm rode in the van of the posse as they loped south out of Ambush. Getting possed up always took some time. So Matt Greene, the stage line's northern manager, had already dispatched a grading crew with a Mormon plow to repair the land-slid post road, which was no more than a wagon trace when you studied on it. Longarm and the other posse riders detoured up the slope around the Mormon plow, which had really been invented by the ancient Romans and didn't resemble a plow as much as it did a barn door out in front of a mule team, held just off the ground by shafts running back to wheels behind the team so the door-like front end could be lowered to scrape and grade loose soil into a flat road-bed. The attempted robbery had taken place less than an hour's ride south of town. When they got there they saw that the Mormon plow had its work cut out for it.

The wagon trace followed a natural contour line along the west-facing slope. So the landslide had roared down out of the east and left a quarter-mile-long by ten-yards-wide scar of blue-gray in contrast to the weedy sod, high chaparral and second-growth saplings to the north or south. The sandy loam that usually lay just under the sod had all slid downhill across clay subsoil, sweeping boulders, trees and everything else down into the brush-choked depths west of the obliterated two hundred yards of trail. As Longarm reined in he saw some total assholes forging up the slope, north of the scar, on horseback.

He swore sincerely and called out, "Hold on! Don't ride hoofmarks over hoofmarks when it's even easier to move up the mountain on your own dainty feet!"

Suiting actions to his own words, Lonagam dismounted, Winchester in hand, to tether Comanchero to a handy trailside hackberry tree as he repeated, "Get them fucking ponies off that fucking slope before you fuck up any hope of cutting sign!"

The county deputy who'd first declared a posse comitatus rode toward the dismounted Longarm on his own paint, mildy observing that Sheriff Peabody had put him in command of the posse.

To which Longarm replied with a weary sigh, "I ain't trying to usurp your leadership. I'm trying to help you lead this bunch somewheres. I scouted some in the war. I've scouted some Indians and outlaws since. I can see I've scouted more than you, no offense, because you've let wellmeaning assholes tear this way and that without looking down at the ground they're tearing across. If you'd rather I head back to town whilst you lead these other gents in circles down this way, I'd be as happy sipping cider through a straw in the Bighorn as I'd be busting ass in vain down this way."

The younger lawman yelled, "Garson and Kellog! Get them ponies back down to the trail before you fuck things up forever!" Then he turned back to Longarm to ask with a boyish grin, "Did I do that right?"

As the county lawman drew his own saddle gun and dismounted, Longarm chuckled and declared, "Couldn't have said it any clearer, myself."

He waited until the local lawman had dismounted and tethered his own mount before he fell in on the county man's left side, the way a junior officer was supposed to. But having put the young squirt in a nominal position of leadership, Longarm softly murmured, "If they left enough sign to matter we ought to find it up around the top of the scar, where we ought to spot such as there might be."

So the nominal leader grunted his way upslope along the northern rim of the landslide as the lawman who knew what he was doing pretended to follow.

When they got to where the highest dirt and rocks had broken the skin of the slope they failed to find anything else. The county man protested, "This hardly seems fair! How could anybody get a landslide going on a soggy mountainside without leaving so much as a fucking heel print?"

Longarm soothed, "Think how tedious our jobs would be if all the crooks left us notes, letting us know where they were headed next. We had all that recent rain, making it easier than usual to get some surface rocks and soil moving with just a little effort."

"Effort *where*?" demanded the local deputy, pointing about with the muzzle of his rifle as he insisted, "I don't see any powder burns or tool marks along this upper edge of the landslide. If said landslide hadn't been aimed directly at another coach I'd be tempted to say it was natural. Big patches of mountain do cut loose for no particular reason after a rainy spell, you know."

Longarm moved gingerly around the upslope apex of the moist raw scar for a better look at the pitted boulder clay under the sandier topsoil. Boulder clay by definition formed from rotten granite off weathered boulders and tended to have more resistant cores of rock embedded in it like the raisins in raisin bread. So those dimples he could make out in the greasy blue-gray slope had been left by rocks large and small busting out to slide down the mountain with all the rest of the topsoil, trees and such. A bathtub-sized pit near the pointed upper end of the exposed clay told him the slide had started with that one good-sized boulder being blasted, pried or washed out of the underlying clay. Any tool or blast marks left on the boulder had rolled on down the mountain with it.

Others were huffing and skuffing up the steep slope to join them, now, and Longarm didn't see them leaving much sign in the springy sod of grama, blue-eyed grass and matted forget-me-nots. He headed higher toward a grove of lodgepole pine laced with aspen, knowing grass grew more patchy in shade and that tethered ponies tended to browse on aspen leaves. As he did so, swinging his Winchester ahead of him for balance, he was aware that another posse member in shotgun chaps and a red checkered shirt was tagging along. He waited until the two of them had made it almost to the tree line before he paused to say. "Great minds must run in the same channels. The gang should have left their mounts out of sight from the trail below and well back from the loose scree they were fixing to dump on it."

The rider dressed more cowboy replied in a deliberately calm tone, "I don't really give a shit about them trying to kill the duchess of Durango. My beef is with *you*, Denver Boy."

Longarm turned to face the obvious cattleman, the muzzle of his saddle gun still aimed polite as he took note of the Schofield .45 riding low against the right chap. He quietly asked, "Do I know you, old son?"

The man in the checked shirt, whose face was smooth-shaven under a slate gray Stetson with its crown crushed cavalry style, raised his own voice a tad as he answered, "You ought to, considering all the talking you've been doing about me and Meg Connors!"

Longarm nodded in sudden understanding and said, "Pleased to meet you, Rory Logan. But Deaf Dave wasn't reading my lips as he peered through the sheriff's window from outside."

He grinned as a sudden thought hit him and he added, "What would you call such sneaky lip reading, eaves peeking?"

The ramrod of the Triple Eight growled, "Call it anything you like. He still says you and the sheriff were talking about me and Miss Meg."

Longarm nodded and said, "Sure we were. They sent me over this way to investigate a string of murderous robberies and I was asking your sheriff about all of you."

"Are you saying me and Miss Meg are suspected of highway robbery?" Logan demanded in a tone of innocent indignation.

Longarm replied without hesitation. "I know it wasn't me as robbed them stages and backshot that postal inspector. That's all I do know for certain. My boss calls what I'm doing the process of eliminating. I start out by suspecting everybody and then I try and eliminate 'em one by one until only the ones I want are left. If it's any comfort to you, I've about decided Meg Connors hasn't knowingly supplied any livery mounts to the road agents I'm after."

Rory Logan looked puzzled and more interested than sore as he asked, "You suspect the robbers don't have their own ponies? How did you come to that odd notion?"

Longarm answered, simply, "Elimination. Two-faces hiding out in town between jobs work better than free-ranging strangers hiding out in these hills with none of you local riders able to cut their sign or spot their hideout. When nobody hunting game or stray stock stumbles over lonesome cabins or abandoned campsites there ain't no lonesome cabins or abandoned campsites to stumble over. I was fixing to scout under yonder shade for any sign any man or beast left under yonder trees. Do you want to help or shall we have us a schoolyard fight over nothing much?"

Logan grudgingly said, "Well, just so you weren't mean-mouthing me and Miss Meg to the sheriff. My intentions toward that lady are honorable and I'll lick any man who says that isn't so!"

Longarm said that sounded fair enough and turned to forge on up to the tree line and duck under some pine branches and discover that, sure enough, the grass and weeds growing in sunlight on the slope had been replaced by a smooth gray carpet of rain-matted pine needles.

Rory Logan trailed after, ducking under a low branch as he asked just what he should be scouting for.

Longarm said, "If I was certain we wouldn't have to scout for it. Thanks to that storm last night we've a clean slate to read under all these trees. Any tracks we spot will have been left this very day and anything bigger than a pack-rat passing through should have left some tracks."

Then, in the same casual tone, he added, "Somebody back in town told me Miss Sharon Rose Slade, the duchess of Durango, is the owner of the Triple Eight you manage for her. Might that be why you don't give a shit whether somebody just tried to kill her or not?"

The rider on the lady's payroll answered with neither hesitation nor any sign of a guilty conscience. "I hate her perfumed greedy guts. I ain't the only one in these parts who could say the same if only they had the balls. The Triple Eight was founded less than a year ago to feed the pilgrims flocking in along Ambush Creek. I was the trail boss for good old Ben Allan. I brung the seed stock over the divide whilst Ben and his part-time hands cut down trees and put up the housing, corrals and such. Ben claimed the home spread along a headwaters branch of Ambush Creek under the government's act of eighteen sixty-three. But he naturally had to borrow some money for notions that didn't grow on trees. Starting a new spread in recent Indian country can nickel and dime you way more than you ever planned on."

Longarm paused and hunkered down to consider a dimple in the pine needle crust as he knowingly replied, "I've noticed that. We'd all be cattle barons if it didn't cost so much to get started. I take it Ben Allan had to borrow the money from someone like Miss Sharon Rose Slade?"

Logan snapped, "Ben and all too many others! That's how she wound up owning the hotel, a smithee, four stores in town and a rival livery she's been building up to under-cut Meg Connors's better one."

Longarm decided the impression in the crust was just a natural slump and rose again to move slowly on as he observed, "Silver Dollar Tabor, over Leadville way, got his start as a storekeeper willing to lend a few bucks to a prospector needing the same to prove his claim. I take it this Duchess of Durango lends at high interest with the property to be improved as collateral?"

Her ramrod made a dreadful comment about the lady's

bowel movements and added, "Poor old Ben and his boys had the Triple Eight just about to start paying off when that miserable cunt and her lawyers, backed by her hired guns, forclosed on his short-term mortgage! It broke the poor old gent's heart and the rest of us would have quit and followed him anywheres, if he'd had anywheres to go and we hadn't needed the money she promised us for staying on."

Longarm nodded and said, "A cattle spread with nobody working it can turn into a lot of empty range in no time. New owners usually keep the crew already on the premises if it's worth its salt. I take it you and those hands who got in trouble at Madame Frenchy's went on riding for the duchess when she took over, lock, stock and barrel?"

"All but that dago, Robles," Logan replied, adding, "We had to. Poor old Ben Allan hadn't managed to meet his last two payrolls in full. We were stuck with I.O.U.s and a little pocket jingle when the two-bit-whore who'd screwed him out of his property offered advances on her offer of a dollar a day and found."

Longarm shrugged and said, "That's about the going rates for a run-of-the-mill Anglo rider these days, with the price of beef going up back East. You and any top hands would be drawing more from this low-down alley whore, I take it?"

Logan reluctantly confessed, "She's paying me more than five hundred a year and nobody I can think of seems willing to top her. Top hands, such as that fucking greaser, Robles, draw the usual forty a month and found. I suspect he eats pussy."

Longarm cocked a brow and asked, "How come? Ain't he a top hand and was it her grand notion to hire him?"

Logan replied witout hesitation, "Yes to both questions. Fair is fair and I'd be lying if I said Rick Robles don't know which end of his pony the shit falls out of. He ropes tolerable, in that flashy Mex manner with his braided raw-hide reata. But it wasn't my notion to hire him. I don't like greasers and they don't like me. It's as simple as that. The Duchess made us take him on as a top hand when she took over. I suspect she planted him among us as a fucking spy."

Longarm said, "Nobody in the landslide business seems to have spent any time up here in this shade. What were the rest of you boys up to that Robles could have reported to the duchess and how come Brewer, Pulver and Wylie say they invited him to go whoring with them if you all suspected him of being Teacher's Pet?"

Logan snorted in disgust and said, "You just answered your own fool question. I suggested it to them when they asked my permit to ride in and get laid. I figured it might make me sleep sounder if I had something dirty on the dago. I never figured on having a *killing* on him, of course. I wasn't there, so I just can't tell you why Robles took it into his head to shoot up that whorehouse like he done!"

Longarm mildly pointed out, "Robles said he never did. He was the only one of the four who denied being anywheres near Madame Frenchy's that night."

Logan shrugged and repeated, "I wasn't there. But if Robles wasn't there, why did them other three boys say he was as they confessed to their own misdeeds?"

Longarm sighed and said, "I reckon I'd better ask him. I don't see anything else I can use up this way."

Chapter 10

After a score and a half of men afoot had failed to cut sign near the landslide, they perforce moved back down to the wagon trace to mount up. But at Longarm's suggestion, they didn't ride back along the same.

Stagecoaches, freight wagons and such had to follow the more or less level double line of wheel-tamped earth divided by a ribbon of grass and weeds. But, like a man afoot, a pony could move along its own contour line along the side of a fairly steep slope. So the posse headed back to Ambush at a walk, spread out like a cavalry skirmish line from the beaten path to the uncertainties of tree line or crest on their right flank. A horse runs way faster, trots at about the same speed and walks a tad slower than the average man, so despite their distance from the sloping ground ahead they all had a pretty fair chance of spotting where an earlier rider or even a rascal on foot might have dug out some sod with a false step after all that rain. More than one rider that afternoon did some serious cussing as he fought to keep himself in the saddle with his pony under him after a divot of soggy sod gave way.

Longarm, riding high on the right flank with that same deputy in nominal command, noticed that the closer they got to the mining camp of Ambush the less the mountain range they were riding looked like Colorado.

In their day the local Utes called the common plantian, with its oval leaves and spikes of bitty green flowers, "The

Saltu's footprint" with Saltu meaning white man and the weed few white men ever noticed a sure sign that white men had passed through Indian Country.

Folk noticed things they weren't used to seeing all about. Plantain grew on every lawn back East and the tiny seeds set by those insignificant flower spikes could travel far and wide in the seams of muddy boots or the cleft hooves of ox teams or beef cattle. It took Indian eyes to notice such odd sights as plantian, crabgrass, dandelions and such. White men paid little heed to honey bees buzzing at any distance on a lazy summer afternoon because you often heard honey bees buzzing on a lazy afternoon, unless you were a Quill Indian raised on your own nation's traditional hunting grounds. Indians seeing European honey bees for the first time had named them "The white man's flies."

As they rode along the west-facing slope Longarm *did* spot some fool bees. Native American bumblebees at first, with more and more smaller amber-colored honeybees as they forged north toward Ambush. It was easy to see why. The bees, foreign or domestic, were foraging on the Dutch clover frosting the freshly rained-on slopes as if there'd been a light snowfall overnight. Old Comanchero wasn't the only pony with the posse who smelled the sweet white clover blossoms and commenced to act like a kid in the doorway of a candy shop.

When the sheriff's deputy called a trail break and Longarm's mount lowered its muzzle to swill clover, Longarm called out down the slope, "Mind none of you let your mounts graze more than a few bites of this fresh clover crop!"

An older rider wearing batwing chaps and seated in a battered roping saddle called back. "Why don't you teach the little red hen to cluck, Denver boy? You're talking to men who ride this range for a living!"

But Longarm was saved when a younger rider wearing the rubber boots of a gold panner asked a pal what they were jawing about. The older mining man he'd asked replied in a soothing tone, "A horse can get a belly ache on

77

green clover the way a kid can get a belly ache eating green apples."

So the green horn said, "Oh" and everybody laughed at him instead of Longarm. They rested their mounts a few minutes after they'd had their heads hoisted out of the clover, and then rode on, slow but sure and not spotting shit.

The deputy on Longarm's right suggested, "What if they just rode them bare ruts down yonder, bold as brass? Nobody has the least notion what they look like, or how many of 'em there might be. What if it's only a couple of riders. Or even one, riding solo, like that famous Black Bart out California way? Wouldn't that explain why he feels the need to kill everybody and then pick through the wreckage for goodies in his own sweet time?"

Longarm reached absently for a cheroot as he mused, "The smaller the gang the less sign it might leave. I can see one or two men making off with the gold alone, provided they had at least one good pack mule tethered within easy reach."

The deputy nodded, "If they'd had any pack or riding stock within a country mile of that slide back there we'd have surely spotted one hoof print or the considerable shit any mule or pony drops every hour or so. So what if they do their dirty work closer to the trail on foot and watch where they plant the same?"

Longarm got his smoke going and disposed of the match stem with care as he replied, "I tracked some outlaws who'd moved in on foot with feed sacks wrapped around their boots, one time. It wasn't so easy. Comanche moccasins leave piss poor sign, too. Comanche on foot drag six- or eight-inch buckskin fringes attached to the heels of their moccasins over their own footprints as they scamper about."

He twisted in the saddle to stare thoughtfully back the way they'd come as he added, "Leave us not forget they missed the coach they were out to crunch, this time. So they'd have had no call to move down off the mountain as far as the trail to begin with and that's likely why none of us saw any footprints of any sort."

The deputy sheriff asked, "Didn't you say you and Rory Logan swept the hillside above that landslide in vain?"

Longarm blew smoke out his nostrils and muttered, "They didn't leave us any sign to read. They were too smart to move across a pine needle crust I had high hopes for. They likely noticed you don't leave enough of an impression to matter on springy green grass."

And so the conversation went, in circles, as they rode ever closer to Ambush with the timber getting thinner and the clover and such getting thicker as they approached what white men considered a better world for his kith, kin and kine.

Riding out from town after another landslide from the east, Longarm had naturally paid more attention to the scenery in that direction. As they got closer to town he found himself paying more attention to the fenced-in pastures and clusters of sod-roofed log construction he'd barely glanced at, headed the other way. For one thing, that Mormon plow and its team hadn't been parked by a cattle guard with the crew over in a kelly-green expanse with what looked like some kids and a woman in a mother hubbard and sunbonnet. They were all gathered in a circle around a calico milch cow, laying on its right side. There were six other cows spread across the pasture like china toys on a pool table. Even as Longarm watched, another cow keeled over. Two of the kids were running over as if to see why.

Longarm asked what he was looking at. The local lawman told him, "That would be the Otis spread and them's the Otis orphans. Poor Ward Otis was riding shotgun for the Durango stage as a sideline whilst him and his kids tried to get their dairy business going."

Longarm started to reach for his notebook. But they paid him to pay attention. So he nodded soberly and said, "Ward Otis would have been killed with the first crew when this string of robberies by landslide started about nine weeks back. I take it his kids have been trying to make a go of it since he was murdered?"

The deputy allowed that was about the size of it. Then he asked where Longarm was going as the taller man aboard Comanchero loped his mount downslope at an angle.

Longarm didn't answer. A man was supposed to help when he saw folk needed help and if none of these range-riding *buscaderos* could see what was going on they hadn't been working with cows as long as some might let on.

Not knowing Comanchero as well as he'd known many a cow pony in the past, Longarm reined in to tether his livery mount to a gate post and stride across the cattle guard of half-buried aspen logs on foot. Having no rifle boot with the hired saddle he perforce had his Winchester cradled over his left elbow as he strode through shin-deep timothy and Dutch clover toward the bewildered looking bunch around that first downed cow. As he approached from the east those two boys of about nine and eleven came bawling back from that other downed cow. One of them yelling, "Poor old Belle's in the same fix, Sis! That Duchess of Durango must have had 'em *poisoned*, like they warned us!"

As he joined the road crew and two boys around a modestly dressed but mighty handsome gal of eighteen or less Longarm told them who he was and added, "This stock is bloated from grazing fresh clover and grass too green by half." He ticked his hat brim to the gal as he asked her if it was safe to assume she was in charge out in the middle of her pasture.

When she smiled at him and graciously allowed she was Miss Gloria Otis, better known as Glory to her friends, Longarm felt like diving into either or both of those limpid blue eyes separated by a turned-up freckled nose. But he handed his Winchester to the oldest boy and reached in his jeans for his pocket knife as he said, "With your kind permission, I mean to try and save your stock. They ain't got time to wait on a vet and gentler methods, Miss Glory.

80

They're fixing to die on you, all of 'em, unless I perform some rough surgery I learned from a Mex *vaquero* along the Goodnight Trail a few years back."

She nodded and assured him she could see desperate measures were called for. But then Longarm dropped to one knee and drove the blade of his pocket knife to the hilt in the drum-tight bloated belly of the dying milch cow.

"Why have you just murdered my cow?" Glory Otis demanded as Longarm moved to one side to escape the warm steaming spout of what looked like creamed spinach and smelled like sauerkraut. One of the road crew opined, above what sounded like a grand protracted fart, that Longarm should have *shot* the poor critter if he wanted to put her out of her misery.

Longarm rose to his considerable height, wet blade at the ready, as he explained, "Cows can't digest grass any better than the rest of us. They depend on little booger bugs fermenting their fodder the way they turn silage and sauerkraut into something critters *can* digest. Things work best when the cow gives them cured hay and a little grass or water to work with. Stuff a cow's multiple stomach with too rich a mixture and the booger bugs produce more gas than any cow can, sorry, Ma'am, get rid of, the natural way out."

Glory Otis dropped to her own knees by the head of the cow Longarm had lanced as she caressed its muzzle to observe, "Bessy *does* seem to feel a little better, but that open stab wound you left in her poor flank can't be good for her, can it?"

Longarm soberly replied, "There's a chance the wound will mortify. If it does, she'll die. She was fixing to die in any case and that acid froth that just shot out of her through said wound has staunched any bleeding the same as a big styptic pencil might have. Do you want to wait a few days and see if she dies before you let me lance that other one down to the north?"

Glory Otis decided a bloated cow with a chance had a bloated cow who was surely dying beat. So they all tagged along as Longarm strode over to the other downed cow and repeated his rough surgery with less of an outcry from his human audience.

The cow only cussed him once as he relieved the pressure with one split second of pain followed by what must have felt like the fart to end all farts and a general feeling of bovine well being.

By this time the first cow he'd lanced was back up on her feet and, being a dumb animal with a suddenly empty feeling, grazing some more on too rich a diet indeed.

Longarm told the girl and her kid brothers, "You have to pen your stock and feed them nothing but half-rations of cured hay until you can mow this meadow!"

Taking the Winchester back from the older boy, Longarm swept the muzzle like a pointer as he explained, "The timothy will cure in the sunlight and dry air you grow at this altitude. But you have to rid yourself of a heap of clover, pronto. Clover don't stand up to mowing like grass does. Couple of passes with a mowing machine, followed by a good raking, ought to have this pasture safe within a few days. But right now it's dangerous as all get out!"

Glory said they didn't have a mowing machine, adding, "Pop said he was out to sell butter and eggs in town, not hay."

One of the road crew who'd left their Mormon plow out by the wagon trace volunteered, "Old Zeb Lansford north of the creek has a mowing machine and horse-drawn rake he might be willing to hire out, Miss Glory."

But his partner nudged him and said, "Old Zeb's Pentecostal and tomorrow will be the sabbath. That's even saying the duchess would let these kids hire anything from old Zeb to begin with!"

The first one sighed and said, "Oh, I forgot she holds the second mortgage on Zeb's hay and feed operation. But there must be somebody in Ambush with a mowing machine for hire!"

Longarm let them sort it out with the gal whilst he and the two boys drove the small dairy herd into a paddock grazed down to bare dirt. Herding milch stock on foot was easy, as long as you didn't have any bull to worry about. Dairy bulls could be more dangerous than screwed-calm beef bulls and no Spanish bull fighter, for all his fancy pants, would face say a Jersey or a Holstein in the ring unless he was tired of living. But dairy cows were bred for gentle manners, as well as overdeveloped udders, so they almost tagged along like pups when it was milking time and you talked nice to 'em.

He had to stab one more bloated belly, once they had the dozen cows penned safely off that dangerous forage. He saw the road crew heading back to their Mormon plow and grading chores as Glory Otis headed toward him and her kid brothers. Before she could get within earshot Longarm asked the Otis kid who'd mentioned poison why he'd said that.

The kid said, "Pop warned us to watch out for that old duchess of Durango before them other villains killed him. He was working for the stage line on the side to keep from having to borrow money from the mean old bitch!"

His big sister had drawn near enough to catch his last few words. So she shook her head and called out, "That's no way to speak about a lady, Wayne! Who were you just now calling a bitch?"

When Wayne Otis, the younger one, told her he'd just been talking about the duchess of Durango the sweet young thing in the sun bonnet made a wry face, laughed bitterly, and said, "Well, in *her* case I reckon bitch is too flattering a term!"

Longarm stared past her at the empty slope to their east. Then he turned to see the others he'd been riding with were clean out of sight to the north. But on reflection he figured he'd have heard if they'd cut sign this side of town and, meanwhile, he wanted to hear more about that duchess of Durango.

He doubted Billy Vail expected him to arrest her for being such a popular gal around these parts. But it was starting to look as if some damned body ought to.

Chapter 11

Glory Otis said any man who'd saved a dairy herd deserved coffee and cake along with a guided tour of the property. So she led Longarm inside to coffee and cake him whilst the older boy, Ward Junior, went to fetch Comanchero in from the gate to water and fodder.

Glory's coffee was Arbuckle brand and her marble cake would have fetched top dollar at a church auction. Later on, as she proudly led him through their milking barn, hen runs and such, he got the whole saga of the Otis family and their misadventures with Sharon Rose Slade.

The day wasn't getting any younger as he waited in vain for some surprises. Glory Otis and the Homestead Act were about the same age, since both had been born during the war betwixt the states. But the late Ward Otis, Senior hadn't brought his bride and baby daughter west from Ohio right off. As a dashing cavalry trooper married to an Ohio farmer's daughter of some substance, he'd tried his hand at this and that along the Ohio after they'd mustered him out of the Union Army and he'd noticed nobody paid you for being dashing.

Glory remembered spending most of her girlhood on that dead-flat Nebraska homestead her folks had settled and proved from half a dozen years after the war to more recent. She sounded as if she meant it when she allowed she liked this mountain dairy spread an easy ride from town way better.

She had more to regret about the more tedious plains of Nebraska than monotony and bitter weather. Her mother had never been really well to begin with and having young Wayne had killed her at thirty or so. Her mother's fading strength had saddled her with household chores above and beyond her years, explaining what Longarm had already noticed about the way she acted more like a mother than even a big sister to her kid brothers.

Glory's mother had died when she was nine and the housework hadn't gotten any easier. Ward Otis, Senior had been away a lot, working in town to make up for the simple fact that a Nebraska homestead two days out from the nearest market hadn't been such a grand notion. You had to be within half a day's drive from a fair-sized town to make a go of truck and other perishables you could sell for real jingle. The amount of wind-winnowed grain you could grow on Abe Lincoln's hundred and sixty government claims didn't amount to much money in the bank at the end of the year. But they'd managed until more recent, when, hearing about the fertile west-slope lands the Ute had lost through foolish abuse of white scalps and pussies, Pop Otis had sold out and headed farther west with his little brood.

The results were to be seen all about. Their new, unproven homestead just south of Ambush had to be one hell of an improvement over any Nebraska homestead Longarm had ever seen. He was glad for all three of the Otis orphans.

Glory was the only one with hair the color of buckwheat honey, once she'd taken that sunbonnet off. She was built sort of interesting as well, from what a man could make out under that loose mother hubbard of floral-print calico.

He waited until they'd rejoined old Comanchero in the log lean-to stable before he casually steered the conversation to the unpopular duchess of Durango, Miss Sharon Rose Slade.

Nothing Glory Otis had to say about her came as an awsome surprise. He'd already noticed the money-lending gal based in Durango liked to offer secured loans at high interest to anyone who'd misjudged a mite on the costs of setting up from scratch in the wilder parts of the west.

As in the case of homesteading too far from your market, the woes of frontier business ventures were all too familiar to a man who rode for the law and sometimes had to foreclose on federal debts.

Everything east or west of the Mississippi cost something, with the price going up as they had to be bought further west. Even the Indians had paid *something*, if only blood, sweat or tears for what it took to stay alive and well. The myth that one could "live off the country" like some Robinson Crusoe wandering through the Garden of Eden was a crock of kid wishes. For while it was true you could whip up anything from a flint ax to a log cabin all by yourself, in time, you never had that much time.

No man, woman or child, as Glory Otis had learned the hard way, had enough minutes in an hour or hours in a day to do more than one thing at once. Mankind had invented paying for things as soon as a heap of overworked and worn-out dwellers in a state of nature had noticed this. It worked out better if everybody did what he or she did best and just paid in cash, kind or wampum for what others did best. A cattleman who tried to make his own boots and saddles from the hides of his own herd would go broke long before the cattleman who raised as many cows as he could and just *bought* the damned boots and saddles.

Folk who thought of themselves as "pioneers" tended to lose sight of such hard facts of frontier life and, hard cash being scarce until you got things going out this way, they tended to be sitting ducks for gold brick salesmen, water dowsers, money lenders and other tempting pests.

Glory told him the duchess of Durango had offered them a secured loan at ten percent, compound, before and after their father had been killed by those other crooks.

Leading his livery mount from the stable, Longarm smiled down at the pretty little thing to ask, "Are you saying your late father was able to prove this claim in less than the usual five years?"

Glory explained, "That was the first question Pop asked her, not too long before he was killed. She said she'd lend us the money for a lien on our goods and chattels, whatever that means."

Longarm grimaced and said, "It means your housewares from beds to bedpans, along with your dairy herd and all them pretty leghorn biddy hens you're running out back. I can see what she has in mind. Raw *land* is easy enough to come by, over on this slope where that's about all anyone has to sell. Livestock that has to be herded or carried over the divide, along with furnishings that can't be druv a step, would be worth way more out here than further east. Have you kids been making a go of your father's butter and egg business since he was murdered?"

She nodded soberly and replied, "We're close enough to town to sell some fresh milk as well. As I told that pushy old baggage the last time she came by, we don't need any help from her to keep this place going."

She gazed past Longarm and Comanchero at the clover-infested green pasture beyond as she added, "Today was the first real emergency we've had since we buried what they left of Pop. You don't suppose that old money lending witch had her hired guns spreading clover seeds whilst we were all asleep at night, do you?"

Longarm laughed and said, "If she did, they were mighty busy. The same clover's growing on the slopes for many a mile to the south. I reckon it came in from civilization along the wagon trace and spread natural. You see all sorts of weeds from back east sprouting beside railroad tracks and wagon ruts after a wet spring like we just had. Folk living back east along railroad tracks are just as surprised to see prairie sunflowers, cactus and such. What almost happened to your dairy herd has to be put down as a natural disaster. We get a lot of them out this way."

Glory Otis neither argued nor offered to kiss him good-bye as he mounted up, sort of wishing she might have. But by the time he rode into town, and it wasn't that far, he'd reflected on the complications of kissing a young and likely virgin gal with big blue eyes and hair the color of buck-wheat honey. So he didn't feel so bad about not having done so.

He reined in by the Western Union and tethered Co-manchero out front to see if the somewhat older Portia Parkhurst had sent any messages yet.

Good old Portia had. Her wire read,

WILL SEE WHAT I CAN DO STOP EITHER WAY
I EXPECT DINNER AT ROMANOS AND DE-LETED BY WESTERN UNION STOP PORKY

Longarm chuckled as he made an educated guess at what the telegraph operator had refused to put on the wire. He'd called Portia Porky that time they'd gone at it dog style because, if anything, her ass was on the boney side. But as some kindly old philospher had said, doubtless in French, meat was inclined to be more tender closer to the bones.

Putting the wire away, Longarm rode on up to the As-sociated Hostler's corral to unsaddle good old Comanchero for a well-earned rest.

The boyish Meg Connors with pale blond braids came out to take over and he naturally brought her up to date on the fruitless search for any sign those landsliding road agents might have left.

Meg said she'd heard as much from the riders coming in earlier and asked him what he and Comanchero had been up to, out on the range all alone until after three-thirty, for heaven's sake.

He explained they hadn't been alone and added, once he'd told her about those bloated milch cows, "Miss Glory Otis tells me that same duchess of Durango who's after this livery seems interested in their butter and egg business as well."

Leading the big gelding into her own much bigger stable, Meg told Longarm, "I'm not surprised to hear that. Our Sharon Rose seems to want everything west of the divide. East of it, too, if the tales we hear about her and her money-grubbing husband over by Pike's Peak are half true."

Longarm nodded calmly and replied, "Heard she was a widow woman, too. Heard she might stand in my way if I wanted to hire a mowing machine off a farmer called Lansford, too. I don't suppose you'd know of anyone else here in Ambush with a mower and say a one-horse rake they'd be willing to hire out on a sabbath?"

Meg heaved the hired saddle over the top rail of Comanchero's cool stall as she calmly replied, "I guess I could lend you our hay rigs. You may find this hard to swallow, but anyone running a livery in the middle of all this open range would be sort of silly not to gather at least some of their own hay. But where were you fixing to mow on a Sunday at the risk to your imortal soul?"

Longarm laughed and said, "My soul will have to take its chances. I doubt I'll have the time, come Monday, and somebody has to get rid of all them timothy and clover tops out to the Otis spread."

Meg was removing Comanchero's bridle with her back turned to Longarm. But he could still feel the drop in temperature as she quietly replied, "Oh? I heard our little Miss Gloria had blossomed some since her late father hasn't been about to chase gentlemen callers away."

Longarm said, "That ain't why I mean to help her and her kid brothers out. It ain't what Billy Vail sent me all this way to worry about, but if I have the time and you'll still hire me the tools, I may as well be doing something useful."

She turned, bridle in hand with a sheepish smile, to ask, "When do you want my hands to haul the mower and rake out for you?"

Longarm smiled back and replied, "Tomorrow morning, Lord willing and the creeks don't rise. I figure I can clear at least their fenced-in fifteen acres by noon. After that I'll likely be too busy for farm chores. Got a lawyer in Denver working to save the day or lose it for me by tomorrow afternoon. You say it's after three, right now?"

Meg Connors said it was in point of fact closer to four.

So he told her he had to get it on down the road and they parted friendly for the time being.

He headed upslope for the county jail, passing the ominous gallows of unpainted lumber in the courthouse square as he weighed the odds on Portia Parkhurst tracking down a stay of executon on a Saturday night. He knew that if anybody could, old Portia with her law degree and trim waistline had the most going for her. He didn't want to think about a slim-waisted pal he called Porky offering that same swell view of her bare boney ass to anyone else, just to save Rick Robles from a hanging he likely deserved.

As he circled the gallows platform he had to laugh at himself. For here he was wondering whether a brunette in Denver would be true to him while, all this time, he'd been wondering whether the boyish Meg Connors or the smaller and softer-looking Glory Otis would look best stark naked in various positions.

He'd just muttered that men and women both deserved something nicer than one another when, as if to prove his point, the vapidly pretty hangman's daughter, Joy Norwich, came tearing around the gallows from the other side to fall into his arms, sobbing, "Thank heavens you have come at last! They told me they'd lost you out on the range. What are we going to do about that vile woman and my true love, Rick?"

Longarm gently but firmly disengaged from the fluttersome gal and held his Winchester at port arms between them as he quietly asked her what in thunder she was talking about.

The hangman's daughter sobbed, "That Slade woman, the one they call the duchess of Durango! She's over at the jail house, talking to my Rick through the window bars! You have to make her stop!"

Longarm sighed and said, "I doubt any federal laws are being broke and it's up to his jailors to see who he may or may not talk to, Miss Joy. But I've been meaning to talk to the both of 'em, sooner or later. So let's just join 'em and see what they have to say."

The hangman's daughter insisted in grabbing Longarm's left elbow as the two of them strode on up to the blocky granite jail on the far side of the frame courthouse. Longarm could see at a glance that while the shape that had climbed down from the coach a few hours back had on a fresh riding habit of chocolate whipcord the shape was much the same, which was to say junoesque.

As he and Joy Norwich approached the shapely gal who'd been jawing through the window bars at someone inside turned to face them, under a big picture hat that matched the rest of her outfit.

The hangman's daughter called out, "You leave my Rick alone, you brazen thing!"

The woman in chocolate brown called back in a calmer voice, "Why don't you hang a wreath on your nose? Your brain lies dead inside!"

Longarm murmured, "Touché!" and tried not to smile as they neared the duchess of Durango. He had to admit she seemed to have the silly gal beside him pegged. As he got closer he had to admit something else he hadn't been expecting.

The chocolate-haired and chocolate-eyed duchess of Durango was just plain downright beautiful!

She was smiling at him friendly, too.

Chapter 12

Longarm knew the Mex looking out through the bars had told her who he was when, still smiling friendly, the duchess of Durango told him, "I've been meaning to have a word with you, Deputy Long. You've taken *my* room at *my* hotel and what have you got to say about that?"

Up close, she had a peaches and cream complexion to go with her chocolate hair and eyes. She had to be older, but just looked *riper* than the tan-haired hangman's daughter in duds a cooler shade of tan. So Longarm's smile was genuine as he ticked his hat brim to the vision in warmer brown and said, "I checked into a hotel, Ma'am. By definition a hotel hires rooms to travelers that nobody else has hired yet. Had they reserved that room for you, me and my saddle would have wound up in another one. We never set out to cause you any upset."

She failed to read him right. It was a failing he'd noticed before in beautiful women who'd been spoiled rotten by other men. Instead of smiling some more and saying pretty please she stuck out her lower lip to pout, "Well, you have, and I want you and your silly old saddle out of my room this instant!"

Longarm had liked her better smiling. He quietly told her, "I got other chores to tend this instant, Ma'am. Speaking as a lawman, would you care to tell me what business you have with this here convicted Mexican?"

The widow Slade blinked in confusion and replied, "Ricardo rides for me. Or at least he rode for me before they accused him of a crime he never committed. That's another thing I have to talk to you about."

Longarm shook his head politely and told her, "Not now, no offense. I'm going inside to talk to the prisoner in private. So both of you ladies had best go share a soda or something, hear?"

The duchess of Durango and the hangman's daughter stared at one another like the gingham dog and the calico cat as Longarm turned to head for the doorway whilst they worked that suggestion out.

The sheriff's deputies on duty that afternoon let him in after he'd whacked the oak door a few times with the muzzle of his Winchester. As one led him along the inner oaken door with barred windows cut out of them for air and observation Longarm commented on the aroma of high-toned cooking that filled the gloom. He asked if it wasn't a day early to be serving fancy last meals.

The turnkey said, "That ain't what you smell. The duchess had some fancy suppers sent over from the hotel just now. All four of the boys we're fixing to hang Monday morn used to ride for her out to her Triple Eight."

Longarm frowned and asked, "Do tell? They never offered to feed me at the hotel when I asked where I could grab a bite. They sent me over to be served my chili at the counter of a dinky beanery. Not that I have any *complaints*, but . . ."

"The duchess of Durango closed the hotel kitchen to the public when she took over the hotel," the local lawman explained. "She travels with a bunch of servants and lickspittles and she hates to make any of 'em wait in line for anything. That's how come nobody but her and six or eight of her private ass-kissers were aboard that coach when the road agents tried to stop it, earlier today."

As he unlocked the door of the doomed Mexican's cell he added with a knowing smile, "Man, they purely fucked up with that particular landslide. Think of the jewelry and

93

pocket jingle they'd have dug out of the mashed up wreckage if they'd mashed *her*!"

Longarm allowed that could account for them trying to stop a coach coming in instead of heading out, this time. Then he was inside with Rick Robles and the turnkey had shut the door after him.

The mighty worried-looking Mex was on his feet in need of a bath and a shave, in that order. A man sure sweat a lot when he could see the gallows from the one window in his cell.

Longarm deliberately took a seat on the one bunk with the Winchester across his knees as he quietly said, "I'm still waiting on a wire from the state capital. If we're lucky, it ain't going to say the governor don't want 'em to hang you. If we're lucky it will say the governor is willing to hear what you have to say about them other killings. So what have you to say about them other killings?"

Robles said, "I had nothing to do with those stagecoach robberies. I had nothing to do with the killings at Madam Frenchy's. I am pure as the driven snow and, damn your eyes, too young to die!"

Longarm started to reach for a smoke, decided not to, and quietly said, "Well, seeing you have nothing for me I have nothing for you and make sure the hangman's noose is snug against the side of your neck, not the back, when they spring the trap under you."

Then he rose to knock on the door as Robles pleaded, "Hold on and hear me out, damn it. I wasn't *with* Buck, Hank and Will when they rode in that night!"

Longarm said, "When you're ready to tell me who you *were* with, let me know. But to tell the honest truth, I suspect it's already too late to save your neck, come Monday morn."

As the turnkey let him out he added, "Look on the bright side. We'd have hung you in a few months, anyhow. So consider the sleepless nights you'll be avoiding by just getting it over and remember what I said about that hangman's knot, old son."

Out in the corridor, he asked to speak in turn to the other three prisoners.

The local lawman said, "We got the three of them together in the same cell. So's they can play checkers, suck one another off and such. Robles is the only one who has to be confined alone. He keeps swinging at the others and vice versa."

As he led the way to another heavy oaken door he added, "We try to keep things tidy, here. How would it look if folk came to town to see a hanging and we had to lead a bunch of busted-up cripples for their enjoyment?"

Longarm handed over his Winchester and removed his gunbelt before entering a cell with three condemned killers. He had his derringer palmed in one big fist as he stepped inside to declare who he was and what he was doing there.

A stocky young cuss was reclined on a fold-down bunk with one of those books that came with a plain brown cover. The skinny kid on the bunk across from him was sitting up straight with his head in his hands and his elbows braced on his knees. A smaller skinny one stood in a far corner with his back to everybody as he played with his pecker.

The one with the book sat up to say, "We heard a federal man was in town. I'd be Buck Wylie and I drew a dollar a day. That asshole jacking off in the corner would be Will Pulver. He never had much sense and lately he's been acting downright peculiar. The crybaby on that other bunk would be Hank Brewer. He believes everything he hears and they told us we were fixing to hang, come Monday morn."

The skinny, red-eyed Hank Brewer snapped, "Why don't you go fuck yourself, Mister Know-It-All?"

Wylie winked up at Longarm and said, "He don't remember that night at Madame Frenchy's, or anything else, come to study on it. Ain't that a bitch?"

Longarm stood with his back to the door as he quietly declared, "That makes it two to one instead of three to one if one of you can't remember shooting up that whorehouse.

95

Rick Robles says he was riding with somebody else that night and it was agreed in court that the three of you were crazy drunk when somebody lost his temper."

Buck Wylie shrugged and said, "That would have been old Will in yonder corner. If I told him once I told him a dozen times that you can't jack off that much and still screw women on a moment's notice."

The slack-jawed youth in the corner turned around, erection in hand, to go on stroking it as he jeered, "You're just jealous because you have to sit down to pee, Bucky boy. Did you ever take it into your head to make money or have you always taken it in the ass? If there's one sort of faggot I've no use for it's a fucking faggot with a big mouth!"

Wylie laughed lightly and replied, "A fucking faggot is a contradiction in diction, Will. The faggot is the one who's *getting* fucked, as if you didn't know."

Pulver started moving in but Longarm snapped, "Stay put! I mean it! I want the three of you to set aside any personal differences and just listen to me tight. You've all admitted in open court that the three of you were so drunk that night of the whorehouse killings that none of you are clear about many a detail. If there was even an outside chance Rick Robles was off stopping stagecoaches with another bunch . . ."

"He was with us. He shot pretty good for a drunken Mex," Wylie cut in and, this time, his partners in crime nodded in agreement.

Longarm said, "I ain't finished. As things now stand all four of you are gonna hang side by side, come Monday morn. But if Robles was to be charged with a federal crime the three of you might well be called before a federal judge in Denver to give evidence."

"What sort of evidence?" asked the morose Hank Brewer in a leery tone of voice.

Longarm explained, "His alibi for not having stopped the stagecoach that same night you boys were shooting up that whorehouse was that he was with you, shooting up a whorehouse. His alibi for taking part in the murders at Madame Frenchy's would be that he was out robbing stage-coaches with some other riders."

Buck Wylie laughed incredulously and asked, "Then what's all this fuss about? Why would the three of us lie about him being with us when they're fixing to hang the three of us either way? What good would it do the greaser if we allowed we didn't know where the bastard rode that night and you got to pin them murders out on the trail to his dago ass?"

The morose Hank Brewer softly but firmly warned, "Stuff a sock in it, Buck! We made a deal and you've always talked too much!"

Longarm refrained from comment as he filed that first serious slip away to see what happened next.

What happened next was Buck Wylie calmly replied, "Talk is cheap. That's how come I talk a lot and mayhaps don't say as much as some assholes I could mention, ass-hole."

Glancing up at Longarm, Buck added, "You were saying it made one bit of difference whether Robles hangs for one killing or the other?"

Longarm nodded soberly and replied, "Like I just told him, it could mean as much as a hundred more days of life. They couldn't hang anyone this coming Monday if he was fixing to stand trial in a federal court on another charge entire, could they?"

Brewer growled, "Buck, I'm warning you!" but Wylie sighed and said, "A hundred more breakfast calls sure has the one we have ahead of us beat. Old Limey Norwich tells me we'll get a swell last supper, Sunday night, but no breakfast before they hang us, lest we shit our pants too much."

It was the self-abusing Will Pulver, not the growling Hank Brewer, who came suddenly flying across the cell with an animal roar of fear and rage to go for Buck Wylie's throat.

But the born mean-mouth must have gotten used to driv-ing others to distraction. For before Longarm could move from the doorway Buck was no longer lounging on his cot but seated, instead, astride the face-down frustrated Will Pulver, who seemed to be trying to beat up the cement floor as he pissed and moaned about last meals and a singular loss of appetite since the hangman's crew had measured and weighed him that very morning.

Buck Wylie calmly told Brewer, as he calmly gathered a twist of hair in one hand and twisted an ear with the other, "They have to weigh us every morning lest they fuck up our execution day. Drop a man who's put on weight too far and you're likely to rip his head off. Drop a man who's lost weight in jail too short a ways and he's likely to dangle there jerking wild as a trout on a hook whilst he strangles a quarter hour or more."

"Stop twisting my damned ear! I give up, you cruel cuss!" wailed the kid on the bottom as Longarm made another mental note that this bunch was not composed of what he'd call responsible adults.

Rolling off Brewer and resuming his seat on the cot, Buck Wylie told Longarm, "I'd be willing to say I *watched* Rick Robles rob the Durango run that night if you're talking about my being a witness at a drawn out federal trial."

Brewer sobbed, "That wasn't the deal, Buck!"

Longarm quietly asked what the deal had been. He saw he'd quietly put his foot in it when Buck Wylie suddenly looked away and muttered, "Nothing. There wasn't no deal. Old Hank, there, says crazy things for a man who accuses others of being windy."

Longarm decided not to press it. He wasn't there to act as a defense attorney for anyone. They wanted him to expose and arrest the outlaws who'd been robbing the coaches packing the U.S. mail.

With no other evidence, getting three irrational gun waddies to change their story wouldn't mean shit. If they'd lied about Robles killing folk in a whorehouse they could lie just as hard the other way. Buck Wylie had all but told him flat-out that his testimony could be altered to suit the occasion, if you made it worth his while.

If these three had been shooting up that whorehouse while that coach was being flattened by a landslide, miles away, they couldn't know one hell of a lot about it. Getting them to say they couldn't say where in blue blazes Robles had been that night wouldn't hang any interference of the U.S. mails on anybody.

Longarm kicked the door behind him with a boot heel until a turnkey opened it. As he stepped out of the cell Longarm suggested they all try and get a good night's sleep.

He knew they wouldn't, knowing it would be their next-to-last night before they got to sleep forever, and that they were missing Saturday night in the only town for miles.

That reminded Longarm that he had needs of his own whilst the sun set slowly in the West. For there wasn't anything more useful he could do than eat, drink and be merry until they wired him that stay of execution.

If old Portia wasn't able to wrangle him one within less than thirty-six hours, now, it wasn't going to matter whether he could get anyone to change their stories or not.

As he paused by the raw lumber gallows platform to light a smoke he noticed he had a hard-on. Thinking about good old Portia Parkhurst with a Saturday night coming on could do that to a man.

But good old Portia was miles away and so, if he aimed to do much about any hard-ons here at hand, unless he aimed to take the matter in hand, he figured he'd best forget about men who weren't going anywheres and see if he could get somewheres with good old Jenny from the beanery again.

Even if she didn't like him anymore, he was hungry as hell and a steak smothered in home fries might be a good way to start a Saturday night in any town.

Chapter 13

Riding the range with a rifle made sense. Taking one to supper sounded silly. So Longarm headed for the hotel to stow the Winchester '73 in its saddle boot. It wasn't getting any easier as the streets of Ambush grew ever more crowded with folk coming in for the multiple hanging slated for Monday morning.

Ponies were tethered rump to rump where carriages and buckboards weren't parked along either side of the crowded main street. You had to watch your step crossing the street itself, lest you step in horse shit or get stepped on by a horse. He elbowed his way through the crowd on the walk outside his hotel to discover the lobby was crowded when he got inside. He was glad he'd hung on to his room key as he bulled his way toward the stairwell with his Winchester held at port arms.

At the foot of the stairs his way was blocked by a giant dressed for Buffalo Bill's roadshow. The vision in fringed and beaded buckskin with his hair worn low and his Walker Colt Conversion worn in a buscadero tie-down holster smiled expansively down at Longarm, which was not a familiar experience for the tall, tanned deputy, as he told him, "I understand you're packing the key to Miss Sharon Rose Slade's corner room, little darling."

Longarm as calmly replied, "No I ain't. I'm packing the key to my own room. Paid for in advance when I got here first."

The giant went on smiling as he said, "I don't think you understand this situation. They call me Twinkle Turner. I'm sure you've heard of me. So would you like to rephrase that unwise remark about room keys, little darling?"

Longarm was aware of the sudden silence all around them as he told the professional bully boy, "I've heard of you. Just as you've heard of me, unless you're a total asshole."

"Who are you calling an asshole, you son of a bitch?" yelled the oversized cover art for a Ned Buntline magazine before he wound up at Longarm's feet, clutching his crotch as he writhed in pain on the carpet while someone in the crowd marveled, "Jesus, did you see that?"

Another onlooker replied, "Not hardly. It happened too sudden!"

Longarm smiled down at the giant he'd lain low with a rifle butt to the balls as he firmly but not unkindly remarked, "I'm sorry I called you an asshole. I didn't mean to flatter you. An asshole performs a useful function and you just ain't worth shit."

"I'm going to kill you if I ever recover!" moaned Twinkle Turner as a very nice familiar figure in chocolate brown moved through the crowd toward them.

While he had the time, Longarm gently told the man writhing at his feet, "No you ain't. The lady you work for can't be dumb enough to want the justice department investigating my demise and her money-lending. She never told you to harm one hair on my chiny chin chin. She told you to see if you could bluff me. You tried to bluff me and you lost. Don't ever call a man with a rifle in his hands a son of a bitch unless you know for certain he's afraid of you."

As the duchess of Durango joined him over her writhing bully boy Longarm ticked his hat brim to her with his free hand and said, "Good evening, Ma'am. Your Twinkle and me were just now discussing the corner room I hired, first, upstairs. Had either one of you approached me more polite I'd have likely let a lady have her way. But since you never

101

saw fit to approach me like a lady you can go to Hell and take this poor excuse for a boogy man with you!"

The willfull but quite beautiful duchess of Durango fluttered her lashes but laughed coarsely as she confided, "All right. I told him I wanted my usual room upstairs and he said he'd see what he could do. He obviously didn't know what he was doing. So let's start from the very beginning. What would you say if I told you I knew Governor Pitkins personally?"

Longarm replied, "Nothing, one way or the other. I don't ride for the state of Colorado and before you say you've been sipping lemonade in the White House with Miss Lucy Hayes, I still hired that room first and, like the Indian chief said, I have spoken."

Then, having nobody but the writhing giant on the floor between him and the stairs, now, Longarm stepped over Twinkle Turner and went on up to put his Winchester away and, whilst he was at it, wash up and dribble some bay rum down the front of his hickory shirt. Making a shirt smell clean was almost as good as changing it when you hadn't brought along that many changes.

When he went back down, wearing a six gun and a wary expression as he palmed the double derringer, Longarm found the lobby crowded as before, but no longer cluttered up with giants in fringed buckskin or imperious women in chocolate riding habits.

He headed for that beanery and good old Jenny Crowfeather to see if she could satisfy some hungers coming on after sundown on most any Saturday night.

The beanery was crowded to where he had to stand at the counter and wait forever until the pleasingly plump Arapaho gal got to him, wiping her brow as she wearily asked what she could do for him.

Longarm said, "I reckon you'd best fetch me some chili from the pot with some of them doughnuts nobody has to cook and I'd like my coffee black, because I wasn't planning on getting much sleep tonight."

Jenny sighed and turned away to fill his order, slopping

an omelet from the grill down in front of another customer before she had Longarm's ready-made grub in front of him. As she shoved the mug of joe across the counter she managed, "My sister and her two kids came in this morning, Custis. They'll be spending the next few nights at my place."

Then she was gone. Longarm ate a spell to let the customers to either side get over any nosey feelings before he took out his notebook, wrote a brief sweet note, and wrapped it around his hotel key. Jenny seemed surprised when he handed it to her, but never let on what it was as she tucked the whole wad in her bodice.

Longarm knew she wouldn't be getting off for hours. So he took his time with dessert before he ambled on down to the Western Union to see if old Portia Parkhurst had had any luck that afternoon.

She must not have. She hadn't even sent him a wire saying she'd failed. She'd likely thought, at a nickel a word, it was a needless expense to state the obvious.

Longarm went up to the saloon to see what else he could do to kill some time. He wasn't sure why he kept picturing the plump and tawny Jenny on one side and the long, lean, pallid Portia on the other as he cuddled them both, murmuring, "Decisions, decisions . . ."

He'd tried three in a bed more than once. It worked better in the hard-up mind of a lonesome traveling man than it did in a real bed. One or the other gal always seemed to get spiteful to the other, when they didn't decide to pleasure one another and leave a man feeling sort of left out. It was just as well Portia was clean over on the other side of the divide. She'd never understand a man could enjoy a younger, less-educated gal no more nor less than a college graduate who'd read the Kama Sutra and such.

As he parted the batwing doors of the Bighorn he saw there was standing room only if one was lucky enough to get to the bar. So he was pleased as punch when he heard himself being hailed from a corner and turned to see Sheriff Peabody and an even older man dressed up like an undertaker, save for his white planter's hat, seated at a table with two younger deputies and, wonder of wonders, an empty chair to spare!

It wouldn't have been polite to say he was glad to see the older lawman had come back to his senses since last they'd been drinking together. So Longarm never did, as he joined the four of them.

Sheriff Peabody said, "We were just talking about you. Heard you busted Twinkle Turner's nuts with a rifle butt. What makes you so mean, old son?"

Longarm calmly replied, "He tried to bully me. Said I couldn't go up to my own room with said rifle because that duchess of Durango fancied it. I've never liked bullies and I've never let them bully me since I got big enough to ball a fist."

Peabody sighed and said, "She sent word to us about that corner room. Says she owns the hotel and wants you arrested for trespassing."

Longarm shook his head and said, "She's full of shit as well as gall. The statute laws of Colorado and many another state say that when you offer lodgings to the public for fun or profit you don't get to throw a paid-up guest back out on the road without just cause."

The stranger in the gloomy outfit and planter's hat nodded gravely and declared, "He's right. He could charge and the courts would likely believe the management of that hotel was out to jack up the prices on a hired room because of all the extra trade in town this weekend. As he just said, that's against the civil code of Colorado."

Sheriff Peabody said, "This would be Major Durwood Scott of the Colorado Militia, Longarm."

The gloomy-looking cuss in civilian duds shook his white planter's hat to say, "Provost Marshal's Office, Colorado National Guard, not Militia."

He might have gone on to explain further if Longarm hadn't cut in with, "We know about the War Department federalizing the old state militias because of what those Southern governors did with Southern militia units after the election of eighteen sixty, Major. Calling the newer organization a national guard takes some getting used to. How come you're over this way in civilian duds instead of at your desk at Camp Weld in Army Blue? Secret mission against the Ute Nation?"

The army man in mufti smiled thinly and replied, "You're not as far off as you may have hoped. I'm on the trail of a heap bad Injun, or a breed, at any rate. Deserted from the Third Colorado with the colonel's thoroughbred and the contents of the regimental safe."

Longarm whistled softly and said, "That must have caused a stir in the officers' club. You say this deserter you want as a safe cracker and horse thief is a breed, Major?"

Scott said, "Texas rider who claims to be part Caddo. We didn't know he'd joined in haste because he was wanted in Texas until we put an all points wire out on him. We put the all points out on him because he never cracked the regimental safe. As near as we can read the sign, he forced the officer of the day to open the safe, then shot him down like a dog. We found two stable hands dead about the same time we saw the colonel's thoroughbred was missing."

Sheriff Peabody said, "They call him Brazos Roy. Brazos Roy Baker, and I'll get you your own glass and another scuttle of suds if ever I can catch that waitress by the eye!"

Longarm asked Major Scott if they might be talking about a rider of say thirty with a swarthy complexion and an army model Colt .45 on each hip, mounted on a blue roan.

The officer perked up to reply, "Can't say what color horse he'd have ridden up this way. He left the stolen thoroughbred tethered in the sun in front of the railroad depot in Pueblo. But you seem to have the rest of him right. We traced him as far as Durango by railroad stubs. None of the liveries down that way recall hiring a mount of any sort to a stranger answering to Baker's description. But a man who doesn't want to leave too clear a trail can buy a pony or

105

more after stealing nigh a thousand dollars in regimental funds!"

The waitress Peabody had been waving for, whose eyes were crossed as a matter of fact in an otherwise pretty face, had apparantly been paying more attention than she'd let on whilst serving other tables. For the next thing Longarm knew there was an empty schooner in front of him and a fresh scuttle of beer in the center of the table.

The pretty little cross-eyed thing even let him have a whiff of her perfume and armpit sweat as she sweetly poured for the new face at the table.

As she left, Peabody laughed and said, "We heard about you and the twats, Longarm. How come the twats admire you so much?"

Longarm said, "For openers I seldom call 'em twats where they can hear me. We were talking about this Brazos Roy and I might or might not have met up with him, earlier today. He was seated in a centerfire stock saddle, dressed trailworn, save for them two .45s and his high-crowned Stetson creased down the front, Texican style. His hat looked new. It was a slate gray Buckeye Model Stetson with a broader brim than this regular J.B. I have on."

Sheriff Peabody asked why he hadn't said anything about such a sinister stranger, earlier.

Longarm sipped some suds and soberly replied, "Didn't meet up with him until after I'd left your company, Sheriff. Didn't know he might be a sinister stranger until just now. We met casual in front of the stage depot during the first flap about that failed robbery to the south. I asked the sort of Indian-looking rider if he meant to posse up with the rest of us. He said he had other fish to fry. I had no call to get exited about that at the time. It would be easier on us lawmen if old boys riding the owlhoot trail would wear a sign directing us to suspect them. But they don't and, for all I know, we're wasting breath speculating on some innocent rider with possible Indian blood."

Major Scott asked if Longarm recalled how that rider on the blue roan had worn those two .45s.

Longarm sipped more suds and said, "Sure I would. They pay me to notice things like that. He was packing a brace of nickel-plated Colt .45-28 Single Action Army Model '73s waist high and cross-draw, like me, Frank, Jesse and lots of old boys who know which end of the gun a bullet comes out of pack their sidearms."

Major Scott opened his frock coat to expose his shoulder holster as he soberly pointed out, "Some of you. Not all of you. Brazos is said to favor a brace of .45-28s carried cross-draw and you say he told you he was here in Ambush on business?"

Longarm shrugged and said, "Not in so many words. He said he had other fish to fry. He might have just meant he had to keep going, if he knows you're this close to him, Major."

The state guard officer replied, "I'm not tracking him in civilian clothes to warn him he's being tracked and there's no *on* to move on to, north of here."

Sheriff Peabody opined, "Unless Brazos Roy was out to corner his fool self in a blind alley. He must have come up our way to fry some fish indeed."

Major Scott saw Longarm was having trouble with that and explained in a more level tone, "Brazos Roy Baker is a professional killer. He joined the guard to avoid a Texas hanging. But the military way of life must not have appealed to him. So he's obviously gone back to his old way of life."

"He's here to kill somebody," said Sheriff Peabody bleakly.

Nobody at the table saw fit to argue. His words made a heap of sense as soon as you studied on them.

Chapter 14

Longarm had to help, seeing he was the only lawman in town who'd laid eyes on Brazos Roy, if that dusky rider out front of the stage depot had been Brazos Roy and not one of Jenny Crowfeather's Arapaho relations. Knowing old Jenny would be getting off work and wondering where in the hell he was at didn't help as Longarm worked his way up and down Main Street after dark.

All the lamps being lit on an unusually lively Saturday night made for flickering tricky light as saloon doors swung and the crowds inside and out on the street milled around, excited about the rare and exotic mass hanging, come Monday morn, or just the excitement of being in town instead of out in the hills working stock, cultivating crops or panning for color.

There were advantages as well as disadvantages for searching in a boisterous sea of strange faces for a wanted man. Faces tended to blur together for both the hunters and the hunted. A man on the dodge was harder to spot than he might have been out on the trail. On the other hand unless he had eyes in the back of his head and wasn't drinking anything stronger than birch beer a lawman could be right on top of him before he noticed.

Longarm and the other lawmen split up to cover more ground, then drifted back together from time to time to compare notes. Major Scott wasn't the only one hunting Brazos Roy that night to suggest that he likely knew they were after him, so he'd gone to ground somewhere out of the bright lights.

It was Longarm who pointed out that whilst they could hardly hope to peer through walls at a sly dog holed up with local pals, male or shemale, they might have better luck looking for that blue roan. When Sheriff Peabody asked Longarm, "Who says that Texas killer has to have friends here in Ambush?" Longarm tersely replied, "Himself, by way of his yellow sheets. Brazos Roy is a thief of opportunity and a killer for hire. No offense, but there's nothing worth stealing up this way that you couldn't steal closer to a railroad getaway in Durango. That reads a hard day on the trail through tedious country to kill somebody here in Ambush. A man who expects to be paid for killing somebody usually has somebody else within reach to point out the victim and pay for the job."

Sheriff Peabody agreed any local residents sending away for a hired gun would likely be willing to hide him out until he'd done a chore or more for them.

Nobody who rode much was dumb enough to ask how come their best bet might be that blue roan the killer had rode up from Durango. You left your horse in a stable, corral or even out in the yard when you turned in for the night and blue roan was an unusual color for a cow pony.

"Roan" was the term for a horse with a frosting of scattered white hairs over hide of a solid base color. Most roans were a sort of sugar frosted doughnut color because brown was the most common basic color. You got a "Strawberry" roan when the white hairs were frosted over a redder shade of chestnut, to where the overall effect looked sort of pink. A "Blue" roan was what you got when the white frosting grew over what would have otherwise been a black horse. It looked blue the same way a black fox with the same white dusting was called a silver or blue fox and, as Longarm pointed out more than once, it didn't really matter why the mount they were looking for had a silvery blue hide as long as they spotted the unusual brute before its rider killed the poor soul he'd likely come to town to kill.

Searching for strange horses as well as strange riders gave Longarm a reason for calling on the Associated Hostlers of Ambush Inc. or, in point of fact, the boyish young widow woman who ran it.

He found Meg Connors ready for bed, alone, he assumed, with a bath robe of maroon toweling thrown over something with lace at the neckline and almost sweeping the floor around her pompom slippers. When he told her he was sorry he'd woke her up and offered to leave, Meg invited him into her kitchen for some hot chocolate and a sit-down about blue roans.

Meg said she'd taken in a score of ponies large and small for the night, but not one of them a blue roan. After that she recalled half a dozen riders who might or might not have Indian blood.

Longarm agreed dusky cowhands were more common than blue roans and conceded, "We could be on a snipe hunt. The town is crowded to overflowing and that breed I spotted wearing crossdraw Colts and a Texas hat could have been innocent as a babe for all we really know."

Sitting down across from him with her own chocolate mug, the ash blonde with her hair unbound for the night said she'd heard others in town were taking in boarders or renting out their hay lofts to whole families who hadn't been able to hire a bed at the hotel, stage depot or any of the few boarding houses in Ambush.

Longarm tried to ignore the tingle in his jeans as he considered what she might be wearing under that robe and whether good old Jenny had that much on, right now, as she awaited his pleasure at the hotel. He glanced at the cuckoo clock on her kitchen wall as he finished his hot chocolate and said, "You just reminded me I'd best get it on home and see if I still have a hotel room. Had a little argument abut that, earlier."

She demurely replied, "So I heard. A rider boarding his mount for the night told us you'd humbled Twinkle Turner, the pet ape of that duchess of Durango. They say he can be dangerous, Custis."

To which Longarm modestly replied, "Anybody can be dangerous. It don't take brains. I've met up with Turner's kind before. He won't really try for anybody his boss lady doesn't tell him to and Miss Sharon Rose seems too smart to tangle with the Denver District Court over a hotel room."

The younger but more weathered tomboy raised a brow to ask, "You've met the Duchess of Durango, then? What did you think of her?"

Longarm answered honestly, "Pretty as a picture. Built like a brick edifice I dare not name. Spoiled rotten as last summer's apples and stubborn as a pit bull used to winning."

"But you did find her attractive?" Meg demanded with the sweet, stubborn logic of womankind.

Longarm set his mug aside and rose from the table as he told her with a clear conscience, "Of course I find her attractive. I'm a man and you just heard me say she was beautiful and built. I find most pretty gals attractive, including present company. Men are like that and would you ladies have us any other way?"

She laughed despite herself and rose to face him in the soft lamplight of her kitchen. So he took her in his arms and kissed her. It seemed the natural thing to do and, for a sweet shuddering moment it seemed she liked it, too.

Then she pulled back and turned her face away, tears streaming down her cheek in the soft light as she pleaded, "Please don't, Custis. I know that was my fault as much as your own, but as I told you, I don't ever want to be involved that way again."

He let her go. It wouldn't have been polite to tell a lady he had no intention of getting all that involved with her. There were good sport gals you could love and leave, and there were romantic-natured gals it was best not to trifle with if you didn't enjoy weeping and wailing. So he thanked her for the chocolate, said he was sorry he'd made her cry, and got out of there before they could wind up engaged.

He headed on back to his hotel. He knew Jenny had

gotten off work over an hour earlier and if that infernal Brazos Roy had wanted to stake himself on the prairie like an Arapaho death singer and take on the whole bunch of them he'd have likely done so by now.

Back at the hotel he found the lobby even more crowded with men, women and at least a couple of children dozing on all the furniture and stretched out on the rugs in bedrolls. So Longarm didn't try for an extra key to his room as he took the stairs two at a time, hoping Jenny wasn't sore at him for making her wait so long. He'd waited a tad longer than he'd ever meant to and sipping chocolate by lantern light with a younger and prettier white gal had left him with hard feelings for women in general.

But when he tapped softly on the door he got no answer. He swore softly and got out his pocket knife. He didn't want to attract attention and when he wasn't using it to lance bloated cows he had another blade that could have gotten anyone but a paid-up lawman arrested.

So it only took a jiffy to pick the lock and let himself in, whispering, "It's me and I sure hope you're half as hot, honey."

There came no answer from the shemale form in the one hired bedstead. You could see at a glance it was shemale because no man born of mortal woman curved under the covers like so in the dim light from a street lamp out front.

He asked her if she'd had a rough night at the beanery as he sat down beside her to hang his hat and .44-40 on a bed post and shuck his boots. By the time he'd stripped to the buff and rolled in under the covers with her he was hard as a rock and hoping he wouldn't come before he could get it in her.

She rolled over limply and kissed back as he took her in his arms to discover she was naked as a jay as well, bless her tawny hide and the swell new perfume she'd sprayed it with whilst awaiting his pleasure. As he tongued her friendly and ran his free hand down her soft smooth curves to gain a better grasp on the situation she twisted her lips from his to murmur in mingled langour and confusion,

112

"What are you doing down there, and who the hell *are* you!"

It was Longarm's turn to feel confused. She'd spoken just as he'd grabbed hold of some pussy he'd never noticed between the bigger but firmer thighs of Jenny Crowfeather! But whoever this particular pussy belonged to, it sure felt warm and wet and it seemed to want him to pet it. So he did so as the duchess of Durango rose on one elbow to say, "Oh, it's you! Have you gone out of your mind? First you put my bodyguard in a sickbed with busted balls and now you're trying to rape me in my own bed?"

Longarm would have removed his hand if she hadn't been pressing it deeper into her lap as he firmly but not unkindly replied, "Like I told your bully boy, Twinkle Turner, this here room was paid for in advance by me, not you. So we're talking about you being in my bed and as for raping you, I'd be proud to take my fingers out of you if only you'd let go my wrist, Ma'am."

She lay back down and began to thrust with her shapely ample hips as she moaned, "It's too late. I'll never forgive you for this, but I'm hot as the Mojave in August and fixing to come with your fucking *fingers* if you're not man enough to treat a lady right!"

So Longarm forked a leg over as in that song about Riley's daughter and as if she'd heard the same dirty words, when she hollered it was for more, so he shoved it in all the way and heard her hiss like the safety valve of an overheated steam engine as she proceeded to move her hot cylinder in time with his pounding piston whilst they huffed and puffed up the grade to Seventh Heaven.

When he'd come for the second time and just had to stop for breath the chocolate-haired gal with peaches-and-cream skin, all over, sighed and said, "I'd forgotten how good that feels. A woman in my position can't get in this position with her hired help and there's only so much my money-grubbing little fingers can do down there. I came with my hand before I went to sleep a little while ago and you still made me feel like I hadn't come in weeks, you brute."

113

Longarm rolled on his back to cuddle her head on his naked shoulder with her unbound hair running over his bare hide like spilled chocolate syrup while she toyed with his limp dick. He asked her why she had to grub for so much money that she hardly ever got laid.

She sighed and said, "Because I never want to be poor again. I grew up poor and they kept me poor while I was working my ass off as the parlor maid for a rich banker and his wife. I fear I'd have died poor if I hadn't taken the rich old bastard away from his dragon of a wife."

Longarm chuckled fondly and softly mused, "Old dragon wives have to be careful about pretty young parlor maids. But wasn't this banking man as deep dyed a villain as his dragon wife? Seems to me most day wages for the hired help are set by the man of the house."

The erstwhile parlor maid began to stroke Longarm's semi-erection harder as she felt it coming back to life while she was saying, "Oh, he was as bad as she was. But she wasn't the one who wanted to do bad things to me. He was. Once I'd let him lick my virgin innocence I had him wrapped around my clit."

"Might you have been a virgin when this wicked banker had his wicked way with you?" asked Longarm with a knowing smile.

She laughed and said, "I *told* him I was and he didn't get to be as wicked as he wanted until he divorced his old wife and married innocent little me. It cost him his job with his stuffy bank and everything he had in any bank. So I came close to leaving him, 'til he showed me how easy it was to start over as a less formal money-lender, further west."

Having worked Longarm almost hard she rolled atop him to calmly impale herself on a no longer at-all soft organ grinder as she went on, "He died in Durango, with a smile on his face, doing this one night after he'd shown me all he knew about *dirtier* ways of fucking people. We were rich again when he died. But I've made ten times as much as he left me because he used to say there were limits to

114

how ruthless any money-lender could be if they wanted to reach old age. Would you like to get on top again, now?"

Longarm suggested dog style as a change of pace. She seemed to like that position. She seemed to like every position. But as he was doing it to her standing up with her beautiful bare butt on the dresser and one of his elbows under each of her knees as he gripped drawer pulls, Sharon Rose Slade calmy observed, "I think I'm about to come again and I've never come this way before. But I hope you know that should word of what we're doing get out, I'll have to have you shot."

Longarm began to thrust faster as he assured her her reputation as a respectable widow woman was safe with him.

The dutchess of Durango laughed like a mean little kid and asked, "What are you talking about? Do you think I give a shit whether anyone thinks I'm respectable or not? I just can't afford to have anyone this side of the Great Divide know I'm soft enough to enjoy a good screwing as much as any mere mortal!"

Longarm laughed and spread her thighs wider as he assured her he wouldn't tell a living soul she had a regular set of private parts, adding, "What are you supposed to be, Ma'am? Some sort of godess?"

She shook her head wildly and thrust her pelvis forward to engulf him to the balls and pubic bone as she growled, "I'm supposed to be the dutchess of Durango and I want all the men to fear me and all the women to hate me and it will serve them all right for treating me so mean when I was little!"

Chapter 15

Once he had her calmed down enough to talk about other folk the vindictive Sharon Rose told him some Indian squaw had been there way earlier that night. Longarm was glad to hear Jenny had been sent packing in one piece. But he wasn't looking forward to explaining such a mean white gal in the hotel room he'd invited her up to.

The chocolate-haired spitfire didn't treat him mean for the next few delightful hours. But along about one in the morning, as she was watching herself in the dresser mirror whilst he long-donged her with three pillows under her ample ass, the Duchess of Durango sudenly told him. "Let me up. I just came and I have to get dressed."

He'd come so many times by then he was only showing off. So he took it out and rolled away, even as he asked if she was going somewhere.

She explained she meant to creep in with her she-cook down the hall lest anyone spy her coming out of a man's hotel room in the cold gray light of dawn.

He didn't try to talk her out of. She was might pretty, built just right, and screwed like a mink, but he'd just about screwed himself out and she wasn't such good company when it came to pillow conversation. When a man wasn't stiff as a poker he didn't feel much like kissing a gal who gloried in tales of evicting families who'd borrowed more than they should have at outrageous interest.

He gallantly rose to kiss her good-bye after coming in

her all those times. But he was just as glad she was gone as he flopped back down across the rumpled sheets to see if he could catch some shut-eye before sunrise and the sabbath bells busting loose outside.

It would have been easy if he hadn't had to take a leak. He lay there naked under a top sheet as he considered the advantages of dropping off before he really had to against the dumb dreams a man tended to have when his brain was telling him to keep dreaming and his bladder was begging him to wake up and for Gawd's sake piss.

He decided it was better to just get it over with than dream of endless interuptions as he tried to find a place to piss in his sleep. But when he reached under the bed for the chamber pot it wasn't there.

"This is one hell of a way to run a hotel!" Longarm muttered as he sat there with his bare feet on the floor, trying to remember which way the hall shitter was, outside.

He cussed himself into his jeans and hickory shirt, leaving his shirt tails out but strapping on his six gun without thinking about it before he let himself out and padded on down to the combined bath and shittery toward the back of the building.

He took a longer leak than usual, thanks to all the extra work he and the duchess had subjected his privates to. There seemed no way to flush the urinal. They likely hosed it down from time to time. Having shaken the dew off his lily, Longarm headed back to his room along the hall runner in his bare feet.

So nobody heard him coming and the first thing Longarm knew of anyone being there was when all hell busted loose. He couldn't jump out of any boots he didn't have on, but he tried to as the hallway was filled with the thunderous roar of more than one .45 six gun going off all at once.

Longarm had his own .44-40 out as he rounded the hall corner near his hired room to spy a dark outline in a haze of gunsmoke, still firing through the doorway he'd apparently kicked open.

Since it was Longarm's hired room, Longarm yelled

117

above the roar of gunplay, "Drop them guns and grab some ceiling!"

But the figure so intent on smoking up the empty depths of a hired room ran inside the same time Longarm put a bullet where he'd last been seen.

Tearing into a dark room after a man with two guns did give one pause if one had a lick of common sense. So by the time Longarm had come up with hitting the rug, rolling, and firing into the darkness from a prone position the hall was filling up with shouting folk of both sexes and there wasn't a peep coming out of Longarm's dark room.

So he called out, "I'm the law. The rest of you stay back," as he gathered his knees under him, sprang forward in a running crouch and crabbed to one side to cover the rest of the room from a corner with the odds more even.

He seemed to have the room to himself. Here and there a feather floated in the air. The first fusilade had been aimed at his empty pillows and feather mattress. Longarm rose to ease over to the open window. He could see how a man in a hurry to leave could have rolled over the sill, dropped to the board-and-baton awning shading the walk below, and simply tom-catted off into the darkness as the hitherto half asleep town and empty main street woke up to ask what all that noise had been about.

Longarm knew what came next. So he'd cussed himself into all his trail duds and reloaded his spent chamber by the time the red-eyed Sheriff Peabody and a night deputy arrived.

The duchess of Durango was about the only hotel guest that didn't seem to be trying to crowd in as Longarm showed the local lawmen how his late night caller had put twelve bullets where they'd have done a heap of damage to anybody in that hired bed.

Sheriff Peabody nodded soberly and decided, "That army man *said* we were searching for a hired killer. It was your grand notion he's been hired by someone around here to kill somebody and it sure looks as if that somebody was you!"

Longarm reached absently for a fistful of cheroots as he quietly mused, "Nobody just shot the shit out of a bed I'd just rolled out of because they admired me. But I'm having a time picturing Brazos Roy as my would-be assassin."

Peabody asked, "Why not? It's what he does for a living."

Longarm shook his head and said, "You just now said why not. Brazos kills for pay, not for practice. If it was him, just now, somebody here in these parts would have had to send him to murder me. The only ones around here with any reason to want me dead would be the outlaws who've been killing stagecoach passengers and crew wholesale. Why in thunder would brass-balled mass murderers send away for a professional who only kills one cuss at a time and expects to be paid for doing so?"

As Longarm doled out the smokes, Peabody's night deputy suggested, "Mayhaps Brazos Roy rid up here on other business, noticed you were in town, and worried about you catching him."

Longarm thumbnailed a matchhead alight as he shook his head to ask, "Why me in particular and not Major Scott or the rest of you lawmen? Brazos Roy must know the third Colorado would send trackers who knew him on sight. I'm just a good old boy they sent over your way to look into them stage robberies. I'm not packing any warrants on him. Even if I was, if that was him I talked to in front of the stage depot, he must have rode off hugging himmself for pulling the wool over my eyes. So somebody else works better and a man makes a heap of enemies, packing a badge for six or eight years."

Peabody asked, "You suspect it could be some old enemy from your past in other parts, then?"

Longarm shrugged and replied, "How do some hate me? Let me count the ways. I've showed my bare face all over town since I got here, looking out for faces I recall. Some old enemy who's changed some, or the kin of some old enemy who recalls me from some courtroom, adds up to lots of possible motives that don't have to motivate Brazos Roy."

They all agreed it was a pisser and then, since it was after three A.M. and nobody they asked had seen more than Longarm, they knocked off for the time being so's everyone could go back to bed.

Longarm lay slugabed for a spell after more than one church bell had invited him to come sing along on a Sabbath. He wasn't smart-ass enough to say there was nothing to such notions, but too well versed in the way the real world worked to buy the Good Book without a grain of salt. So once he'd shit, shaved and showered he got back to work as if it was any other day of the week.

He went down to the Western Union to find no messages at all, good or bad, from good old Portia Parkhurst on the far slope. As he headed for the jail, Joy Norwich, the hangman's daughter, waylayed him near the gallows to haul him into the shade of the platform and plead with him to save her romantic Rick Robles. Breathing warmly in his face in the crisp morning air, Joy promised, "Save my lover and I'll suck your cock all the way!"

Longarm smiled thinly and replied, "I read in the Good Book how Miss Sarah was willing to sacrifice her private parts to Old Pharaoh to save *her* man. I'm sure she never told Old Abraham she enjoyed it, whether she did or not. You don't have to go that far with me to save Robles, Ma'am. Just get him to give me some evidence I can use to carry him off as a federal prisoner."

Joy Norwich sighed and said, "He told me you federal lawmen will only wind up hanging him, too. He's hoping for a better deal."

Longarm shrugged, said, "Hope springs eternal whilst time and tide wait for no man," before he gently but firmly disengaged from her grip and legged it on up to the granite jail house.

Longarm wasn't surprised to find Rick Robles hollow-

120

eyed but up and about at that hour. After that the doomed *vaquero* seemed tedious to talk to as ever.

Longarm cut into his conditions with, "I don't think you follow my drift worth spit, Robles. The sands of your remaining minutes in this world are running out, fast. I'd be lying if I promised you I could get a stay, this late in the game, if you were willing to dictate and sign a full confession, naming Frank and Jesse as accomplices. But if you give me something to go on I'll see what I can do."

"That's not good enough!" Robles insisted, adding that he wanted it in writing that he'd be tried in Denver if he admitted to any offenses at all over here on the West Slope.

Longarm decided not to waste a three-for-a-nickel cheroot on such a stubborn kid. He said, "You must think I'm seriously stupid. Thinking you're smarter than honest johns is a common mistake among your kind. They *have* you and them other Triple Eight riders on offenses committed on this slope. I need a *federal offense* to even consider asking them for you. So you study on that and I'll drop by later. Right now I have to go mow some clover."

He knew that was likely to puzzle the condemned top hand considerably. He wanted Robles puzzled. So he didn't explain a man had to have some way to spend a long dull wait and needed farm chores had early drinking or jacking off all morning beat.

It was going on nine by the time Longarm made it over to Associated Hostlers of Ambush. So he found Meg Connors and her young hands up and about when he got there to see about borrowing her mowing machine and one-horse rake.

Meg led him around to a fenced-in patch of grass on the far side of a log shed, dressed that morning in a more feminine denim smock instead of her riding outfit. She'd had her help set up the mowing machine and rake, without any stock. She explained they hadn't known when he'd be by or whether he wanted mules or draft horses to work with out at the Otis spread.

Longarm said two willing mules would do him fine, explaining how he meant to haul the lighter rake behind the mower by its empty shafts, like a caboose.

She said one of her hands could drive the rake out and walk back to town, seeing the Otis place wasn't too far south of town.

But Longarm said, "I've no call to make anyone walk a good three miles when he don't have to. I can't use but the one team at a time, once I'm out yonder. I figured on mowing that clover-infested pasture first and then letting the mules take turns betwixt the shafts as I rake the treacherous fodder up."

She said that made sense and added, "I'll show you the draft stock on hand if you'd care to come with me."

As he followed, admiring her view from the rear, Longarm reflected that coming with her sounded tempting as all get-out, after a little rest. The duchess of Durango had lit out on him whilst he was still planning on some positions they hadn't gotten around to. But he doubted she meant her remark the way it could be taken.

He was wrong. They were barely out of sight inside her stable when Meg Connors whirled to suddenly blurt, "Why did you ever want to make love to that vicious duchess of Durango, last night, Custis?"

Longarm was glad it was gloomy in there. He chose his words with care before he replied in a desperately casual tone, "Most men would have wanted to. She's pretty. Who says I did?"

He couldn't tell whether Meg was red-faced or pale in that light, but her voice sounded might sore as she replied, "I overheard some riders who came by for their ponies, earlier. They said she went to your room at the hotel and threwed some other woman of yours out! What do you do to them, Custis? Is it something you slip in their drinks?"

He laughed and felt surer of his ground as he lightly replied, "I get my Spanish Fly wholesale from a pal who runs a drugstore. Keeps my harem hopping. I don't suppose these early morning gossips had a name for this other love-starved woman waiting in my one little room?"

122

To his considerable relief, Meg said, "That's not the point. I might not mind you making love to some woman of the town, you being a man and all, but that evil money-lending witch? How could you?"

He tried, "She loaned me some money and when I couldn't pay up she foreclosed on my fair white body?"

The willowy young widow laughed despite herself and said, "Fess up, Custis. Did you or didn't you?"

He shrugged and replied, "What do you think?"

She said, "I don't know. You hear all sorts of things about a very unpopular woman and they say you've a dreadful way with the ladies. I guess there's only one way anyone could prove it, either way, and I told you when you kissed me last night that I don't ever want to start up with another man that way."

Yet even as she was saying this, she seemed to be drifting closer in the shadows of the earth-smelling stable. So he quietly took her in his arms again to softly ask, "How do feel about starting up with a man some other way, then?"

She put her arms around him, nestled her head against the front of his hickory shirt and murmured, "All right. But not down here. Take me up in the hayloft and show me whether you've been with another woman or not since last we kissed, you flirty old tease!"

Chapter 16

Thanks to the duchess of Durango leaving early and the delightfully different ways the two gals were built, Longarm had no trouble getting it up, once he had Meg up in the hayloft to discover she'd put on no underdrawers that morning.

But whether she'd been planning on haylofts or not, he sure had a heap of trouble getting any further with her, once they were in the hay with her skirts up and his jeans half down. For she kissed him willing and reached for his privates once he'd parted her ash blond pubic hair with two questing fingers. But when she felt what he had to offer her she twisted her lips from his own to protest, "Wait! I'm not sure I want to go through with this after all! For I came to my first husband a virgin and neither husband nor anyone since had *this* much in store for me!"

Longarm left his petting hand in place but held it there with her love-slicked clit nestled betwixt his fingertips as he soothed, "You feel like a natural woman down here, no offense, and whilst I don't want to boast or brag, I've had it in tighter places with few if any complaints."

She tried to cross her legs as she pouted, "Pooh, I'll bet that money-grubbing duchess of Durango has a way bigger one."

Longarm thrust his fingers deeper as he replied, "Let's see. How come you keep accusing me of doing this with another lady, Miss Meg? Do you hear me accusing you of messing with the kids who work for you, just because you seem to enjoy kid games?"

She started to cry, even as she uncrossed her legs as if giving in to him. He knew he could have her if he wanted to wrestle some and, had not it been for that last climax with a more willing gal by far, he'd have wanted to. But the day wasn't getting any younger and he'd learned to quit whilst he was ahead with flighty gals who couldn't seem to make up their minds while they swapped spit with a man.

So he gently removed his fingers, wiped them dry on her warm lap fuzz, and gently removed her hand from his hard-on before he smoothed her skirts down over her naked thighs, saying, "They're expecting me out to the Otis spread and you're likely right about this not being such a good notion, once you study on it."

She rolled over in the hay to face the other way as she told him to just leave her be and do what he wanted with her durned old mules.

So less than five minutes later Longarm was driving out to the road behind the team he'd chosen, before their owner could change her mind again. He knew what was eating her. It gave him a hell of a hard-on.

He rode seated in the mowing machine, which looked sort of like a buggy with a short wheel base and a monsterous cross-cut saw pasted to its right side. That wasn't what the serrated mowing bar really was, of course. It folded up out of the way for road travel. Once you got to some meadow to be mown you lowered it out to ride flat, inches off the ground, and connected the gears that could turn with the axle to slide the serrated mowing blade back and forth on the outrigger bar.

Coupled behind the mowing machine he was driving rode the lighter and easier to savvy two-wheeled rake. Like the mowing machine, it was easier to drive along a wagon trace with its yard-long rake tines cranked up level with the axle. When you had a mule hitched betwixt its shafts and wanted to rake with it, you lowered the tines with a lever to drag the ground and gather anything loose. When you wanted to leave a windrow you just hoisted the raking tines some more. It didn't take an engineering degree to drive a mowing machine or wheel-rake.

But as he drove through town that late Sabbath morn he sure got a heap of dirty looks from ladies in sunbonnets and fusty old gents in black suits and ties. But he just smiled neighborly and kept driving. There were times a man had to do chores when he had the time, and he doubted he'd have time to help the Otis kids, once this last Sabbath before the slated executions waned.

He resisted the impulse to stop as he drove past the Western Union. Old Portia had doubtless tried and old Portia had likely failed. He'd wired her too late, bless her heart and black pubic hairs she swore were prematurely going gray.

Thinking about the lean lady lawyer back in Denver didn't get rid of the hard-on Meg Connors had inflicted upon him with her own fickle form. But thinking about sure screwing in the sweet bye and bye had a calming influence and by the time he was out of town on the wagon trace south to Durango he was looking forward to some farm chores to kill an otherwise dull but suspenseful day.

He knew Rick Robles and anyone else who knew toad squat were having as tough a time with the tedious Sabbath as they tried to decide what happened next. Longarm knew it wasn't for him to decide whether Rick Robles cracked or not. He didn't want to think about what he'd tell the condemned *vaquero* if he *did* change his story at this late date. Longarm hated to flat-out lie. But he didn't see what else he could do if a man set to hang within hours agreed to talk for a stay of execution. Longarm knew Billy Vail would never forgive him if he let a little thing like a guilty conscience stand between him and cracking a case. But that Mex was sure going to cuss him when it came time to mount those thirteen steps for Colorado after agreeing to make a deal with the federal government.

The dairy spread owned by the Otis orphans lay less than two country miles south of town, as Longarm recalled, so he considered passing up the two raggedy Indian kids on the wagon ruts ahead until he drew abreast of them as they stepped off the right-of-way. But a mile to walk was a mile to walk and the little gal of four or so, clinging to her eight- or nine-year-old brother's hand, looked mighty weary as she toddled along on her dusty bare feet.

So Longarm reined in and called down, "Howdy, fellow travelers. I'm only going as far as the Otis spread, but if you'd like a lift that far, pile on."

The little girl said something in what sounded like the Uto-Aztec dialect of the recently evicted West Slope Utes. Longarm chose to assume they were assimilated Arapaho as the boy grinned up to tell him, "She says we're not supposed to talk to you *saltu*. But we know where the Otis place is and riding sure beats walking!"

So the two of them got the little gal up on the spring seat to one side of Longarm and her brother climbed up to Longarm's right. Had the three of them had full grown asses it would have been a tad too crowded. As Longarm flicked the ribbons and clucked the team on down the road the boy, who said his name was Todd, asked if he could drive.

Most men would have said no. But Longarm had been eight or nine one time and it wasn't as if he had two trotting thoroughbreds hitched to a light sulky. So he handed the ribbons over to the kid, waited to make sure the grinning young Ute didn't do anything silly with them, and settled back to enjoy the sort of tedious ride.

There were advantages to doing nothing on a lazy day with grasshoppers buzzing out of the grassy center strip ahead and butterflies playing tag above the trail-side pink and yaller mountain daisies. A rider paying less attention to the trail ahead tended to notice hoof beats keeping time with his team, say a quarter-mile back.

Longarm cussed himself for leaving his Winchester behind as he stretched lazy and risked a casual glance over his shoulder.

He couldn't see anybody back there. The wagon trace

wound some between the weedy slopes to the east and the brush-filled draws to the west.

He waited until they'd moved on a good two thirds of the way before he told the kid holding the reins, "I'm going to let you in on a secret, Todd. I'm a lawman and I need your help in playing a trick on somebody."

Being a kid, Todd thought that sounded like a grand notion. He asked what Longarm wanted him and his little sister to do.

Longarm said, "I want you to just drive on to the Otis spread and do you reckon you can stop and wait there, by their gate?"

The Indian kid allowed he could turn in and commence mowing, if he had to.

Longarm shook his head and gently replied, "You won't have to. Just drive on to their gate and rein in. Tell any Otis kids who come out to the road that Deputy U.S. Marshal Custis Long asked you to, and tell 'em I'll be along directly to explain."

Todd gasped, "I know who you are, now! You are the one my people call Saltu ka Saltu, the stranger who is not a stranger! Now that we have met I see why they call you this! You did not have to stop and give us a lift. A lot of Saltu wouldn't have. A lot of Saltu say we don't live around here anymore!"

Longarm filed that away for now. He could worry how many Ute were still haunting these parts after he found out who was ghosting along this haunted trail to Durango behind them!

He told young Todd to just keep driving at a slow and steady walk and neither stop nor speed up no matter what. He waited to see the kid could handle the team the way he was told. Then he waited until they swung around a brushy bend.

As they did so Longarm rolled over the back of the spring seat to flatten out in the grass and weeds of the center strip while the two wheel-rakes to their rear ran over him with its tines just clearing his prone form. The moment he was able Longarm rolled across the bare wagon rut to his left and hunkered in a trailside clump of buckthorn. He didn't look over his shoulder as the mowing rig moved on at the same slow steady pace, Lord love all friendly young Indians.

The rig rolled on, its rumble and rattles fading in the distance as, sure enough, Longarm heard the approaching crunches of a horse being ridden at the same slow pace.

A million years went by. Then Longarm could see Major Durwood Scott of the fucking Colorado Third pussy-footing down the trail on a chestnut barb.

Breaking cover with his .44-40 held politely down the seam of his jeans, Longarm called out, "Howdy, Major. Who might we be following this afternoon."

The military police officer in mufti reined to reply with an easy smile, "Yourself, of course. You don't know how relieved I am to see you spotted me on your tail and got the drop on me."

To which Longarm modestly replied, "It's a gift that came to me in a war they gave one time. Are you saying the national guard sent you all this way to find out if you could tail an old cavalry scout?"

Major Scott replied, "I was trailing you to see who else might be trailing you. They told me about Brazos Roy making a try for you last night. The whole town watched you drive off down this wagon trace with that mowing rig, so . . . Where have you hidden all that rolling stock, by the way?"

Longarm stepped out on the wagon trace to put his .44-40 away as he replied, "I'll show you if you'd care to tag along a few furlongs. How come everybody seems to think that was Brazos Roy smoking up my feather bed last night? Like I told Sheriff Peabody, a man in my line of work makes enemies and that hired gun has no particular reason to be gunning for yours truly, right?"

Major Scott kept pace aboard his mount as he answered, "Wrong. We all agree that breed has to be holed up with someone back there in town. By sundown, last night, his two-faced host or hosts must have told him you'd told everyone you'd talked with him in front of the stage depot. So Brazos Roy knows you and you alone can identify him on sight at a distance!"

Longarm asked, "What about yourself, Major? Are you saying they have you hunting an outlaw you wouldn't know on sight at a distance?"

The officer nodded and confided, "That's about the size of it. Now that I've traced him to this general area I've wired Camp Weld to send me some non coms from his troop who could identify him for me. But I naturally never heard of the murderous shit before he left the officer of the day dead on the floor near an empty regimental safe!"

Longarm whistled softly and almost asked a dumb question. But he saw without asking how Brazos Roy couldn't have known who he was talking to when they'd exchanged those few words out front of the depot.

Longarm nodded and said, "He figured out who he'd been talking to the same way I figured out who he'd been, jawing with his own bunch, later."

Major Scott said, "He did. Then, after we'd all hunted high and low for him and packed it in for the night he came out of hiding to finish you off in the wee small hours. He knows that nobody else in these parts could single him out of the crowd at a glance. He knows that as long as you're wandering around these parts on your own mission he's in no position to carry out his own!"

Longarm had to smile at the picture. He shook his head and said, "I'm likely keeping some poor soul alive, just by being over in this slope, hunting somebody else! They never sent me after Brazos Roy and I can't see him being after the same jaspers I'm after. Brazos Roy would be in line for reward money if he shot any of them road agents who've been robbing the Ambush-Durango stage line. So he'd have no call to gun anyone else who was after them."

Then, before the major could tell him, Longarm chuckled sheepishly and said, "You're right. He'd still be wanted for murder, robbery and horse theft whether he was after those other crooks or not. But you'll have to admit it would be a real pisser if me and Brazos Roy were out to nail the same road agents. They say Billy the Kid started out as a gunslinger hired to track down stock thieves and other hired guns. I sure wish folk out this way wouldn't take the law into their own hands so freely and so often."

They rounded another bend to see the mowing machine and two-wheel rake parked by the gate of the Otis spread, with the mules tethered to a post and neither Indian kid to be seen.

Longarm said, "This is where I was headed, Major. As you can see, yonder pasture is infested with rampant growth and Dutch clover. I told the kids who live here I'd give 'em a hand. Would you care to pitch in?"

The military policeman stared thunderghasted and demanded, "Have you lost your senses? I'm a field grade officer and you, unless I heard Sheriff Peabody wrong, are a senior deputy U.S. Marshal! Why would either of us want to mow a damned pasture for some butter and egg nesters?"

Longarm didn't feel like bragging on all the help he'd gotten in the past from folk too humble for the high and mighty to mess with. He just told the major to suit himself and untethered the team to lead it over the cattle guard as the proud military man in mufti let go a snort of disbelief and wheeled his barb to ride back to town.

Longarm led the team across the cattle guard on foot. As he headed for the log buildings down the slope he saw Glory Otis in her doorway with those Indian kids. As he approached she called out he was just in time for the coffee and cake she'd put on.

It served Major Scott right for being such a stuck-up prick.

Chapter 17

Glory Otis set a swell table with generous portions to make up for the lack of any tablecloth. Her Arbuckle brand coffee was fresh made and the rich layer cake harmonized with her dark honey tresses where the chocolate frosting didn't remind a man of the Duchess of Durango.

Longarm told himself not to think of the hot-natured older woman in the kitchen of a likely virgin and complimented Glory on her cake.

She modestly confessed it was store bought. She'd brought it home from a bakery in town that bought her butter, cream and eggs. So he allowed she was still responsible for the swell cake, in a way.

After she'd coffeed and caked them all Glory insisted in a guided tour of the property before she'd let him chore any of it for them.

A fluffy pup called Tiger tagged along to keep an eye on Longarm as Glory showed him all the work they'd done. Five dog-run cabins went with four log corrals or cattle pens, a chicken-wire hen run with a stout coop and a lean-to stable attached to a fair-sized milking barn.

You called the square one-room cabins connected by covered breezeways dog-run cabins because a yard dog could run back and forth through the open spaces between what functioned as individual rooms. Longarm didn't ask why they'd built with the plentiful local aspen instead of the more widespread and not much longer-lasting pine. The

132

pretty green barked aspen's white wood wasn't much use in a stove and rotted in six or eight years if you managed to keep it fairly dry. But it was easy to cut down when a nester was building with no more help than a budding daughter and two boys not much older than that Indian kid helping them out front with the mules. Once she'd shown both the cows he'd lanced earlier were still alive, chewing safer cuds on bare dirt with their sisters, Longarm allowed he'd better get started if he meant to get back to town before sundown.

Glory tagged along, shyly suggesting he was welcome to stay the night if he had a mind to.

Longarm shook his head politely and explained, "I told the owner of that rolling stock and its team I'd have 'em back before sundown. After that I have a room at the hotel paid up until tomorrow noon and I have to drop by the telegraph office and the jail no later than supper time."

He had no call to explain about last suppers to such a sweet young thing. The sun they'd been talking about was high and beaming down white hot through the thin mountain air. So Longarm hung his hat on a fence post and draped his denim jacket and hickory shirt over the same before he got down to business with that Dutch clover.

Mindful of what Major Scott had said about Brazos Roy Baker, he left his six gun right where it belonged on his left hip.

Getting started was the toughest part when you set out to mow a field right. You needed a clear lane for your rig along the fence line because the mowing bar only mowed a lane over to your left. So Longarm proceeded along said fence line with a two-handed scythe from their tool shed. He faced the fence to scythe to his left along the same, sweeping close to the sod and leaving a short tidy stubble as he worked counter-clockwise in an easy rythm that came back to a body like shucking corn or shelling peas back in West-By-God-Virginia.

The skinny ten- or eleven-year-old Ward Otis, Junior got another scythe and took off his own shirt to commence up

133

the fence line, scything clover like he really hated it.

Longarm called out, "Let the weight of the scythe decide the speed of your sweep, Ward. You'll tire yourself needless if you fight a tool that was designed to work with you, see?"

The kid slowed down, sweeping at different speeds until he suddenly got the hang of it and called back, "You're right! All of a sudden it feels like somebody else is helping me and look at that clover go!"

So with a grown man and a half-grown boy working together they had a five-foot lane along the fence line cleared in a little over an hour and neither one of them argued when Glory called them back to the shade of her kitchen's dog-run for some lemonade she'd just made with genuine ice.

Longarm wasn't surprised to hear she sold butter and eggs to the grocer and ice man over in Ambush as well. He could see that while they likely had to work like beavers to begin with, they had a nice little family business going, now. He could see why the duchess wanted it, and why Glory felt no call to sell.

Sweat dried away sudden in the high dry mountain warmth. That sun was beating down through way less air than it felt like. So Longarm put his shirt and hat back on to finish the mowing less toilsome.

Leaving the rake resting on its empty shafts, Longarm hitched up the watered, foddered and rested team and drove into position next to the fence to lower the mower bar on its outrigger line and engage the gears while Glory and the four kids watched.

Then he mounted to the spring seat, snapped the mules rumps with the slack ribbons and started 'em up. The Indian kids ran away when the steel teeth skimming the ground to his left commenced to snick and snee through the juicy fresh grass and clover stems. Glory and her kid brothers seemed to take modern science in stride as they strolled the swath he was leaving, impressed as well as delighted by the fast results after seeing how slow a man who knew what he was doing could mow with a scythe.

It took Longarm much less time to mow the whole fair-sized field than it had to circle them once with that scythe. But the mower bar had only lain low the dangerous fooder. It still lay there, ready to bloat any stock attracted by the sweet smell of a new mown field.

Glory made him sip some more lemonade as her brothers hitched one of their own ponies to the two-wheel rake. When he idly asked where those Indian kids had gone, Glory said, "Home, I reckon. We don't ask and they don't tell just where they live these days. According to the army the Ute aren't supposed to live in these parts at all since they treated those white women so fresh up by White River."

Longarm made a wry face but didn't comment. He knew the poor Utes were in more danger from the Colorado National Guard than the regular army and, the hell of it was, he could see both sides.

The Indians had been here first. After that they'd been a stone-age folk hogging way more range than other races needed to get by on. A Chinese farmer could feed a big family fairly well on less than five acres, weather and worms permitting. Pennsylvania Dutch farmers lived higher on the hog working eighty acres on the average, while even a hundred-and-sixty-acre Western homestead would feed, clothe and educate a white family if they nested sensible on good soil near water. But a hunting and gathering band of say thirty-odd Indians needed hundreds of square miles to roam. Picking berries here, digging roots yonder, taking out all the game in this valley and moving on to the next as they followed what the poets called the noble savage life.

Longarm didn't doubt it was a good life, or had been, back before even the Indian country of the West started to get crowded. So that was doubtless why Mister Lo, the Poor Indian, just hated to live on a fool reservation smaller than his old hunting grounds. But, as he'd told more than one truculent Indian in the past, the noble savage life was just too savage to last, anywhere. White folk had started out as noble savages and it had likely been fun tò pick berries and track game where cities and farms now stood. But those white noble savages kept on increasing and food gathering until they'd stripped nature's free lunch counter bare and would have starved to death if somebody hadn't come up with farming and other such modern notions.

As he climbed up on the rake and lowered the tines to the sod he considered how much he could do with this simple but clever notion of his own kind, next to even the early farming methods of days gone by.

Driving the draft horse over the mown pasture with the tines under his lazy ass doing the chore for him, Longarm reflected on how long it would have taken Mister Lo to turn into a more civilized critter if Columbus had never taken that wrong turn to India. The pragmatic Pueblo nations to the south were already living at the level of say the Canaanites in the Good Book whilst the Aztec, Inca, Maya and such further south had progressed to the level of Early Egypt or Babylonia. So even if no white folk had ever crossed the main ocean to set up a Bureau of Indian Affairs, armored legions out of Mexico would have marched north to build roads and cities across their own world and the noble savages in these parts would have been in the same fix as those ancient barbarians the Romans had civilized whether they'd wanted to get civilized or not.

He raked the cut greenery into long windrows, lifting the tines to do so whenever and wherever he wanted to. After that it was a cinch to run the rake the length of a windrow to gather a knee-high pile of green hay. Before he'd finished, young Ward and his kid brother, Wayne, had shown they followed his drift. They fetched pitch forks from their shed and started pitching dangerous fodder over the fence before he was half finished.

So they had the whole chore done before supper time and when Glory invited him to supper Longarm allowed he was mighty tempted but had to get it on back to town.

Glory rode the mower as far as her propery line with him, thanking him more than once and pouting that he wasn't giving her half a chance to show her gratitude.

He doubted she meant that the way the smoke signals in her big blue eyes could be read by a less-worldly gent with a natural nature. Young gals who weren't as worldly could get themselves and dirty old men in trouble with false signals because they weren't aware of what they were signaling. He could have sworn she was rubbing her thigh against his like that on purpose, if he hadn't considered how the seat was a tight fit and she didn't seem to have any grown men messing with her out here in the sticks.

When they got to the northeast fence post of her spread Glory repeated her invitation to put him up out there and kissed him on the cheek before she dropped gracefully off, vaulted the fence, and lit out for home, not looking back.

It was a caution how some young gals were natural prick teases before they'd ever laid eyes on a prick. He had to chuckle at the deliberate flounce to her trim young hips under that calico mother hubbard as she traipsed through waist-high weeds that didn't need a mowing in spite of all that rain. He told himself to stop following her with his eyes as he explained how timothy and Dutch clover sprang from heavier grazed sod. He had to get on back to town after killing more time than intended with a girl-child who'd be harder to mess with than the skittish Meg Connors, for Gawd's sake.

Thinking about the more tomboyish young widow woman inspired him to drive a tad faster, albeit not fast enough to endanger Meg's mowing machinery. As he drove up Main Street he saw more foot traffic now that the Sabbath was winding down and everyone was looking ahead to that mass hanging in the morning.

When he drove into Meg's back yard one of her hands came to help him with the team and said they'd see to putting the rolling stock away. Longarm said he had to thank the kid's boss lady. That's when he was told Meg was away for the evening. Her hand couldn't say just

137

where. Longarm was too polite to comment on the window curtain he saw moving in a second-story window.

He headed for the jail house, muttering about womankind even as a tingle in his jeans told him he was recovering nicely from his surprise screwing the night before. He decided to picture old Portia back in Denver taking his old organ grinder in her ring-dang-doo by lamplight. The only natural woman he knew over on this slope was old Jenny Crowfeather and she was likely sore at him, too. He'd find out later, at supper time, when he had an excuse to drop by her beanery.

As he passed by the gallows in the courthouse square he spied the sheriff jawing with some other gents by the thirteen steps up to the platform. Sheriff Peabody hailed him over and introduced the others as interested cattlemen who'd ridden in to watch four cowboys hang.

Peabody added, "We have your saddle, possibles and Winchester over in our own tackroom if you're wondering where they went."

Longarm frowned and said, "I hadn't known they were gone. I just came in from the Otis spread and haven't been by my hotel room, yet."

Peabody looked uncomfortable and confided, "You don't have no room at that hotel no more, no offense. Miss Sharon Rose Slade swore out a trespass warrant and got our district attorney to order to agree that you had no right to keep her our of her own room last night."

Longarm cocked a brow to reply, "I didn't know I had. This is sure getting tedious and who do I have to pistol whup to convince you all the law is on my side when it comes to that fucking room?"

Sheriff Peabody sighed and said, "I wish you'd drop it, old son. I know the law's on your side. The duchess of Durango don't give a shit and she holds a second mortgage on the D.A.'s fancy townhouse."

Longarm decided, "I'll worry about that later. Right now I'm on my way to see Rick Robles, with your permit, of course."

Sheriff Peabody said, "Tell 'em I said to let the two of you argue in private. That greaser sure is arguing, this evening. He keeps on telling us we can't hang him in the morning."

The sheriff winked at one of his visiting voters and added, "A lot *he* knows, the fancy-danding greaser!"

Longarm strode on to the granite jail house, where he found the soon to be late Ricardo Robles literally dancing back and forth in his cell as he blubbered, "Where have you been? I've been trying to reach you all afternoon! Don't you know they mean to hang me in a little over twelve hours?"

Longarm lounged in the doorway, reaching for some smokes as he told Robles, "I've been off making hay whilst the sun shone. How come you wanted to talk to me? Are you ready to talk about those stagecoach robberies?"

He didn't know whether to laugh or cry when Robles gasped, "I'll talk! Just save me from hanging in the morning and I'll give you what you need to hang me and all my pals some other time, see?"

Longarm saw. He felt like a shit-eating dog as he told the doomed *vaquero* there might be time to get him a stay if he sang a really fine song. For in point of fact there wasn't. If he wired that very night that he'd solved that string of robberies along the Ambush to Durango line there wasn't a Chinaman's chance of a reply before the cold gray dawn sent a mighty bitter Rick Robles up those thirteen steps to his double-crossed doom.

Chapter 18

Longarm got out his notebook and sat on the one bunk while the Mexican paced. Robles commenced by swearing he'd taken no direct part in any of the many killings. It wasn't going to do him a lick of good but Longarm took that down anyway and said, "Bueno, you rode along to hold the horses up along the crests whilst your fellow road agents scampered down to finish off anyone left and loot the busted up coaches. Let's hear some names."

Robles replied, "I'm only sure of one. I was recruited against my better judgment by an old boy I used to ride with on the Maxwell grant, down along the Pecos. His name was Roberto Valdez. We called him Bobby. Like me, he was raised an American citizen after the treaty of Guadalupe Hidalgo."

Longarm took down the description of an assimilate Mex about the same age and a little fatter than Robles with a missing pinky finger.

Longarm said, "You *vaqueros* shouldn't dally rope if you aim to grow up with all your fingers. Who else rode with you when you landslided all them poor folk?"

Robles looked away and muttered, "We didn't use last names when we got together out on the hills. There were two others Bobby introduced me to in tricky light. He called one Duke and the other answered to el Aguilar."

"The eagle?" Longarm noted in his book, adding, "Never

mind the tricky light and tell me more about these civic-minded citizens."

Robles said, "I don't think el Aguilar was exactly a citizen. He had an odd way of talking but he didn't speak Spanish."

Longarm didn't ask how Robles knew that. Most riders from New Mexico, Anglo or Mex, spoke a mixture of bad English and Spanish. He asked, "How come this el Aguilar had a Mex nickname if he wasn't Mex?"

Robles shrugged and replied, "¿Quien sabe? Bobby and Duke called him el Aguilar. He was our leader. Tall, lean, hatchet-faced with a dark complexion and, like I said, a funny way of talking."

"Indian." Longarm decided, adding, "Real Indians don't sound like them heap-big stage show Injuns. They talk sort of high-pitched and pissed off. Is that what your boss road agent sounded like?"

Robles nodded thoughtfully and volunteered, "He was the one who knew all the short cuts through the high country all around. Bobby said it was best not to ask too many questions."

Longarm said, "That's what they pay me to do. What did Duke look like?"

Robles said, "Average for la raza. A little older and heavier set than me or Bobby Valdez. Like I said, we only rode together against the stage line, after dark a lot of the time and they had me hanging back with the horses when they were holding still above the trail."

Longarm grimaced and said, "I don't suppose you have any mailing addresses to go with your mysterious pals."

It had been a statement rather than a question. But Robles replied that Bobby Valdez had been riding for the Circle Z up until the time he, Robles, had been arrested for a crime he'd never committed.

He whined, "I don't know why those three Triple Eight riders said I was the one who was with them that night. I was off to the south with Valdez, Duke and el Aguilar.

Why do you suppose they said I was the whorehouse shooter who got away?"

"They might be protecting the one who really got away," Longarm suggested, adding, "On the other hand you could be handing me a line of shit to save your own ass. A lot will depend on what your old pal Valdez has to say when I look him up. You say he rides for a spread called the Circle Z?"

"He was. I ain't seen him since they arrested me out to the Triple Eight. You don't expect him to own up to night riding with me, Duke and el Aguilar, do you?"

"Not right off," said Longarm, dryly, as he got to his feet and put his notebook away.

He banged on the door to be let out. Robles repeated his complaint about those three Anglo hands next door telling fibs about him because nobody out to the Triple 8 had ever liked him.

As Longarm was leaving, Robles asked how soon they might expect a stay of execution. It was a dumb question. The poor simp had less than twelve hours to live if they really meant to dangle him at dawn. Dawn came earlier than five A.M. in summertime at that latitude. Longarm said he'd send a wire directly. He really meant to ride out to that Circle Z to bring Roberto Valdez in *poco tiempo*!

But like that Scotch poet had observed, the best laid plans of mice and lawmen had a way of getting all fucked up. When he went over to the sheriff's department to ask for his saddle, the loan of a pony and directions to an outfit called the Circle Z, the night deputy on duty said, "You won't find anybody out to the Circle Z these days. The duchess of Durango fired half and put the top hands to work on the Triple Eight when she consolidated the two spreads and their brands."

Longarm frowned thoughtfully and asked if the local lawman knew of a former Circle Z rider called Roberto Valdez.

The night deputy nodded and said, "Sure. He's dead. They held the funeral in town for him last week. He was

142

loping after a calf in tall timber when his pony fell and rolled on him. They gave him a swell funeral, even if he was a Mex. Bobby Valdez was a top hand and a good old boy with lots of pals, Anglo as well as Mex."

Longarm shot a murderous glance out the window as he muttered, "One of his Mex pals just told me all about him. I was afraid I was being sold a bill of goods just now. Some men will say anything to get out of dying in the morning."

He added he'd still like his saddle, Winchester and the loan of a pony. So they fixed him up with a high-stepping paint of about fourteen hands with a barrel head and a willing nature.

He rode over to the Western Union to send a night letter to his home office. He knew Billy Vail would want to know how he was doing, even though he was making as much progress as that inky dinky spider climbing up the spout. The easy answer to all that bullshit about the late Bobby Valdez and some even less identifiable riders was that Robles was guilty as charged and good riddance to the big fibber.

So Longarm didn't know what in thunder he was supposed to do when he got to the Western Union and they were holding a wire from Governor Fred Pitkin for him, granting Ricardo Robles a stay of execution while the federal district court in Denver decided whether they wanted him or not!

Longarm rode back to the center of town and tethered the paint out front of the Bighorn Saloon. Inside, as expected, he found old Sheriff Peabody holding court after an early supper.

When Longarm sat down and slid the stay across the table to the older lawman, Peabody swore softly and said, "A heap of visitors from out of town ain't going to like this, you infernal spoil-sport!"

Longarm softly replied, "I know. Might be a good idea if I was to leave town with my prisoner by the light of the moon."

Peabody shook his head and demured, "Ain't nothing in

143

this wire from the governor about turning Robles over to you, just yet. It only says not to hang him until they thrash the matter out in Denver, not over here in these parts."

One of the other older men at the table sounded mighty morose as he chimed in with, "What's this I hear? We don't get to watch that murdersome Mex trip the light fantastic at the end of his rope, come morning?"

Peabody warned, "Stuff a sock in it. When I want everyone all het up I'll announce it my ownself."

He glanced up at Longarm to add, "You'd best let us put you up for the night. Major Scott thinks Brazos Roy is gunning for you and I know for a fact that Twinkle Turner is. He says you suckered him the first time and you'll never get that close to him again, alive."

Longarm shrugged and said, "He sure barks a good fight for a hound on a leash. I don't have to worry about him until such time as that duchess of Durango sics him on me."

Sheriff Peabody said, "She's sicced him on you. When she had your saddle and such dumped in our doorway she sent word she means to have you shot for a trespasser if you ever go near her again. How come the pretty little thing is so sore at you, old son?"

Longarm sighed and said, "Reckon she don't want to be friends no more. I don't have to go to her fool hotel. I want it on record I ain't looking for trouble with the duchess or any of her hired guns. After that the law gives me every right to defend myself if they come looking for me, right?"

The older lawman agreed that was the way *he* read the laws on self-defense and added, "I already told Twinkle Turner and his back-up not to try for you on this side of Main Street. So if you were to let us bed you down at the courthouse . . ."

"I got more comfortable quarters in mind," Longarm cut in, adding, "I always sleep more comfortable when nobody who's sore at me could know where I'm sleeping. What time are you hanging those other boys in the cold gray dawn?"

Sheriff Peabody said, "Well after sunrise, when it won't

be so gray and the crowd will be in a better mood after breakfast. It ain't as if Brewer, Pulver and Wylie will be in any hurry, you know. I want a good turnout with the sun shining bright before we announce that they won't get to see Ricardo Robles die, just yet."

Longarm didn't ask why. He'd faced down more than one ad hoc mob of night riders in his own time. He said, "I'll get there by eight to back your play and see if the ones you'll be hanging have anything new to say about that night at Madame Frenchy's."

Then he rose to elbow his way to the batwings and back out on the street as the sun was setting and the light was in his eyes. He could just make out the outline of a crab-like figure scuttling toward the hotel on the far side.

The beanery Jenny Crowfeather worked in was on his side of Sheriff Peabody's tacit deadline. Since few riders supped that late in the day the counter was empty when Longarm came in and grabbed a seat at the same.

The portly but pretty Arapaho gal moved down the far side to face him with a smoldering look, saying, "You have some nerve, coming here after what you did to me last night!"

Longarm soothed, "I didn't do it to you, Jenny. That money-lending gal who owns the hotel won't let me in that room, neither. When I heard she'd chased you away I was afraid to come across the creek to your place, knowing you had company."

The Indian waitress softened somewhat but said, "I still have company. My sister asked all sorts of questions when I came home from work so late last night. She as much as accused me of dining on white meat!"

Longarm smiled at the memory her words evoked but never pointed out that French lessons had been her own grand notion. He said, "Speaking of white boys, or close enough, what can you tell me about a *vaquero* called Bobby, Bobby Valdez? Got rolled to death a spell back?"

Jenny shrugged her plump shoulders and said without hesitation, "He was all right. I went to his funeral over to

145

the Papist burial ground. Used to come in here on payday with another Mex called Duke. They were sort of flirty, like most Mex tend to be. But they never gave us real trouble. Why do you ask?"

"My boss wants me to," Longarm replied. "How about another pal of theirs called el Aguilar, or the Eagle?"

Jenny thought, shook her head and said, "I'd have remembered anyone with such an outlandish name. Sounds like one of *my* people."

Longarm said, "He might well be. Another Mex tells me el Aguilar knows the rough range all about like he might have grown up in it. How much do you and your Arapaho kith and kin know about the Ute bands who used to roam these parts?"

Jenny replied, "Not much. Most of them were long gone before I got here. I do recall some really ornery hold-out rode rings around the army under a young war chief called Powered Wagon. Funny name for any Indian if you ask me."

Longarm suggested, "Try *Poggamoggan*, which would be Ute for warclub."

Jenny thought, shook her head and decided, "I'm sure the second part sounded more like Wagon. Where did you learn to talk Ute? Have you been fucking *wild* Indians, you wicked thing?"

Longarm said, "All my Indian friends are friendly. I don't speak Ute, or Ho, as they spell it. But I know a few words. So try *Puha Waigon* instead of *Poggamoggan*."

She did and agreed, "That sounds more like it. That heap bad Injun could have been called *Puha Waigon* instead of Power Wagon. What does it mean, Custis?"

Longarm said, "Thunderbird Medicine. He sure must have been mighty modest if he wanted to be called a man with the medicine of . . . wait a minute. Mexicans picture the thunderbird the same as we do, as a big old flappy *eagle* and Robles said el Aguilar spoke no Spanish and talked odd in English."

146

Jenny asked what that might mean and what he wanted for supper.

Longarm said, "It means a suspect I just talked to was lying like a rug or mayhaps telling me the simple truth and I'd like two eggs sunny side up on top of my chili con carne with my coffee black and strong."

As she served the strong coffee Jenny pouted, "Who were you planning on staying up late with, you horny rascal?"

Longarm truthfully replied, "I ain't got another gal lined up, if that was your subtle question. I want to sleep light because I have a hanging to attend in the morning. I've found that when I'm really tired I can drop off full of java and it wakes me up early. So I put in an honest day's work this Sabbath and I'd likely sleep through the most interesting part of tomorrow morning if I just flopped down natural."

Another late diner came in and Jenny moved off to serve him, still muttering to herself about other women while Longarm tried to decide where to head next.

The fickle and vindictive Sharon Rose Slade had made it clear she'd had second thoughts about all those nice things she'd said while he'd been hitting bottom. He wasn't up to any more kid games with another widow woman up at Associated Hostlers of Ambush Inc. He suspected he knew what had poor Meg Connors so mixed up about her lonely independent ring-dang-doo. A slightly older and more level-headed widow woman in Denver had explained it to him, before she'd ever let him strum her old banjo. But it was Meg's misfortune and none of his own. So where would it be safe for a gent as popular as himself to bed down for just a few hours of safe and sound sleep.

When it came to him he laughed, rose to leave a good tip on the counter and headed for the door. Jenny called after him, "Is she pretty?"

To which Longarm could only reply, "Pretty as a picture, but she don't put out, as far as I know."

Chapter 19

It was well after dark and that fluffy little pup called Tiger was baying like a wolf as Longarm led the paint on foot across the cattle guard at the Otis spread. The barks got no louder as he and the pony moved on down the slope. So Longarm knew Tiger was pent or chained for the night. That was a smart move in coyote country.

Glory Otis was outlined in a square of doorlight as she called out, "Who's there? I ain't alone and we've all got guns!"

Longarm called back, "It's me, Custis Long, come to take you up on that invite to stay the night, if it's still good."

The light from behind her outlined more of Glory than her mother hubbard was intended to show as she danced forward to exclaim, "Of course it's still good! Did you think I was just trying to sound like a Christian after all you'd done for us?"

Her two kid brothers boiled out of the cabin to demand the honors of watering, foddering and rubbing down his borrowed pony. Longarm had no call to insult farm kids by warning them you always watered a horse before you fed it. He hung on to the Winchester as he dismounted. As the boys led everything else around to their stable he followed Glory inside, where he saw they were in the square one-room cabin they used as their kitchen and dining space. He told Glory he'd just supped in town but she still sat him at the table and said she'd put the coffee on.

He said, "I don't reckon I'd better drink no more coffee tonight, no offense. Already had some and I'd like to catch a few winks before I have to lope back to town for that hanging. Were you and your kid brothers planning on driving in for the show?"

Glory sat down across from him with a sober shake of her buckwheat honey-colored head. She said, "Ward and Wayne wanted to watch. But I told them it was wicked to take pleasure in the suffering of others."

Longarm felt no call to argue about that. So he kept still.

She read his silence wrong and insisted, "I'm not a big sissy. I'm not. I can wring a hen's neck or stick a pig if either has to be done. I'm sure I could kill a man, red or white, if I had just cause to do so. But none of those four cowboys ever did anything to me or mine and my pop took me to a hanging when I was little. I don't know why. It wasn't any fun at all and the poor man wriggled and jiggled like an earthworm caught on hard ground by the sun!"

Longarm nodded soberly and said, "Public hangings are meant more to instruct than amuse. But looking on the bright side, they're only fixing to hang three in the morning. A lawyer pal of mine got a stay of execution for one of 'em, signed by Governor Pitkin on a weekend! Ain't that something?"

Glory didn't ask and Longarm didn't want to consider what the sort of flat-chested but mighty nimble Portia Parkhurst might have done for Governor Pitkin on a weekend.

Glory only wanted to know which one they weren't fixing to hang.

When he said it was Rick Robles she smiled and said she was glad, adding, "I danced with him at the Greenup Social in May. He was really a swell dancer and ever so polite. I found it hard to believe he'd go crazy mean in a house of ill repute. I only danced with him, myself, but from what I hear tell Rick Robles wouldn't have had to pay for his more manly pleasures at Madam Frenchy's."

Longarm quietly replied, "He claims he was somewhere

149

else that evening. Since you seem to know some of your Indian neighbors, Miss Glory, have you ever heard mention of a hold-out Ute they know as *Puha Waigon* in their own lingo?"

Without hesitation the white girl nodded and said, "That means Thunderbird Medicine in *our* lingo. Utes talk like Mexicans and say Medicine Thunderbird when they mean Thunderbird Medicine."

Longarm cut in, "I've noticed that. What else have you heard of this modest quill Indian who's name might just come out el Aguilar to a less superstitious Mex?"

The gal who lived out on range some Indians still roamed shook her golden head and replied, "He's not a quill Indian, to begin with. They tell us he's been to a mission school and can talk, read and write English better than some white riders. He led the army a merry chase, intercepting dispatches and knowing what the different bugle calls meant. But that was then and this is now. Thunderbird Medicine's band went west to Utah Territory with the rest of their nation before Pop brought us all over the divide to settle these old hunting grounds of the western Ute bands."

Longarm mused aloud, "Robles would have known Valdez was dead, too. I just hate it when all the witnesses to a suspect's alibi are missing or dead. It leaves you way in the middle of the air. Ricardo Robles could have been offering me a bag of wind to keep from hanging in the morning or I could be on the verge of catching the crooks who killed your dad and all them other folk!"

Glory Otis didn't sound excited, considering, as she sniffed and said, "I wish we had a nickel for all the wild guesses on who might have robbed those wrecked coaches."

"Who do you suspect it was, Miss Glory?" he asked.

She answered, simply, "I doubt anyone will ever know. They left no witnesses alive. They started those landslides, looted the busted-up remains and rode off without anyone ever cutting their sign. Since they haven't hit since that Mister Phillips from the post office was back-shot along the trail, I'll bet they've quit for good and won't ever be caught."

Longarm asked if she'd been questioned by Postal Inspector Phillips.

Glory nodded gravely and said, "Sitting in that very chair, earlier of a Wednesday as I recall. He talked nice about Pop being killed in the first robbery but seemed to think my brothers and me should have known more about that stage line than we did. I told him none of us had ever rid to Durango in coach. It was Pop who rode shotgun and that was only when he wasn't out here, building things. You never saw a man for building things like our Pop. There was never enough time in a day or money in the bank to satisfy Pop. He'd get up early to put in a whole day's work before he'd ride the coach down to Durango and back for extra day-wages. Mister Phillips asked us about pals of Pop who might have known what was riding in the boots of those coaches without having to ride along with the same."

Longarm nodded and said, "Good question. What did you tell him?"

Glory asked, "Are you sure you don't want any coffee or mayhaps some hot chocolate? There wasn't anything I *could* tell Mister Phillips. Like I said, it was Pop, not us, working for the stage line, and he was one of the first company men killed when those robberies commenced. I think Mister Phillips was looking for somebody hanging around the depot in town whilst they were loading up for the runs down to Durango. Mister Phillips said there were dozens of ways the road agents could have cashed the gold dust they took along with the hard cash from those wrecked coaches. I've been paid in panned color for butter and eggs myself. Folk in mining country have always used raw gold as money."

Longarm nodded and said, "He was closer to the bone looking for a finger-man around that depot. I see why he asked you about your dad's pals in town. I'd have asked that, my ownself, if you hadn't already volunteered the answer."

"Why do you reckon they killed him if he wasn't getting warm?" she asked.

To which Longarm could only reply, "They must have thought he was getting warm. He might have questioned somebody who knew more than they wanted to tell him. He might have scared somebody skinny just by questioning them. A killer with a guilty conscience might have decided to dry gulch Phillips before he ever *got* warm!"

She repeated her offer of hot chocolate. Longarm repressed a yawn and confessed, "I'm usually just waking up at this hour. But to tell the truth it's been a long day and I didn't get much sleep the night before."

So she rose and said she'd show him to her Pop's cabin, seeing it was the best in the string and nobody was using it anymore.

As he followed her out to the first dog-run she cut around through the dark yard, murmuring that the boys were about to turn in up ahead if they knew what was good for them.

When he commented that she seemed to run a tight ship, or at least a tight dairy spread, Glory chuckled fondly and said they could thank their late Pop for that. She said, "I'm nothing to Pop when it comes to working hard and keeping things tidy. But he taught me true and I reckon he'd be proud if he could see what a go we've been making of a spread that was little more than an aspen grove when we first came to this valley less than two years back!"

She showed him into another dark cube and struck a match to reveal a swamping featherbed with a rolltop desk and shelves of books along its green-gray walls of unpeeled logs. There was a crazy-quilt comforter over the bedding. Glory lit a bed lamp and turned the comforter down to reveal clean muslin sheets under a red flannel blanket. She suggested he shuck his duds and get under the covers whilst she went to make that hot chocolate. He politely insisted he didn't want any. It wasn't clear whether they were in agreement or not as she slipped out to leave him alone with his Winchester and her dad's featherbed.

He leaned the rifle against the logs between the bed and lamp table and hung his Stetson and gun rig on a rustic bedpost before he shucked his boots and duds to tuck his double derringer under a pillow and roll under the covers. He was so tuckered out he didn't get around to trimming the lamp before he was sound asleep.

So the soft glow from beside the bed was still illuminating the herringbone pattern of willow whips betwixt log roof rafters as he was suddenly aware he lay bare as a babe, spread eagle on his back with the covers tossed aside while somebody seemed to be giving him the French lesson of his life!

He glanced down to see with relief it was a naked blonde gal and not a silly young boy sucking on his old organ grinder while she fondled his bare balls. She had him almost there and he didn't want to waste it where it wouldn't do her as much good. So he rolled the two of them over and withdrew from Glory's pouted lips with an audible pop to slide it hard and wet down between her heaving cupcake breasts, the length of her firm young torso, to where her trim thighs were spread wide in adoration.

He kissed her for the first time as he rammed his raging erection into her tight but willing ring-dang-doo. So she wrapped her arms and legs around him, tight, before she got to moan, "Oh, yesss! I hoped it would be big enough to fill my gaping gash!"

Longarm just kept pounding with some of his stored-up passion left over from earlier silly conversations. But once they'd shared a long toe-curling climax together he felt obliged to kiss her again, more gently, and confide, "The man who said this tight little ring-dang-doo was a gaping gash must have been hung like a peanut. But don't tell me who he was and I won't tell you whose pussy I'm comparing this one to."

She moved her trim hips langorously as she murmured,

153

"You don't find me just a little floppy titted and sloppy betwixt the legs, handsome?"

He began to move in her some more, as most men would have, assuring her, "You're built so firm and maidenly I'd have never thought you weren't cherry, even when I shoved it to you, before you commenced to screw back so mature. I like your tits just swell, even though they do seem a tad underdeveloped, no offense. As for the rest of you being sloppy, that's just silly. There ain't an ounce of loose fat on your lovely frame and I just now told you how tight you were built."

She began to move in time with his slow gentle thrusts as she sighed and confided, "That makes me feel so happy, even if it's not true. I guess it's because I got started early, when any grown man's manhood would have filled me down here a lot. Do you suppose I just imagined I was built sloppy betwixt the legs because men seemed to have less to offer as I grew bigger?"

Longarm grimaced and said, "I'd just as soon not hear about the time and place you really lost your cherry, Miss Glory. Suffice it to say you sure seem to have enjoyed it and I take it your dad didn't know you were screwing around, despite your innocent ways, since before you had a full grown twat to screw with?"

She raised her bare knees to hook an ankle over either of Longarm's shoulders as she coyly replied, "Pop would have killed that married cowboy if he'd ever known what we were really doing when he offered to give me those riding lessons. I think the biggest cock I ever had in me, up until now, was that traveling saleman who came by while Pop was working in town, back in Nebraska. At least, I *think* he had a big cock. Now that you mention it, I was only about fourteen and hadn't had much experience, so . . ."

Longarm laughed, called her a little dickens and suggested dog style, seeing she was such a woman of the world despite her girlish ways and shy flutters.

Dog style being the most conversational position in the

Kama Sutra, Longarm casually asked, while long-donging her with his bare feet on the braided rug, whether he had anybody with a peanut-sized dick and a possessive attitude to worry about.

Glory arched her spine to take it deeper, a lovely sight by lamp light, as she assured him she was careful about putting out to gents who weren't married up or just passing through. When she asked why, he confided, "I've had two brushes in town with hot-heads who accused me of messing with other gals."

Glory winked up at him with her pink rectum as she purred, "Why go to strangers, now that you've decided I'm not too sloppy for you down here?"

He laughed and said, "I ain't been with either gal who like to got me into a fight. One fool accused me of messing with a widow woman who doesn't seem to want anybody messing with her. The other even bigger fool accused me of messing with his damned daughter."

Glory panted, "Deeper, faster, are you talking about Joy Norwich, the hangman's daughter?"

Longarm got a firm grip on her hip bones to ram her good as he said, "Matter of fact, it was. Are you saying that happens a lot with Joy Norwich?"

Glory lowered her face to the sheeting as she moaned, "Ooh, that feels so good! Everybody in these parts knows Limey Norwich worries about his daughter. He has good reason. She'd do this with a hound dog, in public, if he didn't watch her like a hawk. Some gals who like to fuck don't know how to do so discreet as the rest of us, see?"

Chapter 20

Thanks to an old leghorn rooster, Longarm woke up before dawn with a fresh morning hard-on. This inspired Glory to get on top and beg him not to leave. As she served him breakfast in bed, an hour later, he told her he'd be back, explaining that he had no better place to stay, he'd be stuck in those parts until he could get a federal warrant he could show the local circuit judge in exchange for Rick Robles, and he wanted her to introduce him to some of their unofficial Indian neighbors.

He said, "I've verified the late Bobby Valdez had a Mex pal called Duke. But if their Indian pal called el Aguilar has been spending much time in town I've yet to meet anyone who noticed. So unless he's got a day job at some nearby spread, under a more natural sounding name, he could be holed up with some of your holed-up Utes who never moved west with the others."

Glory said she didn't know how many Ho-speaking natives of the west slope might still be around and added that they didn't seem to be out to give anyone any trouble.

He told her that was his whole point, explaining, "Lots of ornery local boys blend in with harmless local folk who neither bust the law nor help it out worth spit. There's Frank and Jesse over Clay County way and Tiburcio Vasquez was playing checkers with other Mexicans in the Plaza De Los Angeles when he wasn't stopping coaches over on the Santa Monica post road. But we'll talk about Ute holdouts gone bad once I make sure nobody hangs his Mex pal, Robles."

Glory had told him her kid brothers slept two dog-runs away and for a gal who liked to come she hadn't yelled too loud about it. So Longarm thought nothing of it, at first, when Ward, Junior came out to watch him saddle up the borrowed paint in their lean-to stable. He told the kid he was riding in to see about that hanging and Ward, Junior said, "I know. Me and Wayne wanted to watch but Glory won't let us. It's a good thing for you our Pop wasn't here last night whilst you were fucking Glory. Pop never held with anyone even trying to fuck Glory whilst he had anything to say about it."

Not wanting to confirm nor deny the kid's accusation, Longarm told Ward, Junior he never did anything a gal's father might not approve of. He said, "The hangman I'm about to meet up with in town told me not to fuck his daughter and I said right out I'd never."

The Otis kid snickered and said, "Oh, her? Joy Norwich would fuck most anybody if they weren't afraid of her father. He sells shotgun shell and dynamite in his hardware store when he ain't hanging folk!"

Longarm led the jug-headed cowpony outside and mounted up before the sassy kid could steer the conversation back to his own dad's views on gentleman callers.

He rode into Ambush a little after eight, with the sunlight crisp but bright, to see some earlier risers gathered around the gallows in the courthouse square. Some country folk had brought along picnic baskets and an enterprising townsman had set up a beer and pretzel stand. Longarm left the borrowed pony back in its stable and stored his saddle and possibles in the sheriff's tack room, but hung on to his Winchester.

He mosied over to the jail to find Sheriff Peabody trying to calm another beer-bellied gent in a rusty black broadcloth suit.

He turned out to be the district attorney who owed money to that duchess of Durango. It wasn't too clear why

157

he wanted all four of her erstwhile riders hung that morning.

The sheriff was holding, correctly, that the Colorado constitution said the county sheriff and nobody else had the local say in all public hangings. As Longarm joined them Peabody said, "Talk to this federal lawman if you want to talk about Robles. I ain't about to hang no dago son of a bitch the governor just pardoned!"

The D.A. and county prosecutor sniffed and said, "I read the same wire from Denver. There's not one word about a *pardon*. Explain that mere stay of execution to Lem, here, Deputy Long."

Longarm shrugged and said, "We've all read the same telegram. So what are we arguing about? Like you just said, it's a stay of execution ordering us to just sit tight and not do anything to that Mexican until he's had time to sort things out with the court I ride for."

The prosecutor snorted, "What could there be to sort out? There's not a word in that wire about new evidence and people have come from miles around to watch all four of those killers hang!"

Longarm said, "I just saw some early birds out front. Robles has confessed to more serious crimes and I'm still looking for evidence to back his play."

The prosecutor, who, like the sheriff, would be up for re-election in the fall, protested, "He was found as guilty as the other three by a jury of his peers. He should have confessed earlier to other crimes if he didn't want to hang this morning."

Longarm turned to the sheriff and murmured, "Life's too short to argue with women or politicians. When were you fixing to start the show?"

Peabody said, "Limey Norwich and his crew are with Brewer, Pulver and Wylie now. They'll be bringing them out, all set to dance, and once they do we'll get on with it. I wasn't planning on any formal announcement about that stay from the governor unless someboy raises a fuss."

The prosecutor tagged along, assuring them there would

be a fuss, as Longarm and the sheriff strode back to the cell the three Anglo riders had been sharing apart from Robles.

As they entered Longarm saw the self-proclaimed professional from London Town had Wylie and Pulver on their feet with their hands tied behind them and what looked like barrel staves lashed along their spines by other ropes around their waists and upper chests. Longarm didn't ask why. Some U.S. Army hangmen favored those lengths of hard wood to immobilize the spine and assure the neck snapping where it was supposed to.

The pale-eyed and washed-out looking Limey Norwich glanced their way but didn't say anything as he and the two teenaged youth with him proceeded to secure Hank Brewer the same way. Brewer just went on looking sheepish as a kid caught with his hand in the cookie jar while they prepared to stretch his neck those few fatal inches. It was Will Pulver, standing helpless in a puddle of his own piss who suddenly wailed, "I don't like this at all! This wasn't the way they told us things would go if we just stuck to our story!"

Hank Brewer stared ahead while they adjusted the stave against the base of his neck but snarled, "Don't crack now, you ninny! You know how this is supposed to turn out if we just hang tough!"

Will Pulver moaned, "We ain't fixing to hang *tough*! We're fixing to hang, *period*! Can't you see we've been sold down the river? If they were really going to save us . . ."

"Shut up!" snapped Buck Wylie from behind him, kicking him in the rump with his unbound right boot as he added, "These old boys ain't in on the deal. They think they're really going to hang us, and they *might*, if you break faith at this late date!"

As he finished with Brewer Limey Norwich dryly remarked to the sheriff, "They've been talking like that for a while. If I were you I'd be on the alert for a last-minute rescue attempt."

Peabody considered, then said, "Nobody is about to get at 'em in here." Then he turned to Longarm to ask, "Out front, do you reckon?"

Longarm shrugged and said, "Might tie up some loose ends if they did. No way in hell they're going to move these cowboys through that crowd with the rest of us shooting down from all around."

Will Pulver sobbed, "You see? It's a durned old double-cross! We ain't about to be saved! Dead men tell no tales and all three of us are fixing to hang by our necks until we are dead, dead dead!"

Limey Norwich was the one who suggested it was getting late and the three of them would never be more ready to go. So Sheriff Peabody nodded and said, "Let's get cracking, then. You three get a move on. The preacher is waiting out front with the others."

Will Pulver didn't want to go. The other two moved willingly from a cell they were likely tired of. But Pulver had to be half carried, trying to dig his heels in, as he babbled about none of this being fair.

Longarm fell in beside Pulver to grip him gently by one upper arm as he carried the Winchester in his other hand, aimed at the floor. He told the prisoner, "I spent some time in a drunk tank when I was younger and wilder. Every time one of my cell mates got bailed out he swore he'd get word to my own pals to come and post my bail. But none of them ever, once they were out, showed themselves. Might that be the sort of situation we have here? That one pal who got away the night of the whorehouse killings promised you boys he'd do something grand for you as long as you never gave him away to the law?"

It might have worked. But Wylie, behind them, snarled, "Don't fall for that lawman's bullshit! He ain't going to let you go if you talk!"

Pulver whined at Longarm, "Will you let me go if I tell you what really happened that night?"

Longarm tried. He called to the sheriff. But now they had the preacher praying up ahead as they all paraded the short distance to the front door and Peabody called back that they'd talk about it later, when they had more time.

Longarm tried, "You'd better tell me pronto. You see how little time I have to work with if you want me to try and save you!"

Pulver moaned, "I want you to save me so bad I can taste it! I want you to save me so bad I'd suck your dick and be your punk for a year and a day! But you have to promise, as a man, before you get anything more from this child!"

"I sure hate animal cunning," Longarm muttered under his breath as they reached the doorway and stepped out into the morning dazzle. He tried to stay in step with Pulver all the way but when they got to the narrow stairway he was elbowed aside by the hanging crew so's they could manhandle the three of them up those thirteen rickety steps of raw lumber.

Longarm followed right after them, hoping to have another word with the weak sister in the bunch once they were lined up on the trap. It was the usual custom to let a condemned man say a few last words. Sometimes they got to go on to tedious lengths. But Sheriff Peabody, or mayhaps Limey Norwich, thought it best to just get the thing over with. So Longarm had just mounted the platform and Will Pulver was yelling something with his feet lashed together and a black poplin sack over his face, when Norwich yanked a lever and all three of them dropped as one while a rifle shot rent the air to pluck whisps of oiled hemp from the stout rope Will Pulver was stretching with all his heart and soul.

Longarm dropped his Winchester to the planking and sprang forward as he whipped out his pocket knife, grabbed the taut rope with the other hand, and tried like hell to cut through that much horn-hard hemp before it was too late.

Limey Norwich dryly asked, "What do you think you're doing? The prisoner is dead and I'll thank you not to ruin that expensive rope."

Longarm saw it was already too late and stopped, stepping back from the open trap door as he pointed to said rope and said, "Somebody else did that much damage with a rifle round."

The hangman grimaced and said, "We all heard the shot. I've read your American Wild West magazines and it's still not possible to cut a full-inch of oiled Kentucky hemp with a single bullet."

Staring down at the three gently swaying forms below the platform, Longarm said, "Don't suspect anyone was out to cut this rope before me just now. Suspect the shot was aimed at Will Pulver's chest, which was at this very level when you sprung the trap before he could yell out who it was who'd double-crossed the three of them!"

Sheriff Peabody had heard some of that and moved closer to hear more as the hangman stiffly asked, "Are you accusing me of springing the trap to shut somebody up?"

Longarm shook his head and replied, "Hanging the three of 'em was the chore the county hired you to perfrom this morning. Their false-hearted friend with the rifle couldn't have been depending on you to shut Pulver up. Have you always walked around with that chip on your shoulder, Mister Norwich?"

The morose Englishman didn't answer. Down below, the deputy coroner called up to declare the three of them dead.

Sheriff Peabody asked what they were talking about.

Longarm said, "Try her this way. Four riders off the Triple Eight rode into town that Saturday night to get laid. One thing led to another and when the smoke cleared those three you just now hung were caught on the scene with smoking guns. They said the one who got away was Ricardo Robles. They said that because they didn't want to say who it really was and nobody out to the Triple Eight liked Ricardo Robles. He was a top hand of the Mex persuasion who didn't join in their fun and games. He'd been hired by the duchess of Durango and none of them liked her all that much, either."

Peabody stared thoughtfully at the frayed rope Pulver

still dangled from as he asked what that more recent rifle shot had meant.

Longarm said, "The one who got away feared that sooner or later one of them might spill the beans to see if he might save himself. I know that for a fact because whoever it was just tried to silence Will Pulver before we could hang him. I suspect from earlier slips of the tongue that he or someone smarter covering for him promised the three we just hung that they'd never hang as long as they stuck to their story about that fourth rider being Rick Robles."

In the meanwhile, as Longarm jawed with the sheriff and the hangman atop the platform, the assembled crowd was making restive noises about the short and likely disappointing show they'd just seen. The numbers three and four were muttered back and forth until someone with a more authoritive voice called out, "How come you only hung three? Where's that fucking Mexican?"

Several others joined in a chant demanding a fucking Mexican but Sheriff Peabody showed they'd voted smart by stepping around those gaping trap doors to fire a shot in the air for silence and then yell, "Cut the crap and help us catch that other one who fired a rifle just now! Don't any of you have ears? Couldn't you tell the rascal was out to throw us off the trail?"

"What trail are you talking about, Sheriff?" yelled a voice from the crowd.

Peabody yelled, "The trail of the road agents who murdered all them other folk! Do you want to see that Mex hang for shooting up a whorehouse or robbing all them stagecoaches? None of you all fired that shot. I figure it must have come from a roof top down the slope along Main Street. Fan out and question everyone over yonder as you search for spent brass!"

It worked. As the crowd began to disperse Peabody turned to Longarm with a sly grin to add, "I still say that fucking greaser is lying like a rug!"

Chapter 21

The rooftop sniper who'd aimed at the hangman's rope, or the man being hanged, had left no sign and seemed to have gotten away clean, for the time being.

Back in the cell of the one surviving prisoner, Longarm saw Robles had stopped pacing and sat down on the one bunk to rest his doubtless worn-out legs. So Longarm remained standing with his back to the cell door as he said, "*Bueno*, let's start over from scratch. I hope you understand you're still alive because I got you a *stay*, not a pardon."

Robles stared at the floor, weak with relief, as he mumbled, "You told me all that. We go to Denver now for another trial, right?"

Longarm shook his head and said, "Only if they let me carry you a country mile away from that county gallows out front. You've still been found guilty of that whorehouse dust-up in the eyes of the county law. You weren't there, so I'll tell you a few last words out of the late Will Pulver left me half convinced you might have been falsely accused to save the real fourth rider who got away that night. You'll have to convince us tighter than that if you expect them to transfer you to federal custody on them other charges."

Robles shrugged and said, "I confessed to robbing them coaches."

Longarm asked, "Are you sure? If I buy those other Triple Eight riders naming you to save an Anglo they liked better, I'll expect you to tell me why you couldn't be playing the same game. Bobby Valdez is dead. He was dead the other day when somebody tried to landslide that coach the duchess of Durango was riding in. If Valdez was dead and you were in jail we're talking about a Mex-American called Duke and your mysterious leader, el Aguilar."

The prisoner on the bunk looked up with a sad little smile to ask, "How should I know whether it was just the two of them or they got somebody else to join them? Nobody from the bunch has come anywhere near me since I was arrested the night of that last robbery I know anything about!"

Longarm said, "Tell me some more about Bobby Valdez. I have placed him in the real world, albeit dead as a turd in a milk bucket with no reputation as a troublemaker."

Robles replied, "Like I told you, we worked on neighboring spreads and we knew one another from down New Mexico way."

Longarm nodded and said, "I understand the duchess of Durango owns both the Triple Eight you rode for and that Circle Z Valdez was riding for, too fast, when his pony went down and rolled him."

The taller high plains rider shook his head wearily and opined, "If I've told you *vaqueros* once I've told you a hundred times that them form-fitting dally saddles you favor can be widowmakers. By the way, did Valdez have a *mujer* I could talk to about that other *amigo* he called Duke?"

Robles looked back down at the floor as he replied, "I don't know. The Triple Eight and Circle Z lie over an hour's ride apart, with a lake and some timber between. You know how you graze cows up here along the West Slope. You file a claim on a hundred and sixty acres with a choice mixture of parkland, timber and water. Then you range your stock on the public land all around. I reckon that money-lending gal wants to sew up all the open range between the two home spreads by owning 'em both."

"You're changing the subject," Longarm cut in. "How come you're changing the subject, my informative guide to the cattle trade? Might there be someone out to the Circle Z you just don't want me to talk to?"

Robles shook his head and said, "Ride out there and talk to anyone you like. I told you I've never been on that spread."

Longarm couldn't decide what the *vaquero's* Mona Lisa expression might be hiding, but you never got them to tell you by asking. So he allowed he might just do that and kicked the door to be let out.

He didn't head for the tack room and sheriff's stable just yet. He ambled over to the stage depot and asked wiry little Matt Greene how he'd go about talking to the crew of that coach the duchess of Durango had come in aboard.

Greene tore a slip of notepaper off a pad on his desk to scribble a mite as he confided, "Our jehu quit and headed for Silverton. Says we don't pay a man enough to outrun landslides. Our part-time shotgun messenger works a placer up the creek a ways when he ain't guarding color on its way to the smelter in Durango. You're looking for a bearded gent called Gimpy Powell. Lives with a handsome squaw called Walks in Beauty Betty. Some say she's 'Pache. But Gimpy is the one you have to watch for if you mess with her. This note's to tell 'em I want 'em to treat you neighborly. You can't miss their tent, about a furlong out of town to the east. Walks in Beauty Betty likes to paint medicine signs on anything they'll fit on. Look for an officer's field tent painted to look like a drunken Indian's bad dreams."

Longarm said he would and left to stroll over to Ambush Creek and follow it upslope to the east, past half a dozen more natural looking claims where Anglo, Mex and in one case a Chinese with his pant legs rolled up was shoveling wet gravel into sluice boxes or cradles. It was easier to sluice gold-bearing sands. But you got more of the gold dust out with the cradles you had to rock until your arms felt like they were on fire.

He wasn't surprised when he passed through some creek-side box elder to see a willowy gal with straight black hair and a lot of tawny skin showing, rocking a placer cradle in shin deep muddy water as she stood in it with her Navaho skirts kilted just above her knees. He'd thought that name sounded more Navaho than 'Pache. But lots of old boys couldn't see much difference, including the Indians so-called, themselves.

The big doghouse-shaped tent upstream a few yards had indeed been decorated with symbols Longarm recognized from his visits to the *Diné* or Navaho reserve to the south-west. The nation white men knew as the Apache called themselves *Déné* or *Na Déné*, meaning the people, and that was about as much difference as there was, save for a more sensible approach to changing times on the part of the so-called Navaho.

But Walks in Beauty Betty's big sloe eyes went 'Pache enough as she saw Longarm approaching her, and the color in her cradle. She called out and a big once-handsome man with a silver-fox beard and a game leg came out of their tent with a Parker ten-guage and thoughtful expression.

Longarm called out, "I ain't a claim jumper. I'm the law and I got a note for you, here, from old Matt Greene."

So the next thing he knew they had him seated on a dynamite box while Walks in Beauty Betty made the coffee.

After that, the part-time shotgun messenger couldn't give Longarm much help about the close call of the coach he'd been crewing when all that mud and rock came roaring down the mountain at it.

Gimpy said, "We'd just passed Coolie Camp, less than six miles south of town, and I was only staring up the slope because I'd noticed a deer in the open up that way. Four-point mule deer it was. Too far off to try for with this Limey shotgun. But it was just as well I was staring up-hill, for all of a sudden a boulder the size of a house come bounding down the mountain to spook that deer and bust other rocks loose to follow it on down!"

"You saw the mountain giving way *ahead* of you?" asked Longarm.

Powell nodded and said, "I thought Doc, driving the team, was out of his mind, too. He told me later he didn't think he could stop and turn around in less than ten seconds. So he whupped the mules on with the slack in his ribbons and we got lucky as all hell. That one big boulder passed in *front* of us and others rolled under or bounced over us as Doc drove to beat the devil and most of the landslide crossed the trail behind us after all."

Longarm nodded soberly and said, "I heard all that the other day. You say it happened right after you'd passed Coolie Camp?"

Powell nodded casually and explained, "Ain't a gold camp. Ain't no color in that occasional creek running north along that stretch to join this bigger one, further west. Ain't no Coolies there no more, either, come to study on it. When white men first struck color in these parts a short spell back we naturally had a bigger crowd at first. Some of 'em were sort of rough. The usual sorts of bully boys you see in any gold rush. So the dozen or so Chinee who came in from the Arkansas River headwaters to try their luck set up camp a safer distance from our Main Street saloons."

The old timer who'd been there at least eighteen months took his tin cup of coffee from Walks in Beauty Betty with a silent nod of thanks and added, "Once things settled down to more modest numbers of honest men willing to work for their color the Chinee drifted in to set up their own tents closer to the claims they were working. Some of 'em, that is. For every Chinee panning for color you see half a dozen doing laundry or stirring chop suey."

"Then the cluster of shelters you call Coolie Camp would be deserted, now, official?" Longarm asked as Walks in Beauty Betty handed him his own too-hot tin cup.

Her bewhiskered squaw man said he reckoned and went on, "The brushy drainage to the west of the trail swings south toward the lower reaches of this here creek before it gets to the Otis place. I mind them Otis orphans standing out in a pasture with a sort of hang-dog looking dairy cow as we tore past them, lickety split with the crazy duchess of Durango screaming at us in the back."

Longarm didn't ask what Sharon Rose Slade had been screaming about. They'd established her first night in town that she was used to just giving in to her emotions like the spoiled brat she'd made of her fool self.

He said, "There's more brush along a shallower run this side of the Otis spread. But you'd have noticed if anyone had charged down the mountain to cross the trail and lay low on that side. I find that mule deer a puzzlement. The rascals laying for your coach just up an open slope from it must have been quiet as church mice if the critters had come back out of hiding. The pussy-footing sons of bitches failed to leave us one damned footprint up that way as well. So we can't be talking about a big gang. Did you hear anything like dynamite or the duller thump of black powder just before that one big rock began to move?"

The man who'd seen it just in time took a thoughtful sip, shook his head, and decided, "Nope. It was naturally making enough noise for a stampede by the time I spotted it in motion. But I suspect the road agents just pried it out of the mountain and gave it a good hard shove."

Longarm said, "I think I found the hole in the clay your big rock came out of. I didn't see any tool marks or powder burns. Maybe that Indian or part Indian member of the gang does have strong medicine."

Walks in Beauty Betty stuck her head out of her painted tent to ask what he'd just said about Indians. So Longarm told the two of them what he'd heard about el Aguilar, or Thunderbird Medicine, depending on who you asked.

The handsome Navaho gal came out to hunker down by her man's round cheese box while she soberly told Longarm, "The people *my* people named the Utes, or Hill Dwellers—they call themselves Ho—do not have the medicine of real people. They boast of how they beat us Diné and drove us before them like the deer they hunt. But the Ute never beat anyone. The Ute served as hunting dogs for Star

169

Chief Carleton and the little Eagle Chief we called Rope Thrower. You called him Kit Carson."

"The long walk of the Navaho Nation is ancient history, no offense," tried Longarm.

Walks in Beauty Betty said, "I have not finished. I was there, I was little but it was not so long ago the boastful Utes helped Rope Thrower herd us like sheep to the Bosque Redondo near Fort Sumner. Hear me, we were not happy there and we asked the great white father many times to let us go home."

"As he did, back in eighteen sixty-eight." said Longarm, gravely.

The Navaho woman said, "We were talking about Utes with medicine. They have none. I would call them dog shit if dog shit was not nicer to smell than they are. Any Ute who calls himself a thunderbird is a boastful child. Any Ute who says he has the medicine of the storming eagle who splinters tall trees and shatters rocks is crazy, drunk, or both. Ute drink like fish and lie like Mexicans. You people found out how your hunting dogs could be trusted when they turned on that white agent and raped all those white women a little while ago."

She got back to her feet and went back in the the tent, muttering to herself in her own lingo.

Gimpy Powell chuckled fondly and confided, "She keeps telling me she just can't see how anyone as dumb as us keeps winning. But I can't say I recall any Ute medicine men being famous for flinging thunderbolts about."

Longarm patted the dynamite box he was seated on, thoughtfully, as he asked, "Could you tell me where you buy your dynamite, and how come you need any, working a placer claim?"

The part-time gold digger replied without hestitation, "We get our dynamite the same place I bought this fine English shotgun, off old Limey Norwich. Like me and lots of others up this way he wears more than one hat to get by. He'd starve waiting for customers to try on his fine knotted nooses. We ain't *that* wild over here on the West

170

Slope. So he mostly runs a hardware and mining supplies store in town, around the corner from Matt Greene's stage depot."

Nodding at the box Longarm was seated on, Powell explained, "You don't blast gold bearing placer grit, if that's the question. But you do blast bigger rocks in the creek to get 'em out of your way and to see what might lie under the same. Gold dust is way heavier as well as way finer than sand and gravel. So it settles deep, near the bedrock your placer lies over. It's a total waste of time to pan the grit you can see right off through sunlit water. You dig down to where your spade grates on solid rock and then . . ."

"I've tried my hand at panning gold." Longarm cut in, adding, "That's another reason I ride for the justice department for a living. Is it safe to say that if you buy dynamite in town most anyone along this creek could buy dynamite in town?"

Gimpy Powers nodded to reply, "Sure they could. All they wanted, to blast most anything they had a mind to."

Chapter 22

It had taken time and its toll on a naturally active man, but back in the Denver Federal Building Longarm had learned from his deskbound boss, Billy Vail and their prissy paper-pushing typewriter player and file clerk, Henry, not to stampede like a steer with a turpentined asshole. So by asking questions around the town Bobby Valdez lay buried in, Longarm saved himself a tedious and likely fruitless ride out to that Circle Z spread the dead *vaquero* had been riding for when he busted himself up.

A kid sister, Ysabella Valdez, had been listed as next of kin by the county on the death certificate Longarm found on file at the courthouse. After that and even better, they gave her address as a boarding house on F Street, over on the unfashionable side of town. In a world run on burning coal and sweating men and beasts, the downwind side of any town was always where the rents were lower.

But no matter where you boarded, in any town you were expected to pay *some* room and board. So Longarm suspected he knew why the Mex-American landlady, who reminded him of a horny toad in a purple housedress for some reason, sounded mighty sullen when she said she'd fetch Señorita Valdez and left him to cool his heels at her front door, standing on tamped-down cinders because she had no front porch.

When Ysabella Valdez came to the door she kept one foot inside it as Longarm introduced himself and asked if

172

he could have a few words in private with her.

The dead *vaquero's* sister was a familiar Mexican type in her gathered fandango skirts and sleeveless low-cut blouse of lacey cotton. Longarm figured she'd be drab and shapeless by the time she was thirty. But nature had provided for the continuation of the mestizo peon's bloodline by allowing them to be blandly pretty, with tempting tits, in their teens and early twenties. Longarm had never laid eyes on her brother, who'd ridden with Robles, Duke and el Aguilar unless Robles was full of shit, but if there'd been any family resemblance it seemed safe to picture the late Bobby Valdez as short, dark and handsome up until he turned into one of those familiar thickset and moon-faced mestizos you met up with in the southwest, working cows or robbing folk.

Longarm noticed her landlady was hovering just inside the doorway and suggested he and Ysabella go for a stroll along Ambush Creek.

The girl made one excuse and another in English until he asked her in Spanish, "*¿Qué le pasa? ¿Está tarde con la renta?*"

The young Mex gal covered her flushed face with her hands.

The landlady behind her snapped. "*¡Ay! Sin duda, Dios mio!* Her brother owed almost a month's room and board when he killed himself riding like a maniac! She keeps telling me she has money coming from their family in New Mexico. Do you see any money coming from New Mexico? I do not see any money coming from New Mexico!"

Longarm reached in his jeans for a double eagle to shove past the embarrassed gal betwixt them, and gravely said, "Miss Ysabella may be called as a government witness. We'll want her to stay here whilst I find out. Twenty dollars of good faith gold ought to maintain the status quo for now, if you know what's good for you. Come on, Miss Ysabella, we've got family matters to discuss in private."

Her landlady seemed to find this a grand suggestion as she put the gold coin away for safe keeping betwixt her big tits. The younger Mex gal let Longarm escort her away as if she was on her way to her public execution, tears streaming down her smooth brown cheeks.

Longarm asked what was eating her. Ysabella sobbed, "I was afraid it would come to this. A woman who has no man for to take care of her eating must let other men abuse her body while she does what she can for to keep it alive."

She shot him a sidelong glance through her tears and added, "Is not that I find you too ugly, Señor. Is *porque* you are so big and I have never been with any *gringo* before. Where do you intend for to have your way with me? Surely not in the open along that *arroyo* so many others will be walking along at this hour?"

Longarm laughed and led her over to a grove of box elder shading a fallen log on the south bank of the creek. He sat her down, put a booted foot up on the log beside her, and said, "I ain't looking to *hacer el amor*, no offense. Like I told both you ladies when first I came to your door, I'm a deputy U.S. Marshal investigating those stagecoach robberies you've been having in these parts."

She looked sincerely puzzled as she smiled up at him to ask, "For why do you think I would know anything about those poor people being killed and robbed. I remember my brother and others speaking of it in the days before he was killed and left me too worried about myself for to worry about dead strangers. But Roberto was the one who read your Yanqui newspapers, not I. Forgive me, I mean no disrespect, but your English spelling makes no sense to me and I find it too difficult for to read!"

Longarm smiled down at her and said, "I used to tell my teachers the same thing when I was dragooned into spelling bees against my will and inclinations. But I know what the newspapers and more formal reports have to say about all that. I'd like to talk to you about your late brother's pals. Did he ever introduce you to Ricardo Robles, and what can you tell me about him?"

The dead rider's sister didn't hesitate. She said, "Ricardo and my poor Roberto rode together back in New Mexico.

My brother naturally introduced all his friends to me when he rode in for the dances in town. My brother was most surprised and upset when Ricardo Robles was arrested for getting into a gunfight in a *casa libertina*. He told me that even if they let Ricardo go I was never to answer if he addressed me in public."

Longarm nodded, started to overshoot his line of questioning and backed up to say, "I'm trying to picture the situation before Robles was arrested and your brother had his fatal accident. How come Bobby had you boarding here in town instead of out to the Circle Z with the other dependents of the hired help?"

She answered, simply, "I was not welcome. My brother sent for me when I wired from back home on the Pecos that my husband had deserted me and our parents would not take me back for because they had told me not to marry a man who drank that much in the first place."

Longarm grimaced and said, "Once any woman tells you she married up with a drunkard you know the whole story, save for a few tedious details that never make any real difference. So your big brother sent for you and how come you weren't welcome as the other *mujeres* out to that Circle Z?"

She said, "They were not hiring and they told the riders they had not to bring any more dependents to their rancho because it was up for sale and they were trying for to show more profits on the books."

Longarm nodded thoughtfully and said, "I heard they sold the Circle Z to the duchess of Durango and combined the holdings. Rick Robles tells me he and your brother were good pals, right up to his arrest."

The dead rider's kid sister replied, without hesitation, "I thought I just explained that to you. Roberto did not know Ricardo was a bad man before the night he went bad."

Longarm insisted, "Robles says your brother was riding with him, not those Anglo boys, that night. Your turn."

Ysabella shrugged her half-exposed brown shoulders and replied, "I was back there at *la casa de huespedes* where you found me. Roberto never told me he had been with Ricardo Robles that night. If he had been with him, somewhere else, for why did he not say so at the trial they held right here in *el tribuno codado*, eh?"

It was a good question. If she had any answer she wasn't offering it. He asked her if her brother had ever introduced her to riders he called Duke or el Aguilar. The dead rider's sister thought, shook her head and thoughtfully replied, "I heard *vaqueros* of *la raza* speaking of some rider called *el Duque*, which would be Duke in English, no?"

He said, "*Sí*, so what about him?"

She shrugged and said, "Is all I know. I never met him. I think they said el Duque was looking for a job after being in prison for a time because of some argument about the ownership of a horse."

Longarm shoved the mysterious Duke to the back of the stove because he knew if there was any truth at all to that part about prison he'd be able to track the rascal as well or better on paper.

He repeated his question about her brother knowing a rider called el Aguilar. She or her late brother had to have been good actors if the mysterious breed had been known to anyone in the Valdez family.

He thanked her and allowed he'd get back to her if ever he came up with any more sensible questions about her brother. He could see she was trying not to cry again. He didn't ask why. He said, "You've no doubt noticed by now you'd be better off down New Mexico way among more kith and kin, no matter how New they may feel about your unfortunate marriage, Miss Ysabella."

She sighed and replied, "You do not know how stubborn my people can be when you have told them they are *burros* and you are off to a castle in the sky with the *caballero* of your dreams!"

Longarm smiled gently down at her to say, "Yes, I do. A dad who's been crossed by a willsome child can be almost as stubborn as a daughter who can't find it in her heart to swallow some pride, eat some crow, and tell her old dad he was right about the rascal. But we'll talk about your future later, after I've studied your brother's past some more. I may as well tell you he's been accused of being a road agent. Before you cloud up and rain all over me, others I have asked told me he struck them as an honest young cowhand who's only known vice was a tendency to ride too fast in a tight-fitting dally saddle."

As he helped her back up with one hand he reached in his jeans with the other, adding, "Things look darkest before the dawn and it's tough to plan your day without any pocket jingle at all."

He gave her a handful of loose change, not counting it, as he continued, "They ain't fixing to throw you out on the street and if you don't cotton to the grub at your boarding house they serve pretty good chili con carne at the beanery betwixt the stage depot and that one hotel on Main Street. We'll talk some more before I leave town, with or without some answers. You'll be hearing from me sooner if I have any more questions for you. In the meantime, you'd best study some on whether you want to go home, stay here if you can find a job or head most anywhere else in this world you fancy."

She grabbed his hand and kissed it as if she thought he was some sort of big shot. He said, "Aw, mush, I haven't saved you from all that much. You're still going to have to do some serious thinking. I only gave you the breathing spell it takes to start. Nobody thinks natural when they're too worried about where their next meal may be coming from or how they're going to make it through the coming night."

He took her back to her shabby boardinghouse, where the ugly old landlady greeted her like a long lost daughter.

Longarm walked off smiling in mild disgust at human nature and the way money could be not only the root of all evil but the font of so much friendliness. Given enough pocket jingle a good old boy from West-By-God-Virginia could likely wind up on mighty friendly terms with half the high-society tidewater belles of *Old* Virginia. But it took a mite less to get laid in other parts.

Not sure of his next logical move, since the morning had flown but he wasn't hungry yet, thanks to that swell breakfast in bed out to the Otis spread, Longarm mosied nonetheless toward Main Street as the Colorado sun reached the zenith and some churchbell tolled high noon.

Main Street ran north and south with neither side more shady at that time of the day. He was thinking about dropping by the hardware store run by their part-time hangman when he spied Rory Logan and two other riders dismounting out front of the Bighorn Saloon just up the way.

That reminded Longarm of questions he might have asked out to the Circle Z if he hadn't caught up with Ysabella Valdez in town. So he ambled up that way as the three riders tethered their mounts and went inside.

The Bighorn Saloon wasn't crowded that time of day during the workweek, now that the mass hanging was over and most of the country folk had headed home to their own chores. But as Longarm's eyes adjusted to the change in light he not only recognized the red shirt and shotgun chaps of Rory Logan but also the more portly figure of Sheriff Peabody down the bar by the free lunch layout.

Longarm was more interested in the late Bobby Valdez than pickled pigs' feet or deviled eggs. So he bellied up to the bar next to Logan and said, "Howdy. You boys figure on riding on out to the Triple Eight, now that the hanging's over for the day?"

"What's that supposed to mean?" asked the ramrod of the Triple Eight in the same tone he'd used when accusing Longarm of sparking the shy Meg Connors.

Longarm said, "Don't get your bowels in an uproar, old son. It ain't for me to say whether you're in town or not on a workday. As a matter of fact, you're being in town saves me a ride clean out to your cattle spread."

He signalled the barkeep and allowed he'd start with Maryland rye and a beer chaser.

Logan asked what business Longarm might have out at

the Triple 8. Longarm said that through no fault of his own he was paid to ask all sorts of dumb questions. By this time the barkeep had slid the shot glass of rye his way and started to fill a beer schooner for him.

Rory Logan stepped clear of the bar to demand in an ominous tone what sort of questions Longarm had in mind. But he referred to Longarm again as "Denver Boy" in a way that made the two Triple 8 hands with him exchange glances and move further away from the bar while Sheriff Peabody, to Longarm's rear, quietly but firmly declared, "I hope you young gents understand the two of you ain't alone in some schoolyard!"

Logan repeated, "What sort of questions might you have for anyone riding for the Triple Eight, Denver Boy?"

Longarm raised his shot glass in a friendly way as he replied in a soothing tone, "I only wanted to go over some names with you, now that the duchess of Durango has put all the surviving riders of both the Triple Eight and Circle Z under you, Logan. You'd be the man I'd want to talk to about who might have been riding where, with whom, that night a whorehouse got shot up and a stagecoach got landslid and robbed, at about the same time."

Rory Logan must have been worried about Longarm asking him such questions, long before Longarm could. For he went for his gun without a word of warning and, seeing his Schofield was riding low in a side-draw rig, there was no way in hell Longarm was going to beat him with his own gun riding crossdraw.

Chapter 23

A man did what he could with what he had to work with. So whilst Longarm's gun hand moved from right to left through air as thick as glue his other hand tossed the glass of rye whisky in Rory Logan's snarling face.

So Logan still beat Longarm to the draw but he fired wild as he screamed like a woman with both burning eyes tightly shut. Then he fired wild some more as Longarm crabbed away from the bar with his own .44-40 in hand at long last.

Three six guns roared at the same time as the sobbing Logan fired blind at nobody in particular while Longarm put a bullet over his heart and the grazed and outraged Sheriff Peabody fired the length of the bar from behind Longarm to gutshoot a man who was already dead on his feet.

Once Rory Logan collapsed to the sound of crumpled leather and metallic clunks it got mighty quiet in the literally smoke-filled saloon. As Longarm stayed where he was, reloading, the portly older lawman waddled forward to join him over Logan's sprawled cadaver, quietly asking, "How come we just done that? I mean, I know somebody had to shoot the loco son of a bitch before he shot somebody, but what did you say to set him off like so?"

Longarm holstered his .44-40 as he stared down through the haze of drifting gunsmoke at the remains of Rory Logan and decided, "He must not have been following my drift. I was fixing to question him about riders working under him under the combined holdings of the duchess of Durango. You were here. You know I never accused him of toad squat, but a guilty conscience is a heavy load for a troubled man with a hair-trigger temper to bear and he must have thought I was getting warmer than I really was."

Sheriff Peabody knew all the local riders better than Longarm. So he told one of the younger hands who'd come in with Logan to go fetch Doc Palmer, the local sawbones and elected coroner.

The other hand, who'd moved away from the bar with him, declared his intent of going along to help. Other regulars drifted closer, now that it seemed safe to do so. Sheriff Peabody spoke for more than one of them when he asked Longarm what Logan had been afraid a federal man might have on him.

Knowing it was an election year and not wanting to do any more of the paper work than he had to on a local case, Longarm included the local law on purpose as he expansively stated, "Those naughty boys you hung this morning told you all a big fib about the one killer who got away that night."

He nudged the dead man's fallen Schofield with the toe of his boot as he continued, "Logan just now showed us how he tended to go *loco en la cabeza* when he felt crossed, and that was *sober*, just now. We can only guess at what set him off that night when he was likkered up in that whorehouse."

Sheriff Peabody whistled and decided, "Well, I never, but that *works*! This nasty-tempered son of a bitch got them boys who rode under him to name a Mex none of them fancied as the man who got away!"

Longarm nodded and said, "Will Pulver was trying to tell us that when Limey Norwich sprung the trap under him. I suspect that rifle shot aimed Pulver's way just before he dropped came from the saddle gun I just noticed out front. Logan favored U.S. Army issue shooting iron. That Schofield he just blazed away with is chambered for Army .45-

181

28 pistol rounds. The old Springfield Conversion he was packing as his saddle gun is chambered for .45-75 rifle rounds. Slow shooting, but with more range than most saddle guns. That's how come he got away a second time after trying to silence a pal who was already done for. Like I said, hair trigger tendencies."

It was the bartender, who'd likely overheard many a conversation on the subject, who asked, "How could Logan, there, get those other two to stick to their story once they'd been tried, found guilty and sentenced to die this very morn?"

Longarm shrugged and said, "Hope springs eternal. From the little I got out of Pulver on his way to the gallows I suspect the ramrod they'd been riding under promised he'd somehow save them in the end. Whether they bought the whole wagonload of manure or not, they knew they'd hang whether they turned him in or not and, like I said, hope springs eternal."

Peabody exclaimed, "Then they were ready and willing to let us hang Robles alongside 'em, knowing the poor Mex was innocent?"

Longarm said, "None of 'em liked Rick Robles. He was drawing the wages of an Anglo top hand and it hadn't been the notion of this dead ramrod of the Triple Eight to hire him. The jury is still out on just how innocent anyone may be."

One of the customers assembled, dressed more country than urban volunteered, "That's right! That fancy-roping Robles was one of the new riders the duchess of Durango imported from other parts after she fucked poor Ben Allan out of his Triple Eight, lock, stock and barrel!"

A sporting type dressed more for town laughed and opined, "That pretty-boy Mex likely fucked that duchess of Durango to get top hand wages Ben Allan never would have paid a greaser! But I fear I owe Robles an apology. I was on the jury and I never bought it when Joy Norwich swore he was fucking her the night Madame Frenchy died. I wish I had thick greasy hair and chili peppers on my breath. Women just can't seem to resist fandango-dancing pretty boys who look like pimps, if you ask me!"

The cowhand laughed and pointed out, "No greaser ever asked you to dance with him. But you could likely get Joy Norwich to fandango with you, lying down, if you wanted to tempt fate and her old man's wrath, speaking of hair triggers."

It was just as well the coroner and some other county big shots came crowding in as the conversation was drifting way the hell off the subject at hand, or seeping into the sawdust covered floor, least ways. By this time Sheriff Peabody had grabbed the ball Longarm had offered him and run with it, declaring to one and all that having shot it out with the killer of Madame Frenchy he had wrapped up all the loose ends of the mystery and suggested they ought to let Rick Robles go after they'd passed the hat for him by way of an apology.

Before too many there could agree, Longarm announced, "Me and the federal government would be much obliged if you'd hold Robles right where he is until I can check out some other ways this whole thing might have worked."

He saw he had their puzzled attention and explained, "I'm pleased as punch that Sheriff Peabody, here, has solved the murders in your own notorious house of ill repute. But we've still got those stagecoach robberies to solve and, try as I might, I just can't tie this poor dead asshole and the others you hung earlier to a single damned act of highway robbery! As a matter of simple logic, the fact that Logan, Brewer, Pulver and Wylie were acting wild and wooly over in Madame Frenchy's at the time of that one robbery miles to the south lets them off that hook entire!"

Peabody once more proved his worth as a lawman despite his girth by declaring, "I follow your drift. If Rick Robles wasn't riding with this dead cuss and his pals that night, he was riding with some other night riders. For we did establish he wasn't in the bunkhouse out to the Triple Eight until just before the rest of us rode in!"

Longarm allowed that was about the size of it. Since the *federal* offenses over this way were all his, he felt no call to pontificate about any evidence pointing toward the late Bobby Valdez and his no-doubt innocent kid sister. But he did try casually asking if anyone there knew another Mex rider called Duke.

He wasn't surprised to hear nobody in the Bighorn had ever heard of *any* Mex rider they wanted to remember that much.

The coroner directed some kids in work duds to carry the cadaver of Rory Logan over to his clinic, but for God's sake to stow it down in the root celler until he could perform a pro-forma autopsy and have the remains embalmed for more proper display.

He tossed in some comments about impanelling a coroner's jury after he talked to the undertaker and any next of kin who came forward.

Longarm didn't ask why. He knew a dead body was usually treated with the respect its owner had rated in life. A big shot with a heap of kith and kin rated a thorough investigation and a formal hearing. A dead drifter often got to rot where he lay if it wasn't too close to civilization. Rory Logan, having just died in some disgrace as a self-confessed whore shooter, would likely be dealt with somewhere between the extremes of current forensic science.

As the sheriff and his admirers expanded on how he'd saved the town from a mad dog armed with a six gun, Longarm saw nobody seemed all that interested in him and so, the afternoon not getting any younger, he drifted out of the Bighorn to get back to his own beeswax.

He wired his home office that it seemed certain Ricardo Robles had not been in any way involved in the crimes he'd been convicted of and hence it seemed more certain he'd been telling the truth when he'd confessed to riding with those road agents.

At a nickel a word Longarm felt no call to explain he needed more evidence against Robles than an unsupported confession. One of the road agents Robles had named was

184

dead. The other two seemed nowhere to be found. No public defender worth his salt was going to let a client's unsupported confession stand unchallenged. All Robles had to say in federal court was that he'd been forced to confess by a slick federal deputy and all bets were off.

Longarm didn't head for the jail house to ask Robles whether he still felt guilty or not. There was no point in suggesting ways out to a man who'd already agreed he'd done it. Thanks to that stay of execution good old Portia had wrangled for them, Robles was still alive. Thanks to Sheriff Peabody owing him a favor, if Peabody knew what was good for him in an election year, Robles would be kept on ice for the time being. Longarm figured he had two or three more days before he had to arrest the young Mex on a federal charge or tell the local law they had to let him go.

In the meantime, the less Longarm had to do with the local law the better. So he headed up the now-shady west side of the street to the livery run by Meg Connors. For whether she was still ducking him or not she *was* in the livery business and her hired help could fix him up with discrete transportation in place of another mount from the sheriff's remuda, along with his McClellan saddle in their tack room. It served him right for storing his Winchester there before he'd known Rory Logan was fixing to make him more famous on the West Slope that summer.

He was mildly surprised but not dismayed when the tomboyish young widow came out front, flushed and glowing in a thin summer frock, as she asked him where he might be riding on the heat of a lazy summer afternoon.

Longarm ticked his hat brim to her and replied, "I was just now studying on rolling this denim jacket behind the cantle of another hired saddle, Miss Meg. I know it's hot and getting hotter. I still want to ride off to the north and poke about all that consolidated range the duchess of Durango foreclosed on."

Meg said she'd show him some saddles before they picked out a fresh pony for him. He didn't ask about good old Comanchero. He'd ridden that mount hard forty-eight hours back. It was only in books about black beauties that you rode the same pet pony every day like a rocking horse. Like their riders, ponies needed to rest up a few days after they came home feeling something like a human athlete might have after running a marathon with a full field pack on his back. He wasn't so sure why Meg expected him to be choosy about his hired saddle. The roper she'd hired out to him the last time had been good enough and he said so as he followed her into the shade of her tack room, where saddles galore rode sawhorses lined up like a cavalry platoon going nowhere in the stillness of the leather-polish scented privacy, illuminated only by an overhead skylight.

Meg Connors turned to face him, her face glowing redder than the warmth at that altitude really warranted as she braced her shapely derrier against a cordovan vidalia showsaddle to suddenly blurt out, "We just heard about you and Rory Logan. I didn't know you were that serious about me, too."

Longarm managed not to laugh, but it wasn't easy as he tried to conceal his surprise, stiffly assuring her, "We didn't have it out over you, Ma'am, no offense. I'm still working on exactly why Logan thought he had to kill me. That's how come I want to hire harness, a saddle and another pony."

Meg glanced down between them, fluttering her lashes as if she could see through the fly of his sun-faded jeans as she sighed and said, "I know why he went after you. He told me he'd kill any man I gave the least encouragement to. But how could he have known about . . . us? You didn't blab around town about those stolen moments over in the hayloft, did you?"

Longarm truthfully replied, "I'd clean forgot about 'em by the time me and Logan were slapping leather over in the Bighorn. I know Logan fancied you, Miss Meg. He told me so his ownself, earlier, and we've just established he got mighty emotional about womankind at times. But your name never came up in the conversation we were having in that saloon when he and he alone chose to go for his gun without any declaration of war."

Meg sighed and murmured, "Men!" as if that meant something and she'd been paying attention.

Then she raised her eyes to smile timidly and murmur, "As I told you over in the hayloft, it's not that I don't find you attractive. It's not that I never feel tempted. It's just that the way I lost my poor husband left me with such conflicting emotions and, oh, Custis, I don't ever want to feel that way about any man again!"

He said that sounded fair, not knowing what she was getting at.

The tomboyish young widow stood taller, swaying toward him as she sighed and said, half to herself, "Oh, if only there was some way to just tear off a piece now and then, without getting all tangled up with somebody you're stuck with! If only we girls were allowed to love 'em and leave 'em, the way you durned boys are!"

So Longarm gently but firmly took Meg in his arms as he assured her as one pal to another, "There's nothing in the U.S. Constitution that says only us boys are allowed to tear off a carefree piece of ass, now and again, if that's what you really feel like doing."

Chapter 24

She must have really felt like doing it. For the next thing Longarm knew she'd backed him against another saddle with one surprisingly strong arm around his waist whilst she fumbled at the buttons of his jeans with her free hand.

A man as tall as Longarm could half-sit, sidesaddle, if he bent his knees a tad. So he did, even as he asked her if it wouldn't be wiser to take all this upstairs.

Meg hoisted her summerweight skirts to fling one slim but muscular thigh up and over the saddle swells to wedge it between his denim-clad hips and the horn as she sobbed, "Hold me up against you. No man born of mortal woman will ever share my bed again but I just have to satisfy this craving!"

It would have sounded dumb to ask her what she had against men as she hauled his hard organ grinder out of his jeans and threw her other leg up to wedge her thigh betwixt Longarm's hip-bone and the forward facing grips of his .44-40. She had her gaping gates to Paradise against his lap as he grabbed her firm ass in both hands to help her impale herself on his raging erection.

She got around to kissing him some more after she'd measured the extent of his virility by sliding up and down the full length of it a few times. He kissed her back sincerely. Their position was wilder than some. But it sure beat pissing. So a good time was had by all and he'd just shot his wad in her when there came a tapping on the tack-room door.

The gal who was screwing him sidesaddle bit down with her innards to keep him hard as she demurely called out, "Don't come in. I'm changing from my riding habit. What is it, Tommy?"

A youthful voice replied through the unlocked door, "It's Jimbo, Ma'am. There's a gent out front wants me to saddle up old Baldy for him."

Meg kept moving her hips, faster, as she called back, "Just one minute, then. I'll tell you when I've finished in here, myself!"

Then in a whisper she confided to Longarm, "It's no use. I'm too out of practice or maybe too tense in here. We'd better go upstairs, but don't get any ideas. I mean that, Custis!"

Longarm had no idea what she meant, but he went along willing, as most men would have when a beautiful young widow woman was leading them out another door by the pecker, as if she thought he was her overgrown pull-toy.

As they left the tack room she called back her permit for Jimbo to enter from the front. She hauled Longarm along a darker corridor and up a flight of steps to her shuttered dormer room under the roof peak, repeating, "Don't get any ideas. Don't even think about staying the night and don't you dare make any promises, because nothing lasts forever and all lovers' vows end in shame or sorrow!"

Longarm tossed his hat aside, unbuckled his gun rig and assured her he was only after an afternoon quicky.

So she gave him one, with icing on the cake to spare once they had all their duds off and got down to brass tacks across her bedstead with a pillow under her firm ass.

Longarm came in her again, as most men would have, and he knew he'd made her come at last when she tried to bust his spine with her crossed horsewoman's legs, dug her nails into his bare buttocks, and proceeded to bawl like a baby.

He kissed her gently without asking what was eating her.

189

He knew what was eating her when she suddenly tried to suck his tongue out by the roots, shuddered all over as if she'd been splashed with ice water, and went stiff under him, hissing, "Take that nasty thing out of me, you brute!"

Longarm did no such thing. He'd been over that trail before. So he puckered his own rectal muscles to make it twitch inside her as he neither moved it in or out, softly saying, "You ain't ready for me to take it out, honey."

She thrust her pelvis upward as she protested, "Don't call me that! I'm not your honey! I was *his* honey and we loved each other dearly until he came down with cancer, in his crotch, and we never got to enjoy this sweet feeling anymore because he was dying, dying slow and dirty with his privates burning like fire whilst I fetched and carried and did what I could to comfort him whilst he cursed me for not making the pain go away."

Her emotional outburst had gotten her hips to moving again. So he commenced to thrust in and out some more as she moaned, "Oh, yesss! That feels so good when your privates are halfway healthy and so pointless when they're not. I wish I could forget how good it felt, all the times my man, Steve, shoved it in me just like so!"

He spread her legs wider with an elbow hooked under either knee as he pounded harder whilst she kept begging Steve to touch bottom on their wedding night, this time.

Longarm managed, even though the thoughts of another man going where no man had gone before hardly helped. Meg enjoyed another long, quivering climax, stiffened up, and then went limp as an old dishrag under him to murmur, "I'm sorry if I hurt you by pretending you were someone else, just now."

Longarm kept going as he shoved her thighs wider apart, assuring her in a neighborly tone that he wasn't done and, come to study on it, he was fixing to come in a pal named Sally.

He did so, flopping limp atop her as he explained sort of breathless, "We called her Roping Sally when I was fucking her up Montana way. She rode a heap, like you, and really

190

knew how to give a man a ride in her own muscular love saddle. Her tits were a tad bigger than yours, though, no offense."

Meg calmly replied, "None taken, just so we understand we're not doing this for anything but the pure pleasure."

So once he had his breath back he suggested they try some doggy style and once he had her talked into it, on her hands and knees across the mattress whilst he planted his bare feet wide on the rug to tickle her clit with his nuts, Meg allowed she liked it that way because it left her feeling so impersonal while it went so deep.

Then she arched her spine and lowered her face to the covers as she asked in a desperately casual tone whether he'd ever done it that way to this Roping Sally.

Gripping a hip bone in either hand as he moved in and out of her at a slow comfortable lope, Longarm explained in as calm a tone, "I sure did. I fucked her laying and I fucked her lying and if she'd had wings I'd have fucked her flying. But then she got murdered by this outlaw before we'd counted all the ways a man might have with a maid."

He gazed down in the dim light at the pretty little rosebud rectum winking up at him in time with his thrusts as he sighed and mused on, "I follow your drift about lovers' vows ending in shame or sorrow. I felt just awful when that land-grabbing son of a bitch murdered poor Roping Sally. I went on missing her, a heap, after I killed the son of a bitch who'd killed her. I may as well confess I got something in my eye when I dropped by her grave to say *adios* and I saw these Indian kids had left a mason jar of cornflowers by her marker. Her eyes were blue as cornflowers and her hair was the color of wheat ripe for harvesting."

Meg muttered in an icey tone, "You don't have to rub it in. I said I was sorry, you sarcastic thing."

Longarm withdrew to flop down beside her, saying, "I wasn't out to sound sarcastic. I said I followed your drift. Had Roping Sally lived I'd likely recall her today with shame instead of sorrow. I've met other gals I admired as much, at first, only nobody murdered them and nobody ordered me to move on while we were still sweet-talking one another. So they're the ones I'm ashamed of ever feeling so foolish about. It sure makes a man feel dumb to recall sweet-talking a sharp-tongued shrew who started nagging him to look for a better-paying job so he could keep her in the style she wanted to be accustomed to."

He rolled on his gut to fumble a cheroot and some matches from his shirt on the rug as he continued, "I suspect that's how come married men who soldiered during the war get all misty eyed when they hear the strains of Lorena, Aura Lee or the Yellow Rose of Texas. None of them made-up gals we used to sing about around the campfires during a lull in the blood and slaughter ever asked us to beat the rugs out back or tell us she had a headache and preferred to sleep alone. So despite all the blood and slaughter, old soldiers look back to the gals they left behind them, and never got stuck with, later."

He rolled back beside her and lit the smoke as Meg stared up at the ceiling to softly remark, "We all get stuck if we don't keep moving. The first boy I ever really loved betrayed my love by bragging to his pals that he'd fucked that stuck-up Margaret Fitzsimmons and I'd let him feel my virgin titties!"

Longarm put the lit cheroot to her lips as he observed, "I had a gal back in West-By-God-Virginia brag on the size of my tool when I was young and bashful. I'd never known gals could talk dirty as the rest of us. But you did find our true love, old Steve, right?"

She took a shallow puff on the cheroot, blew it out without inhaling and said, "First there was Curtis, after Teddy had betrayed me. Curtis told me he loved me and promised we'd be as one forever and ever, and then he took to drinking and getting arrested in whore houses! You know what I mean about it always ending in shame or sorrow?"

Longarm took the smoke back, lest it be wasted, and told her he'd just been trying to make that point. He said, "We love and lose or we love and wonder what in tarnation we ever did to deserve so much vexation. You told me you just got it right with your good old Steve, when he up and died on you."

She repressed a shudder and said, "If only! I'd have been devastated if Steve had been killed outright while our marriage still seemed made in heaven. But he wasn't killed outright. He died slow and there were times near the end where I didn't know whether I wanted him to live or die!"

Longarm gently suggested, "You wanted both. It's natural to want things both ways, even when it ain't possible. Nobody wants to lose a loved one, just as nobody wants to get stuck with nursing a dying invalid past the point of no return. I suspect I know how you must have felt."

She propped herself up on one elbow to casually reach for his limp manhood as she replied with some heat, "No, you don't. You were never there when I needed some of this. I was all alone, night after night to empty bloody bedpans or change cruddy bandages, with the bad smell of death in the air all around for the ages it took death to get there. It was awful, but I'd vowed to stick it out in sickness as in health and not to have a lick of fun with others until death did us part. So once death did, I made up my mind then and there I'd never feel anything for any man again. For all such feelings end in dislike, disgust or, even when you get it right, cruel death!"

She began to stroke him as she felt an awakening in his interest. As she beat his meat she sweetly told him, "This just isn't worth it. Not worth all the tedious shit that goes with it, I mean! In exchange for seldom as much as an hour's satisfaction around bedtime we get to clean and cook and sew and listen to the same old stories from the same old bedmate whilst the two of you grow ever less tempting to look at whilst you both tire of the same old familiar feeling until one or both of you gets too frail to fuck and . . . Jesus, I want you to go, now! It was fun whilst it lasted but nothing lasts long enough to pay for those first few minutes!"

She'd let go of his shaft. But it remained at half-mast as he told her, "I'll go as soon as I finish this smoke. I only came here today to ride somebody with four legs. But, for the record and speaking as a man who's been accused of loving and leaving 'em, I have to declare your sad tale of woe is leaking like a sieve."

He took a luxurious drag on the cheroot, snorted smoke out both his nostrils, and said, "You ain't the first young widow woman I have met up with. Some of them have been more honest with me and mayhaps their ownselves. I know for a fact that many a fairly well-off widow, or widower, chooses to stay single for the same reasons I've never seen to marry up to begin with."

She murmured, "You told me about the lost love you still mourn as she waits for you under cornflowers that match your memories of her eyes."

He snorted more smoke and said, "Aw, mush, I said Roping Sally was murdered whilst I still admired her. I'm single today because, like you and some other pretty widow women I know, I don't want to give up my freedom. It ain't my fault. I never made the rules. But this is a man's world and gals who try to live free and easy as men get called a lot of names, unless, that is, they're poor widow women, free to live alone, free to manage their own affairs, because the man appointed by fate ain't around to guide their dainty footsteps no more."

She turned away, murmuring, "Take any pony in my remuda and saddle it with any rig we have downstairs. I want to go to sleep, now. When I wake up I want to find myself alone."

Longarm chuckled, said he was almost done with his cheroot, and sat up to swing his bare feet to the rug as he said, "Thanks, I mean to take you up on that. For you're the proud and independent owner of this whole livery operation, free to say yes or no to any business deal with nobody to say you're right or wrong, just because he's been in bed with you under more formal rules of conduct."

He snubbed the smoke out as he fumbled for his duds on the floor, asking, "Could you tell me more about that duchess of Durango offering to buy this place, speaking of independent widow women with minds of their own?"

Meg didn't answer. She was pretending to be asleep. He wasn't sure why. Women tended to have headaches or get sleepy when they wanted you to just leave them the hell alone.

So he got dressed, went downstairs, and helped himself to that saddle they'd been screwing against, along with a mild-bitted bridle.

Then he went out front to choose a spunky black mare with four white stockings and a blaze. Young Jimbo, the hand who helped Longarm rope and saddle her, said her name was Mittens.

Longarm led her out front on foot, meaning to mount up and ride off to the north, a tad later in the afternoon than originally planned. But then young Ward Otis, Junior came loping up Main Street, bareback, on that old draft horse from their dairy spread. Longarm had sort of forgotten he'd assured Glory Otis he'd be by to fondle her some more after sundown. He was wondering if he'd still be man enough when her kid brother blurted, "They told me they'd seen you up this way! I've been looking all over for you! My big sister sent me into town to fetch you. She says she needs you, now!"

Longarm glanced up at the afternoon sun, still fairly high to the west, as he sighed and asked if Ward, Junior knew just what his sister had in mind for that afternoon.

The kid said, "We got trouble. That duchess of Durango is out to sieze our property. Glory said you might be able to do something to help us save Pop's homestead!"

Chapter 25

Longarm told the Otis kid he'd just been talking about the duchess of Durango and added that he meant to pick up his Winchester from the sheriff's tack room before they rode out. For a gal gone greedy to the point of crazy sounded bad enough without her own private crew of hired guns.

As they trotted their mounts the short distance up the slope Ward, Junior told Longarm the money-lending Sharon Rose had sent some of her hirelings out to his place to serve eviction papers on them. She wasn't out there at the moment, herself.

Longarm glanced over his shoulder toward the Main Street they had just swung away from but decided you could only eat an apple one bite at a time and grown men menacing women and children ought to be dealt with first.

He left Ward, Junior seated on his drafthorse as he dismounted and tore into the sheriff's tack room for his rifle. He met Sheriff Peabody and Major Scott from the Colorado Guard as he was coming out.

The sheriff said, "Afternoon. Me and the major, here, are on our way to your hotel. We just got word a stranger answering to the likes of Brazos Roy Baker was pussyfooting around your lobby, asking about room rates but not checking in, even though there's plenty of rooms for hire there, now that the hanging's over."

Major Scott added, "They say he's not there, now. But

you never know and the breed's a killer. So we could use some company as we go there to question your room clerk."

Longarm shook his head politely and replied, "It ain't my hotel no more and I ain't after Brazos Roy. They sent me out this way to catch them road agents to begin with and now I have to ride out to the Otis spread with Ward Otis, Junior here. He tells me they're having trouble with that duchess of Durango and you may recall somebody trying to rob her coach the same as them others, earlier. So I reckon I have at least a lame excuse to look into her serving another eviction notice on folk in these parts."

Sheriff Peabody looked puzzled as he asked, "What eviction notice, to be served on who by whom, Dad blast it? My sheriff's department serves all such civil court orders issued in these parts, and collects a fee for such services."

Longarm glanced up at the kid seated bareback on the draft horse to quietly say, "It's your turn, Ward, Junior. Didn't you just tell me they were serving you Otis kids with such papers?"

The barefoot boy of eleven or so said, "Trying to. Glory won't take nothing off nobody or let 'em on our property and she and my kid brother Wayne are both packing shotguns. I can't tell you any names because we never seen either of 'em before they showed up less than an hour ago waving papers none of us wanted to read. Glory said to ride into town and fetch you. So I did. It wasn't easy."

Longarm muttered. "They're trying to buffalo the kids with some sort of high-tone bullshit written pretty on fancy paper. I'd best ride out and see what this is all about."

Sheriff Peabody said, "Wait 'til I can get to my own mount and I'll ride with you. Ain't nobody has the right to serve eviction notices in these parts unless he works for me!"

Major Scott protested, "What about Brazos Roy?"

Sheriff Peabody answered, "Fuck Brazos Roy. You just heard me say he ain't at the hotel, right now, and after that he's wanted in other parts, not here. I'd be proud to help you catch him when I have the time, but that money-lending bitch from Durango is pestering folk who might *vote* for me, someday, if only I can keep 'em on their own damn land!"

He scurried off with the odd grace of the overweight as Longarm untethered Mittens and mounted up, telling Ward, Junior, "He knows the way. Let's ride and he can catch up whenever he has a mind to."

The kid swung his draft horse around with a broad grin and some bare-heeled rib thumps. Longarm just let Mittens have her head. Good riding stock tired slower when you treated it gentle. Bad riding stock got you there late no matter how you treated it.

But since the Otis dairy spread was a short ride out of town in any case, Longarm and Glory's kid brother rode in to join the tense scene around the open Otis gate in no time.

Glory Otis was standing with one foot on a cross-log of her cattle guard and the other braced on the bare dirty between. She was wearing that same thin dress she'd shucked for Longarm the night before, with her buckwheat honey hair unbound and the ten-guage double Greener in her dainty fists covering the two gents who'd dismounted out front to lead their ponies across the cattle guard, or try to. Glory was being backed up by her youngest brother, the bitty nine- or ten-year-old Wayne, aiming a twelve-guage Whitney breech loader over the fence at the same unwelcome visitors.

Longarm reined in and dismounted within pistol range but not within *easy* pistol range when he saw Glory's visitors were Twinkle Turner and a shorter, hungrier-looking individual in old jeans and a shiny new shirt of black sateen. This professional bully boy was showing off an old horse pistol worn low in a brand new buscadero holster. Hired guns had to earn their hire less when they made others think twice about slapping leather.

As he ambled over to the tension by the gate, his own .44-40 higher on his own left hip lest it fall out of its holster whilst he was scaring somebody, Twinkle Turner called, "Stay out of this, Uncle Sam! This ain't a federal matter!"

Longarm moved in with a smile to reply, "Yes, it is. These orphans tell me their late father claimed this quarter section under that federal homestead act of eighteen sixty-three."

It wouldn't have been polite to ask a man how his balls felt in mixed company. But Twinkle must have still felt bad about that rifle butt in the balls because he wasn't smiling back as he said, "Our boss lady ain't foreclosing on no homestead land. I guess Miss Sharon Rose knows the law as well as any federal *deputy*! She grubstaked the late Ward Otis after he put up his goods and chattels as security. That's what they call a dairy herd and everything that ain't nailed down on a dairy farm, goods and chattles."

Longarm said he knew the difference betwixt personal and real estates as he held out his left hand and added, "Let's just see what you got, there."

Glory Otis gasped, "Don't take it, Custis! As long as nobody takes it it hasn't been served, see?"

Longarm gently responded he wasn't her lawyer or a member of her family and explained, "I ain't *accepting* nothing from nobody. As an officer of the law I'm *demanding* to see what this is all about."

The befringed giant clutched the bond paper closer to his buckskin breast as he protested he hadn't been instructed to serve it on anybody but Miss Gloria Otis in the flesh.

Longarm calmly drew his .44-40 and threw down on the hired gun before he asked with a cold thin smile, "Pretty please with sugar on it?"

Twinkle Turner gasped to anyone within earshot, "The man's gone out of his head total! First he tries to turn me into a falsetto forever with a rifle butt and now he's pointing a gun at me whilst demanding private papers! What are we going to do about this maniac, Omaha?"

Omaha, if that was the name of the one in the shiny black shirt, answered, "We give him the infernal eviction notice! The boss lady told us to give it to somebody, didn't she?"

Turner protested, "Not to no lawman! To these here Otis orphans who owe her money, Omaha!"

Glory Otis spat. "We don't owe her sour milk and Pop never said a thing to me about borrowing money from her or anybody else! Why was he riding shotgun when that landslide swept him away if he could borrow so much money from the duchess of Durango?"

Longarm soothed, "Calm down and let me see if I can find out, Miss Glory. Tinker, here, was just about to let me read that impressive-looking writ he's getting all wrinkled with his sweaty fingers."

He cocked the gun in his hand, even though it was double action, as he added, "Ain't that right, Twinkle?"

The hired gun got the message of the needless hammer click of a serious six gun. He handed the sheaf of bond paper over, even as he growled that the duchess wasn't going to like this.

Longarm used the muzzle of his .44-40 to turn the pages of the sheaf he held in his left hand. It only took a few seconds and he was grinning when he shoved the double-folded eviction notice in a hip pocket, announcing, "I'm holding this tomfoolery as legal evidence. I sort of doubt the federal land management office is going to like what your boss lady has been trying to pull out here in newly opened country. I've seen slick and I've seen raw. But she don't even know how to bust eggshells halfways lawsome! Who has she been using as her lawyer, that Baron Munchausen I've heard so much about?"

He half-turned to Glory, explaining, "Baron Munchausen was this High Dutch noble who lived back around George Washington's time. They say George Washington never told a lie. The same can hardly be said for Baron Munchausen. He told some real whoppers before he went to work writing loan contracts and eviction notices for the duchess of Durango."

"There's nothing wrong with them papers you took from me against my will!" protested Twinkle Turner.

Before Longarm could answer they all heard hoofbeats. So Longarm turned to stare up the trail past Ward Otis, Junior and the horseflesh to see Sheriff Peabody coming their way, along with that Major Scott and a couple of deputies.

Longarm waited until the older lawman reined in and naturally had to ask what was going on before he declared, "You're just in time to arrest these two confidence men, Sheriff. I got here just as they were trying to rob these three orphans with a writ of Mother Goose legal jargon."

Holstering his gun and hauling out the folded papers, Longarm asked, "Have you ever heard tell of a cuss employed by neither one government entity nor a member of any bar association serving legal papers signed by no judge to back a legal contract neither notorized nor registered with any county clerk I've been able to find amid all this poetry?"

The portly older lawman dismounted to take the papers in hand as he muttered, "Like I said back in town, ain't nobody but us supposed to serve any sort of writs in these parts."

Then, because he'd been alerted by Longarm or because he was the old pro he seemed, Sheriff Peabody snorted, "Jesus H. Christ! Sorry, Miss Glory, this fool loan contract says Ward Otis, Senior borrowed five hundred dollars, putting up all his livestock, farming gear and house furnishings as security!"

"So she drives a hard bargain," tried Twinkle Turner.

Sheriff Peabody conceded, "That's for sure. I had to serve better-looking papers than this on old Ben Allan when she foreclosed on the Triple Eight. But that was then and this is now. Ben Allan and all of the witnesses to his taking out the loan were alive and well when Ben and the Duchess thrashed it out in circuit court. I don't see nothing here about no court proceedings."

Twinkle Turner said, "She tried to take these stubborn Otis kids to law, Sheriff. But they ignored the summons and we all know that circuit judge won't be back this way for six or eight weeks."

"You mean you were counting on that." Longarm cut in.

Sheriff Peabody waved a hand to hush them all as he

read on, wadded the papers up before getting to the end, and declared, "You two are under arrest. Like Longarm says, you were out to rob orphans with this worthless flim flam inscribed on pretty paper. I don't know whether that signature ascribed to the late Ward Otis looks like his or not. I do know most every responsible citizen in these parts, at least by name on the voting rolls, and there just ain't no qualified witnesses named Upshaw or Thornline in these parts!"

Twinkle Taylor tried, "Old Ward Otis took out that loan when he was down Durango way at the far end of his coach run, see?"

But the sheriff said, "Not hardly. If you're so smart about legal documents, suppose you tell us why a loan his survivors deny would have been taken out in any county without being notorized? Then, if you can accomplish that wonder, explain how her nibs got this mighty officious eviction notice from no judge of any county named by hand or by typewriting machine?"

After a moment of awkward silence Sheriff Peabody nodded curtly and said, "I didn't think so. The two of you can ride back to town with me like men, with your hands free, if you'd care to surrender your shooting irons to Deputy Terry, yonder."

As the younger lawman indicated heeled his pony closer the gunslick called Omaha gasped, "Hold on, Sheriff! I only work for the duchess, or that is to say I did until she must have gone loony! I don't know nothing about a single event leading up to this discussion. She told me after noon, today, to ride out here with Twinkle and back his play. I never even read that fool paper you're waving around there!"

Sheriff Peabody looked at Longarm and asked, "What do you think, pard?"

Longarm asked Omaha if he thought any of his other pals riding for the duchess of Durango might feel the same way about backing the play of a gal gone ga-ga with greed. When Omaha said he sure meant to tell them just that, Longarm suggested to Peabody, "I'd throw that one back and just keep Twinkle. I doubt you have enough to hold anyone who's yet to have done all that much, and who cares where the bits and pieces wind up when you defang a sidewinder?"

So Sheriff Peabody told Omaha he was free to go as long as it was somewhere else by sundown. Then he told Twinkle Taylor he was under arrest on suspicion of molesting orphans. In the weeping and wailing confusion that followed, Glory Otis moved clean across the cattle guard with her shotgun held more polite as she joined Longarm in a wagon rut to purr, "I knew we could count on you, darling! As soon as they leave I mean to drag you inside and make you come until you just can't come no more!"

Longarm glanced up at the low sun to the west as he replied with a thin smile, "That might not be as hard as you think. But just hold the thought, for now. The sheriff and the sunball just gave Omaha time to ride into town for his possibles and pals and still ride out of these parts before dark."

She said she had shades on her windows and a lock on her door. But he insisted, "I don't want anyone to know where to find me tonight as I lie slugabed. So I'll be back after dark, once I do some riding my ownself. We've still got some daylight left and I noticed, scouting for the army, hoofprints and other sign gets easier to read closer to sundown."

Chapter 26

Omaha had already lit out of town, his pals and possibles at a dead run. Longarm followed the sheriff's party and Twinkle Taylor as they loped at a more comfortable pace. Longarm trotted Mittens to let everybody gain a good lead on him. They were out of sight by the time he reined in out front of the Western Union and dismounted to enter without company.

He'd been expecting answers to his earlier wires or further instructions to go with that stay of execution. For the state governor hadn't *pardoned* Robles for the murders in that local whorehouse. The stay had only instructed the sheriff not to hang the son of a bitch or let him go whilst the powers that be made up their minds.

But with the shooting of Rory Logan and Sheriff Peabody helping himself to the credit for solving the mystery of the killer who'd gotten away that night at Madame Frenchy's, the sands of due process were running out on holding Robles in Durance Vile. For unless they charged him with something else, sudden, it was only a question of time before some pal of Robles showed up with a writ of *habeas corpus* on the grounds that since he hadn't shot anybody in that whorehouse, after all, it hardly mattered whether he'd been pardoned officious or not. A sheriff running for re-election in the fall could only do so many favors for a fellow lawman. Holding a suspect for the federal courts without a fool federal indictment was asking for an egg in your beer and then some!

Seeing the workday was about shot and knowing Western Union would not be able to deliver to a federal building shut down for the night, Longarm used more words than usual and sent a night letter at off-hour rates explaining his need for most any sort of wire from Denver to show the local authorities if anyone wanted Robles held on suspicion of most any federal offense the legal eagles in the federal building came up with. He sent a shorter but more to-the-point straight wire at a nickel a word to Marshal Vail's home address on Capitol Hill. He wanted Billy braced for the shilly-shally in the marble halls of justice once he got to work in the morning. He knew that Billy Vail would know he had a mighty slippery grip on Ricardo Robles, now that the *vaquero* had to know that unsupported confession no longer stood betwixt him and that gallows Limey Norwich had built there in Ambush.

Coming out of the telegraph office, Longarm felt no call to go on over to the jail and say goodnight to his one and only likely suspect. For the longer it took Robles to repudiate his confession the longer Sheriff Peabody was likely to hold him, and Longarm wanted him held lest he ride off forever to parts unknown with those two surviving pals, Duke and el Aguilar.

He felt no call to have supper at the beanery where good old Jenny Crowfeather worked, for a younger, prettier white gal had supper on the stove for him out to the Otis spread, even if old Jenny had managed to get shed of her Arapaho kin.

He felt no call to return Mittens to her owner and see if old Meg had gotten over her moody second thoughts about some innocent slap and tickle. Life was too short to waste any of it arguing with moody gals and he needed *some* damned mount to get back out to the Otis spread, where the grub was good and the slap and tickle was less complicated.

So he was standing there on the plank walk in front of

the Western Union, lighting a thoughtful cheroot as he tried to recall if he had any other late afternoon errand in town before he rode out of the same to take his beating like a man when a totally strange sparrow bird asked if he was by any chance Deputy Custis Long.

On second glance the sparrow bird was a little gal of about forty, peering out from under her drab summer boater of dark straw through thick specs. Longarm ticked the brim of his coffee brown Stetson to her and replied, "It ain't by chance, Ma'am. I carry a U.S. Deputy Marshal's warrant to go with my badge. Who told you I'd be here by the Western Union, waiting for you, Miss . . . ?"

"Zimmer, Ernestine Zimmer, my friends call me Ernie," she replied in a breathless tone, adding, "I wasn't expecting to find you here, I was about to send a wire but this is a stroke of luck! You see I work for Mrs. Sharon Rose Slade."

"My heart goes out to you," said Longarm. "But she surely never told you to track me down, here at the telegraph office. The last I heard, the Duchess was sore at me."

Ernie Zimmer sighed and said, "She still is, I'm afraid. I know her better than to ask her just why. I work as her secretary and legal advisor. I was on my way here to wire friends in high places for a writ of *habeas corpus*. But maybe if we put our heads together we could save her from another ill-advised maneuver. You were the one Omaha Joe just told us about, weren't you?"

Longarm nodded soberly and said, "I didn't know his name was Joe but I'm glad he made it back to town, speaking of ill-advised maneuvers!"

She sighed and said, "I told them that eviction bluff wasn't liable to work. The plan was for Twinkle to offer a gracious way out, once he had Gloria Otis on the ropes. I told them the girl was too smart by a half. I'd already tried to negotiate a straightforward buyout and you have no idea how hard it can be to buy people out when they don't want to sell and don't need the money!"

Longarm dryly remarked, "I suspect I do. Glory and her

kid brother were holding Twinkle and Omaha at bay when I got there. We know how that turned out. You ain't about to get Twinkle out on a writ because the Latin words *habeas corpus* simply mean why are you holding the body and we've got plenty of just cause to hold a confidence man who tried to rob orphans with worthless scribbles on a wad of expensive paper. If I was advising her nibs on legal matters, this evening, I'd advise her to get out of town along with Omaha Joe before the circuit judge gets back here to hold the trial!"

The tiny, once-pretty and doubtless well-paid lady in waiting to a self-styled duchess quietly said, "Mrs. Slade doesn't always take my advice. I warned her that attempt to frighten Gloria Otis into a distress sale could bring down the roof on us as it did and now Omaha Joe and the other two men who came up here with us have quit her like rats deserting a sinking ship!"

"I don't find that hard to believe," said Longarm, dryly, before he asked, "How come your willfull boss-lady wants the Otis dairy operation to the point of just plain silly?"

Ernestine Zimmer sighed and replied, "You just put your finger on it. She's used to getting her own way and inclined to get willful when she doesn't. She's conceived a real dislike for young Gloria Otis and when she's really down on someone she tends to lose her head."

"I've noticed that," said Longarm, looking away to avoid her eyes and check how much daylight they had to see with. Kicking himself for even a veiled remark to a hireling who'd likely brought the wet towels on other such occasions, he asked how come the duchess was so vexed with such a pretty little milkmaid.

The woman who worked for the pissed-off duchess replied, "I suppose it's partly because Gloria Otis is young and pretty, but it's mostly because she runs the best butter and eggs operation for a day's haul from Ambush. The Otis orphans sell clean butter, cream and milk from high-grade milking stock, along with Grade A leghorn eggs and they'd have poultry to sell as well if they didn't give spent hens and those cockerels they have no use for to begging Indians. Mrs. Sharon Rose thinks that's a poor way to do business and when she tried to beat the Otis orphans down on the produce they'd been selling to the hotel she bought, Gloria Otis told her to go buy her butter and eggs from the devil in Hell."

Longarm smiled fondly and remarked, "I've noticed Glory Otis has her own emotional streak. I thank you for being so frank about those tense moments out at the Otis spread. So I'll be frank with you, now. You ain't going to get Twinkle Turner out on no writ before the circuit judge come back this way to try him as a confidence man."

"He was only acting on orders he said might not work!" she cut in.

Longarm hushed her with a wave of his hand and said, "I ain't done talking. Now that you've helped me see the picture I'm in way better shape to offer friendly advice. I take it you would like some friendly advice with night coming on and you ladies a long way from home with no hired guns to guard such a popular pair?"

The little gal in fusty dark poplin said, "I'm listening. But I've told you how hard it can be to advise Miss Sharon Rose."

He said, "Advise her this. I can't speak for Omaha and two others I don't know. But Twinkle Taylor would likely stand by her if only he was out of jail."

She nodded at the Western Union doorway and said that was the main reason she'd come over from the hotel.

Longarm shook his head and said, "The only way you're going to get him out in less than the seventy-two hours we can hold anyone without an indictment calls for Glory Otis to drop charges. I know you and your boss-lady found Glory a tad sassy. But I know how to get on her good side and she might just drop the charges against Twinkle if I can assure her nobody will ever pester her about her dead dad's old homestead ever more."

Ernestine Zimmer thought before she decided, "I'll carry your offer to her. She might accept it. She's awfully worried right now. For you're so right about us being alone and a long way from her home base in Durango with night coming on. Can I tell Omaha Joe the war is over if I can catch up with him and the others before they ride out?"

Longarm glanced at the low sun to the west as he shook his head and said, "I can't ask Sheriff Peabody to let Twinkle Taylor go until I see Glory Otis and she'll likely turn in for the night early. You know how milkmaids are when they have to milk the stock around three in the morning and three in the afternoon."

It was none of their citified business that Glory had those kid brothers doing the early chores so's Glory could be a more gracious hostess with her perky bare breasts all silvery by the gray light of dawn. He wanted Twinkle Taylor and those other hired guns right where he seemed to have 'em as he casually asked, "You said Omaha and the others still at large were fixing to *ride*, as Sheriff Peabody just suggested. I figured he and Twinkle had hired the stock they rode out to the Otis spread. Didn't they ride up from Durango with you ladies in that coach that almost failed to get here?"

She shook her mousy head and replied, "The four men rode ahead on horseback for several reasons. We'd heard about those bandits up this way and Omaha Joe once scouted for the cavalry. All three of the others, as you might imagine, rode for one side or the other during the war."

Longarm nodded and said, "Makes sense, even if they did ride past the sneaks fixing to landslide the coach. You said she had more than one reason?"

Ernestine Zimmer replied, simply, "She likes to travel in comfort. She hired that coach from the stage line that day for a special run with no other passengers allowed."

The mousy little gal looked away and supressed a giggle as she sort of half whispered, "It was a warm, muggy ride after all that rain we'd been having. So neither of us were, ah, fully dressed when they sent half that mountain downhill at us."

Longarm smiled at the mental picture and replied, "It's

just as well they failed, then. Those poor road agents might have gotten an awful shock when they came down the slope to glean the wreckage."

He saw she was bound and determined to send a wire before she did a thing he'd suggested, and so, seeing he had some unexpected chores of his own to tend to before he enjoyed a swell supper and an even sweeter dessert out at the Otis spread, Longarm suggested she suggest another private coach back to Durango for now and added, "I'd let things cool some and come back with a politer crew and a nicer way of talking to country folk around a mushroom town. Glory Otis ain't the only one in these parts with a just grudge against her nibs. Nobody can have everything they want and when you bully folk who don't want to sell it's more likely to make them give you the business than to do business with you."

Leaving her with that advice she mayhaps didn't need, since the duchess was the self-spoiled brat, Longarm ticked his hat brim to the lesser evil of the bunch and led Mittens on foot as far as the nearby stage depot.

Tethering the black mare out front, he went in to find scrawny little Matt Greene fixing to leave for the day. When Longarm said he'd just found one raisin in a slice of otherwise disgusting cake, the manager of the northern run invited him back to the office for some bourbon he had on file under "B".

Longarm said, "I'll take you up on that another time. I'm likely to be late for supper as it is. I just now had a talk with the lady's companion of that duchess of Durango and she just now told me they were riding in one of your un-scheduled special runs. How come I got the impression that day that the road agents had tried to squish your regular run up from Durango?"

Greene answered easily, "Because that was the only run that day and you weren't familiar with our time tables, I reckon. We don't have the trade for a daily run in either direction. We offer the regular coach service every other day, with or without a paying load of passengers, mail or light freight. The same coach crew works every day but the Sabbath, driving north one day and south the next, see?"

Longarm said, "I do now. But if the duchess and her own crew were coming north that afternoon while your regular coach was heading south to Durango, who was driving that special she hired for her ownself?"

Matt Greene said, "Standby help, of course. You don't run even a modest stage line with no back-up, should a mule go lame or a jehu get drunk. We've many an experienced teamster and even some coachmen laid off by Banning, Overland and such, panning gold or swamping out saloons these days. You take old Ward Otis, the shotgun messenger we hired for that special they robbed first. He'd worked as an armed guard on payday nights back in Nebraska and . . ."

"Hold on!" Longarm cut in. "Are you saying that first stagecoach they smashed to kindling and looted was making a *special* run down to Durango?"

The man who'd no doubt sent Glory's dad to his grisly fate nodded cheerfully, considering, and said, "All eight of 'em were. Didn't you know that?"

Longarm swore softly and replied, "I sure wish gents who write up crime reports would dot the Is and cross the Ts. For there the answer to a heap of questions hangs, like gravy down the front of a banker's vest! I've been busting a gut trying to figure out who was tipping the outlaws off to the coaches worth robbing! I had it pictured in my mind the way the notorious Sheriff Henry Plummer and his Innocents were doing it up Montana way. But with you sending special runs with placer gold under extra guard in the boot, the bastards didn't *need* any confederates in town! They only had to watch for one of your coaches heading south when the regular run was headed north and . . . Have you ever looked high and low for your keys and suddenly seen they were there on the bed where you'd tossed 'em, all that time?"

Matt Greene said, "I follow your drift. It never occured to me to tell those other lawmen we'd run special coaches packing the way more valuable pokes of color instead of mail sacks. It seemed so natural to me that nobody would rob a run-of-the-mill regular coach. So now that we have that straightened out, what does it mean?"

Longarm said, "It means I can avoid a heap of questions I wasn't looking forward to asking a heap of folk I don't have to question anymore. My boss calls this the process of eliminating. You pare away the suspects who seem most innocent and spend more time on the ones who don't."

He glanced out the window and added, "Thanks to sheer shit-house luck in meeting up with a suspect I never had on my list, I suspect I just narrowed the field down considerable. So I'd best get cracking."

They shook on it and parted friendly. He went out to untether and remount the black mare he'd hired off Meg Connors. He considered a trot over to the jail house to confront Rick Robles with what he'd just found out. But he felt no call to tell a road agent how he and his pals had singled out the coaches to be robbed and, the less the prisoner knew he knew, the easier it might be to trip him up with an innocent sounding remark.

He decided he and the setting sun were in agreement about quitting for the day and giving everything time to sort of simmer on the stove.

He reined Mittens around to ride south, looking forward to some of Glory's down-home cooking and inspired slap and tickle. He didn't care to wonder where such a young gal with no steady swain courting her had learned to fuck so fine.

He cared even less to wonder whether she'd been practicing with a lot more than one special swain in her short spell as an independent young woman of means. But if nobody in town knew he'd been in bed with her, who was to say how many others might have been in bed with her on the sly?

As he rode down the lonely wagon trace to spend another

night with her as at least one of her secret lovers, Longarm made a mental note to make sure the door was locked and he'd wedged his derringer betwixt the mattress and the headboard before she took his pants down for him.

Chapter 27

The sky pilots who said virtue was its own reward didn't know much about human anatomy. For it was usually tougher to come in old familiar surroundings when you hadn't come anywhere else a few hours earlier. But fortunately little Glory was an unusually great lay and she seemed to take Longarm's unusual extra effort as a compliment.

"I'm so happy that you really really like me!" Glory gushed as she cuddled softly in her birthday suit against Longarm's heaving chest whilst he got a smoke going in the dark.

Longarm took an extra drag on the cheroot to give himself time to choose his words before he patted her bare ass with his free hand and told her, "Anyone who didn't like you would have to be mighty mean in spirit, Miss Glory. For you sell swell butter and eggs at fair cost, you cook better than many a Chinaman, you screw better than many a French lady and you're kind to Indians."

Glory kissed his bare shoulder and fondled his limp dick while she replied, "Aw, I only do what seemes natural. Who bragged on me and the Indians down the trail?"

He said, "I heard in town how you let Indian beggers have unwanted cockerels and spent hens. Many a butter and egg outfit on the edge of Denver sells such poultry for such petty cash as it's worth."

Glory shrugged, her bare shoulder slithered swell along

his sweaty rib cage, and explained, "I showed you my leg-horns. Leghorns are bred for laying, not eating. Leghorn eggs are big, rich and white as snow. Leghorn meat is stringy and tasteless next to other chicken breeds. But the poor Indians find any sort of chicken a welcome change from jack rabbit, and it ain't fair to call them beggers. Ute never come right out and *ask* for anything. They drop by in their sneaky neighborly way and just stand there 'til you notice them. I learned how to deal with Indians from Momma, back in Nebraska where the Pawnee acted the same around white folk."

He said he knew most Indians took their time about say-ing anything much. The one who spoke first was considered the loser.

Glory said, "Momma told me. But we had house chores to do and we couldn't hold out as long as your average Pawnee. So she'd look up at the sky and ask if they thought it looked like rain. Then they'd allow that sometimes it rained but most times it didn't and ask her if she had any yard work they'd be proud to do for her."

Longarm exhaled and assured her he knew that. "So it goes until it comes time to leave and the lady of the house allows she might have had some work for them if they'd come earlier. Then they tell her not to be so foolish as she presses some grub on 'em in payment for the work they might have done if only she'd known they were coming."

Glory said, "Sometimes I open the door in the morn to find something left on the sill. I don't know how they get by our yappy dog, Tiger, in the dark. But they do. Some-times it's a bitty basket. Ute women take their time and make baskets tight enough to hold water. Other times they share some venison with us. Ute used to live off the deer, the elk and the bighorn in these parts the way the Sioux still live off buffalo. But white men with rifles nail high-country game at ranges no Ute arrows can match, then scare away any game they fail to bring down from a mile away. So you can see why the ones I know are in the market for leghorn drumsticks. They only share a deer or elk with us

215

once in a blue moon. But the point is that they *try*."

Longarm kissed the part of her hair and toyed with her tail bone as he softly remarked, "You got to respect them as try. It's the best a heap of folk ever get to do. How do you go about getting word to the remaining Ute in these hills, should you need to?"

Glory purred, "Move your fingers down a mite and tease my asshole. I've never needed to get word to any Indians of any nation. My momma said and my pop agreed it was best to try and get along with friendly Indians. So I always have, ever since Momma died when I was twelve and left me the woman of the house. How come this ain't hard, honey lamb? I'm playing with it nice and you have a finger in my asshole and yet you're still limp as a durned old dish rag!"

"I'm worried about my job," he lied. He knew they weren't going to fire him if he failed to pin those robberies on Ricardo Robles with some material evidence to back his confession. His words were a mite more truthful when he explained, "I've reason to suspect at least one member of that outlaw gang who killed your dad might be an Indian and, after that, I did spot deer up above the trail the other day. So Ute could still be hunting deer up along the ridges and a Ute who might know anything is a Ute I'd sure like to talk to. I haven't found any white folk, yet, who can back a word of that one suspect's unsupported confession."

Glory forgot to stroke his semi-erection as she asked with interest why any man with a lick of sense would confess to a crime he hadn't committed.

Longarm explained, "It happens all the time. Lonesome lunatics own up to robbing a bank or cutting off a school-marm's head in the hopes of being better known to the world for a while. Smarter crooks tend to confess to things they never done, just to get out of jail."

Glory laughed incredulously and demanded, "How does a body get out of jail by confessing to a crime? Don't they build jails to lock the crooks up for committing crimes?"

Longarm explained, "You only stay in jail, or swing from

216

the gallows tree, by a court order from a judge and jury. Looking back on it, now that I wrangled a stay for Robles on the strength of his confession, I ain't as sure who was foxing whom. I figured I'd use his admissions to round up his pals. But the one pal he named is dead and I can't seem to locate the two left. The kid sister of the late Bobby Valdez, the one name Robles gave me, swears her big brother was an honest *vaquero* and, so far, I ain't found anyone but Robles who says different."

Glory began to stroke him again as she quietly asked what this kid sister he'd been talking to looked like. She gave his limp dick a good squeeze as she sweetly asked, "Have you had this in her, you rascal?"

"Not yet," said Longarm, truthfully, as he wound up to assure Glory that Ysabella Valdez was sort of plain and dumpy, next to her. But on reflection, few if any kid sisters were too plain and dumpy to consider and so he put his cheroot out as he considered how much fun it might be to frolic with the two of them there with the coal oil lamp glowing off their chocolate and vanilla hides.

Glory said, "You did screw that Mex gal! I can feel you getting it up again, just thinking about her!"

To which Longarm could only reply, "I told you I never and even if I had, she ain't here. So this is all for you, if you want it. Otherwise, let's get some sleep. For I fear I have a long day ahead of me, come sun-up."

She said that reminded her she had a dairy spread to run and so a good time was had by all as they started missionary style, switched to doggy style and somehow wound up in a corner with his bare feet braced wide on the floor boards and her shapely legs around his waist whilst she braced her bare back against the angled logs.

They did it some more at cock's crow, after a few winks of sleep, and then she served him breakfast in bed and scampered off to look after her stock as he got washed and dressed.

Out in the lean-to stable, as he backed Mittens from her stall to saddle, Longarm found himself in the admiring company of young Wayne, who allowed he meant to have a black pony with white stockings some day. When he asked where Longarm was headed on such a fine steed the grown man who'd once been a kid smiled down to reply, "That's a good question, pard. I wanted to jaw with the elders of those Indian kids you may recall from the other day. But Glory says she doesn't know just how I'd get in touch with 'em."

Wayne said, "That ain't so tough. No Utes are supposed to be living in these parts no more. A bunch of Utes fucked some white gals up by White River and got everybody mad as hell at their whole nation. But the ones around here ain't like that. Their chief told Glory that if any Indians fucked her she only had to say the word and they'd take care of them good."

"Then you do know how to get in touch with them?" asked Longarm.

Wayne said, "Glory may not. She's told us not to get too friendly. She said our momma taught her the best policy with Indians was live and let live without acting nosy. But I know where that Ute kid, Todd, lives."

Longarm threw the livery rig over the saddle blanket on Mittens as he quietly asked if that was a state secret or if Wayne might let him in on it.

The nine-year-old came back from staring into space as he told Longarm, "I was thinking back to my momma, dying in Nebraska after giving birth to me. I don't remember her, of course, but I've seen her tintype and Glory says she was really nice to her and Ward, Junior as well as everything in the world to our poor old pop."

Longarm gently remarked, "You were fixing to tell me where those Indian kids lived, remember?"

Wayne said, "Oh, that's easy. You just ride south three miles or less. You'll see three . . . no, four bare patches left by them landslides. I'd forgot that last one. The Indians have holed up in that shanty town the Chinamen built for themselves a safe distance out of town. Ain't no Chinamen there, now, though. Just a couple of families of ragged-ass

Indians who didn't want to go west to Utah Territory with the others."

As Longarm cinched the saddle, the kid added, "I don't know why. If I was an Injun and had the choice of living on a reservation and drawing rations from the government or squat in a brushy draw, eating such wild grub as I could find, I reckon I'd be over in Utah Territory right now."

Longarm led the black mare outside as he confessed he just didn't know which sort of life he'd choose, if he had to, since both sounded mighty tedious. Then he swung himself gracefully into the saddle, waved his hat as he passed Glory coming from the cow pens, and rode out at a lope to let Mittens get some night kinks out of her legs, as her kind had to after spending a tedious night indeed as a horse.

Horses slept no more than most grazing critters, doomed by Professor Darwin to catch no more than a few winks at a time in a world filled with meaner critters who ate meat. It was the meat-eating critters such as dogs and cats who got to sleep sound, sprawled comfortable, in a world where grazing critters felt no call to sneak up on sleeping meat-eaters. Lions and tigers could sleep as long as they felt like and they felt like sleeping a heap. Wolves, coyotes and other members of the dog family slept about as much as their human masters, which worked out just fine. Professor Darwin and the jury were still out on why two-legged members of the monkey family slept as long as the more ferocious critters such as bears, lions and wolves. Longarm sort of liked the notion that sleeping all night when you couldn't see, and having a natural fear of the dark, seemed the safest policy for anyone who bedded down for the night high in a tree.

As he loped south aboard a poor grazer stuck with many a night just standing there in the dark, waiting for dawn, Longarm recalled how Indians and other country folk still tended to go to bed and rise with the chickens whilst he, albeit born and raised on a hard-scrabble hill farm in country much like these Colorado hills, had already sort of "evolved" as Professor Darwin put it, into more of a night

219

critter, thanks to lamplight and piano music not to be found in your average tree or Indian camp.

He passed the long, bare scar where the mountainside had slid down to cover the right of way and nearly squish the duchess of Durango. He saw that crew with the Mormon plow had cleared the way for the regular coaches nobody seemed interested in or those special runs those road agents had stopped eight times. Thanks to Matt Greene, Longarm now had a better idea how the killers, red or white, could tell which coaches they wanted to stop.

"But what about the duchess and her bitty pal, Miss Zimmer?" he asked his mount as he reined to a walk.

He hadn't expected the pony to answer. He'd reined her in so he could study the brushy draw following the route south to his right. Just riding along on horseback, coach or rail, you could miss a whole heap of shit in a tangle of trail or trackside stickerbush, even when it wasn't in full leaf, as it was that morning thanks to all that recent rain. Lots of Indians liked to camp in brushy draws for the same reasons those Chinese had likely had. White men didn't cotton to camping where they might have to cope with damp firewood, skeeters and flash floods. Indians burned damp wood for the smoke it gave off to drive bugs away. Indians admired burning eyes more than they did bumps or flies in their food.

So it was a blue haze of smoke he spotted, hanging low above the scrubby tree tops past that fourth landslide scar, that told Longarm young Wayne's directions had been on the money. As he walked his mount in he reflected on how far barefoot kids, red and white, could scamper along. He figured he really was close to three miles south of the Otis spread by this time.

Nothing happened. There wasn't a sign of life as he walked Mittens along the wagon ruts as far as the source of all that smoke. Once he had you couldn't see shit from the roadway unless you stood tall in the stirrups and studied downslope through the fluttering leaves at more square patches of gray-brown. Then, having spotted where they'd dragged some brush across a turn-off gap betwixt two clumps of aspen, Longarm dismounted to lead his mount down the slope through the scrub on foot. He left his Winchester in its boot to avoid giving needless offense to folk who'd likely already spotted him.

He wondered whether he should have done that when a shot rang out and an hysterical voice cried out through the sticker-bush, *"Ta soon da hipey, tai va voney!* She has done nothing to you! You have no good reason to be here! She did not want you to know she was here! Go away and leave us in peace! Go away or I shall have to kill you!"

Chapter 28

Longarm stopped but stood his ground amid the greenery whilst he called back, "Hear me! I come in peace! If you kill me I will never speak to you again and there will be no peace. My chief knows where I have ridden this morning. If I don't come back he will send blue sleeves, with field guns, and my heart hangs heavy to think of all these green trees blown to bloody splinters."

The Indian packing a smoking Henry allowed himself to appear out of the stickerbush, like a fish swimming closer in soupy water. He was a man of say forty, wearing faded jeans as well as a loose cotton smock. His hair was shoulder length and parted in the middle with no headband. He wore no paint. His height and stature gave him away as a pure-blooded member of the widespread Ho Hada, or Real People.

The Indian who'd asked Longarm to take pity on them and just go away before they had to kill him called out in the boyish accent the stage actors never got right when they tried to sound like Indians, "I am called Honapombi. I am not a renegade. I have never touched my hand to any agent's pen. I have never been given a ration number by your BIA. I do not follow the Eyototo of my people or the Jesus ghost of your people. I have learned to think for myself. I took no part and I know nothing, nothing about the fighting up around the White River Agency. When the blue sleeves said all the Ho who had killed Saltu men and fucked

222

Saltu women had to go across the Green River to live I did not see how they could mean us. So we stayed."

Longarm nodded soberly and replied, "That sounds sensible enough to me. I don't ride for the BIA. I am not after any of the people who paint themselves, as long as they haven't broken the laws of my own kind. They call me Custis Long. I have come to talk to you about the wrecking and robbing of those stagecoaches."

Honapombi waved the muzzle of his rifle graciously as he nodded and said, "We will share food and tobacco while we talk about that, then. None of my people, none, had anything to do with that."

Longarm followed the older man through the tanglewood to a clearing where half a dozen bitty log cabins seemed to be gasping for breath in a haze of pungent woodsmoke. As that same kid, Todd, came out of one cabin to take care of the pony for him, Longarm saw such a stream as there was a few paces down the slope was a muddy trickle betwixt the occasional mountain rains. It was a safe bet the Chinese who'd built the cabins had located them above the usual flood stage of the draw. Chinese were known for the study they put into siting anything before they built it. So the reluctant Ho had chosen a fair place to hole up until the BIA lost interest in them. The state of Colorado didn't give a buffalo fart where Indians lived as long as it wasn't on land any white man with pals in the statehouse wanted.

Honapombi showed Longarm to a cabin with a doorway so low they both had to duck inside. Once they had, the floor was dirt, partly covered with mats of woven sedge. The fire filling the cabin with acrid, eye-watering smoke burned puny in a ring of stones set in the middle of the one square room. So it was tough to make out just what that was sort of shimmering against the back wall until it bade him welcome in Ho and he suspected from the wavering high pitched voice it had to be a mighty old woman. He knew he was likely right when the man of the house introduced the old lady as Yatahotey and allowed she was their grandmother. Longarm knew by their own logic they meant everybody's grandmother, including him. Ho speakers set great store by respect for their elders and called the Arapaho dog-eating grandmother murderers, with some justice. Arapaho did eat dog meat, the same as most plains nations, and tended to leave old folk behind when they got too weak to keep up.

So old Yatahotey was likely lucky she'd been born or adopted as a Ho. She didn't look spry enough to follow anyone through snow drifts as she sat there in better weather, wrapped in a braided rabbit fur robe as if she had the shivers despite the season.

Another Ho woman, a younger one dressed traditional, for summer, with her tits hanging free, came in with a bowl of corn and chicken stew for them to share. Longarm knew he was supposed to swallow some grub and offer a cheroot before he asked any serious questions. So he soon discovered Glory had been right about leghorn drumsticks. But the old lady across the fire gobbled her share and more as if she thought she was that famous cannibal owl they scared bad children with.

Longarm didn't try to talk to her, beyond addressing her as "Umbeah" as required by the courtesies of her kind. So he was surprised when it was she, rather than the apparant leader of the small band, who asked him in fair English why he'd come to them for help in hunting those road agents. She said, "None of our young men, none, have ever hurt any of your people. I warned them not to, even before Colorow, Canalla and Nicaagat went crazy, crazy and gave you people a good excuse to start picking on us!"

Longarm nodded gravely and fished out some cheroots as he assured her he knew most of her folk had good hearts. He said, "I have smoked with your high chief Ouray. He has told me the same things. Ouray has never made war on us Saltu and none of us have ever made war on him or his bands. I have heard Ouray is not well and this makes my heart heavy because he is a good man and as long as he lives he will keep the peace he made with us."

The old gray-haired lady in gray rabbit fur suddenly

smiled, not a pretty sight, and decided, "I know who you are, now. Ouray calls you his *tua* and we Ho Hada know you as Saltu Ka Saltu, the stranger who is not a stranger. You ride for the men in black who hang those who do not follow the same *puha*. Is this not so?"

Longarm conceeded, "Close enough," as he handed out cheroots to both older Indians. Splitting hairs over the differences between the law and medicine sounded too tedious to get into. So he simply told her busting up stagecoaches with landslides was bad medicine indeed and both Ho seemed to agree on that as they all lit up.

Happily adding more smoke to the haze between them, Yatahotey confided, "We have been wondering who might be doing that. The blue sleeves are quick to blame us when any of you manage to get killed. But we know no more about those robberies than you do."

Longarm blew some smoke of his own at her with a shake of his head and said, "My *umbeah* has to know more than I do because I know nothing."

Pleased to hear a white man make such an astounding admission, the male Ute smoking beside Longarm said, "We know that nine times rocks and soil have slid down across the trail to crush eight coaches and kill everybody. That ninth time nobody was hurt. We think this might have been because *Tanapah* was shining high in the sky. All the other times it was dark or almost dark. That last time the evil doers had to move carefully above the trail so nobody would see them. After that the one driving the coach had more time to see the mountain coming down at him."

"Why were those other coaches on a dangerous trail after midnight?" asked old Yatahotey, adding, "Most of your coaches move through these hills when the light is good. Can't they see that the evil doers are waiting for one to come along after dark?"

Longarm said, "That ain't exactly the story, my *umbeah*. Those road agents don't set on the ridges like owl birds, waiting for a coach to come along. They know the coach line sends extra special coaches south to Durango with gold dust from the placers along Ambush Creek. I mean to ask Matt Greene, but I reckon he's been dispatching them before dawn, not after midnight, to avoid meeting northbounds on the trail or in a vain try to keep such runs secret."

Then he blinked, grinned, and added, "I just told myself something I hadn't thought of. Them outlaws are neither waiting along the trail like buzzard birds nor marking coaches for robbery in town. It's less complexicated than either as soon as you study on it! Matt Greene *told* me all them coaches they crushed were extra specials! All any outlaw with a lick of sense would have to do would be to take note of any *extra* coach coming *up* the trail from civilization. Once the coach line had one standing by out back, the gang would simply have to assemble after dark, ride to an ambush site of their choosing, and wait for old Matt to send them more goodies before dawn!"

Honapombi shook his somewhat oversized head and firmly stated, "I don't think they ride. I think they move along the game trails on the ridges on foot. Those robberies are none of our business, but we hunt game along those same trails and hunters are curious abut everything."

Longarm gravely allowed, "We weren't able to cut any sign above that last landslide. I figured they'd left their ponies at some distance and moved in afoot."

The local deer hunter insisted, "They left your town on foot. They returned to it on foot with the things they stole from the wrecked coaches. Hear me. All the robberies and the one that failed happened between the town of Ambush and the next stage stop south at Slippery Rocks. That is the distance a pony can run in one of your hours."

Longarm thought and decided, "A tad more. A coach team moves at an average of nine miles an hour. As I recall that last team-swap we made at Slippery Rocks we had a tad more than an hour to run before I got to climb down from that discomforting old Concord. But I follow your drift. Saying they set up that stop at Slippery Rocks with that springwater there more important than a few extra minutes' running time, we're talking around a dozen miles.

Less than that from the landslide farthest to the south but well north of that armed station crew down to Slippery Rocks. So, sure, a legged-up desperate man could get himself and say sixty pounds of color back to town on foot by the time anyone possed up to ride out of the same!"

He added in his head without consulting his notes, nodded, and told the two Indians, "Four fairly strong men on foot could pack two hundred and fifty pounds of loot and I doubt that much color was ever taken in one robbery. But I suspect I just caught one of 'em in a fib. He told me he'd only come along to hold the horses. If there were no horses to be held and a heavy load of loot to be shared by one four-man crew, he was in on it up to his bloody elbows!"

The old lady sighed and siad, "That yellow iron you people search for along our creeks seems to drive you crazy, crazy. We have always known the shining stuff was there. We have eyes. Sometimes our little ones brought home bits the size of beads. It was pretty. But that was all it was good for. It was too soft to pound into knives or arrow heads. Yet, ever since you people heard about the yellow iron in our shining mountains you have been killing one another, and us, over it!"

Longarm had been raised to treat his elders with respect. So he didn't tell old Yatahotey she was either shitting him or the living proof that her band was resisting the BIA as the innocent children of nature they wrote poems about, back East.

Most Indians knew damned well that placer gold sold for twenty an ounce and that a twenty-dollar golden eagle could buy heap firewater or enough play pretties to get laid by more than one pretty squaw. In one impassioned plea for the Black Hills his own Lakota had taken away from weaker nations as they moved west from the Great Lakes, Red Cloud had set a price of seven million dollars on the real estate in question and bitched that his BIA annuity had been held back by the government whilst he war danced. Longarm resisted telling Yatahotey or host, Honapombi, that *wampum* was an Indian word.

He politely said, "My heart hangs heavy when I say this. But I have been told one of those road agents may be Ho."

The two Ho exchanged stricken looks. The old woman sobbed, "That can not be! That *must* not be! We have lost almost everything because those Ho Hada went crazy up at the White River Agency! Now we play the children's game of *nanipka* with your blue sleeves while we wait for them to forget those weeping Saltu women nobody really hurt! How could any Ho who wasn't crazy do such a thing to his own people?"

Longarm quietly suggested, "He might think he's helping them by resisting the spread of civilization on this slope. Buffalo Horn did, up in the South Pass country a short spell back."

"Buffalo Horn is dead," snapped the husky Honapombi. "Your blue sleeves killed him and all those young Ho you call Bannock when they tried to drive you *Taibo* from their hunting grounds!"

Longarm knew enough Ho to know Honapombi was starting to get pissed off. For just as white folk could refer to colored folk they admired as colored folk, or describe those they didn't care for as niggers, Ho speakers had the choices of *Saltu* or strangers, *Tai Va Voney* or totally outside humanity, or *Taibo*, which was short for the same the way "Spic" could be short for Spaniard.

So he tried to sound soothing as he told them both how Robles had named an Indian or part-Indian he called el Aguilar. Then he went on to explain how another Indian had assured him there was a resisting Ute leader called Thunderbird Medicine, which seemed close enough.

The two Ho rattled like sidewinders back and forth in their own tongue-twisting lingo before the old lady said, "Hear me, Puha Waigon is no more. Nobody listened when he offered to lead them against you people the way Red Cloud led his own nation, through good fights and bad, until in the end there were not nearly as many of them, doing what Little Big Eyes of the Interior Department tells them to do. The one we *used* to call Puha Waigon is now known as Cameahwait because he no longer dances, or even walks. He sits alone in a cave above the timber line, singing his death song even though we still feed him because he was a good man before he went crazy."

Honapombi volunteered, "Our dream singer who never walks anywhere anymore, hates your people too much to walk or ride with any of you. He has been up there in his cave since the last moon of the falling leaves. Only *Taiowa* knows how he lasted through the snow moons. Some say this may mean he has strong medicine, after all. I think it must be because Ho Hada of other hidden camps visit him to hear his songs of better times and naturally bring some food along."

Longarm said, "A medicine man perched high in the mountains with Ho from all over calling on him might know heaps of things the rest of us are just guessing at. Do you reckon this great one who never walks might sing to *me* if I was to visit him with say a side of bacon or a sack of flour?"

"He would probably try to kill you," his male host replied in a casual tone, considering.

The old lady sighed and said, "Don't look so sad, my *tua*. I will send word to Cameahwait that the Saltu Ka Saltu who has stood up for other Ho wants a word with him. I think he will say no. If he says yes I will send those children who are not afraid to go into town to tell you. May I have another one of these nice smokes before you ride back to fuck the Otis girl some more?"

Chapter 29

Longarm didn't ask how the Indians knew. They'd naturally be keeping an eye on a friendly white family, good for handouts now and again. Glory hadn't bragged on it, but Longarm suspected she'd handed out more than stringy chickens now and again. He was way more concerned about her generosity in bed as he rode back toward town that morning.

He knew it was neither polite nor useful to ask any woman how she'd learned to screw so fine. When women talked about other men they tended to low-rate them if they were still alive or elevate 'em to sainthood if they were dead. Before he'd learned not to be so nosy Longarm had heard many a tedious tale of husbands with peanut dicks, pot bellies and a tendency to snore whilst a gal was still hot. The tales of magnificent studs who marched off to death in battle after the most romantic night in the history of womankind could get sort of tedious, too.

Longarm wasn't interested in how a young spinster had learned to blow such sweet tunes on the French horn because he was jealous. He was worried about some jealous lover feeling jealous enough to shoot him in the back. It was easy to shoot a man in the back when he had no idea you had any reason to. He recalled what might have been a slip the night before, when Glory had confided with a giggle that nine out of ten married women had sucked at least once, whilst that tenth married woman was a liar.

A married man paying a call at a dairy spread now and again made a heap of sense, both ways. Glory had clearly been broken in by a gent who knew more than your average cowboy about the anatomy of human shemales. After that any man who'd broken in a gal that tight and pretty would be coming around more often if he didn't have some other woman he was required to service more often.

Longarm wrinkled his lip in distaste as he pictured some two-faced married man driving out from town to pick up some butter and eggs for the wife and kids. But fair was fair and he wasn't sure he approved of a confirmed loner with a tumbleweed job, and no future to offer a gal, fooling around with anyone that young and, well, innocent *looking*.

Then he came upon the still visible signs of an earlier robbery. The third, according to his notes, Longarm reined in, tethered Mittens to a box elder beside the wagon trace, and forged up the slope afoot to scout for sign.

Thanks to the rains they'd had since the third pre-dawn landslide, Longarm didn't bother to look for footprints in the thick green sod to either side of the still-fresh gouge down to hardpan clay. But at the peak of the sort of Gothic window-shaped scar he found the still clear signs of blasting. Black powder blasting when he stuck a finger in damp blue clay and sniffed it. Dynamite fumes smelled medicinal and tended to make your head throb if you breathed too deep. Black powder blasting left a smell something like kitchen matches and the residue tasted salty. Lots of prospectors packing black powder and wanting to travel light didn't bother packing salt. They just used a pinch of black powder on their grub, instead, and it wasn't true that the potassium nitrate or saltpeter in black powder kept a man from feeling horny, as many a lonesome prospector had doubtless wished it might as his burro kept resisting his advances.

He knew better than to scout for hoofprints high on the slope, no matter what Robles had said about holding horses. Staring soberly down the giant slide of rocky gray clay, eroded some by the real thunderbird, he could see how

231

they'd repaired the roadway and run over it with many a steel-rimmed wheel until it was tough to make out where the landslide had crossed over it. But you could see what it had done to a furlong of stickerbush and tanglewood on the far side. Tons of rocks and even more tons of clay had rolled down into the draw beyond, along with many a tree branch, a team of six mules, a Concord coach and everyone and everything aboard it. So he could see bits and pieces of painted wood, maroon and yellow, from way in the middle of the air. So he headed back down, digging in his heels on the grass-slick slope.

Getting to the streambed through the tanglewood was no problem in that stretch of the occasional creek. There was nothing standing from the roadway to another treeline up the lower slope to the west. The landslide had dammed the watercourse and likely resulted in some fair-sized mill ponds for the first few rains. But the floodwaters had cut through the loose clay betwixt granite boulders and now there was only a big marshy patch to the south to show how things had been.

The six mules were still there, minus their harness and hides and smelling just awful in spite of a half-ass attempt to bury them, too shallow, where summer showers could expose a bodacious amount of blackened, fly-blown, rotten meat. The human dead, coach crew and the fortunately few passengers taking advantage of extra special early morning runs, had naturally been hauled into town aboard the first buckboards. Their killers hadn't left anything more valuable to be loaded aboard with their bodies. The more useful bits and pieces of the wrecked coach had been salvaged by Matt Greene and his help, Longarm could see. He didn't need to ask. He knew different coachwork, busted up by different rocks, would be busted up different, for any good wheelright or cabinet maker to patch the sounder bits and pieces into a new whole. He found a six-inch splinter of hardwood, chrome yellow where it wasn't raw hickory, and didn't ask himself why they hadn't bothered picking it up. They'd salvaged the sound spokes to be mixed with others

232

inside a new wheel rim for a new, or sort of new patchwork coach. Mayhaps more, considering the bastards had wrecked eight in all, so far.

Splinters of maroon softwood siding and some already rusty twisted tie rods told the same story. Longarm didn't much care what they'd done with the remains and wreckage. As he moved north along the mess he saw more heelprints and hoofprints than he wanted to. The posse had done a real job on any sign before the rains they'd had since had erased any left.

Longarm moved back up to the wagon trace to spare his ankles by following surer footing back to his tethered mount. He almost passed a wadded lump of nothing much in a patch of rabbit bush near the edge of the healing landslide. But nothing much was more sign than nothing at all. So he hunkered down, picked it up, and gingerly unwadded it as he strolled on to where Mitten stood tethered.

It was a buckskin pouch about the size of a good-sized cock. But it hadn't been fashioned as a crude condom. It was a gold digger's poke. It had the initials, F. R. B. branded into the paler buckskin with a hot iron. When he probed its depths with his trigger finger he found one tiny, shiny speck of color under his fingernail. One was enough.

Putting the gold poke away in a saddle bag, Longarm told the placid Mittens, "Forget what I said about numbers. Any number can play when slick road agents loot a wrecked coach, hide the loot nearby under the soft bottom of a draw and come back for it later with pack mules, a wagon or most any form of transportation you'd care to name on a day betwixt robberies when nobody is naming nothing along a public right of way!"

He mounted up and rode on toward town as he asked the black mare, "What's that, you ask? How did I get so smart about gold pokes? Let me count the ways. *Numero uno*: gold is heavier than lead and so we've all been picturing the looters loaded down with the same as they made eight getaways. *Numero dos*: the gold pokes Matt Greene was shipping to Durango for their owners were all marked with the names or initials of said owners, and no outlaw with a lick of sense would want to get stopped with evidence like *that* on him. So let's say they wrecked the coach back yonder, buried the gold pokes and other valuables they took from the coach and passengers where the trickling creek would pond over any sign they failed to erase, and then scampered on, empty-handed and acting innocent around town or, shit, riding with the posse, until the coast was clear and, oh, yeah, *numero tres*: somebody in said posse would have spotted that wadded-up gold poke if it had been laying by the wheel ruts all the time they were scouting for sign and picking up the pieces. We only found it this morning because the robbers left it there well after the robbery, see?"

Mittens didn't answer, but she moved right along at a mile-eating trot and when they passed the Otis spread Glory waved at them from the dooryard. He waved back, even though he'd told her not to expect him before suppertime, if then.

He rode on into town, stopped at the telegraph office, and found a wire from Billy Vail waiting for him there.

His badge-toting boss had wired that old Judge Dickerson down the hall wanted more on Ricardo Robles than an unsupported confession and the names of confederates who were dead or unknown by other witnesses. Judge Dickerson was inclined to instruct mere federal deputies not to spit into the wind.

He stopped next at the stage depot to show Matt Greene the empty gold poke he'd found at the site of that third robbery. The older man agreed at least somebody in such a crowd should have seen it lying in plain sight if it had been there. Greene confirmed the poke, and such color as was missing from it, had been the property of one Frank R. Burnside with a claim just up past Zeb Lansford's, if Longarm wanted to talk to him about it.

Longarm allowed he'd take the stage line's insurance underwriter's word on just how much any particular customer had lost.

Matt Greene sighed and confessed they didn't have insurance, and not as many customers, as before the robberies had commenced. The older man added, "It's as if them murdersome sons of bitches set out from the beginning to put us out of business! They could have just stopped the coaches and robbed them without hurting nobody, the way civilized road agents do it! You take that mysterious Black Bart who's been stopping the Wells Fargo coaches out California way. Lord knows how many Black Bart's stopped since back in seventy-six or seventy-seven but, so far, he's yet to rob a passenger or harm a single soul! He just orders them to throw down the box and drive on. Which they do, with nobody getting hurt! Why couldn't those mean-hearted sons of bitches robbing *this* line take the damned gold the same simple way?"

Longarm volunteered, "You just suggested they were mean-hearted. They may have a better reason. They may be well-known in these parts. I know they say Black Bart stops coaches wearing an ankle-length travel duster and a flour sack mask, but someone who knew him intimate might have still recognized him by his voice or body motions if he was from that particular neck of the California woods. Since he's been getting away with highway robbery and leaving bad poetry behind in taunting notes to the law, it's safe to say he's robbed folk who've never met him anywheres else, so far."

Anxious to move on, Longarm added, "They'll get Black Bart sooner or later. He ain't the road agent the Denver District Court sent me out your way to catch. I got to have another word with my own prime suspect before I swap my livery mount for another. But I have one last question before I move on. I want you to think hard instead of dirty when I ask it."

The wiry older man grinned and said he liked to think dirty if they were talking about the duchess of Durango.

Longarm smiled thinly and said, "I ain't expecting her to stay in town long. I want you to understand I ain't accusing nobody of nothing and then I want you to tell me whether Miss Gloria Otis has been spoken for by any gent in these parts."

Matt Greene did, then he shrugged and said, "Little Glory? She's not courting. Keeps to herself on that busy dairy spread most of the time. Her kid brothers deliver eggs and dairy produce to their regular customers in town. My wife and me included. What gave you the notion Glory Otis . . . Hold on, there *was* a swain, last summer. He ain't up this way no more."

Longarm chose his words carefully before he asked, "Do you recall the name of this beau Glory had while her father was still alive out yonder?"

Greene said, lightly, "Sure I do. Fired him myself. His name was Larry Frank and he was of the Pennsylvania Dutch persuasion. He was nineteen or twenty and a good-looking kid in a big, blond, goofy way. He aspired to drive a jehu, but we only had him wrangling the mules out back."

"How come you fired him?" asked Longarm, writing down the name in his notebook.

Matt Greene said, "Glory was how come. That is to say, her father, Ward Otis was. He never said exactly what he caught the two of them at but he must not have liked it much. He told me it was him or Larry Frank as had to go and, being old Ward was an experienced shotgun hand and Larry was just a fool kid who hadn't learned you didn't shit where you et, I learned him. Told him to watch where he waved his pecker if he ever got another job."

Longarm put the notebook away. He had no call to *write down* how a youth fired to keep him from getting at anything as great in bed as Glory might have stormed off mighty bitter at her father, and the line her father rode for.

But he didn't head right back to the telegraph office to put the name of Larry Frank out on the Western Union web. He had a suspect a heap closer at hand and he had a few bones to pick with Rick Robles.

So he rode Mittens the short distance upslope to the jail house, dismounted, and tethered her out front. But before he could go in, the hangman's daughter, Joy Norwich, popped out the front door like a cuckoo clock bird to breathlessly gasp, "Thank heavens you came back! I was just speaking to my poor Rick! He tells me you mean to take him back to Denver and have him stand trial for other things he never did!"

Longarm ticked his hat brim to her and said, "That's what they decide at a trial Ma'am. They decide whether you did or didn't."

The vapidly pretty gal with the light brown hair looked around as if to make sure her father wasn't watching from the still-standing gallows in the center of the square. Then she took Longarm's left hand and said, "Come with me. I have something to show you!"

"Come where to be shown what?" Longarm asked as she sort of towed him after her toward a side door of the nearby courthouse. She told him they were headed for the file room, where she meant to show him something to prove her Rick innocent.

So he went along and the next thing he knew they were sure enough in a small room, inside, outfitted with filing cabinets and a flat-top desk. Joy Norwich shut and barred the door after them as she said, "Nobody ever comes in here when the circuit court is not in session."

He asked her what she had to show him. When she peeled her summer-weight dress off over her head he failed to see how such a sight made Robles look innocent. It sure didn't make *her* look innocent. For the hangman's daughter was built like a brick shithouse!

Chapter 30

It seemed just as well it was only mid-morning and he'd had a French lesson from a prettier face with his breakfast. For even though this gal had to be teched and Matt Greene had been right on the money about not acting dumb on the job, he'd have been tempted as hell by the outstanding charms of the hangman's daughter, now that none of her interesting curves were covered by a stitch!

Feeling no call to ask a crazy lady why she was acting crazy, he turned to the nearest filing cabinet to calmly say, "I've been meaning to ask your county clerk for a look through your records on mining or homestead claims, business charters, title transfers and such."

As he got out his notebook, placed it atop a cabinet and opened a drawer, Joy Norwich tossed her dress over another, cupped her firm breasts in both hands to aim their nipples at him, and demanded, "If you had all this waiting for you over at the hotel would you be riding to a house of ill repute with cowboys you didn't get along with?"

Longarm knew better, but he sighed and said, "Miss Joy, we know Rick Robles wasn't with Rory Logan and his pals at Madame Frenchy's that night. Logan was the killer who got away and Sheriff Peabody is still bragging on killing Logan."

"Then why is my Ricky still in jail? Why?" she demanded, letting go one tit to part her light brown pubic hair with two fingers as she added, "He was in here, at the hotel,

238

like I told everyone in court! Why won't any of you believe me?"

Longarm patiently told her, "That's likely because the room clerk on duty at the hotel at the time told the same court he never laid eyes on either of you that night."

He hauled out a file folder of property transfers as he reluctantly went on, "That was before I got here and Robles confessed to me he'd been night riding with somebody other than yourself, no offense. We figure the bunch never rode that far out of town on horseback. It's commencing to look as if they followed game trails on foot along the ridges, where neither man nor beast is inclined to leave footprints on the natural part to the mountain's hair. Game follows such bare and hard-packed strips because the going is easier and the game can see farthest in all directions. They only had to worry about leaving heel marks betwixt the ridges and the hillside boulders they'd chose to blast loose above the wagon trace. But why am I telling you all this and won't you please put some duds back on, Miss Joy?"

She moved around him to plant her bare bottom on the flat-topped desk and lean back with her knees raised high and parted in welcome to either side of the pink slit she was fingering as she purred to him, "Fess up! You want some of this more than words can say, but like all the others, you're afraid of my father, aren't you?"

Longarm smiled thinly and confessed, "That's for damned sure! I'd hate to think of the questions I'd have to answer under oath after I shot it out with the crazy father of a crazy daughter! This just ain't going to work, Miss Joy! I don't know what in blue blazes you're out to prove by this shocking display of your old ring-dang-doo, but I reckon I'll be on my way, now."

Suiting actions to his words, Longarm put the file folder away, shut the drawer, and unbolted the door to leave as Joy Norwich rolled off the desk top to chase after him, stark naked, as she babbled at him about nobody understanding her.

He didn't expect her to follow him out of the file room, clean out to the sunlit courthouse square, until she did so.

Longarm reversed directions to herd her back inside before the whole blamed town could ask him why a naked lady was chasing him around the gallows platform in broad daylight.

He grabbed her wrists as she beat on his chest, sobbing dirty words that didn't add up to anything. Thanking his stars there was nobody in the hallway despite all her demands to be ravaged and despoiled like the depraved sluts of Sodom Town, Longarm got her back in the file room and kicked the door shut after them as he soothed, "Take it easy, Miss Joy. Nobody is going to hurt you."

She raised one naked leg to wrap it around his denim-clad rump and gunbelt as she wailed, "But I *want* to be hurt, by a really big cock touching bottom with every stroke! Won't somebody, anybody, take pity on a girl who only wants to have fun?"

By this time they'd somehow wound up with her bare butt against the desk again as she kept trying to tear her wrists from his grasp. He had an educated hunch about what she'd be reaching for if he let her and even though she had to be mad as a hatter he knew he was only a natural man.

Doing his best to ignore the stirrings in his own loins, Longarm asked in as reasonable a tone as he could muster what this sudden invitation had to do with her true love, Ricardo Robles.

She perched on the edge of the desk to wrap both bare legs around Longarm's waist as she replied in the rational tone of the insane, "Everything in the world. Can't you see how tempting I am? Do you really think any man I offered all this to would ride off with other *men* and pass up the chance to make a woman of me?"

A sudden wild notion struck Longarm. But how did you ask a woman rubbing her moist pussy hairs against your fly whether she was still a virgin or not, even though that would sure explain a heap of crazy talk from both this hangman's daughter and the hangman!

There was a way to find out, albeit he knew neither he nor Billy Vail would ever forgive him if he did pop the cherry of any insane virgin. He settled for letting go one of her hands and running his own down her smooth curves as she moaned, "Oh, yesss!" and grabbed for his fly buttons.

But it was easier for him to reach inside of her than it was for her to reach inside his tight jeans under a gunbelt. So before she could get his old organ grinder out he'd established by hand that her organ had been ground some.

She moaned, "Make me come!" as she literally sucked on his fingers with her well-educated labia. So he did. It seemed common courtesy to finger-fuck anyone in such obvious need. But when she tried to haul his erection out for a hand job he politely declined, glad his stiffness made it tougher to get the fool thing out of his jeans and knowing that some lonesome evening with nobody's hands but his own on tap, he was surely going to cuss himself for passing on the chance to just whip it out and shove it in where they both really wanted it at the moment.

But one of the few things that made the difference betwixt a man and a beast was that a man could control where he shoved it, if he really tried. So Longarm jerked the crazy gal off and even kissed her while she came, clawing at his crotch in a manner to sort of calm things down in those parts. Then, when she wound up on the floor with her dress clutched to her naked body, sobbing that he surely knew what a bad girl she was, now, Longarm got the hell out of there before she could come after him again with talk of Sodom and Gomorrah.

He'd read in the Good Book how the Lord had rained down fire and brimstone on Sodom because the Sodomites had wanted to corn-hole some angels visiting old Lot. He'd never figured out what the folk over in Gomorrah had been guilty of. He didn't ask the hangman's daughter—he was afraid she'd try to show him!

He never asked Meg Connors when he rode Mittens on up to her livery, even though Meg came out of her office smiling as if nothing had ever happened betwixt them to upset her so.

He figured Meg might be putting on some calm feelings when she asked him, cool as a cucumber, where he'd been all that time. She said they hadn't expected him to keep Mittens away overnight.

He knew what she was asking, but he said, "We've done us some serious riding and she's earned a rest. I'd like to leave my Winchester in your tack room 'til I'm ready to ride out again. I have to ask around town before I'll be certain just where that'll be."

Meg called one of her hands out to lead Mittens inside and store Deputy Long's personal property. Then she invited Longarm into her office for a drink.

He went, poker-faced. For life was too short to waste arguing with gals who couldn't make up their minds and it had been her grand notion for him to leave her be whilst his privates still smelled like her own.

Great minds seemed to run in the same channels. As soon as they were alone in her office Meg turned to him with a sheepish smile and said, "I suppose I owe you an explanation for the way I behaved upstairs, yesterday."

Longarm shrugged and said, "That was yesterday. This is today and I told you I'd met other widow women who didn't want to give up all that sudden freedom just to get laid."

She made a wry face and confessed, "That's putting it crudely and I hadn't been thinking about how free that long nasty death might have left me until you pointed it out and made me feel . . . ungrateful."

Longarm didn't answer as he simply stood there with his back to the door. Meg took a fifth of sloe gin and two hotel tumblers from a desk drawer as she mused, half to herself, "I had a good marriage and we were the bee's knees in bed and comfortable with one another as old shoes when we weren't being awfully naughty. I was thinking about my late husband while I was coming with you upstairs, Custis. I wanted him inside me, desperately, while I was giving myself to you. Please don't think I'm telling you this to be cruel. I'm telling you things I've seldom admitted to myself because I want you to understand!"

As she poured the shemale drinks Longarm nodded soberly and told her he followed her drift, adding, "There's this thing we call Love and there's this thing we need called Sex. Sometimes they ride together and just as often they don't. Many a man who sincerely loves his wife would rather screw a painted woman who knows how to move her ring-dang-doo better and feels less shy about statute crimes against nature. I have been known to wish my lady of the evening was Miss Ellen Terry or that redheaded Princess of Wales."

As he accepted the slug of gin she held out to him he added with a wistful smile, "Sometimes I wonder what the Prince of Wales must be thinking whilst he ruts with the real Princess Alix. For they do say he fools around on her with that stage actress, Miss Lily Langtry."

Meg held her own glass up but didn't sip from it as she sort of stared through him, saying, "They raise us from childhood to marry our own Prince Charming and live happily ever after. But nobody lives forever and we give up so much we never knew we had when we settle down with another adult, just as we were breaking free from adult supervision!"

Longarm took a cautious sip of gin, wishing it was Maryland rye or, hell, plain draft beer, as he let Meg hold the floor. He figured she'd get to the point sooner or later, if she had one.

She said, "I never knew until the only man I ever loved was dead how much of me I'd been giving him, day and night, year after year as neither of us got any younger and then he got terribly, terribly sick."

She took a sip, followed it up with a gulp, and continued, "I'm not talking about giving him my *body*. You know how much I like *that* part of being with a man. I'm not even talking about the cooking and cleaning or helping him run our livery business back home. Such chores have to be done and such chores can help you pass the day whether you live with a big family or all alone. But, Custis, when you live alone you don't have to think of anyone else while you go about your life at your own pace. You get to eat exactly what you feel like eating at every meal, any time you choose and, should you feel like turning in early after a hard day or staying up late with a good book, or even a dirty one, you don't have to account to anyone else on Earth. Nobody else on Earth knows or cares whether you're improving your mind or abusing yourself with a penny candle and I'm so afraid of giving all that up again for any man! Does that sound so crazy to you?"

Longarm sipped a little more of her girlish offering to be polite and set the glass aside on a book shelf as he said, "It sounds to me as if you've discovered a pleasure called *privacy*. I know it well. I get to spend more time alone than my married-up boss because I'm the one he sends out in the field whilst he goes home for supper up on Sherman Street. Both ways of ending a workday have their good points and their bad. It usually hits me riding on a train at twilight how all them lamplit farmhouse windows I see passing through my life in the distance will soon be winking out for the night as happy couple after happy couple get under the covers to get . . . happy."

Then he shook his head wearily and added, "Or vice versa. I suspect many a man or woman listening to my train passing through their own lives late at night wishes they could be aboard it, heading almost anywheres, as long as it's away from where they feel stuck. If any of us had the power, if the truth be told, we'd all roam the world over with a magic lamp and just whip up a friendly sex maniac whenever we felt horny. Then we could clean up the mess and have our great lovers vanish in a puff of smoke so's we could go find some other pleasures. But none of us have such powers. So we're stuck with the possibles and we have

244

to consider the feelings of others if we want them to be there when we feel any need for them."

Meg sighed, drained her own glass and moved closer to Longarm with sloe gin on her breath as she smiled shyly up at him to ask, "What if we both agreed to live in one another's magic lamp, Custis? I'd sort of forgotten how good it felt, dog style and talking dirty. The first man I gave myself to after my husband died made me come so hard that I fainted. I hadn't been getting any, nursing a dying man for months and turning in too tired to even play with myself. But the man who'd been our boss wrangler wanted me to marry him, too, and I almost did until I caught myself wondering whether I should ask him about money matters and suddenly felt the slippery slope I was on."

Longarm said, "He might have had honorable intentions. He might have figured you'd expect a man to propose, once you'd been talking dirty, dog style."

She sighed and said, "We'll never know. I never hung around to see. I sold out and came here to Ambush to start over. As you see, I've done well with no advice or consent from anyone else and I mean to keep it that way. But if you'd like to . . . come out of my lamp and take me upstairs again, for just a little while . . ."

Longarm managed not to grin like a shit-eating dog when he quietly replied, "I'd like to. I can't. I'm on duty, trying to cut a trail that might hold up in court and not having much luck. But I'll sure keep your kind offer in mind."

Then he left before she could make him a better one. For it sure beat all how horny a man could feel before noon after turning down more than one rub at that magic lamp, even though pretty little Glory Otis had been rubbing her own, or his balls, less than eight hours earlier.

Chapter 31

Longarm strode back down Main Street feeling pleased with his old organ grinder as a Turkish pasha with a private harem to pick from. For it never seemed to rain but it poured and Longarm suspected there might be a vast she-male secret society agreed to send men to bed all alone or totally worn out. For he'd spent many a payday night in trail towns bigger than Ambush, buying drinks for the other boys while he wondered where all the *gals* had gone. Yet here he was turning down two pieces of ass within the hour, with two more sure lays and likely a third if he'd read little Ysabella's smoke signals right, whenever he had the time and felt up to it!

Such feast or famine situations made a man suspect he saw why women liked to lead men on with the premeditated intent to turn them down. It felt sort of *good*, as well as *different*, to say no when someone was expecting you to surely say yes.

He liked old Jenny Crowfeather too much to throw cold water in her smiling dusky face. But the way-prettier Glory was expecting him for supper. So he figured he'd best not order dinner at the beanery where Jenny worked. They'd told him there was a dining room at the hotel, even though the duchess of Durango had been hogging it. Longarm knew at least four members of her entourage were in jail or no longer on her payroll, now. So he headed that way to see if they might be able to squeeze another armed man in.

As he ambled along the plank walk toward the hotel entrance that bitty sparrow bird, Ernestine Zimmer, popped out moving faster, without her fusty hat or specs. So she blinked at him owlishly when he howdied her. She ran over to him, gasping, "Thank God it's you! I was just on my way to fetch the sheriff! We need a lawman, bad!"

He ticked his hat brim, saying, "I was just now talking about how bad a lawman ought to act, Miss Ernie. What seems to be the trouble?"

She told him her boss lady, the duchess of Durango had yelled at her to go for the law without telling her just why. So Longarm went inside and upstairs with her to that corner room he and the duchess had fought and fornicated over.

They found the lady in question half dressed with her chocolate hair down, and showing. The front of her brown brocade kimono was hanging ajar under its hastily tied sash. Longarm had forgotten that patch of pubic fuzz in adding up available womankind. She'd said *she* didn't want to give him any more of that.

But she seemed to have forgotten she was sore at him when she saw him and his six gun in her doorway with the gal she'd sent for help.

Swinging her bare, shapely legs off the bed she rose, barefooted on the rug, to move over and grab hold of his hickory shirt, sobbing all sorts of things about feeling too young to die and sorry she'd ever been such a little piggy.

Longarm gently shushed her and said, "Ain't nobody here but me and Miss Ernie and we're not here to hurt you, Miss Sharon Rose. So why don't you simmer down and tell us who you're worried about, and how come."

She sobbed, "It's Brazos Roy Baker! He's here in town! I just saw him out that very window! He was across the street and looking up at the front of this hotel. So I know he saw me too. For the fresh thing ticked his hat brim to me before he turned away to make his escape before we could call the law!"

Longarm told her, "The law's been looking for Brazos Roy for some time, now. There's a military police officer already here with more state troopers who know Baker on sight headed our way."

He moved around the two women to the window. He stared soberly down at the sunlit street, murmuring, "Going on high noon on a business day and he surely knows Major Scott and some local lawmen are keeping an eye out for him. So what do you reckon he was looking for over yonder in front of that ladies notions shop?"

The duchess of Durango answered, bleakly, "Me! It has to be me! For I don't mean to brag, but I'm the most important guest in this hotel and that was what he was doing across the street, casing this hotel, as my late husband and his associates used to put it when Brazos Roy was working for *them*."

"Your money-lending husband needed the services of a hired gun?" Longarm asked.

She replied, "What can I tell you? It's a rough business. You make more enemies than friends when you lend money to win. Don't ask me any details about such collection chores as that breed may have done for us. I never dealt with him, myself. I only remember him for his visits, after dark, to pick up unmarked envelopes I never looked inside of. He used to tick his hat brim and smile at me that same way, the way you'd expect a fox to smile through the fence at plump chickens, waiting for it to get dark."

Longarm asked, "How come you fear he's waiting for it to get dark, Ma'am?"

She started to answer, locked eyes with the mousy Ernie Zimmer, and curtly told her she wanted a word with the law in private.

The little sparrow bird, who looked more like a gal without her specs, as her mousy brown hair commenced to come unpinned, smiled as game as any gal who really needed a job might and allowed she'd be in her own room next door if they needed her.

As soon as he and the duchess of Durango were alone,

she hauled over to the bedstead he remembered fondly and sat him down beside her, holding one of his hands in both of hers, in her lap, as she confided, "I'm sure Brazos Roy has been paid to follow me up here and murder me most foul in the middle of nowhere! My enemies know there's only a fat senile sheriff, a district attorney with a drinking problem and a circuit judge who's hardly ever here!"

Longarm pet her bare pussy, since that was what she seemed to want with that hand, as he calmly said, "Sheriff Peabody knows his onions and I told you about those military police after the gun-toting breed. I'd be lying if I said I thought nobody would want to see a swell kid like you pushing up the daisies. But he could be after somebody else and even if he is after you it won't be dark for hours and Miss Ernie got to us with time to spare."

"To do what? Could you put your fingers in a little deeper or, better yet, make sure that hall door's locked and give me what a girl really needs at times like these!"

He shoved her on her back to strum her old banjo right for her as he soothed, "We got all afternoon to stake this hotel out if you're his chosen target for tonight. As for your other invitation thanks just the same but I ain't interested in you that way no more."

This was not the whole truth. For just as most other men might have, Longarm was developing a raging erection in his jeans as he tried to comfort a lady in distress, soothing, "You just go ahead and come if you've a mind to. Feeling tense, or even getting wounded, seems to make folk hot and horny. I've oft suspected war and rape ride so near each other because scared men, and heaps of scared women, feel like fucking whilst they still have the chance."

She shut her eyes and spread her thighs as she begged him to stop teasing her and finish right. But he only strummed harder until she suddenly went stiff all over, deflated like a punctured balloon, and moaned, "God will get you for that!"

He laughed, rolled off the bedstead, and rose to glance out the window again as he said, "Got to see if I can fuck

Brazos Roy, now. What were your own plans for this afternoon, Ma'am?"

She sat up, gathering her kimono around her sated form as she told him, "I'm not budging from this room until the extra hands I had Ernestine wire away for can get here! I don't know why I seem to be so unpopular up this way. I haven't fired anyone working for any of the businesses or spreads I've taken over!"

He said, "You're all heart. Somebody's sure to put a bullet through it at the rate you've been taking things over. But they never sent me out this way to regulate commerce. I'm frankly doing you a favor by sticking my nose into this business with Brazos Roy. But it ain't as if we were exactly strangers and I'm running out of crooks I can talk to. So on the outside chance a dusky hired gun from Texas knows other dusky riders from New Mexico, I reckon I'd best help Scott and Peabody round the rascal up."

He moved to the door, warning her to lock it after him and not to open to anyone but him, her Girl Friday or other voices she knew for certain. Then he went next door to knock on Ernestine Zimmer's door.

When the smaller gal let him in his hard-on didn't feel quite so pointless. She'd changed into a cooler house dress of thin ecru pongee that buttoned, or unbuttoned, down the front. She hadn't put those glasses back on, either. When she asked him what she could do for him Longarm said he wanted to look out her window.

When she let him, the view was much the same. He nodded and told her, "I'm going out just long enough to fetch my Winchester and some extra backing. Is it true they have a kitchen open downstairs and do they offer room service?"

She answered yes to both questions but wanted to know why.

He said, "I was on my way to dinner when we met out front just now. I'd like 'em to send up some nibbles with a pitcher of black iced coffee to keep us going after dinner. I'd like steak and potatoes first, if they got 'em."

Ernie looked away and smiled like Miss Mona Lisa as she softly replied, "Miss Sharon Rose described you as a steak and potatoes man. What would you like for dessert?"

He said most anything sweet and interesting would do. Then he lit out to cover some ground before Brazos Roy came back.

Being it was noon dinnertime helped. The streets of Ambush were nigh deserted and there was nobody in the tack room when he helped himself to his own Winchester '73. Then he cut across town catty-corner to the sheriff's office. A lone, hungry-looking desk deputy told him the sheriff had gone home to dine, but he'd be proud to take any messages. So Longarm tore a sheet from his notebook and wrote a message inviting the sheriff and Major Scott to help him stake out the hotel.

Out in the square, he saw they'd started to take down the gallows but had knocked off to go eat. As he circled the remaining framework of raw lumber he was hailed by a childish voice.

When he stopped and turned he saw it was that little Ute kid they called Todd. The little Indian caught up with him to say, "My *umbeah* sent me into town to tell you she has been singing. Yatahotey means She Who Sings While She Winnows. She has been singing to Eyeototo while she winnows the words you had with her. Eyeototo sang to her that the other spirits have heavy hearts because one of our own has done bad things. But when she asked Eyetoto how much she and my other elders should tell you, they sang it was wrong to tell any saltu, even a saltu ka saltu more than he really needs to know."

Longarm glanced at the noonday sun and swore softly before he decided, "It never rains but it pours! I reckon I'll just have to get on out to your camp and back before quitting time. I doubt the outlaw I'm hunting here in town will make any moves before he feels he has some escape routes all to himself."

Young Todd shook his sort of pumpkin head and said, "None of the elders you want to speak to will be there, now. They have gone higher in the mountains to ask that medicine man, Cameahwait, how much you need to know."

"All of them, even your grandmother?" asked Longarm with a bemused smile.

The Indian kid looked smug as he replied, "*Our* old people can *ride*. They do not just sit there, waiting to die, like some. But I think if you come to talk to my *umbeah* early in the morning, before sunrise, they should be there with Cameahwait's answer."

Longarm nodded and said, "In that case I may be able to cover two bases after all. Could you take a message from me out as far as that Otis place where you and your baby sister had that coffee and cake?"

Todd said, "Sure. What do you want me to tell the woman you have been fucking there?"

Longarm knew better than to lie to an Indian who knew the simple truth. He said, "Tell Miss Glory not to hold supper on me because I may be here in town all night. Tell her I may have cut the trail of someone mighty bad and that I'll explain when I get the chance to ride out yonder."

The little Indian nodded gravely and said, "I will tell her. Are you going to arrest that hangman's daughter?"

Longarm blinked in surprise and asked, "Why in thunder would I want to do that, Todd?"

The kid replied, "I don't know. I only heard my elders arguing out there in our hidden camp. I am too young to understand all the words. But my *umbeah* said the least they could tell you about was the hangman's daughter. She said once you knew about the hangman's daughter you would understand everything, everything, because you are Saltu Ka Saltu and so you are much smarter than others of your kind."

Chapter 32

That was all he could get out of a little kid who likely didn't know any more. Things looked brighter once he got back up in Ernie's room. The target's Girl Friday had gotten the hotel staff to hang a set of fresh cotton lace curtains clean across the window so's you could stare out unseen from across the way. After that Room Service had wheeled a linen-covered table close to said window, with silver bowls over all the grub, the way they did it on Pullman dining cars.

When Longarm hung up his hat and braced the Winchester's barrel against the window frame with its butt plate on the rug his gracious hostess shut and barred the door without being asked and came to join him at the table with her hair let down total, seeing she wouldn't be going out on the street and hadn't et her ownself.

When Longarm got the covers off on his side of a table bigger than one needed but snug for two, he saw his steak was rare and the mashed potatoes had been mashed with butter and formed into a little volcano with its crater full of mushroom gravy. There were two pitchers on the table. Iced black coffee for him and iced tea for her. He saw she was having grilled trout, bitty boiled onions and string beans for dinner. It was a free country.

Ernie turned out to be one of those citified gals who liked to talk whilst she et. Like most raised country, Longarm had been taught as a kid to just put his grub away and get back to his chores. But thanks to some of the fancy company he'd shacked up with since, he managed to talk and eat at the same time without sounding rude or choking to death. As they chatted, et, and kept an eye on the empty street out front, Longarm learned the gal across the table had been sent to a fancy business school back East. She didn't have to say they'd been out to improve the chances of a little sparrow bird who hardly seemed slated to marry up with J. P. Morgan or Jay Gould. Albeit she might have turned out a mite prettier than expected, now that she'd filled out just a mite and learned to leave her glasses off when it wasn't all that important to see what she was doing.

What she'd been doing for the duchess of Durango had been almost everything for an overgrown spoiled brat. She'd already told Longarm she'd been against that phoney eviction notice that Twinkle Turner had tried to serve on Glory Otis. But when pressed she admitted she'd filled out the form. She did all the paper work for her money-lending boss lady.

But when he asked if she'd brought any of her filed-away loans up to Ambush she told him she hadn't. She explained she had blank loan contracts in her baggage. They weren't up this way, this time, about outstanding loans. They were out to lend new money or simply buy more properties the duchess fancied.

Washing down some grub with cold black coffee, Longarm glanced out the window as he asked, "Are you saying that notion to foreclose on the Otis orphans was a spur of the moment impulse?"

The gal in position to know hesitated, then sighed and confided, "If the truth be known, I don't see how Miss Sharon Rose is about to put Glory Otis out of business. That's what she's really after. I've warned her not to lend money on unproven homestead claims."

Longarm asked, "How comes she's at feud with Miss Glory and, off the record, did she ever loan the late Ward Otis a bean to begin with?"

Ernie lowered her eyes to her more delicate dinner plate

as she softly replied, "Off the record or on the record, no. He was killed months ago before we'd ever heard of him or his sassy daughter. Miss Sharon Rose never knew she was alive until she took this hotel over last month, tried to get a better price on eggs and dairy products for the kitchen downstairs, and didn't much care for the answer."

Longarm asked, "Do tell? I've heard from others here in Ambush that Miss Glory peddles good produce at a fair price. What's wrong with that?"

The hotel owner's Girl Friday answered, simply, "Depends on what Miss Sharon Rose consideres a fair price. She seems to feel that since a hotel kitchen buys in greater quantities it deserves a break on the bulk sales. What's wrong with that?"

Longarm said, "Nothing, if you're talking real bulk. But the Otis orphans only milk so many cows and run so many hens. So they can sell all the butter and eggs they have to sell without cutting prices for anyone. Her nibs likely noticed Miss Glory is younger and prettier as well. So I get the picture and I thank you. My boss calls such nosy questions the process of eliminating. Speaking as a federal lawman, you ladies were on mighty thin ice, trying to grab an unproven homestead the U.S. Bureau Of Land Management still holds title to."

She dimpled across the table to reply, "Speaking as the one who drew the silly papers up, there was no mention of *land* in that sort of fuzzy foreclosure. The state of Colorado may have a valid charge against us. But as you'll see when the charges against Twinkle Turner are suddenly dropped, one needs a few friends in the state house if one is to engage in money-lending in any part of the same. What was that you said before about having to ride down past the Otis place as soon as you knew what was going on up this way? Have you been having a . . . feud with that pretty Gloria Otis?"

"We ain't mad at one another," Longarm replied, which was the simple truth as soon as you studied on it. He glanced out the window some more as he added, "I got to

255

ride farther than the Otis spread. To pay a call on some Indians."

She naturally wanted to hear more and so, seeing folk were coming back out on the streets again and the duchess had been warned to stay away from her own corner windows, he figured he had more than enough time to bring her up to date on his own mission. So he did, leaving out Jenny, Meg and just how well he knew Glory. He was glad he had when she demurely asked if he'd made love to Ysabella Valdez.

Figuring the duchess next door had been bragging some on him, he assured her, "Miss Ysabella is no more than the kid sister of a possible suspect. I say possible because it's easy to name a dead man as crook when he ain't around to defend himself. Those I've questioned who knew Roberto Valdez in life have defended him as no more than a top hand who rode too fast through timber. I've yet to sleep with the hangman's daughter, either, since you seem so curious."

She favored him with another Mona Lisa smile and murmured it seemed only a question of time. Then she asked more seriously, "What do you suppose those Indians mean about Joy Norwich being the key to solving those murderous robberies?"

He shrugged and got to work on the fancy dessert as he told her he hadn't asked them, yet. He explained, "If they headed up above timber line to consult a medicine man in a cave they won't be back in that shanty town to the south for a spell. Meanwhile, Joy Norwich and her secrets are right here in Ambush. If she has the least notion what an Indian kid was jawing about, and if she's willing to tell me, I might save myself a few hours in the saddle. What do you call this stuff I'm eating?"

She allowed it was a Spanish notion called *flan* and reminded him he'd requested something interesting. It looked and spooned like glue and tasted of eggs and caramel. So he allowed he'd had worse and dug in as Ernie mused, "She might not know what to tell you. From what I hear of the poor thing, she's not too . . . rational."

Longarm washed the too-sweet taste away with some black iced coffee and said, "I've already considered her being *loco* as the connection them Indians are expecting me to make. I can't make it fit with any other pieces of the puzzle. The only connection I see betwixt her and them road agents is that she keeps saying she's the true love of Robles and Robles admits to a small role in them robberies. But after that Robles and the night clerk of this very hotel agree she lied like a rug when she swore they were here together on the night he either shot Madame Frenchy or rode with them outlaws. *He's* lying, too, if he insists he was only holding their horses at a distance. Them same Indians had no more luck cutting sign than the rest of us. The gang pussyfooted out of town and back *without* any horses. As I put it together they ran ridges less than twelve miles out of town, dropped some mountain on a pre-dawn special, plundered the wreckage, cached the loot nearby, and scampered back to town empty-handed, acting innocent until they had the chance to drive out in broad daylight and gather up the goods after the scene of their crime cooled down."

Ernie said, "We've been over all that. Let's get back to what those Indians could have meant about you understanding everything as soon as you understood . . . what? That Joy Norwich is a big fibber with a dirty mouth?"

Longarm said that was about all he could come up with, adding, "From what might have been a slip of that Ute kid's lip I suspect his folk are torn betwixt not wanting to be accused of another crime against us white folk and not wanting to turn in one of their own. Robles told me the leader of his gang is a breed or assimilated Indian he only knew by a nickname. The Indians have assured me the eagle or thunderbird I had at the head of my list won't work. That still leaves a whole flock of big bad birds willing to smash a coach and its contents to bit and pieces and pick over the broken bones for scraps."

There came a rap on the door. Ernie started to rise from the table but Longarm silently signalled her to stay put as he got to his feet and moved over to the door with his six gun drawn. But when he opened up it was the portly Sheriff Peabody and Major Scott. They wanted in on the stakeout. So Ernie ducked out while Longarm filled the other lawmen in. Then she came back with a hall porter and some keys to show Peabody and Scott to yet another unoccupied room a couple of doors down. When Longarm asked the porter who was in the rooms between the porter confided, "Whisky drummer who goes in and out and a honeymoon couple who don't. *He* comes downstairs now and again for a fresh bottle or some sandwiches. Ain't seen *her* since they checked in yesterday. I can't say if they're cheap or just don't know about room service. They look to be country folk."

Peabody said he didn't care and left with the porter, Ernie and Major Scott. She came back in a few minutes, saying she was glad she had the authority from her boss lady, seeing Sheriff Peabody *had* been told about room service.

Longarm knew she'd had that porter put in a few words downstairs when another one came up to clear away all the dinnerware so's they could sit by the window with just soda crackers and peanuts to go with their iced tea and coffee.

The afternoon would have dragged even more tedious if the little shy sparrow bird across the table hadn't talked so dirty.

Longarm was certain he was on to her game. Other fully dressed but foul-mouthed little things had played the same game with him in many a railroad club-car or standing by a steamboat rail with a man who wasn't allowed to touch. He knew that she knew he couldn't take her up on it if she got buck naked and lay down on the rug with her legs spread wide. So he wondered, idly, why that mental picture gave him such a hard-on.

She never came right out and suggested *they* do anything naughty. That wasn't the way the game was played. She'd adopted a clinical tone of voice as she suggested many a dirty little secret that hangman's daughter might be hiding.

Longarm stared out at the busy afternoon street, wishing it was way later, as he dryly remarked, "I somehow doubt Miss Joy is very good at keeping anything about herself secret." He tried not to think once more about that mighty pretty little Mexican nun who'd chewed his ear off about whether her vows of chastity had been the right choice or not, with her Padre and an older nun lazing in a seat across the aisle as their train took forever to cross the Chihuahua desert. It was cruelty to animals. But mayhaps some ladies had some of that left over from childhood to get out of their systems. You hardly ever saw little gals in pigtails torturing kittens or tossing earthworms on ant piles.

Once she'd considered whether Joy Norwich might be claiming to be a Mexican's lover just to cover up for a real Indian lover, the speculating sparrow bird went on to speculate whether those whores at Madame Frenchy's could have been murdered because they knew too much about other crimes. She said she'd heard most riders of the owlhoot trail led shocking private lives.

She asked if it was true most professional criminals were queer from being alone so often, for so long, with other wild sinners.

Longarm spotted something interesting, decided it was only one of the local Mex riders coming out of that notions shop across the way and told her, "I suspect some are and some ain't. It takes all kinds to ride herd or rob stagecoaches. I know the last time Jesse was spotted he was married up lawful."

He kicked himself for bringing up other unsolved puzzles on a lazy afternoon. He had enough on his plate without rehashing the possible comings and goings of the James brothers since that disasterous Northfield raid had wiped out half the James–Younger clan and taught the survivors to hide out like bark beetles betwixt robberies.

But as the afternoon wore on, with Ernie on the subject of the men who'd used and abused her back East, now, his mind kept drifting back to Jesse James and his wife, Zerelda

259

Mimms. But try as he might, he couldn't see why. Despite all the headlines, those James boys and their kin, the Younger Brothers, had never robbed any stagecoaches, or anything else on the West Slope of the Rockies. Yet them alienist docs over in Vienna town held that when your brain kept buzzing back to the dumb buttercup it was trying to *remember* something you might not care to think about. He knew the little sparrow bird he was spending so much time with seemed to look less plain as the time passed, with her telling him the story of her life and him trying not to take her up on it. For by sundown he felt sure he had to be the only white man, east or west, who hadn't used and abused the poor little little thing as a play-pretty.

She seemed even prettier as the shadows lengthened out front whilst they shared a room service supper. By the time they were putting away another fancy French dessert, named after a Miss Suzy, the lamps were winking on in windows across the way. But when Ernie asked Longarm if he'd care to light the wall lamp he shook his head and explained, "I want us looking *out* through these curtains. I don't want anybody out there in the gathering dusk looking *in*!"

She said she followed his drift. But then, as if to prove his point with a vengeance, a fusilade of shots rang out in the distance, some window glass shattered closer, and then it got ominously quiet for the time it took Longarm to leap to his feet with his six gun in hand.

Chapter 33

There was just enough lamplight in the hall outside to keep Longarm and Sheriff Peabody from throwing down on one another. Some gal inside was screaming fit to bust as Peabody pounded on the door of that honeymoon couple with his own gun. Major Scott was covering the same door with his own sidearm. Longarm called out to them, "Shots came from outside. Me and Miss Ernie were closer to the north end of the building. Heard window glass getting shot out, closer."

The sheriff gave the honeymooner's door another lick for luck and followed as Longarm strode the short distance to the corner room he'd told the duchess to stay in and only knocked once.

When she didn't answer he kicked the door in and entered fast and low to trim the bedlamp she'd lit before he paused to look at anything else. As he noted the bullet-riddled window shade facing north he saw it had stopped most of the shattered window glass. He warned everyone to stand out of line as he raised the shade to gaze out over empty rooftops and a street filled with puzzled faces staring up toward him.

He pulled the shade down again, just in case, and moved a table lamp to the sill of the same before he lit it, where it couldn't cast any fatal shadows against that linen shade.

The duchess of Durango had only been hit by one of the six rounds fired through her shadow on yonder shade. But once was enough when it caught you just over the left eyebrow. She lay spread eagle on her back with her kimono wide open and a sleepy little smile on her face.

Sheriff Peabody stared soberly down at the still mighty tempting cadaver to state, "Lord have mercy, there's a swell piece of ass shot to hell. Sorry, Miss Ernestine, I didn't know you were standing in the doorway. You'd best go somewheres else. I was lying when I said we had a prett sight in here!"

The small but spunky Girl Friday moved past them to kneel by the body and arrange the kimono more modestly as she quietly asked what the three lawmen looming over her meant to *do* about all this.

It was a good question. Major Scott said, "We have to cordon off all the trails out of here, now that we know who Brazos Roy was hired to kill."

Sheriff Peabody asked, "How? I doubt he'll be leaving by rail or any other form of public transportation. We know he rode in aboard a pony he stole in Durango. What's to stop him from stealing another up this way and just drifting off through the trees in most any of many a direction?"

Longarm said, "I don't expect him to make a run for it, tonight. If he's the professional he's supposed to be he'll go to ground and wait for things to cool down before he comes out of his hidey hole again."

"But where could he be hiding?" the portly sheriff demanded, putting his six gun away as he added, "We've hunted him high and we've hunted him low in a settlement of fewer than a thousand souls. There ain't but this one hotel and a score of houses where they take in boarders. My boys have visited every one and searched some other houses known for wicked doings but willing to help us out with a killer. We know he has to be somewheres close because he was spotted coming in, never spotted going out, and just now assassinated that lady on the floor! But after that I'm just plain stuck!"

Ernestine Zimmer got back to her feet, asking, "How can

any of you be certain the assassin was this Brazos Roy? What if it was somebody else?"

The three lawmen exchanged looks. Longarm said, "If it wasn't the hired gun Miss Sharon Rose spotted from that other window and called the law on, we're in a real pickle, Miss Ernie. I've read them mystery stories where the killer is the last one anyone would suspect. But in real life it ain't always so complexicated. That lady lying dead at our feet told us she feared a known hired gun was after her and now she lies dead at our feet. So what more do you want, egg in your beer? The major, here, tracked Brazos Roy up here from Durango. I saw the wanted cuss up close here in town. Miss Rose Sharon saw him earlier today and when he saw she'd seen him he lit out. Pro tem. He could have fired from most any of them rooftops across the way and just lit out some more."

Sheriff Peabody sighed and said, "Well, here we go again. I'll get my boys together for another sweep of the usual haunts for strangers here in Ambush."

Longarm shook his head and said, "I doubt he's been hiding in any of the usual transient flops, Sheriff. I'm almost certain he's been holed up with somebody respectable, in a private home."

Major Scott allowed that sounded reasonable to him. The older and fatter sheriff said, "I wish you boys wouldn't say things like that. We can't make a house to house search without warrants in an election year!"

The military police officer said, "Those troopers who know Baker on sight should be here by tomorrow afternoon. If we can't search for him house to house we can still stake out the likely places he might steal a horse, see?"

Sheriff Peabody seemed to cotton to the notion. Longarm didn't feel any call to toss cold water on it. He knew a gunslick hiding out with unsuspected local folk wouldn't have to steal a pony up at this end. When the time came for him to ride out, his secret pals could sneak him out of town a dozen ways and see him off with a pony of their own. But since Longarm had no idea who the son of a bitch

263

would be hiding out with that night, he suggested they start by calling in the coroner's crew.

As they tidied up next door, Longarm took Ernie aside in her own room to confide, "It narrows down to motive. Most anyone out there in the dark with a six gun had the means and the opportunity. So let's talk about folk up this way with a good reason to hate your late boss that much."

Ernie sat wearily on the bed in her dimly lit room as she laughed bitterly and asked, "Would you care for me to list them numerically or alphabetically? It was a good job while it lasted but we both know she was a nasty piece of work, just asking for what she just got."

Then she glanced up at him, smiling that Mona Lisa smile in the faint light from a street lamp outside, to ask, "How could you have layed such an evil bitch, Custis?"

He was glad the light was so tricky. He only had to keep a poker voice as he replied in a matter of fact way, "It was easy. The gent usually gets on top. She was a *great looking* evil bitch and I'm a single man with nobody to account to about such matters and not one damned apology, neither."

"Was it . . . good for you, Custis? She told me you made her come with your tongue."

Longarm didn't bite. He said, "What happened betwixt me and a lady who ain't here to defend herself happened in private. If you want to find out how I make ladies come, I suggest you take off your dress whilst I make sure they're through, next door."

She gasped and told him he was just horrid.

He shrugged and said, "I wasn't the one asking whether *you* et pussy or not. You're starting to wear my patience thin with all this horny talk and no action, Miss Ernie. I told you before I was sorry as all get out that your first engagement didn't work out, once he'd had his wicked way with you. I told you before I didn't really care to hear about that villain who lured you West with promises of a job and then turned out to have no business but money business. If it's of any use to your curious mind, I'm a natural man who likes to fuck women and I'd like to fuck you if that was what you really wanted."

She made a bo-peep noise, leaped to her feet, and ran over to the door to shrink against it all atremble.

Longarm stayed where he was, astride one of those room service chairs, as he snorted, "I really have to hand it to a gal who can dish it out but can't take it. I was hoping, if we put our heads together, you could help me figure a few likely hiding places to search for that hired gun. Since you only want to play kid games I reckon I'll just go spend the rest of the night with a kid I know."

As he rose to his considerable height, the tiny Ernestine Zimmer dashed over to wrap her arms around him, sobbing, "Don't leave! I'm afraid to stay here alone in the dark!"

He relented enough to sound more gentle as he told her, "They ain't after you. They got the one they were after and the streets of Ambush will be crawling with lawmen and volunteers looking for excitement 'til those other riders you sent for show up to carry you safely away to the right interesting life you've been telling me about for hours."

She hugged him tighter, saying, "I didn't meant to tease you. I was only trying to tell you I'm sort of natural, too. Don't run off and leave me for some kid. Who's this kid you're talking about? What can she do for you that I can't do for you?"

Longarm allowed there was only one way to find out and this time she didn't bo-peep as he ducked out in the hall to see if the coast was clear. They'd taken the body away next door. Turning back, he ran into a young jasper in jeans, an undershirt and no boots. When Longarm asked, the honeymooner who'd been taking a crap down the hall told him those other lawmen had just left. He said Sheriff Peabody had asked him who he was on his way to the crapper.

Longarm just wished him and his bride well and ducked back into Ernie's room, where he discovered she was in bed in the dark with her own ecru outfit over the chair he'd been using. So he shut and barred the door to sit down at the foot of the bed whilst he shucked his boots and such.

She was crying softly when he got under the covers with her. He didn't ask why. There was only one natural way to treat a naked lady who'd got into bed with you willing, whether she was *loco en la cabeza* or just out of practice.

He decided it had to be the latter as he gingerly rolled into position above her wee but well-shaped form. It felt sort of like mounting a ten-year-old with great tits as she thrust her compact pelvis up to swallow his throbbing erection to the roots, sobbing, "Ooh, she was right! You *are* hung like a fucking horse!"

So, seeing she seemed to have gotten over her shyness, Longarm proceeded to dong her deep as it would go, with her taking every inch and begging for more.

You couldn't tell a book by its cover and good old Roping Sally had been tall as most men with a way tighter ring-dang-doo. But if this little used and abused sparrow bird had more capacity betwixt her legs than most, she made up for it by amazing muscular control to go with incredible gyrations. When she said she wanted to finish on top, and he let her, it felt more like someone was jerking him off skillfully with a well-lubricated hand. A *strong* hand when she bit her lip, as well, and allowed she was coming.

That made two of them and when she felt him shooting his wad up into her she laughed and told him to just let Mamma treat her baby right. So he did and those tales of woe she'd told about being left in the lurch by false-hearted lovers began to make sense. Many a man in the market for a little sprarrow bird to nest with must have gotten one hell of a jolt when the shy little thing commenced to wring his cock out like a dish rag!

Longarm enjoyed such efforts now and again, in moderation. As he lay there picturing how Glory would look, and feel, in the very same position, the tiny, tighter Ernie made him feel sort of sheepish about a gal who, after all, was pretty young and petite in her own right.

He'd warned Glory there was no saying just how long he'd be doing this with her, and here he was already doing it with somebody else who was surely going to add him to

266

her list of rascals who'd loved her up and left her singing her sad little sparrow songs.

But how come he was thinking about Frank and Jesse James at a time like this?

It made no sense. He said so, later, as they were going at it in a more conversational dog style. He confided, "Please don't think I don't admire your swell little ass, Miss Ernie. You look more like a grown woman in this position in this light as I slide it in and out of you, but . . ."

"Ooh, yesss, slide it in and out of me fast and hard!" she moaned.

He did, but said, "I ain't finished. Your bare ass in this soft lamplight is trying to tell me something about Frank and Jesse James. Hold on. Just Jesse, as I close my eyes and picture wanted posters as we fornicate."

She arched her spine like a cat in heat, marveling, "I must say this is surely a new experience. I've had men say lots of odd things as they were having their wicked ways with me. But Jesse James? I don't know anything about Jesse James, you adorable goof! Are you suggesting I could be harboring a criminal where you seem to be so interested in exploring?"

Longarm laughed and rotated his hips to screw it around in her the way she liked it as he decided, "I don't suspect you of nothing but money-lending, now. Whether that landslide that almost got you coming in was occasioned by hoof beats below rain-slicked dirt and rocks or premeditated black powder, I can't see you or the late Sharon Rose Slade planning such a close call. I can't see her hiring Brazos Roy to murder her this evening, either. Roll over and let me finish right again as we consider Jesse James."

She was willing to roll over, and lock her ankles around the nape of his neck for more gyrations, but she assured him he was crazy if he thought she knew anything about Jesse James. She thrust her hips up and let them slowly drop to suck him skillfully as she tossed in, "The last I read about the James gang in the Rocky Mountain News they were said to be hiding out somewhere in Missouri."

He kissed her collar bone and decided, "Hideout must be what's been trying to bust out of the back rooms of my mind. The Pinkertons have hunted high and low for Jesse, Zerelda and their two kids in all the known outlaw strongholds. So they figure they're living somewhere more respectable, pretending to be honest folk. Your pretty behind got me to thinking of them because Brazos Roy has to be holed up here in Ambush at a respectable address."

"My bare ass told you that?" she demurely demanded as she moved the same a whole new way, Lord love her.

Moving in time with her, Longarm said, "I ain't one of them head examiners. But I might have been considering how dull this evening might have turned out if Brazos had shot you in the ass instead of nailing the shadow of your boss through the head. It's likely as well for you that the folk he's working for didn't know how much of the dirty work you did for the less popular duchess of Durango."

She protested, "I was only following orders. None of the money loaned out was mine. None of the property we foreclosed on will ever be mine, if that's what you're hinting at!"

He patted her reassuringly and soothed, "I ain't one for hinting when I suspect somebody. I make the charge or play my cards close to my vest 'til I'm ready to play 'em. As they read right now, even if you had the motive you had neither the means nor the opportunity. It was her nibs, not you, who spotted Brazos Roy scouting her room. Had he been in cahoots with you there'd have been no need for him to risk a peep in broad daylight. There were too many ways a confederate here in the hotel could have got word to him she'd be in that room next door. After that I don't see how you could be hiding Brazos Roy Baker here in Ambush. You don't have no other quarters up this way and he purely ain't in this bed with us."

She laughed, said that sounded like fun and then, as if inspired by her own dirty mind, suddenly gasped she was coming and suited her shudders to her words as Longarm

268

wisely decided to pass on that one and settle for some restful smoking.

Ernie said she didn't smoke but didn't mind. So Longarm lit up to enjoy a cheroot as she snuggled against him with her mousy brown hair spread across his bare chest while she toyed with his old organ grinder, her head pillowed lower than most gals who wound up on his shoulder.

As he blew smoke rings in the dim light he gave serious consideration to how come Jesse James kept creeping into his thoughts while he was screwing women miles and miles away. It made no sense. The James boys weren't suspects in the case he'd been sent out on. He had no call to suspect little Ernie, here, or any of those other new friends he'd made out this way had anything to do with Jesse James and . . . Hold on, his wife, Zerelda?

He'd seen a tintype reputed to be the image of Zerelda James née Mimms of Clay County, Missouri. If that was really her, she was sort of pretty and he could see why Jesse James had wanted her. But she didn't look at all like any of the gals he'd gotten to know better in the biblical sense. The one he was in bed with was blowing bubbles against his chest because she'd dropped off after some screwing she'd doubtless felt overdue for.

So he snubbed out the smoke, gently removed her hand to give his own overworked privates a well-earned rest, and let go to just drift off in the arms of Morpheus with a naked woman in his arms until all of a sudden someone was wanging away on an alarm triangle and they both awoke in the cold gray dawn to hear hell busting loose outside.

Ernie gasped, "My God, what's going on?" so Longarm rolled out of bed to stick his head out through the lace curtains and yell the same question down at the men and boys gathering in the street below.

A kid Longarm recognized as one of Peabody's deputies called up to him, "We're fixing to posse up and ride! They've done it again! Rider from the south just came in with the news. Them outlaws just sent the whole side of a mountain sliding with malice aforethought!"

"On who?" Longarm demanded, adding, "I've studied the time tables. There ain't no coach supposed to be rolling either way this morning!"

Another face in the crowd called up, "Wasn't a coach they landslid, this time. You know that Chinee camp to the south filled with Indians? Well the sons of bitches just buried the same under tons and tons of dirt and rocks!"

Chapter 34

Truer words had never been spoken. In the clear mountain air you could see the mile-long barren scar of the landslide long before you could get to it. When you got to it the wagon trace was blocked by earth and rocks to treetop height, while a furlong-wide swath of the tanglewood hiding the old Chinese camp had been swept away, along with the camp and anyone in it when all that crud came rolling down on it in the wee small hours before dawn.

As Longarm dismounted and tethered his livery pony near the north end of total destruction he saw others who lived closer were already on the scene. As he and other posse riders gingerly worked their way across the tangle of cabin-sized boulders with cabin logs and worse sticking out of the mud betwixt them, like the stubble on some awful gray giant's jowels, Longarm found Gloria Otis on her knees in a muddy denim work dress, holding something in both hands as tears ran down her mud smeared cheeks.

When he hunkered down beside her he saw she was holding the tiny hand of a bitty baby. The tiny brown arm from one elbow up was all of the rest there was to see. When Glory saw who'd joined her she told him in a numb voice, "I'm afraid to pull. I pulled on another child's feet over yonder, and they both came out of the dirt like a couple of carrots. Carrots rooted red instead of orange."

Longarm put a gentle hand on Glory's wrist and soothed,

"Leave this one be. Men and boys with picks and shovels will be coming to dig them out right."

Glory sighed and murmured, "To what end? We're only going to have to bury them again. I don't think a single soul escaped. But how come, Custis? This couldn't have been a natural disaster. The boys and I heard the explosion in the distance as we were getting up to milk the cows before dawn. We knew right off it was black powder. A heap of black powder. Pop used black powder to blast stumps when we first came out here to prove his claim. But Lord knows he never used that much to blow anything out of the ground!"

"Could have been set with a slow fuse. I asked on the way down. The rider who came tearing into town before dawn was named Tex Dillon. Might the name mean anything to you? I was sort of wondering why anyone would be riding anywhere at that time of the dark."

As she let go the infant's hand but remained on her knees, Glory told him, "We know Tex Dillon. He's all right. Farms down the other side of all this mess with his wife and kids. They say his wife has lots of headaches and female complaints. Tex was likely in town last night to . . . see a doctor about her condition."

She smiled down bitterly at the tiny dead hand by her knees as she added, "I doubt he set off all that black powder just to block his way home so's he'd have an excuse for riding in so late. This was mass murder in cold blood, Custis. Who do you suspect, the same ones who landslid them coaches and that duchess of Durango?"

Longarm shrugged and said, "The late Sharon Rose Slade won't be bothering you or anyone else no more, honey. That was how come I wasn't able to sup with you last night. You did get my message I'd be tied up in town for a spell, didn't you?"

She said, "Yes, but young Todd never said anything about anyone being *dead*! What happened to her?"

He said, "What I stayed in town for in the hopes of preventing. She was shot just after sundown in the privacy of her own hotel room. She'd told us someone was after her. We thought we had her guarded tight. But like that Scotch poet said, the best laid plans of mice and men don't always go the way they were supposed to. None of us thought to warn the duchess not to light a lamp and stand betwixt it and a window shade. So she did and the killer got lucky with one of six bullets through said shade!"

"I didn't do it," Glory flatly stated, adding, "You can ask my two brothers. I was serving a late supper around sundown, seeing nobody else had ridden in to share the chicken and dumplings someone had been slaving over all afternoon."

He put an arm around her shoulder and hauled her to her feet as he said, "I told that Indian kid to get word to you *en poco tiempo*. I know you didn't sneak into town to murder the duchess. She told us who was after her and you were the least of her worries."

As he carefully guided her across the treacheorus footing toward the firmer ground north of the slide he added, "I talked to the late money-lender's Girl Friday about the trouble you'd been having with them. She admitted your dad never mortgaged nothing with them. She said that clumsy eviction ploy was the pure notion of a pest you'll never have to worry about no more. So what say you agree to drop the charges against Twinkle Turner?"

"If you want me to," she agreed in a puzzled voice, but naturally added, "Why? I don't see as I owe that big bully any favors!"

He pushed through some still-standing aspen to the firm wagon ruts beyond as he explained, "He won't spend enough time on the county roads to make it worth all the bother. We'd both have to appear before the circuit judge, when and if he ever gets back this way, and then Twinkle would likely be sentenced to Time Served. But if we let him off the hook he's no more than a bully without a job and I'd like him to carry Miss Ernestine Zimmer, that Girl Friday I told you about, down to Durango and off this cluttered chessboard. I still have to help Sheriff Peabody and the Colorado Guard catch the rascal who shot their boss lady."

Glory asked, "How come? Didn't you tell me the only case Uncle Sam was interested in was . . . all this?"

As she swept the scene of death and destruction with her waving arm Longarm said, "Like I said. Complexicated chessboard. Before I sent him back here to his own death, damn my hide, that Indian kid said something about a gal in town holding the key to this whole big mess. So, seeing I have to nose about town in any case . . ."

"Todd told you the Indians knew who those road agents were?" she cut in.

He shook his head ruefully and replied, "I wish I had a million dollars and a pony that could fly, too. But all I got out of young Todd was that his elders didn't feel right about giving away one of their own. That does tie in with what my only jailed suspect told me about the leader of his gang being an Indian or part Indian. After that I haven't been able to confirm a single thing he's told me. I'd suspect he was just fibbing about robbing coaches to keep from hanging for the murder of Madame Frenchy, if we hadn't already caught the murderer of Madame Frenchy."

They saw the portly Sheriff Peabody ponderously moving their way and Longarm hailed him. As the older lawman got within earshot Longarm told him Glory wanted to drop the charges against Twinkle Turner.

The sheriff said, "If you-all don't want him we sure don't want him. I can't stand a man who cries and spills his bread and beans on the floor. What about that greaser, Robles? How long do you expect us to hold him with neither a federal nor local indictment?"

Longarm smiled thinly and said, "I can take him off your hands this morning and we'll be on our way, if you don't want me helping you with anything else around here."

The sheriff blanched and said, "Hold on. I never said nothing like that! Ain't this mess out here the likely work of them road agents and didn't they try to landslide the duchess of Durango before they just up and shot her and . . ."

"I reckon me and my prisoner can stay a spell if you want us to," Longarm cut in, adding, "I'm as curious as most cats my age and whilst we could likely get the whole story out of Robles in time I'm working on a fresh hint these folk out here offered, late yesterday."

The sheriff stared soberly through the gray-green aspen trunks at the sunlit acres of jumbled dirt and rocks as he marveled, "They told you who them landsliders were? It's small wonder they just got landslid!"

Longarm grimaced and said, "If only. All I got was two conflicting suggestions. The kid who said they wanted to mull it over before they told me more did make mention of one or more members of the gang being Ute. They wouldn't have called an Arapaho or Mex one of their own. But then they named a white gal in town as the key to the whole puzzle!"

"Hot damn!" the sheriff exclaimed, "Who is she and why don't we just run her in?"

Longarm said, "I ain't ready to say who she might be. I want to ask her some questions in private, first. I suspect she's innocent if by innocence we mean robbing coaches. The lady they named ain't amazingly bright. But I suspect I know how to get her to talk, if only I come up with some sensible questions. She's already said she doesn't know who's been landsliding folk in these parts."

Sheriff Peabody asked, "Do you reckon your mystery lady might be able to help us with our search for Brazos Roy?"

Longarm shook his head and said, "Not hardly. Brazos Roy may be one of the few men in town she ain't made a play for, yet."

"You're talking about the hangman's daughter, ain't you?" Peabody demanded with a knowing smile.

Longarm mentally kicked himself for forgetting how smart some fat old farts could be and said, "I'm fixing to see Miss Glory, here, as far as her own spread. Then I'll be riding on to town for a look at the county clerk's files."

Peabody said the clerk in question was seldom there, being he was a part-timer, like their hangman and many a deputy. The full-time sheriff explained, "It's hard to make ends meet on a county stipend when you have a family. So our pencil pusher, old Pete Boyle, spends most of his time panning for color along the creek."

Longarm didn't want to mention that one blade on his pocket knife to a lawman. So he said he'd look the part-time file keeper up. The sheriff said he had to stay out there until the coroner and some gents from the BIA got there to bless the clean-up.

Longarm got Glory to the paint pony from her stable and set her to ride sideways, bareback, as he forked aboard the bay he'd hired off Meg Connors. As they rode north cavalry-style, trotting a furlong and walking a furlong at a steady mile-eating pace, Glory asked questions he didn't want to answer about his being in town while she'd been feeling so alone in bed.

During a spell of walking, when he couldn't pretend he couldn't answer, Longarm soberly said, "I'll likely be able to join you there this evening, Glory. But I warned you when we first started up that I'm a no-good tumbleweed who ought to be whipped with snakes for fooling with anyone as young and starry-eyed as yourself."

She sighed and said, "I know you'll be moving on, in time. I only want such time as you can spare me. I promise I won't cry when you take that swell thing out of me for the last time."

He said it might take a spell to wrap up such a tangled web of treacherous crimes. She said she sure hoped so and asked, "Does she fuck as good as me, that hangman's daughter you're riding into town to see some more?"

Longarm laughed easily and said, "You have my word as an enlisted man and gentleman that I have never fucked the hangman's daughter. I hoped by this time you'd understand my old organ grinder and me have better taste than that!"

She shrugged and asked, "Then who were you with all last night, that Meg Connors you hired that bay from? Or does she let you ride her stock as well as her for nothing?"

He sighed and said, "I told Miss Meg to bill the justice department for her livery services to me. I wasn't riding her last night, either."

This was the simple truth as soon as you studied on it and it seemed to cheer Glory up. It was just as well she'd never met up with Ernie when Ernie had her specs off and her hair down.

When they got as far as her dairy spread Glory invited him in for some coffee and cake. But he told her to hold the thought and rode on. He knew how one slice could lead to another and the morning was already slipping away from him.

With the sheriff and most of the able bodies in town out at that muddy bloody mess to the south, Longarm had the courthouse square to himself as he reined in there, noting they'd finished taking down and carting the gallows away.

He tethered the bay to a horsehead hitching post near that same side door and, finding it unlocked, went on in. But when he turned the knob of that file room door he found the door locked.

But that was how come he'd had a Denver locksmith file one blade of his pocket knife after some argument. The locksmith had warned him Denver P.D. would arrest anyone caught with such a burglar's tool on him. But that was one of the advantages of packing a federal badge. You got to bend a few local statutes.

So he got out the knife, slid the trick blade into the latch of the file room, and jiggled it a few times until he felt the simple bolt mechanism give.

Then he just opened the door and stepped in, expecting to find himself alone in there with all those filing cabinets.

But he didn't. Joy Norwich, the hangman's daughter, half reclined across that desk at the far end, braced on her elbows with her head thrown back as she went on gasping, "More! More! Don't ever stop!" as he kept her bare legs wide apart with her skirts up around her bare ass perched on the edge of the desk.

The figure on its knees in bib overalls had its back turned to Longarm and the hitherto locked door. He kept his bullet head right where it was between Joy's thighs as if he was unaware the doorlatch had just snicked open behind him. He likely wasn't. They'd told him Deaf Dave could read lips but you had to get in front of him if you wanted him to know you were there.

The gal he was servicing on his knees had better hearing. Everyone had better hearing than Deaf Dave. So when she tore her gaze from the ceiling to see Longarm in the doorway she gasped, "Oh my God! It's you!"

To which Longarm modestly replied, "I ain't your god, Miss Joy. I'm just a public servant who'd like to go through some of these county files as soon as Deaf Dave gets done with licking your pussy."

Chapter 35

The two of them must have been too bashful to finish with Longarm watching. Deaf Dave was blushing like a rose and didn't look him in the eye as Joy led him out by the hand to doubtless finish somewhere else in the deserted court-house.

Longarm left the door open to avoid any further surprises as he hauled out the file drawer he was interested in. He found the filed copies of the foreclosure on the Triple 8 cow spread easily. But that wasn't what he was looking for. He put that drawer back and started scouting for a city directory as he tried not to picture Joy Norwich getting licked somewhere in another part of the same building. He failed to see how the simple fact that she was a sex maniac and tall-story teller tied in with road agents led by a breed or fullblood.

Robles had denied he'd ever fooled with the hangman's daughter. So it hardly seemed likely he'd told her he was a road agent. On the other hand it hardly seemed likely she'd shame herself in open court to save a man who'd spurned her total. Longarm didn't feel any call to brag on giving the crazy thing a hand job and he doubted Deaf Dave was going to tell anyone in sign lingo that he'd been eating her old ring-dang-doo.

Longarm muttered, "Shit, there ain't no city directory on file. You put city directories where folk who need directions can find 'em."

He put everything back the way he'd found them and locked up again as he left. Then he took his time considering where he aimed to search next. He didn't want to walk in on Deaf Dave and the hangman's daughter a second time. He knew by this time Deaf Dave should have made the gal come with his mute tongue and mounted her proper for his just rewards atop some other desk or, if they were lucky, an office settee.

Not wanting Joy Norwich to suspect he was after sloppy seconds, he went outside and walked over to the jail to see if they had a copy of the city directory.

They did. It was only six pages of addresses inside a cardboard cover; Ambush wasn't that much of a city. He found the address he was looking for and wrote it down in his own notebook. As he handed the directory back the desk deputy asked when he meant to take that Mex they were holding for him off their hands.

Longarm said, "I was just now talking to the sheriff about that. The lying bastard will keep, here, 'til I find out what he's been lying to me about."

Then he went back out to his livery bay and rode it over to Meg's livery. He had to tell her what all that excitement off to the south had been about and she invited him in for some coffee and cake while he told her the whole story.

He didn't have the time or the hard-on, thanks to good old Ernie just down Main Street. But he brought Meg up to date and when she asked why anyone would do such a thing, even to Indians, he said, "Might have been an Indian who did it. That poor little Indian kid told me they'd been arguing about how much they ought to tell us white folk about one of their own. If one of their own heard about the argument he'd have had no trouble guessing what they'd decide in the end. The Ute Nation took one hell of a beating when only a small handful of them killed a handful of white men and raped three white women without further harm. This breed, renegade or such, has killed way more whites than Colorow and Nicaagat combined."

"That's the Ute *we* called Captain Jack, isn't it?" she asked.

He shrugged and said, "A bad Injun by any name will smell as sweet once the army gets through with him. I suspect they were gonna tell me the whole story. Only now they can't and their mass murder is a federal crime as well."

He left Meg with her coffee and cake untasted and passed by the hotel to grab a bite at the beanery beyond. He was keeping an eye on the clock and he knew little Ernie couldn't see anyone passing the front entrance under the plank awning below her window.

Jenny Crowfeather acted mighty glad to see him as Longarm took a stool and allowed he just had time for some ready-made chili with a cup of joe. He was the only customer there just an hour before noon on a workday. So she was able to come right out and tell him her sister and her brats had cleared out at last.

Pretending not to savvy the invitation, Longarm said, "First I'm going to tell you a tale about Indians. Then I'm going to ask you some questions about Indians."

So he brought the Arapaho waitress up to date about that mass murder to the south as she served him a bowl of chili with oyster crackers and a mug of black coffee.

Once he had, Jenny agreed with his reading of the killer's likely motive. She said, "I know little or nothing about Ute customs. We never liked them much. But my people speak the same tongue as the South Cheyenne and we often rode with them in our shining times. So I know what happened when some South Cheyenne under Woquina killed some of you people after the other chiefs had made peace."

"Are we talking about Roman Nose?" asked Longarm.

She freshed his coffee as she calmly replied, "You people called him Roman Nose. He was killed in the Beecher Island fight after your blue sleeves and gray sleeves stopped killing one another. But before he was killed, Woquina got a lot of South Cheyenne killed at Sand Creek. Hear me, they had done nothing to you people, nothing, but a blue sleeve out for blood after white people have been killed is ready to kill any member of the same nation. The Utes are smart enough to understand such simple facts. If they knew one of their own was behind all that wrecking and plundering I think they would tell you. They wouldn't *want* to. They'd try to make their wayward brother behave. But if he wouldn't listen, as Woquina refused to listen to the older Cheyenne leaders, they would have no choice."

Longarm said that was likely what someone with a keg of black powder and a ruthless disposition had likely figured. Then he glanced about to make sure they were alone and confided, "You were there that time Limey Norwich accused me of messing with his daughter. You were the one who saved us both from a likely gunfight. Since then I have learned her old man has just cause to worry about her fooling around. I suspect she'd fool with most anybody. Have you heard anything about her fooling around with Indians, preferably Utes?"

The Arapaho gal dryly replied, "Thanks. Where might you rank us *anybodies*, above or below a sheep?"

He soothed, "I was talking about some Ute who don't think much of me, neither. With such a strict father and such a warm nature it's occurred to me she might be loudly proclaiming her undying desire for a confused Mex to protect some other dark-complected gent, see?"

The dark-complected waitress shook her head and told him, "Not an Arapaho. We consider it dangerous to have anything to do with crazy folk. In our shining times we never fought 'em or fucked 'em. We left them to wander about on their mysterious missions for Ma'tou. You call Ma'tou a Great Spirit. Close enough. I can't speak for any Ute with a hard-on. I've never let such a pathetic excuse for a human being near me. Want some apple pie, now?"

He told her he had to get it on down the road and left more than enough on the counter as he rose. Jenny asked if he'd be coming back for supper, or anything else he fancied, later.

He told her he might be tied up and left before she could ask what he meant. He strode south past the stage depot and cut over along a more winding side street. He saw they'd cut down all the old growth timber when they'd laid out the bitty mining town. Them street trees you saw on postcards of Paris, France, depended on wide-paved avenues and high stone curbs in a world where axle hubs stuck out a mite further than their rolling steel-rimmed wheels. Along narrower cinder paved streets with no raised sidewalks it was easier to just cut the fool trees down to begin with, lest they do some damage when, not if, they got knocked down by a passing dray.

But as he drifted slowly along Longarm saw nobody had bothered of late with the second-growth saplings and sunflowers along the alley fences behind the straggle of dog-run cabins and frame cottages facing north. So he mosied that way and drifted slowly up the alley, neither sneaky nor purposeful, until he was behind the double dog-run he was looking for, glanced casually around, and hunkered down in a tangle of burdock and sunflower, shaded by some quaking aspen that helped him blend in better under fluttering shadows that drew no attention with their constant but natural movements.

Longarm consulted his pocket watch before he drew his .44-40 and loaded the sixth chamber he usually left empty lest he shoot himself in the foot. For he doubted he'd be aiming that way and they'd told him Brazos Roy was good. Longarm knew for a fact he loaded six in the wheel, for the proof had been poked through that window shade over to the hotel the night before. Longarm could only hope that like most men, good or bad, Brazos Roy tended to take a shit just before or just after he sat down to his noon dinner. For he had a swell field of fire betwixt the backs of those two dog-runs and the single shithouse standing closer in the middle of the weedy backyard.

Nobody with a lick of sense came rapping on a front door, alone or with backing, when it was just as easy to pussyfoot around to the back fence and stake-out the shithouse.

Longarm had to grin as he thought back to that poor soul

who'd been waiting out back for *him* in the shitter behind his own boarding house back in Denver. Laying for an intended victim where you'd left yourself no room to dodge if he spotted you in time could add up to a fatal mistake, as that killer he'd caught in his crapper had found out. So a million years went by as Longarm began to fear the wanted man he wanted had to be constipated or just not there at all.

Then he stiffened as he spied movement in the deep shade of one dog-run. Then a fat lady in a polka dot blue dress waddled out across the yard and Longarm had to wait forever while she seemed to be enjoying a long lazy crap.

But as all things must end, even fat ladies crapping, he was jolted back to attention as she flung the door open at last to waddle back to the string of log squares.

Brazos Roy had likely been watching. For he was the next customer and Longarm noticed the lean and hungry-looking rider with the dusky complexion had left his Tex-ican hat indoors but meant to take a shit with his six gun riding low.

So Longarm let him step in and releave himself. It seemed the considerate thing to do and, as the hired gun stepped back in sight, his back was to Longarm, now.

Longarm called out, "Freeze, Mister Baker. I got the drop on you at can't-miss range and you are purely under arrest, if you know what's good for you!"

The swarthy owlhoot rider froze still as a wooden Indian, but kept his hands down. As Longarm caught the drift of that gun hand he said in a calmer tone, "Don't try it. I don't want to brag, but others have and I'm still here. I'd be Deputy U.S. Marshal Custis Long of the Denver District Court and I reckon you know why you're wanted federal. So would you care to just unbuckle that gunbelt and let it fall as it may, Mister Baker?"

Brazos Roy quietly replied, "All right. My mamma never raised a total fool and I know your rep, Longarm. Kindly note I am not going for anything but the buckle of this gunbelt, polite as shit."

Longarm continued to cover the professional gunslick as, sure enough, the gunbelt fell around his ankles, open, and Brazos Roy took one step away as if to clear his feet.

Then that same fat lady came out in the yard to call out, "What's going on, Roy? Why are you standing there so strange?"

The gunslick so addressed must have thought, or hoped Longarm's attention would be drawn away from him for at least a split second and a split second was all Brazos felt he needed.

But it wasn't enough. Longarm fired as the Texan whirled like a ballerina and crabbed sideways, raising the derringer in his right hand, a split second too late.

Brazos Roy fired, too, up at the clear blue Colorado sky as he stopped one of Longarm's slugs with his belly button and a second with the part of his straight black hair as he jackknifed backwards to sprawl limp as a discarded rag doll in the weeds.

Longarm stayed put. He'd attened the funerals of men who'd broken cover to approach downed foe. Brazos Roy wasn't any danger to anyone, now. The son of a bitch who fired from a back window past that bewildered fat woman was the clear and present danger, now!

Longarm yelled, "Run sideways, Ma'am!" and then changed positions as, sure enough, the unseen rifleman inside put another round through that first patch of burdock and sunflowers.

Longarm gingerly raised his head as he lay prone in the alley dust behind some wooly sulphur flowers and sand lilies. The fat lady was two yards over, moving with amazing grace, and Brazos Roy still sprawled dead as he was ever going to get. When his unseen enemy fired at the same sunflowers from the same window Longarm held his fire. He figured it was about time they took somebody alive for a change.

That was the way it turned out. With a dead house guest out back and the lady of the house jumping fences in the distance, the local man who'd been hiding Brazos Roy all this time stayed put at a rear window whilst a quartet of Peabody's deputies left in town to keep the peace moved in on the sounds of gunplay, as Longarm expected, and simply moved in from all sides to recover that stolen blue roan in the carriage house and disarm the fuming Ben Allan in his kitchen.

When Longarm joined his fellow lawmen inside they already had Ben Allan handcuffed. Longarm said, "That's the late Brazos Roy Baker out by the shithouse. He was paid by Mister Allan, here, to murder that duchess of Durango."

The senior of the two young deputies said, "The sheriff said Baker might have done that. How did you figure old Ben, here, had hired him and hid him out, here?"

Longarm smiled modestly and said, "Process of elimination, along with means, opportunity and motive. Heaps of folk the duchess diddled had the motive. But most she'd cleaned out seemed to be long gone. So I only had to consider a man who'd lost his beef operation but still panned for color up the creek and had a private home here in town. It was all in your city directory. So what say we carry this murderous old son of a bitch over to the jail and see if we can get a statement out of him before his woman gets back with a lawyer?"

Chapter 36

They could. It was easy. The bitter Ben Allan was still so sore about losing his Triple 8 to the duchess of Durango that he went on spitting bile and gloating over her murder all the way to the jail. So the young senior deputy had a signed statement with Allan locked alone in the cell block, by the time Sheriff Peabody and the others rode back to town that afternoon.

Major Scott was happier about Brazos Roy over in the coroner's celler on a slab. He'd been worried about how those troopers from Camp Weld were supposed to get there with the only public right of way blocked by that landslide. But since he no longer needed them he headed for the Western Union in hopes they hadn't left Durango yet.

Sheriff Peabody agreed with Longarm that it hardly seemed likely there was any connection betwixt the killing of Sharon Rose Slade and those stagecoach robberies, save for them trying to rob her coach as well.

Longarm suggested they talk about it sitting down with some suds at the Bighorn Saloon and on the way he confided, "I don't reckon we can hang that one landslide on the road agents who caused all of the others. If you'll recall, it had been raining fire and salt. So the clay hardpan was slickery under all that waterlogged topsoil and wet rocks when the duchess and her party came along down below, in a hurry in a heavily laden special coach, drawn by twenty-four pounding hooves as it rumbled on steel wheel rims."

The sheriff said, "I like it. That would account for none of the keen-eyed rascals being able to cut any sign."

Longarm nodded and observed, "I've often noticed that when there ain't no sign to read nobody's left no sign. I found the depression where the key boulder to the whole cascade of rocks came out of the clay, unaided by tool marks or powder residue. The vibrations down to the bottom of the slope wiggled a boulder that was primed to roll out of its soggy bed and, since the coach doing the vibrating had done so fairly close, the crew had time to see what was coming down the mountain at them and barely get on by before the roadway was wiped out right behind them."

They entered the Bighorn and took a corner table with a pitcher of suds, a fifth of Maryland rye on Longarm and the glassware to handle the situation. Longarm didn't care if the sheriff got drunk on duty again. He wasn't on duty, himself, at the moment.

He said so, once he'd washed down a shot of rye with a sip of suds. He said, "I wired in the news about Brazos Roy before you got back with the major. Billy Vail wired right back that I'd done good but that wasn't what he'd sent me out here to accomplish. He feels that a bird in the hand is worth a village of dead Indians and no leads at all. So he wants me to just bring Robles in and see if he can't be persuaded to turn state's evidence."

Sheriff Peabody said, "I'm glad. We're tired of holding him on a federal charge of suspicion and your boss makes sense. I know the greaser has a sassy mouth and a sarcastic smile. But he may change his ways once he's facing a hanging again. You remember how that one Triple Eight rider started to talk just as we'd put the rope around his neck, the other day?"

Longarm nodded and said, "Rory Logan must have suspected he'd be a weak sister. But Will Pulver and the man who tried to shoot him from a distance are both dead. So let's stick to Robles. Do you agree everything he's told anyone, so far, smells like red herrings without enough salt?"

Peabody downed his second shot as he asked, "On what occasion? The greaser changes his story every time you talk to him."

Longarm nodded soberly and said, "I noticed. I've been trying to find out why. Had he just gone along with that fib about spending a murderous night with the hangman's daughter, one damned place or the other, he'd have never been charged with that first murder to begin with."

Peabody suggested, "He's likely proud of his rep as a ladies' man. Nobody but a village idiot with a hard-on would mess with that crazy Joy Norwich."

"I noticed," Longarm replied, truthfully enough.

The local lawman explained, "It ain't that she ain't good-looking in her own childish way. It's just that she ain't good-looking enough to be worth the risk of crossing old Limey Norwich!"

Longarm said he'd noticed that, too, confiding, "Your hangman and me almost came to slapping leather over his daughter the other night. I managed to convince him, with a little help from a friend, that he had the wrong man. But the poor old cuss has a hard row to hoe with a daughter so flirty and untruthful. She'd somehow convinced her old man I'd demanded her favors up in my hotel room that evening. Lord knows what he'd have done if he'd really caught us in any hotel room!"

Sheriff Peabody chuckled and said, "He hardly ever does. To say Joy is clever would be to go too far. Let's just say old Limey is too dumb to see through that maidenly ploy."

Longarm asked, "She told him I was out to screw her as a maidenly ploy? What am I missing, here?"

The local man who heard all the local gossip said, "She aimed to meet someone else that night. She told him it was you, hoping things might turn out as they did. Nobody got hurt. Not you. Not her overly protective dad. Not the one she was really getting together with that night."

289

The portly sheriff took another swig, belched, and explained, "It ain't as if Joy Norwich needs much time for such secretive slap and tickle. With a dad like hers, she and Deaf Dave have to sneak in their quick fucks hither and yon in just a few stolen minutes."

Longarm stared thoughtfully down into his whisky glass as he asked, "How did you know about her and Deaf Dave? I thought that was our own little secret. How many times has he been caught with her if the two of them have been sneaking around so clever?"

Peabody sighed and said, "Limey Norwich only caught them once in the back of his supply store, going sixty-nine, stark naked, behind some black powder kegs. It was Limey who exploded and the judge fined him a hundred dollars on top of poor Deaf Dave's medical expenses. Limey took his belt to his daughter pretty good, too. But the circuit court had no jurisdiction over family discipline, within reason, and she wasn't hurt near as bad as Deaf Dave. Limey like to killed that fool kid. Swore he'd finish him off total if he ever saw him anywheres near his daughter again."

Longarm downed that shot but refrained from pouring another as he mused, "That's odd. When your hangman confronted me about his daughter he allowed he wasn't so worried about her flirting with young gents, as he put it. He said he was sore at me for trying to force a diddle out of her. But, of course, all this was after he'd been charged with assault and fined for whupping an earlier diddle. He might have just decided Joy was old enough to decide for herself who she diddled."

The local lawman shook his head and said, "Don't you believe it. Limey Norwich is strict as hell and not even Deaf Dave will go near his flirty daughter anymore. You should have seen the mess he made of that poor dumbell. They brought him to the dispensary as naked as he'd been caught, eating Joy Norwich's pussy. He was covered from the knees up with black, blue and bloody belt-buckle marks. Her teeth marks were on the pecker he'd had in her mouth when her father walked in on them. She'd likely been taken by considerable surprise."

The older man chuckled ruefully and added, "The Lord giveth and the Lord taketh away. I reckon I'd as soon be hard of hearing if only I could have a pecker like Deaf Dave. There's more to that boy than meets the eye when he'd grinning at gals foolish in them bib overalls. Lord knows how Joy Norwich found out he was hung like a horse but she must have. I ain't seen that Mex with his pants down. Have you?"

Longarm grimaced and replied, "Robles swears he's never had a dick of any size in Joy Norwich. I'm commencing to see why. Whether Robles ever fooled with her or not, all that bullshit about Robles being her great love was designed to protect Deaf Dave, see?"

"But she ain't seeing Deaf Dave no more. Her father swore he'd kill the long-donging dimwit if he ever caught him offering a flower to his Joy."

"I just said that," Longarm replied. "Don't ask me how I know, but Deaf Dave has other ways of pleasuring a gal than with his overly manly manhood. So I'll tell you where Joy Norwich was when she swore she was at the hotel with that Mex rider off the Triple Eight. She was shacked up, longer than usual, with her real true love, good old Frenching and fucking Deaf Dave! Her dad had been badgering her about where she'd been, with whom, that night. So her courtroom dramatics were designed to throw him off the obvious suspect."

He treated himself to some weaker suds and declared, "It worked. More than she might have expected. Whilst her father and the rest of us were trying to figure out why she'd say such a thing whilst a man with his life at stake would say she was full of shit, not a one of considered her fucking somebody else entire that night."

Peabody must have remembered getting stone drunk in his office that time. He declined the silent offer of another shot of rye by placing his hand over his glass as he said,

"Makes more sense than anything I can come up with. But who cares?"

Longarm said, "I do. Before she was murdered before dawn, this morning, a wise old Indian woman said that hangman's daughter held the key to those other landslides. Limey Norwich sells black powder when he ain't hanging men or beating the shit out of them for messing with said daughter. But heaps of folk in these parts could have bought all the black powder they needed, months ago, and the Indians said something about not wanting to turn in one of their own. Limey says he hails from London town and his daughter don't strike me as a breed. Could Deaf Dave have any Indian blood and, if so, might it be Ute?"

"He's Scotch-Irish, I hear. Works down around the stage depot as a baggage handler for the little it takes to keep such a simple soul in eating money. If he's been robbing stagecoaches there must not be as much profit in it as we've been led to believe. How would the Ute know anything about Deaf Dave to begin with? Joy's own father never knew they were secret lovers until he caught them in the act."

Longarm said, "No Indians I know of ever said anything about Deaf Dave holding any keys. They said that once I understood the hangman's daughter I'd be slick enough to work the rest of the puzzle out. So what could a well-hung deaf mute eating any gal's pussy have to do with them nine cold-blooded mass murders by landslide?"

Since Peabody was no help with that, Longarm allowed he'd go ask his federal prisoner, Ricardo Robles. But when he found himself alone in a side room at the jail house, sharing smokes across the writing table with the mysteriously moody Mexican, Robles said he had no idea what Longarm was talking about.

Blowing smoke out his nostrils like a pissed off bull, Robles told him, "I've seen that deaf half-wit around town. I've never spoken to him and vice versa because he can neither hear nor speak, as far as I know. If you say he's the true love of Joy Norwich it just goes to show I was right about her being a half-wit, too! When are you going to take me back to Denver with you, so we can get this bullshit over with?"

Longarm blew a thoughtful smoke ring and replied, "I'm getting a mite tired of this bullshit, too. I suspect you've been bullshitting me from the beginning about your secret gang. You picked a reckless riding but otherwise innocent pal out of a hat, knowing Bobby Valdez was dead and could neither be arrested nor questioned worth shit. His kid sister, Ysabella, told me he did have a nodding relationship with another rider called Duke. Nobody else in town recalls a Mex called el Duque as anyone but an out-of-work *vaquero*, looking for work for a spell before he drifted on. That leaves your mysterious Indian, el Aguilar, and all the other Indians I've asked seem to share my suspicion that you're full of shit. You made that bandit leader out of whole cloth."

"Why would I want to do that?" asked Robles, not meeting Longarm's unwinking gaze.

Longarm said, "Early on you confessed to things you'd never done to keep them from hanging you for things you'd never done. You knew no federal judge and jury would ever hang you unless I could produce proof you'd done doodly shit with Valdez, another innocent *vaquero* and some mythical mastermind combining the dramatics of say Crazy Horse and Jesse James."

Robles shrugged and demanded, "Why would I be sticking to such a confession, now that you know Rory Logan was the one who shot things up at Madame Frenchy's that night, if it wasn't the simple truth?"

Longarm said, "Why indeed? That part's easy. The question before the house is why I keep picturing Jesse James and his wife every time I study on this other case entire? I suspect you've been sticking to your confession because you know how tough it would be for a pissed-off father to beat you to death or gut-shoot you on your way out of here with me. But how do Jesse James and his wife, Miss Zer-

293

elda, fit in with all this bullshit about the hangman's daughter?"

Robles said, "I thought I read somewheres it was his
mother, not his *wife,* with such an odd name as Zerelda."

Longarm nodded but said, "Her, too. Frank and Jesse
were born to Robert and Zerelda James neé Cole in Clay
County, Missouri. So *that* Zerelda married a second husband when her first one died and now we have her down
as Zerelda Samuel. The younger Zerelda married to Jesse
is his first cousin, Zerelda Mimms, named after his mother,
who's her aunt. I know it sounds compexicated. That's
likely one of the reasons we have laws against incest. Think
how tangled family trees might wind up if relatives even
closer than first cousins were allowed to marry up or even
fornicate and . . . Son of a bitch, that's it! That's the key
them Indians were hinting at and they were right about
things falling into place as soon as you twist it say a
quarter-turn!"

Chapter 37

Glory Otis caught up with Longarm that evening as he was coming out of the Western Union. She said she'd carted a load of produce to town and added, "I heard all about the busy day you've had. Why don't you come home with me and after supper I'll see if I can rub the kinks out of your weary bones for you."

Longarm smiled weary indeed and replied, "I'd like to. I can't. I just now sent a night letter to my home office, telling them I've done about all I can out this way. They'll be expecting me to show up with my one prisoner and I have to drop an innocent Mex gal off along the way so's she can catch a train home to New Mexico."

Glory lowered her lashes and softly asked, "Just like so? What about us, Custis?"

He told her gently as he knew how, "There ain't no us, if you're talking about happy-ever-after. You knew when first we met that I was only passing through your life like a railroad whistle in the night."

Then he put out his hand to raise her chin up as he added with a smile, "I want you to study on that whilst I'm away. I have to come back in a week or so to tie up some loose ends. I'll understand if you don't invite me out to your spread for . . . supper. If you're fool enough to ask for more . . . well, I'm only a natural man."

She smiled up at him to say, "I've noticed that, and it

feels so good. But why are you coming back if Rick Robles is your man?"

Longarm grimaced and said, "He says he was riding with others and them Indians told me nobody was mounted up when they set off all them black powder charges. They told me something else, about the hangman's daughter holding the key to all them murdersome landslides. But Robles says he's never even held hands with her and the only possible charge we have on her, if we could prove it, would be incest."

Glory blinked and asked, "Incest? You mean you caught her screwing somebody in her family?"

He said, "It happens in the best of families. The Egyptian pharaohs married their sisters or their daughters by preference. But we figure the case of Joy Norwich was more like that of that other English lady, Elizabeth Barrett Browning. It was never proven, but there was a lot of talk when a forty-year-old spinster, devoted to her dear old dad, up and eloped with a younger and likely more lusty poet at the age of forty. Her daddy behaved mighty jealous, too. I reckon it's tough to start over when the loving daughter you'd thought you'd raised right gets to kicking up her heels with younger bedroom athletes."

Glory stared owl-eyed, then grinned like a mean little kid and said, "We just thought she was sort of feeble-minded. But what could such a scandal have to do with those stagecoach robberies, Custis?"

He sighed and said, "I'll be double danged if I *see* any connection. But there must have been one or that wise old Yatahotey never would have said there was."

Glory nodded, then softly said, "But poor Yatahotey is dead."

Longarm replied, "I noticed. But young Todd told me she and some of the others were going up into the mountains to pow-wow with a medicine man. So when I come back in a week or so I mean to ride up yonder on my own to see if he can tell me what Yatahotey was hinting at."

•   •   •

Sixteen hours later Cameahwait was seated at the mouth of his cave with a dogskin drum between his knees, beating the drum with one hand while he gnawed on the roasted venison rib in the other. He Who Never Walks was naked, even though Tanapah never shone in the mouth of his cave, high in the sky above the slopes where trees could grow, because it was summer and his tanned skin was more enured to colder winds than those of summer in the high country.

After he'd gnawed away most of the meat on the venison rib, He Who Never Walks tossed it overhand out the mouth of his cave, across the stone ledge just beyond, to land somewhere on the snow-covered slope facing north below his chosen place of visions. He Who Never Walks did not have to crane to see what happened to the discarded food scrap. No matter where it landed on the steep slope of summer snow, it would slide down and down and then down some more to the jagged rocks of the glacial moraine where the downward-creeping snow mass melted, to trickle into the crevasses and feed a spring at an even lower elevation. He Who Never Walks understood these things because once, when he'd been younger and thought there might be some answers, he had learned to read as well as speak in the saltu way.

As he held the drum while he beat it harder, He Who Never Walks chanted, "Hear me, Taiowa, whom our enemies call Ma'tou, Wakan Tonka or God, hear me and tell me what to tell my people. For my heart is made heavy and my eyes weep blood when I think of giving one of our own to the cruel laws of the Tai Va Von. But the wisdom of my years tells me who will be blamed for so many bad things. Send me a vision, Taiowa! Show me something I can hang my thoughts on! As I gaze out at your blue sky to the north I see nothing, nothing, not even a soaring eagle or a wisp of cloud. Take pity on a dream singer who has lost his *puha* and no longer sees the future clearly. Let me see or hear some sign from you, Taiowa, Eyeototo, any *other* spirits out there in the mocking mountain breezes!"

As if in answer to his chanted prayers, He Who Never Walks heard a distant voice call out in English, "Cameah-wait, is that you I hear up yonder, beating on that drum? I heard you were up here, somewheres, but you're a hard man to find, noisy as you seem to be!"

The no-longer-young medicine man went on drumming as he called back to his distant visitor, "Up this way. Be careful as you come closer. I am prayer-chanting on a flat ledge above a dangerous drop. It is not a very big ledge. But there is room for more than one as long as you watch your step."

So a few minutes later Glory Otis came around a curve in the wind sculpted rock-face, wearing a sheepskin jacket over her denim work dress and carrying a brace of leghorn pullets in one hand as she braced herself with a fathom of peeled aspen sapling. As she took in He Who Never Walks and his view to the north over a heap of nothing much the white girl whistled softly, grinned impishly, and hunkered down by the old Ute, saying, "Brought you some chickens for supper. I'm a friend of Honapombi and his *umbea*, Ya-tahotey."

He Who Never Walks stopped drumming just long enough to toss her offering over his shoulder into the dark depths of the cave behind him. Then he started to softly drum some more as he gravely told her, "You mean you *were* their friend, my pretty *saltu* who gives food to the hungry. Honapombi and Yatahotey are dead. All of the Ho Hada in that band are dead. How could they be your friends? Have you the *puha* to speak with ghosts?"

Glory stared owl-eyed as she asked the medicine man, "How did you know that? How *could* you know that? Who could have told you so soon?"

He Who Never Walks said, "Hear me, I know a lot of things. You are called Glory Otis. You and your two broth-ers live just north of where the band of Honapombi was holding out, where those yellow men used to stay. You often gave them your white birds to eat, along with butter-milk and other good things you had left over. In return they watched over you and your brothers. They let no Ho Hada steal anything from you, even though you were saltu, holding land that had once belonged to Ho Hada. They thought your heart was with them, even when you did bad things to others. They treated you as one of their own, and in the end you did bad things to them as well. I told them you might. I asked them how they could trust any woman, of any nation, who would murder her own father."

Glory Otis sat still and silent for a time. Then she nodded and softly said, "I was afraid they knew. I was hoping they hadn't told you, even though one of your children came out to my place with a message from a lawman who is sweet on me and let it slip that he'd already told this lawman what Yatahotey had said about the hangman's daughter having a father who deserves to die. But you don't know what I'm talking about, do you?"

The near-naked Indian stared out over the yawning gulf to their north as he softly replied, "Yes, I do. She Who Sings While Winnowing wanted Saltu Ka Saltu to give much thought to the hangman's daughter. She didn't want to tell him more than that before she spoke to me and the spirits I know. She and some others were up here at moonrise the night you murdered them, along with many others, many who knew nothing about your crimes against your own people, nothing."

Glory sighed, "I was wondering how you could know so much, beating on that infernal drum. I knew my Indian neighbors were nosy. But how could they have seen me, alone in the dark up above the wagon trace before dawn? I thought I was being ever so careful."

He Who Never Walks said, "You were greedy, too. Nobody ever saw you setting off any powder charges high on the slopes in the dark. It is not true we Ho Hada can see in the dark like that owl-eyed evil spirit, Piamuhmpitz. You were seen when you came back later in the daylight to recover things from the wreckage you had hidden away like a pack rat."

Glory nodded grimly and deided, "Then I was right.

They had figured things out and you did tell them to turn me in to the law!"

He Who Never Walks put aside his drumstick to smile sadly at her as he said, "You were right about them suspecting the simple truth. We are a hunting people. We have always been good at reading sign. You were wrong about my telling them to tell the Tai Va Von what you had done. Did you think we loved the Tai Va Von for their big blue eyes and generous ways? Hear me, when I was young and strong I led raids against the Tai Va Von! I hate them. Most of them, at any rate. I told the people who asked me what I thought—that I thought you were generous and had a good heart to the Ho Hada. So I thought it would be wrong to turn you in, as you put it, for killing many Tai Va Von and letting them think saltu robbers had done it. I told them to tell the Tai Va Von that one dark rider they'd heard about was a dog-eating Arapaho and then just watch you unless you did something bad to them."

He turned to stare at her reproachfully and add, "Then you did do something bad to them. You started a landslide that wiped out that whole band. Men, women and children who'd considered you one of their own. They understood why you'd felt you had to kill your father. We think men like that are very wicked. They didn't care about those other Tai Va Von as long as they didn't get blamed for it. I just told you how I told them to avoid being blamed for it. I think it was bad and foolish for you to murder friends who understood why you had to murder your father."

Glory rose slowly to her feet, walking-staff in hand, as she softly said, "I figured you might feel that way about it if you ever found out. Lord knows how an old cripple banging on a drum found out so much. But seeing you have, I'm afraid I'll have to kill you, too."

The medicine man calmly asked, "How? I was expecting you to bring a gun when it was revealed to me that you might be coming. I do not mean to insult you, but you are not very big. Neither is your stick."

Glory Otis raised the six-foot length of sapling to one

300

shoulder like a baseball player as she replied in a conversational tone, "You'd be surprised how strong a girl can get, working from Can't See to Can't See under a stern taskmaster. But it's nothing personal, Cameahwait. I never killed anyone out of malice, once I'd rid myself of Pop. The extra money just came in handy as I set out to run our family business right!"

Since she was getting set to swing, Longarm called out, "Don't do it, Miss Glory!" as he stepped into view from the darkness of the medicine man's cave.

Glory gasped, "Custis, darling! What are you doing here? You told me you were taking that prisoner back to Denver before you came up this way to talk to this old Indian."

Longarm drifted closer as he morosely replied, "I lied. I wanted to talk to this witness before somebody killed him. I wasn't dead certain you'd be that somebody, Miss Glory. There was a chance the one who'd murdered all them other Indians had heard they meant to pow-wow here with their medicine man. But you were the one I sent poor little Todd to with that message that evening."

Glory tried, "Todd did make mention of Joy Norwich in passing. I paid no attention at the time. But after he and all those others were murdered I rode up all this way to see if this old man could tell me what Yatahotey might have meant."

He Who Never Walks sang in English, "Coyote did bad things to his own daughter, so they tell. But Coyote is neither a true spirit nor a real man, so they tell. Coyote eats shit, so they tell. This child's father was not Coyote. He should have known it is bad to fuck a little girl, even when she is not your own daughter!"

Glory pleaded, "Custis, make him stop singing such things about my poor Pop! It sounds so dirty and me and my brothers all loved our poor old lonesome Pop!"

Longarm soberly said, "How a nine- or ten-year-old felt about a grown man sticking his full-sized cock in her is neither hither nor yonder. As in the case of Joy Norwich there came a time when you commenced to weary of an aging lover's ways, in and out of bed. Your own dad made Matt Greene fire Larry Frank just as you'd managed to find romance or at any rate variety, out to your spread whilst your father was riding shotgun down Durango way. Like another gal I know, you also thought up your own notions on how your family business could be run, if you and you alone were the head of said family. So one wet spring morning when your dad was guarding a coach along that trail past your spread you simply murdered him and everyone else aboard that special run and, as this wise old man just pointed out, you'd have never been spotted if you'd been content to settle for murder on top of incest. But it takes money to make money in the butter and eggs trade. So you helped your-ownself to the color your dad had been guarding. Then you did it again and again, accounting for the gold dust by saying you'd been paid that way by your steady customers along the creek."

Glory had dropped her staff and clapped both hands to her ears as if she didn't want to hear as Longarm relentlessly continued, "It was too late to quit by the time Postal Inspector MacPhillips showed up. Or at least you thought it was, Miss Glory. Did you fuck him before you shot him in the back and helped yourself to that paint cowpony?"

Glory never answered. She cut short Longarm's accusations with a shrill scream of mingled shame and terror as she dove headfirst out of sight over the rim of the rock ledge.

She was still screaming like a banshee sliding face-down on a kid's sled as Longarm made it to the gut-wrenching view over the edge. And then Glory hit the rocks at the bottom and seemed to silently explode in a cloud of blood and brains before the sickening wet crunch could get back up to the suddenly sick lawman.

Longarm swallowed the green taste in his mouth and asked the hermit behind him if there was any trail down to the bloody scraps steaming on cold gray granite.

He Who Never Walks said, "No. But why would anyone

want to go down there? You can do nothing for her, and do you really want a closer look?"

Longarm softly replied, "Not hardly, Lord rest a poor little twisted body and soul!"

Chapter 38

By the time Longarm got back to Ambush, Matt Greene's grading crews had the line running again. So Longarm got Ysabella Valdez down to the depot, tended to some paperwork, and frog-marched Ricardo Robles there from the jail in handcuffs.

The others who boarded the southbound coach, a mining man and his woman, stared thunderghasted as Longarm removed his prisoner's irons as they were rolling out of town. Longarm assured them, "He ain't quite as dangerous as he looks, folks. He's been trying to get a free ride to Denver out of me, meaning to repudiate some confessings as soon as he felt safe from the vengeance of a man with a dangerous rep and a crazy daughter. But he's really fixing to escort this señorita home to New Mexico Territory, if he knows what's good for him."

So the mining man produced a bottle, which saw them in some comfort to the railhead in Durango. By the time Longarm and his party got off in Del Norte to change from their short-line the Mexican kids were openly flirting with each other.

So while they were having a last supper together across from the Del Norte junction Longarm waited until Ysabella went to take a crap before he told Robles, "My train for Denver will be coming in before you and Miss Ysabella will be boarding for New Mexico. So I'd better hand over your tickets and some pocket jingle in case she wants some soda pop or whatever before you can carry her home to kith and kin. They weren't being cheap when they held back the usual five dollars as I checked you out of jail in Ambush. They thought you were federal."

As he slid the envelope across the bare wood table, Robles said he aimed to return the money by wire if he ever got another job.

Longarm said, "Aw, mush, it ain't that much and I want you to spend it on Miss Ysabella. The kid's had a rough time since her brother got rolled. I'd tell you to treat her with the same respect *I* might, but I ain't sure how much respect I'd show any young widow woman if I'd been locked all that time with just my fist for company. So just try to remember she was the sister of a pal and let your conscience be your guide."

The Mexican gravely replied, "I won't do anything she does not want me to do. You could have had her, yourself, you know. She told me all about the money she owes you. She confessed while you weren't listening, aboard the train from Durango, that she expected you to demand some favors in return. She was surprised when you did not. Surprised and, *¿Quien sabe?* Perhaps a little disappointed. Don't you find her *linda?*"

"Muy linda," Longarm replied, going on to explain, "But I knew a gal who owed me money might think she owed me more and neither one of us would ever be certain I wasn't treating her like a *puta*. Don't try to understand the way my head works, now and again. Sometime I don't understand myself, myself."

As the gal they were gossiping about returned, wearing some fresh war paint and a sweet little smile, the *vaquero* she'd be riding on with held out a hand to Longarm and soberly said, "I think I understand you very well, Don Quixote."

So they parted friendly and, try as he might, Longarm couldn't get started with the only good-looking gal aboard his own train up to Denver. But he didn't care. It gave him time to organize his notes into a handwritten officious report for old Henry in the front office to type up in triplicate and he was saving some passion for Portia Parkhurst of the Colorado Bar Association, skinny as she might be. For he knew both he and that lying Ricardo Robles owed her more than either could ever repay.

Had she not wrangled that stay from the governor, Robles would have swung that Monday morn and never told those swell lies to send a stuck lawman floundering on toward the truth.

He told her so once he got back to Denver, filed his report late in the day and showed up on her doorstep smelling of bay rum and fresh underwear with a bunch of store-bought flowers in his hand.

Portia Parkhurst smelled good, too. She was a willowy-going-to-gaunt brunette going slightly gray, a few years older than Longarm but still good-looking for such a smart old gal. She usually wore black to and from her tough chores as a shemale lawyer who wanted men to take her serious. But that evening she had on a summer dress of lavender linen and pinned a sporty straw boater atop her upswept silver-streaked hair when he told her he'd reserved them a table at Romano's.

Romano's was this Eye-talian restaurant, close enough to walk, with checkered tablecloths, candles in Chianti bottles and jars of free bread sticks on every table.

They had all those empty Chianti bottles because everyone ordered some Chianti wine, imported all the way from Italy with the olive oil, to sip whilst they studied the outlandish bills of fare. Chianti went well with most everything on their menu, once you got used to sipping what looked and tasted something like red ink.

Portia said she liked the wine and knew what spaghetti with meatballs tasted like. But when she allowed she liked Swedish meatballs better Longarm suggested the veal Parmesan with carbonated pasta on the side.

Portia said she didn't see that on her menu. Then she laughed and told him, "It's *Pasta Carbonara*, Cowboy. Does it have garlic in it? I understand a lot of this dago food leaves a body with garlic on her breath."

Longarm shrugged and asked, "What difference will it make if we both enjoy some garlic in our grub? Who else were you planning on kissing, tonight?"

She said she wanted to eat first. So they did and then he took her to the vaudeville show at the Apollo Theatre to show he wasn't only interested in her body and then he took her home to show a heap of interest in her body.

Portia showed enough interest in his to leave her lavender linen dress and straw boater on the rug in their wake as she hauled him into bed with her and allowed she didn't mind the garlic on his breath at all.

He found the mingled odors of garlic, perfume and crotch sort of inspiring, the way the mingled odors of buck-skin, sweetgrass and smoke on a pretty Cheyenne could inspire a man to forget and not much care what white gals smelled like.

Being an educated woman of a certain age and independent means, Portia liked to see what she was doing at such times and told him not to trim the bedside lamp. So he was able to consider how little like an Indian, or any other recent bedmate, she reminded him of as he held his weight above her on locked elbows to gaze down between them as he admired the sight of his love-slicked erection sliding in and out of her through that sort of silver-fox welcome mat betwixt her lean ivory thighs. It felt good, too, and when a man gazed down at her flat pale belly and modest but firm turgid tits, he was inclined to decide she was going gray premature. For few teenagers could have moved her hips any better or clung to pal's pecker more friendly, as they flew on up over the moon together.

Once they had, and paused for some smoke and pillow talk, Portia shyly confided, "I think I see what they mean about Latin lovers. The combination of your heavy mustache and all that garlic when we sucked each other's tongues just now got me all exited."

He didn't think it would be polite to say gray hair and bitty tits helped him put away any lingering regrets about

Ysabella Valdez. He just lit a cheroot for them to share as they snuggled, propped up on pillows, to rest up for some more.

He thought he'd told Portia the tale of his adventures on the far side of the divide, or at any rate those parts it was safe to tell a lady you aimed to spend the night with.

So he was glad he was smoking when Portia suddenly asked him in a desperately casual tone, "So tell me, was that incestuous brat behind all those landslides as good in bed as me?"

Longarm carefully sent a big fat smoke ring rising in the lamplight before he replied just as carefree, "Gloria Otis never caused the one that almost killed that duchess of Durango and her traveling companion. That's how come she and her brothers were more interested in a bloated cow that day. I'd have likely had a tougher time meeting up with them if she hadn't been feeling innocent for a change."

Portia cuddled closer to insist, "That's not what I just asked you and you know it."

He tried, "What makes you suspect I was playing slap and tickle with a prime suspect who'd been broken in by her own father at a tender-twatted age?" Which was a fair enough answer when you studied on it.

Portia laughed, dirty, and decided, "Something like that *could* give a milkmaid a good head start on your average giddy teenager. How big does a little girl have to be to take a full-grown cock?"

Longarm felt on surer ground as he snorted, "How in the hell should I know? I told you that twelve-year-old orphan I rescued that time was turned in to the orphanage as pure as I found her. Even though her pimp had broken her in somewhat younger. Going on the few medical reports of rape victims I've read, a dirty daddy using care and a little butter could likely get an average-sized organ grinder into a nine-year-old. But it would sure feel big as hell to her."

Portia murmured, "How nice for both of them. But even as she grew to seem more mature her unnatural lover would be . . . receding from her?"

Longarm didn't feel he ought to mention what Glory had said about needing a heap of man to satisfy what she described as a sloppy gash. He said, "Incest is likely the most common unreported felony, with most of the few complaints being about father-daughter incest. I suspect you just nailed one reason. Should a widow woman catch her son beating his meat and decide such family secrets be shared, *his* old organ grinder and her old ring-dang-doo would fit together ever tighter as she raised her darling boy right."

Portia cooed, "Ooh, yum yum yum! But you said that was only *one* reason abused daughters were more likely to turn on their fathers?"

He said, "Kids grow up in every way. It's only natural that any kid experienced beyond his or her years would be curious about the other side of the hill and less shy about exploring. But whilst a boy can leave home, or mayhaps only come home for another slice of his Mom's old pie now and again, or a brother and sister can split up as easy as any other couple, a possessive head of the house and legal guardian can crimp the style of a budding belle of the ball. Glory said she'd had more advanced notions on producing butter and eggs, too. But I doubt I'd have tumbled to her motive, which led as the sunrise leads to the day to her means and opportunity, if it hadn't been a mite more obvious that hangman's daughter had been driven to distraction by her own daddy's aging back and ever-more-disappointing dick."

Portia reached absently down between them as she teased, "It's a wonder you brought any of this back for little old me. Did that poor Joy Norwich say this sleeping monster made her feel young again?"

He laughed innocently and replied, "You have my word under oath I never laid the hangman's daughter. She has an eager young lover and enough to worry about with her jealous father trying to catch them at it some more. The crazy lies she made up to protect Deaf Dave helped me a heap, though. I wasn't the least bit interested in a *vaquero*

309

they were fixing to hang for a local crime until one big fib after another led me to the truth at last."

The trouble with getting in bed with a lawyer was that even when a lawyer was playing with your cock you had to watch what you said around lawyers.

Portia decided, "So you only fucked Gloria Otis, along with anyone else in skirts around a county seat. I was wondering why you let her off the hook as the only likely but never-charged sole perpetrater."

He snubbed out the smoke as he calmly replied, "Two good reasons, having nothing to do with that poor virile member you're pulling on a mite too hard, this early. To begin with you *can't* indict a smashed-up corpse with anything, even if you bring it in, which I never, because I agreed with that medicine man it would only be a messy waste of time to scrape only some of her off a jumble of jagged-ass rocks. After that I was considering Glory's innocent kid brothers, Ward, Junior and Wayne."

Portia blinked and confessed, "I'd forgotten about those poor kids. Whatever will become of them, now?"

Longarm said, "Nothing. I knew they wouldn't want to talk to myself about driving their big sister over that edge. But I got together with other grown-ups around Ambush and they'll be all right. A pot-bellied district attorney I wound up friendlier with worked it out with a part-time county clerk to leave them be, as wards of the county, with this widow who owns a livery business in town acting as their legal guardian and running their family business for them until they come of age. Miss Meg will get to share the profits with them in the meanwhile, but that's only fair. She has to keep up the taxes on the property whilst she feeds both them growing boys and all their stock. Had I taken Glory Otis in for trial, she and her kid brothers would have had all her property siezed as restitution when they sentenced her to hang for wrecking all them coaches and killing all them people."

"You'd have had to testify against a girl you'd diddled,

310

too," the older woman playing with his cock calmly decreed.

He said, "You sure have a mind to go with your naughty hands. Have you heard me ask you how you wrangled that stay of execution out of Governor Pitkin on a weekend with his office officiously closed?"

Portia didn't answer. She couldn't. For her mouth had become too full, after one long slithering kiss the length of his naked belly.

As he felt himself rising fully to the occasion, Longarm smiled down at the bobbing part in her silver-streaked black hair to assure Portia, "I ain't as jealous as some folk I know. But I asked you a question and I'd sure like to know how you and that lying Mex accidentaly aimed me wrong in some right directions. So fess up, what did you have to do for old Fred Pitkin to get us that last-minute stay?"

Portia lifted her head from his lap with a sheepish smile to tell him, "I never had to do anything. He'd left by the time I got up to the statehouse. But you'd wired it was important for you to save that Mex and it occured to me neither the governor's seal nor signature could be sent by wire. So I guess I fudged just a teeny weeny bit."

Longarm gasped, "A teeny weeny bit? You could have been disbarred for a stunt like that, you sweet ass-risking lawyer-gal!"

Portia shrugged her pale bare shoulders to demurely demand, "How? It was Governor Pitkin's name I signed to the wire, not my own, and who was going to turn me in, you?"

To which he could only reply as she proceeded to suck him harder, "Not hardly. But I hope you understand that what you're doing to me right now is legally defined as a crime against nature. So you'd best let me roll you over and finish this as a mere misdemeanor."

JAKE LOGAN
TODAY'S HOTTEST ACTION WESTERN!